Unbridled Spirits

Unbridled Spirits

Short Fiction about Women in the Old West

Edited by

JUDY ALTER AND A. T. ROW

With an introduction by FRED ERISMAN

Texas Christian University Press
Fort Worth

Library of Congress Cataloging-in-Publication Data

Unbridled Spirits: short fiction about women in the Old West/edited
  by Judy Alter and A.T. Row: with an introduction by Fred Erisman.
       p. c.m.
    ISBN 0-87565-124-0
    1. Women — West (U.S.) — Fiction. 2. Short stories, American.
  3. Western stories. I. Alter, Judy, 1938- . II. Row, A. T.
  PS648.W6B49 1994
  813'.010832041—dc20   93-14335
                                                                    CIP
                                                                    Rev

The cover art, "Target Practice," is by Tom Lovell, courtesy of
the National Cowboy Hall of Fame, Oklahoma City.

Book and cover design by Barbara Whitehead.

Acknowledgements

"Pioneer Women" by Mari Sandoz. Published in its entirety for the first time courtesy The University of Nebraska – Lincoln, Archives and Special Collections of the Libraries.

"Marlizzie" and "Martha of the Yellow Braids," by Mari Sandoz. Copyright © 1959 by University of Nebraska Press. Copyright © renewed 1987 by Caroline Sandoz Pifer. Reprinted by permission of McIntosh and Otis, Inc.

"On the Art of Fiction" is from *Willa Cather on Writing* by Willa Cather. Copyright © 1949 by the Executors of the Estate of Willa Cather. Reprinted by permission of Alfred A. Knopf, Inc.

"A Wagner Matinee" by Willa Cather is reprinted from *Willa Cather's Short Fiction, 1892-1912*, edited by Virginia Faulkner, introduction by Mildred R. Bennett, by permission of the University of Nebraska Press. Copyright © 1965, 1970 by the University of Nebraska Press.

"Journey to the Fort" and "Flame on the Frontier," from *Indian Country*, copyright © 1950 by Dorothy M. Johnson. Reprinted by permission of McIntosh and Otis, Inc.

"Lost Sister" from *The Hanging Tree* copyright © 1957 by Dorothy M. Johnson. Reprinted by permission of Ballantine Books, a Division of Random House.

"The Man Who Lied About A Woman" from *One-Smoke Stories* by Mary Austin. Copyright © 1934 by Mary Austin. Copyright © renewed 1961 by School of American Research. Reprinted by permission of Houghton Mifflin Co. All rights reserved.

"Kittura Remsberg" by Jack Schaefer is reprinted by permission of Don Congdon Associates, Inc. Copyright © 1952, renewed 1980 by Jack Schaefer.

Contents

Introduction

∽∼∽∼∽∼∽∼∽∼∽∼∽∼∽∼∽∼∽∼∽∼∽∼∽

We would be lost without our myths. In a world that for generations has only become more complex, contradictory, and confusing, myths give us a core of certainty to cling to, for they are the mechanisms by which we interpret and dramatize the dominant, unifying values of our culture. Drawn initially from actual episodes in our history but retold and embellished over the years, these historically dramatic stories and images gradually grow to take on an authenticity all their own, until they become more "real" and more evocative than the historical realities that spawned them. And in that compelling "reality" is their importance, for they are the "history" we remember and use to guide our actions.

Take the case of Paul Revere's ride. We all "know" that on the night of April 18, 1775, Revere rode from Boston to Concord, crying "The British are coming!" to all within earshot. It doesn't matter that Revere barely reached Lexington, nor does it matter that Samuel Prescott, not Revere, actually carried the news to the defenders of Concord. What matters is the enduring image of the democratic individual, driven by the courage of his convictions in the face of imperial injustice, to set down his tools, leave his shop, and risk life and fortune to alert his comrades of the oncoming British forces. In that image we find the essence of American self-determination, linking the good of the individual with the good of the community, and it gives us, as a people two centuries later, a reassuring model to follow as we seek justification for our own principled actions.

Because they are so memorable and so satisfying, myths can also be seductive. We "know," just as assuredly as we know of Revere's ride, that men settled the American West. We know it so well, in fact, that we've made the knowledge a part of our national imagery, populating American history with a whole gallery of masculine figures working in concert to civilize the wilderness. They take many forms, to be sure. There's the hunter, with his moccasins, his buckskins, and his long rifle, moving silently through the forest. There's the pioneer, carving clearings from the underbrush in the name of settlement but ready to move on the moment he hears the sound of a neighbor's axe. There are the trapper and the miner, interchangeable in their shagginess and their search for the riches to be found upon and underneath the earth. And there's the cowboy, lean, laconic, and lethal, who as he rides the range becomes an emblem of national attitudes and values as unmistakable as the American eagle. But one and all they're men, and they seem to populate the mythic record to the exclusion of all others.

Mythic "knowledge" notwithstanding, a moment's reflection reminds us that where there are men, there are women as well. Historical data bear this out; with the exception of Montana and Wyoming, where there was a dramatic shortage of women for much of the period of settlement, the male/female ratio between 1830 and 1890 throughout much of the West averaged anywhere from 3:2 to 5:4. Though men did indeed outnumber women, the West was far from the womanless wasteland of legend. Just who those women were is less clear, however, and it comes as no surprise to discover that Americans over the years have translated the demographic data into a cluster of myths as persuasively memorable as any that surround the men who won the West.

Within this version of the nation's history there are five women who share the West with the men. Three are white, two are not, and all are to one degree or another overshadowed by their male counterparts, but their mythic stature is as established and as recognizable as that of any of the men. At the forefront of the white women is the genteel, educated woman who, be she officer's lady or spinster schoolmarm, is the epitome of high culture, social sophistication, and eastern values for all the region. She may be initially unwilling to confront the realities of the West, like Owen Wister's Molly Stark Wood or Grace Kelly's Quaker wife in *High Noon*; or she may be as forthright as any of the heroines played so memorably in the films by Maureen O'Hara, but she stands unflinchingly as the voice of civilization in a rough-and-ready world.

Just as familiar is the mythic mate, the married woman whose locus is the home. Whether workworn and beaten down by frontier life, as are the farm wives that populate Hamlin Garland's short stories of the agricultural West, or the superhuman earth mother found in John Steinbeck's Ma Joad, she stands with her basket, her bonnet, and her Bible as the emblem of domesticity and family cohesion. When she is defeated, we see the poignant waste of a human life; when she triumphs, we recognize a victory for the power of the home. In either case, she speaks for the maternal and humane qualities of womanhood. Her darker counterpart is the woman of questionable virtue, the frank manipulator of sexual allure and mercantile power who uses her will and her body to shape the lives of men and women alike. She may be one of the good-hearted whores scattered through Bret Harte's tales of Gold Rush California, or she may be the entrepreneurial Mis' Kitty of *Gunsmoke* notoriety, but she is everything the lady and the homemaker are not. She reminds us all of the baser urges within and the power such urges can command, whether unleashed or channeled.

Among the non-white women of the mythic West, two figures stand out. One is the squaw, American Indian by birth and culture and in many respects comparable to the white man's helpmate, although her domesticity is uncontaminated by his civilization. Shaped and controlled by generations of custom, she stands in the background, an essential participant in the internal economy of the tribe. She is passionate in love, loyal in wedlock, and ruthless in war, and her occasional liaisons with white men mean only that she is removed from the organic confines of the tribe. The other is the princess, like the squaw usually of American Indian birth, although frequently Hispanic in origin. She may be Sacajawea, whose knowledge of the land and its ways saves the white, male explorer from his own ignorance, or she may be the border-town señorita in *rebozo* and *mantilla*, whose pure-hearted love is seduced away by the callous Anglo. In either form, she speaks for the other cultures whose lives and values are as much a part of the West as those of the whites.

Whatever form she takes, the woman of the mythic West offers us the same comforting certainty that we find in her male counterparts. We "know" that the cowboy, in from the range, sowed genteel wild oats with the commercially friendly saloon girls of Tombstone or Medicine Bow, but learned from them what true manhood meant. We know that Maureen O'Hara and Shirley Temple brought books and music to Fort Apache as assuredly as we know that nine out of ten farm wives steadfastly kept bacon and biscuits on the table while doing the laundry, bearing the children, and standing off the occasional Indian raid — often, it seems, all at the same time — throughout Nebraska and the Dakotas (the tenth, unable to stand the rigors of farm life on the Plains, went mad and hanged herself in the kitchen). We know all these occurrences for a fact and we're comforted by them; this is the West as it ought to have been, and it gives us models of womanly behavior that are appropriately satisfying complements to those supplied by the men.

Like all good mythic figures, these women originate in historical reality. There *were* cultivated eastern women who followed their army-officer husbands from one barren encampment to another, there *were* countless farm and ranch wives whose lives became a never-ceasing round of drudgery and privation, and there may even have been the occasional pure-hearted hooker whose ideals helped her to transcend the occupational hazards of cirrhosis and syphilis. But the irresistible progress of myth-making, fed by a century's worth of writers (and later by film-makers), has focused our attention upon the categorized types to create a picture of women's life in the West as simplified and as stylized as the account of Paul Revere's ride. What results is a portrayal of western life not necessarily *wrong* in either spirit or fact, but without question incomplete, and we owe it to ourselves and to the whole grand sweep of history to explore the sides of western life that the myth overlooks.

The historical record is once again the place to start, for there, for all to see, are the data that challenge the myth's simplifications. Women, as we've already seen, trekked westward in numbers almost equivalent to those of the men. As they did, they took up the challenges of western life as readily as the men. Many were, to be sure, no more and no less than the wives and schoolmarms that we know so well. But many others made their marks in ways that the myth would do well to heed. The record shows women parlaying their domestic skills into profitable businesses, creating the laundries, the tailor shops, the dry-goods stores, and the eating-places so much a part of western settlement. The record shows them holding land and managing farms and ranches, sometimes by necessity when a husband died or deserted them, but often of their own volition; Eliza Jane Wilder, the autocratic schoolmarm of Laura Ingalls Wilder's *Little Town on the Prairie*, in historical fact not only taught school in DeSmet but also worked a homestead claim she held in her own name throughout her tenure in Dakota Territory.

The record shows women putting their education to use in ways reaching far beyond teaching the three Rs in the one-room school beloved of myth. More than one western schoolmarm moved up to teach in the academies (and at times to lead, like Mary Atkins of California, who founded what was to become Mills College) and seminaries that sprang up in the aftermath of settlement. The record shows them entering the sciences and the professions traditionally considered the exclusive preserve of men, with female physicians, clerics, and attorneys far from unknown throughout the West. Mary Elizabeth Lease, who achieved immortality by exhorting farmers to "raise less corn and more hell" during the heyday of Populism, was a qualified attorney and a member of the Kansas Bar, while Colorado's Martha Maxwell gained national prominence as a naturalist and zoologist.

Indeed, the record shows women playing an integral role in bringing the West into the larger national picture. Women wrote for and owned western newspapers, helping to shape public opinion and the progress of their communities. Women were at the forefront of some of the region's most compelling social movements; Iowa's Annie Turner Wittenmyer was one of the founders of the Women's Christian Temperance Union and Kansan Carrie Nation achieved nationwide notoriety with her saloon-busting efforts. And women helped to make the West the most politically progressive region of the times; they were active and prominent in the Patrons of Husbandry, the Populist Party, and the Farmer's Alliance, and the efforts of others led Wyoming to become the first of the states and territories to grant the vote to women. One cannot talk about the West without talking of its women, and they are far from being solely the women of the myth.

These are the women that *Unbridled Spirits* seeks to recognize. In the pages that follow there are, to be sure, women recognizably cast in the mythic mold — a farm wife who forces herself to repress all that music once meant to her, a California señorita whose youthful love for an Anglo officer evolves into tragically noble spinsterhood, a pregnant wife who takes up a rifle to defend the homestead alongside her husband, or a widow who defies cholera and custom to find love among the trials of a wagon train. But there are other women as well, who remind us of the roles played by the women of history. There are women who run ranches, and run them well — one driven by memories of a childhood *faux pas* in front of her father, another because she has no other option if she is to survive, much less retain her self-esteem. There are Indian women, neither squaws nor princesses, who use the traditions of their people to challenge injustices and protect tribal interests.

Along the way we meet cultivated eastern women who come West with their eyes open, knowing full well what they will encounter but determined to make the best of it. We meet a tomboy on the brink of womanhood, who's not at all certain she wants to accept the part that her society has set out for her. We meet women who experience life among the Indians as well as life among the whites, and who discover that there are merits to both cultures. We meet women who strive to put up with abusive or indifferent men, but who at last are driven to take affairs into their own hands. We meet an army wife who's more concerned with making a home for herself and her husband than she is with culture, and a couple whose dream of California is slowly overwhelmed by the trials and tragedy they encounter in West Texas; their resilience augurs well for the future of both families, as each finds that home and love are where one finds them.

Through these stories we get a clearer sense of women's lives in the West, and they are as compelling as any found in the historical record. Children of their culture and shaped by their experiences though they are, the diverse characters who populate the stories are individuals who struggle to take charge of their own destinies. Some are young; others are old. Some are innocent, others experienced. Some are single, some married. Some know the West; others are experiencing it for the first time. But, whatever their heritage and whatever their circumstances, they are linked by a common human thread. They accept the realities that life presents them with, yet, drawing upon women's skills and women's values, they endeavor to shape those realities into a life that has substance and meaning and worth.

Myth has its place, even in the presence of reality. The women of western myth have without question played their part in helping us to think about the past and consider questions about the future, and our sense of the region's history would be the poorer without them. Fascinating though the myth has been and remains, however, we need to recognize that the reality is far more complex and tantalizingly more intriguing. The time has come to look behind the myth to consider its origins, for in them are the *people*, men and women alike, who actually did the work of settling the West. And when we do look beyond the myth, using the record of fiction to complement and expand the historical record, we find that alongside the mythic figures stand the real ones, as ready to help us understand the past and interpret the present as any of their mythic counterparts. Throughout the period of settlement and ever after, as the stories in *Unbridled Spirits* remind us, women were *in* the West, they were *of* the West, they helped *shape* the West, and they *wrote* about the West. It is time for them to share the stage with their mythic counterparts.

— *Fred Erisman*

Apologia

A truth about compiling anthologies: everyone you ask has a different opinion about what should be included. At the outset of this project, we asked scholars and teachers to give us their ideas about a book that would refute the traditional notion that women in western fiction were mere stereotypes, either the soiled dove or the pure schoolmarm. Some advised the largest number of authors possible; others wanted several selections each by a limited number of authors; some insisted that only selections written by women were eligible; some said use only fiction, others said nonfiction, and a few suggested excerpts from novels. We finally took a little of this advice and a little of that and compiled what we hope will be a useful table of contents.

Our subject is the Old West, which gave us, we thought, some immediate criteria: stories set before the turn of the century and west of the Mississippi. Selection turned out not to be that simple, and while the stories are all set west of the Mississippi, some creep into the twentieth century. The criteria became intangible: we chose frontier stories, those with the feel of the Old West.

Because we wanted to present the image of women as it was created — rather than lived — we narrowed our selections to fiction. And because we thought excerpts from novels difficult to deal with outside the context of the full novel, we confined the list to short stories. Our choices were narrowing.

The number of women who have written or are writing today about the American West is simply not great. Believing that four names stand out historically — Mari Sandoz, Willa Cather, Mary Hallock Foote, and Dorothy Johnson — we included several selections by each and, where possible, essays revealing their ideas about writing and/or the American West. Some of Sandoz' selections are sketches — technically nonfiction — but Sandoz used fictional techniques to develop her characters, and we believe the pieces fit the spirit of this collection.

In the section entitled "Other Women's Voices," we unhappily found that our choices were few. Many women have written factually about the American West and their lives in it; some have written novels but no short stories. The seven stories in this section represent our pick from a relatively slim field.

If the stories in this collection seem too heavily weighted toward the Anglo experience of frontier settlement, slim pickings is again the reason. There are relatively few good short stories focusing on Native American and Hispanic women. Gertrude Atherton wrote about California's Hispanic culture, and Jack London of the American Indians of the Northwest. Dorothy Johnson often wrote of the Plains Indians, but it was with an Anglo as protagonist, as in all three selections by Johnson chosen here. We found no usable stories about black women. So the selection does not necessarily imply that we consider the white experience on the frontier of primary importance; it does indicate that the Anglo experience has gotten much more creative attention.

Our subject is writing about women but not necessarily by women. One aspect of the myth of the stereotypical woman is that all western fiction was written by men who were incapable of creating lively, rounded, believable women. We wanted to counter that by including some among many outstanding stories written by men. To have excluded these stories because of the gender of their authors would, in our view, have amounted to chauvinism of the worst kind.

In a few instances, copyright restrictions and high permissions fees kept us from including stories that we greatly admired.

Readers will notice great inconsistencies throughout this text in spelling, punctuation and capitalization. As closely as possible, we have reprinted the stories as they appeared in the original texts, without imposing contemporary editing standards on them.

We are most grateful to those who offered advice, both that which we took and that which we finally had to reject. Among them are Jim Byrd, Sue Hart, James Maguire, Jim Lee, Joyce Roach, Lou Rodenberger, Ann Ronald, Sue Rosowski, Dale Walker, and, of course, Fred Erisman whose constant interest and suggestions — and written introduction — are much appreciated.

Many thanks to Gary Rogers, who read countless stories in the library and helped greatly with the final selection. We're sorry that circumstances took him too far afield for him to remain a part of this project, as originally intended.

Cathy Thomason deserves special credit for spending weeks and weeks — and too many weekends — putting these stories on computer, sometimes by scanner and sometimes by old-fashioned typing, not an easy chore when she had to deal with aged original materials.

~~~~ *I* ~~~~

The

Classic

Women's

Voices

Mary Hallock Foote

≈≈≈≈≈≈≈≈≈≈≈≈≈≈≈≈≈≈≈≈

*E*asterner *Mary Hallock Foote (1847-1938) followed her mining-engineer husband west in the 1870s. Her fiction consistently reflects the viewpoint of the eastern woman transplanted to the West and learning an entirely different way of life. In her early works, the East is home — safe and cultured — while the West is a masculine place, full of adventure but lacking in the finer things of life, a wilderness to be endured while one longed for home; in later works, she saw more promise of civilization in the West. But for Foote, the West provided a changing experience, and once having lived there, her heroines cannot return to their former, eastern lives. Foote's fiction, however, never relies on the stereotypical characters of the West nor on stereotyped responses, and some of her love stories are anything but genteel and happy.*

Formally schooled as an artist, she began her career as an illustrator in New York City where she met and knew some of the leading literary lights of the day. When she moved West, her friends encouraged her to write of what they saw as her bizarre experiences. In stories in Scribner's Monthly, Atlantic Monthly *and* Century Magazine *and in novels, she told in fiction the story of her own life. In recent years later works —* The Ground-Swell (1919), Edith Bonham (1917) *and her memoirs,* A Victorian Gentlewoman in the Far West — *have been recognized as of more significant literary value than early fiction such as her best-known novel,* The Led-Horse Claim (1883). *Ironically, Foote's literary importance comes almost more from the novel based on her life —* Wallace Stegner's Angle of Repose — *than from her own works.*

Although her work is sometimes dismissed for its melodrama, wooden plots and out-of-place gentility, it is a mistake to overlook the importance of Foote's record, from a feminine point of view, of the coming of civilization to the West.

A brief review of Foote's writing can be found in "Mary Hallock Foote (1847-1938)" American Literary Realism 5 (Spring 1972), pp. 144-150. The best overall assessment of her work is Mary Hallock Foote, *by James Maguire (Boise, Idaho: Boise State University Western Writers Series, 1972). Rodman W. Paul's introduction to the 1972 edition of* A Victorian Gentlewoman in the West *(San Marino, California: The Huntington Library) also gives a helpful assessment of her life and work. Readers may also want to explore* The Idaho Stories and Far West Illustrations of Mary Hallock Foote *(Idaho State University Press, 1988), edited by Barbara Cragg, Dennis M. Walsh and Mary Ellen Walsh.*

"The Pretty Girls in the West," while not a reflection of Foote's ideas on writing, does reflect her feelings on women who lived in the West and those — the pretty girls reared in the genteel traditions of the East — who were not suited to life in the West. The essay was written to accompany one of a series of full-page woodcuts by Foote, a respected artist as well as author, which appeared in Century Magazine *in 1888.*

The Pretty Girls in the West
Century Magazine, 1888

The wish so often expressed by mothers in the West that their daughters should have a "good time," suggests an inquiry as to what precisely is meant by this fond aspiration.

A mother's idea of a "good time" for her daughter usually signifies the sort of time she has failed to have herself. If she has been a hard-working woman, with many children to care for, she will desire that her daughter shall live easy and be blessed, in the way of offspring, with something less than a quiver-full. Where in the past labor has urged her, often beyond her strength, pleasure in the future shall invite her child.

So the mothers of the West, women of the heroic days of pioneering, unconsciously tell the story of their own struggles and deprivations in the ambitions in which they indulge for their children.

Along the roads over which her parents journeyed in their white-topped wagon, their tent by night, their tabernacle, their fortress in time of danger, the settler's daughter shall ride in a tailor-made habit, or fare luxuriously in a drawing-room car. Where the mother's steadfast face grew brown with the glare of the alkali plain, the daughter shall glance out carelessly from behind the tapestry blind of her Pullman "section." Where the mother's hands washed and cooked and mended, and dressed wounds, and fanned the coals of the camp-fire, the daughter's shall trifle with books and music, shall be soft and "manicured" and daintily gloved.

It is one of the curious sights in the shops of a little town of frame houses — chiefly of one story, where the work of the house is not unfrequently done by the house-mother, not from poverty, but from the want in a new community of a servant class — to behold about Christmas time the display of sumptuous toilet articles implying hours spent upon the care of the feminine person, especially the feminine hands. This may be one of the indications of the sort of good time that is preparing for the daughter of the town. There are other and more hopeful suggestions, but none that seriously counteract the plainly projected revolt, on the part of the mothers, against a future of physical effort for their girls.

There are girls and girls in the West, of all degrees and styles of prettiness, but here, as elsewhere, and in all her glory, is seen the preeminently pretty girl — who by that patent exists, to herself, to her world, and in the imagination of her parents. The career of this young lady in her native environment is something amazing to persons of a sober imagination as to what should constitute a girl's "good time." The risks that she takes, no less than her extraordinary escapes from the usual consequences, are enough to make one's time-honored principles reel on the judgment seat of propriety.

It is true she does not always escape; but she escapes so often that it is quite impossible to draw any wholesome deductions from her. The only thing that can be done with her is to disapprove of her (with the consciousness that she will not mind in the least) and forgive her, because she knows not what she does. Why should she not take the good time for which, and for little else, she has been trained — the life of pleasure for which some one else pays?

In the novels she goes abroad and marries an English duke; in real life not quite so often; but she is an element of confusion, morally, in all one's prophecies with regard to her. She may have talent and make an actress or singer if she has any capacity for work; or she may marry the man she loves and become an exemplary wife. That which in her history appeals most deeply to one's imagination is the contrast between her fortunes and those of her mother.

If Creusa had survived the fall of Troy to accompany Aeneas on his wanderings, with a brood of fast-growing boys and girls, whose travel-worn garments she would have been mending while her hero entertained Dido with the tale of his misfortune, it is not unlikely that much-tried woman would have had her ideas as to those qualities in her sex that make for a "good time," and those which mostly go to supply a good time for others. And we may be sure that in planning the futures of the Misses Aeneas she would not have chosen for them the virtues that go unrewarded; rather shall they sit, white-handed and royally clad, and turn a smiling face upon some eloquent adventurer — who shall not be, in all respects, a copy of father Aeneas.

Whoever has lived in the West must have observed that here it is the unexpected that always happens; therefore it will be a mistake to take the pretty girl too seriously, or to regard her as a fatal sign of the tendency of the life she is so fitted to enjoy. She is merely a phase, — an entertaining if not an instructive one, — for which her parents' hard lives and changes of fortune are mainly responsible. Her children will reverse the tendency, or carry it to the point of fracture, where nature steps in, in her significant way, and rubs out the false sum.

But as often as not nature permits the whole illogical proceeding to go on, and nothing happens of all that we have prophesied. We see that the fountain *does* rise higher than its source, that grapes *do* grow upon thorns and figs upon thistles, on some theory of cause and effect unknown to social dynamics.

The pretty girl from the East is hardly enough of a "rusher" to please the young Western masculine taste; but there will not be wanting pilgrims to her shrine. Her Eastern hostess will be proud of the chance to demonstrate that she isn't at all the same sort of pretty girl as her sister of the West, — it is the shades of differ- ence that are vital, — and she will receive an almost pathetic welcome at the hands of her young countrymen, stranded upon cattle-ranches, or in railroad or mining camps, or engaged in hardy attempts of one sort or another wherein there is room for feminine sympathy.

Whether she takes her pleasure actively, in the saddle or in the canoe, or sits out the red summer twilights on the ranch piazza, or tunes her guitar to the ear of a single listener who has ridden over miles of desert plain for the privilege, she will be conscious that she supplies a motive, a new meaning to the life around her.

All this is very dangerous. She is in a world of illusions capable of turning into ordeals for those who put them to the proof — ordeals for which there has been no preparation in the life of the pretty girl. Even the ordeal of taste is not to be despised — taste, which environs and consoles and unites and stimulates women in the East, and which disunites and tortures and sets them at defiance, one with another, in the West.

The life of the men may be large and dramatic, even in failure; but the life of women, here, as everywhere, is made up of very small matters — a badly cooked dinner, a horrible wall-paper, a wind that tears the nerves, a child with something the matter with it which the doctor "doesn't understand," an acquaintance that is just near enough not to be a friend; it is the little shocks for which one is never prepared, the little disappointments and insecurities and failures and postponements, the want of complete- ness and perfection in anything, that harrows a woman's soul and makes her forget, too often, that she has a soul.

So let our pretty Eastern girl remember, before she pledges herself irrevocably to follow the fortunes of some charming young man she has had a "good time" with on the frontier, that — all good times and masculine assurances to the contrary notwithstanding — the frontier is not yet ready for her kind of pretty girl. There is more than one generation between her and the mother of a new community — unless she be minded to offer herself up on the altar of social enlightenment, or for the particular benefit of her particular young man. This is a fate which will always have a baleful fascination for the young woman who is capable of arguing that, if the frontier be not ready for her, the young man is.

The pity of it is that these young gentlemen will always pick out the pretty girl, when a less expensive choice would be so much more serviceable and fit for the conditions of their lives so much better. But they are all potential millionaires, these energetic dreamers. They do not pinch themselves in their prospective arrangements, including the prospective wife. Between them both, the girl who expects to have a good time, and the young man who is confident that he can give it to her, there will probably be a good deal to learn.

The Fate of a Voice
Century Magazine, 1886

There are many loose pages of the earth's history scattered through the unpeopled regions of the Far West, known but to few persons, and these unskilled in the reading of Nature's dumb records. One of these unread pages, written over with prehistoric inscriptions, is the cañon of the Klamath River.

An ancient lava stream once submerged the valley. Its hardening crust, bursting asunder in places, left great crooked rents, through which the subsequent drainage from the mountain slopes found a way down to the desert plains. In one of these furrows, left by the fiery ploughshare, a river, now called the Klamath, made its bed. Hurling itself from side to side, scouring out its straitened boundaries with tons of sand torn from the mountains, it has slowly widened and deepened and worn its ancient channel into the cañon as it may now be seen.

No one can tell how long the river has been making the bed in which it lies so restlessly. Riding towards it across the sunburnt mountain pastures, its course may be traced by the black crests of the lava bluffs which line its channel, showing in the partings of the hills. From a distance the bluffs do not look formidable; they seem but a step down from the high, sunlit slopes, an insignificant break in the skyward sweep of their long, buoyant lines. But ride on to the brink and look down. The bunch-grass grows to the very edge, its slight spears quivering in light against the cañon's depths of shadow. The roar of the river comes up to your ears in a continuous volume of sound, loud or low, as the wind changes. Here and there, where the speed of the river has been checked, it has left a bit of white sand beach, the only positive white in the landscape. The faded grasses of the hills look pale against the sky [it is a country of cloudless skies and long rainless summers] — only the dark cañon walls dominate the intensity of its deep unchanging blue. The broad light rests, still as in a picture, on the fixed black lines of the bluffs, on the slopes of wild pasture whose curves flatten and crowd together as they approach the horizon. A few black dots of cattle, grazing in the distance, may appear and then stray out of sight over a ridge, or a broad-winged bird may slowly mount and wheel and sing between the cañon walls. Meanwhile, your horse is picking his way, step by step, along the bluffs, cropping the tufts of dry bunch-grass, his hoofs clinking now and then on a bit of sunken rock, which, from the sound, might go down to the foundations of the hills; there are cracks, too, that look as if they went as deep. The basalt walls are reared in tiers of columns with an hexagonal cleavage. A column or a group of columns becomes dislocated from the mass, rests so, slightly apart; a girl's weight might throw it over. At length the accumulation of slight, incessant, propelling causes overcomes its delicate poise; it topples down; the jointed columns fall apart, and their fragments go to increase the heap of debris which has found its angle of repose at the foot of the cliff. A raw spot of color shows on the weather-worn face of the cliff, and beneath it a shelf is left, or a niche, which the tough sage and the scented wild syringa creep down to and fearlessly occupy in company with straggling tufts of bunch-grass.

One summer a party of railroad engineers made their camp in the river cañon, distributing their tents along the side of a gulch lined with willows and wild roses, up the first hill above it, and down on the white sand beach below. The quarters of the division engineer, who had ladies with him in camp that summer, the tents of the younger members of the corps, the cook-tent, and the dining shed made a little settlement by themselves on the hill; while the camp of the "force" was lower down the gulch. Work on that division of the new railroad had been temporarily suspended, and the engineer in charge, having finished his part of the line to its junction with the valley division, was awaiting orders from his chief.

It was September, and the last week of the ladies sojourn in camp. They were but two, the division engineer's wife and the wife's younger sister, a girl with a voice. No one who knew her ever thought of Madeline Hendrie without thinking of her voice, a fact she herself would have been the last to resent. At that time she was ordering her life solely with reference to the demands of that imperious organ. An obstinate huskiness which had changed it since the damp, late Eastern spring, and had veiled its brilliancy, was the motive that had sent her, with her sister to the dry, pure air of the foot-hills. In the autumn she would go abroad for two or three years' final study.

It was Sunday afternoon in camp. Since work on the line had ceased there was little to distinguish it from any other afternoon, except that the little Duncan girls wore white dresses and broad ribbons at lunch instead of their play frocks, and were allowed to come to the six o'clock dinner in the cooktent. Mrs. Duncan had remarked to her husband that Madeline and young Aldis seemed to be making the most of their farewells. They had spent the entire afternoon together on the river beach, not in sight of the camp, but in a little cove secluded by willows, where the brook came down. Mrs. Duncan could see them now returning with lagging steps along the shore, not looking at each other and not speaking, apparently. The rest of the camp was on its way to dinner.

"I told you how it would be, if you brought her out here, you know," Mr. Duncan said, waiting for his wife to pass him, with her skirts gathered in one hand, along the foot-bridge that crossed the brook to the cook-tent.

"Oh, Madeline is all right," she replied.

But Aldis was missing at table, and Madeline came down late, though without having changed her dress, and during dinner avoided her sister's eye.

"You're not going out with him again, Madeline!" Mrs. Duncan found a chance to say to the girl after dinner, as she was hurrying up the trail with a light shawl on her arm. "All the afternoon, and now again! What can you be thinking of?"

Mrs. Duncan could see Aldis walking about in front of the tents on the hill, evidently on the watch for Madeline

"I must," she said hurriedly. "It is a promise."

"Oh, if it has come to *that*" —

"It hasn't come to anything. You need not be troubled. Tonight will be the last of it."

"Madeline, you must not go. Let me excuse you to Aldis. I cannot let you go till I've had a chance to talk with you."

"That is what I have promised him — one more chance. You cannot help us, Sallie. Go back, dear, and don't worry about me."

These words were hastily whispered on the trail, Aldis walking about and gloomily awaiting the result of his flying conference between the sisters. Mrs. Duncan went back to the house only half-satisfied that she had done her duty. It was not the first time she had found it difficult to do her duty by Madeline, when it happened to conflict with the inclinations of that imperative youngest daughter of the house of Hendrie. However, it was not for Madeline that she was troubled.

The path leading to the bluffs was one of the many cattle trails that wind upward, with an even grade, from base to summit of every grass-covered hill on the mountain ranges. Madeline and Aldis shortened the way by leaving the trail and climbing the side of the bluff where it jutted out above the river. It was a steep and breathless struggle upward, and Madeline did not refuse the accustomed help of her companion's hand, offered in silence with a look which she ignored. Mechanically they sought the place where it had been their custom to sit on other evenings of the summer they had spent together, — one of those ledges a few feet from the summit of the bluff, where part of a row of columns had fallen. Cautiously they stepped down to it, along a crevice slippery with dried grasses, he keeping always between her and the brink.

The sun had already set to the camp, but from their present height once more they could see it drifting down the flaming west. Suddenly, as a fire-ship burns to the water's edge and sinks, the darkening line of the distant plains closed above that intolerable splendor. All the cool subdued tones of the cañon sprang into life. The river took a steely gleam. Up through the gate of the cañon rolled the tide of hazy glory from the valley, touched the topmost crags, and mounted thence to fade in the evening sky. The two on the bluffs sat in silence, their faces pale in the deepening glow, but Madeline had crept forward on the ledge, nearer to Aldis, to look down. It was the first confiding natural movement she had made towards him since the shock of this new phase of their friendship had startled her. Aldis was grateful for it, while resolved to take all possible advantage of it. At his first words she drew back, and he knew, before her answer came, that she had instantly resumed the defensive.

"Everything has been said, except things it would be unkind to say. Why need we go over it all again?"

"That is what we came up here for, is it not? To go over it all once more and get down to the very dregs of your argument."

"It is not an argument. It is a decision and it is made. There is nothing more I can say, except to indulge in the meanness of recrimination."

"Go on and recriminate, by all means! That is what I want, — to make you say everything you have on your mind. Then I shall ask you to listen to me. What is it that you are keeping back?"

"Well, then, was it quite honest of you to seem to accept the conditions of our — being together this summer, as we have been, and all the while to be nursing this — hope, — for me to have to kill? Do you think I enjoy it?"

"The conditions?" he repeated. "What conditions do you mean? I knew you intended yourself for a public singer."

The girl blushed hotly. "Why do you say 'intended myself?' I did not choose my fate. It has chosen me. You must have known that marrying" — the word came with a kind of awkward violence from her lips — "anybody was the last thing I should be likely to think of. A voice is a vocation in itself."

"I did not propose marriage to you as a vocation. As for that hope you accuse me of secretly harboring, I have never held you responsible for it. I took all the risks deliberately when I gave myself up to being happy with you, and trying to make you happy with me. You have been happy sometimes, have you not?"

"Yes," she confessed; "too happy, if this is the way it is to end."

"But it is not? Perhaps I ought to thank you for being sorry for me, but that is not what I want. I want to make you sorry for yourself, and for the awful mistake you are making."

"Oh, the whole summer has been a mistake! And this place and everything have been fatal! But if you had only been honest with me, it might have been different. I should have been on my guard."

"Thank heaven you were not! Do you suppose the man lives who would put a girl on her guard, as you say, and endure her company on such terms?"

"You know what I mean. I am not free; I am not — eligible. I thought you understood that and admitted it. We were friends on that basis."

"I never admitted anything of the kind or accepted any basis but the natural one. When you make your own conditions for a man and assume that he accepts them, you should ask yourself what sort of an animal he is. Most of us believe we have an inalienable right to try to win the woman we have chosen, if she is not bespoken or married to another man."

"I am bespoken then. Thank you for the word. My life is pledged to a purpose as serious as marriage itself. You need not smile. Love is not the only inspiration a woman's life can know. I shall reach far more people through my art than I could by just living for my own preferences."

"You still have preferences, then?"

"Why should I deny it. I don't call it being strong to be merely indifferent. I can care for things and yet give them up. I don't expect to have a very good time these next three years. I dare say I shall have foolish dreams like other girls, and look back and count the time spent. But what I truly believe I was meant to do, that I will do, no matter what it costs. There is no other way to live. Listen!" — she stopped him with a gesture as he was about to speak. She raised her head. Her gray eyes, which had more light than color in them, were shining with something that looked like tears, as she gave voice to one long, heart-satisfying peal of harmony, prolonging it, filling the silence with its rich cadences, and waking from the rocks across the cañon a faint eerie repetition, an echo like the utterance of a voice imprisoned in the cliff. "There," she said, "are the two me's, the real me and what you would make of me — the ghost of a voice — and echo of other voices from the world I belonged to once calling in the wild places where you would have me buried alive."

He smiled drearily at this girlish hyperbole. "I think there is room here even for a voice like yours. It need not perish for want of breath."

"No, but for want of listeners. I could not sing in an empty world."

"You would have one listener. I could listen for ten thousand."

"Oh, but I don't want you. I want the ten thousand. There are plenty of women with sweet voices meant for only one listener. You should find one of those voices and listen to it the rest of your life." There was a tremulous, insistent gayety in her manner which met with no response. "As for me," she continued, "I want to sing to multitudes. I want to lean my voice on the waves of great orchestras. I want to feel myself going crazy in the choruses, and then sing all alone in a hush — oh, don't you know that intoxicating silence? It takes hundreds to make it. And can't you hear the first low notes, and feel the shudder of joy? I can. I can hear my own voice like a separate living thing. I love it better than I love myself! It isn't myself. I feel sometimes that it is a spirit that has trusted itself to my keeping. I will not betray it, even for you."

This little concession to the weakness of human preference escaped her in the ardor of her resolve. It was not lost upon Aldis.

"Do you think I wish to silence you," he protested. "I love your voice, but not as a separate thing. If it is a spirit, it is your spirit. But I could dispense with it, easily!"

"Of course you could. You don't care for me as I am. You have never admitted that I have a gift which is a destiny in itself.

If you did, you would respect it; you could not think of me, mutilated, as I should be if you took away my one means of expression."

"Oh, nobody who has anything to express is so limited as that. Besides, I wouldn't take it away. I would enlarge it, not force it into one channel. I would have the woman possess the voice, not the voice possess the woman. I should be the last to deny that you have a destiny; but I have one too. My destiny is to love you and to make you my wife. There is nothing in that that need conflict with yours."

"I should think there was everything!"

"You have never let me get so far as a single detail, but if you will listen."

"I thought I had listened pretty well for one who assumes that it is her mission to be heard," Madeline again said, with a piteous attempt at lightness, which her hot cheeks and anxious eyes belied.

"Granting that it is your mission, this part of the world is not so empty as it looks. The people who would make your audiences here are farther apart than in the cities, but they have the enthusiasm that makes nothing of distance. They would make pilgrimages to hear you — whole families in plains-wagons with the children packed in bed quilts. And the cowboys! they would gather as they do to a grand round-up. It would be a unique career for a singer," he continued ignoring an interruption from Madeline, asking who would evoke this wide-spread enthusiasm, and whether he would have her advertised in the "Wallula News Miner."

"There would be no money in it for us." (Madeline winced at the pronoun.) "I would not have your lovely gift peddled about the country. There would be no floral tributes or press notices you would care for, or interviews with reporters or descriptions of your dresses in the papers. You might never have the pleasure of seeing your picture in the back of the monthlies, advertising superior toilet articles; but to a generous woman who believes in the regenerating influence of her art, I should think there would be a singular pleasure in giving it away to those who are cut off from all such joys. I know there are singers who boast of their thousand-dollar-a-night voices; I would rather boast that mine was the one free voice that could not be bought."

"There are no such vagrant, prodigal voices. A beautiful, trained voice is one of the highest products of civilization. It takes the most civilized listeners to appreciate it. It needs the stimulus of refined appreciation. It needs the inspiration of other voices and the spur of intelligent criticism. I know you have been making fun of my ambitions, but I choose to take you seriously. My standard would come down to the level of my audiences — the cowboys and the children in bed-quilts."

"Oh, no, it wouldn't. Your genius is its own standard, is it not? You would be like the early poets and the troubadours. They sang in rather an empty world, did they not, and not always to critical audiences? The knights and barons couldn't have been much above our cowboys."

"Oh, how absurd you are! No, not absurd, but unkind; you are making desperate fun of me and of my voice too, because I make so much of it — but you force me to. It is my whole argument."

"I'm desperate enough for anything, but I'm hardly in a position to make fun of my rival. Madeline, sometimes I hate your voice, and yet I love it too. I understand its power better than you think. It has just the dramatic quality which should make you the singer of a new people. Oh, how blind you are to a career so much finer, so much broader, so much sweeter, and more womanly! Your mission is here, in the the camps of the Philistines. You are to bring a message to the heathen; to sing to the wandering, godless peoples, — to the Esaus and the Ishmaels of the Far West."

"That is all very fine, but you know perfectly well that your Esaus and your Ishmaels would prefer a good clog-dancer to all the 'messages' in the world."

"Oh, you don't know them, — and if they did, it would be the first part of your mission to teach them a higher sort of pleasure."

"And I am to go to Munich and study for the sake of coming out here to regenerate the cowboys?"

"That isn't the part of your destiny I insist upon," Aldis said, letting the weariness of discouragement show in his tones. "But you say you must have an audience. And I must have you."

"But does it occur to you," Madeline interrupted quickly, "what a tremendous waste of effort and elaboration there would be between the means and the effect?"

"I don't ask for the effort and the elaboration. That is the part you insist upon. All I want is you, just as you are, voice or no voice. You need not go to Munich on my account."

"You expect me to give up everything."

"You would have to give up a good deal; I don't deny it. But is there any virtue in woman that becomes her better?"

"Perhaps not, from a man's point of view. But it is no use listening to you. You haven't the faintest conception of what my future is to me, as I see it, and all this you have been talking is either a burlesque on my ambition, or else it is the insanity of selfishness — masculine selfishness. I don't mean anything personal. You want to absorb into your own life a thing that was meant to have a life of its own, for all the world to share and enjoy. Yes, why not? I won't pretend to depreciate my gift! I am only the tenement in which a precious thing is lodged. You would drive out the divine tenant, or imprison it, for the sake of possessing the poor house it lives in."

"Good Heavens!" Aldis exclaimed, with a sort of awe of what seemed to him an almost blasphemous absurdity. "What nonsense you young geniuses can talk! I wish the precious tenant would evacuate and leave you to your sober senses, and to me."

"And this is what a man calls love!"

Aldis laughed fiercely. "Has there been any new kind of love invented lately? This is the kind that came into the world before art did."

"Art is love, without its selfishness," said Madeline, with innocent conclusiveness.

"Where the deuce do you girls learn this sort of talk?" Aldis demanded of the girl beside him.

She answered him with unexpected gentleness. She leaned towards him, and looked entreatingly in his face. "This is our last evening together. Don't let us spoil it with this wretched squabbling."

"She calls it squabbling — a man's fight for his life!" He turned and gave her back her look, with more fire than entreaty in his eyes.

"There is the moon," she said hurriedly. "It is time to go home."

The fringe of grasses above their heads was touched with silver light, and the shadow of the bluff lay broad and distinct across the valley.

"We must go home," Madeline urged. Aldis did not move.

"Madeline, would you marry me if I had a lot of money?"

"Oh, hush!"

"No, but would you? Answer me."

"Yes, I would." She was tired of choosing her words. "For then you would not have to earn a living in these wild places."

"You would take me then as a sort of appendage? You don't want a man with work of his own to do?"

"Not if it interferes with mine."

"That is your answer?"

"Can I make it any plainer?"

"You have not said you do not love me."

"I don't need to say it. It is proved by what I do — I might have been nicer to you, perhaps, but you are so unreasonable."

"Never mind if I am. Be nice to me now!"

"I meant to be. But it is too late. We must go home." She felt that she was losing command of herself through sheer exhaustion; any hint of weakness or hesitation now could only mislead him and prolong the struggle. "Come," she said, "you will have to get up first."

He did not move.

"Oh, sit still a little longer," he pleaded. "I will not bother you any more. Let us have one half hour of our old times together — only a little better, because it is the last."

"No, not another minute." She rose quickly to her feet, tripped in her skirt, and tottered forward. Aldis had risen too. As she reeled and threw out her hands, he sprang between her and the brink, thrusting her back with the whole force of his sudden spring. The rock upon which he had leaped regardless of his footing gave its final quake and dropped into the abyss. It was the uppermost segment of a loosened column. The whole mass went down, narrowing the ledge so that Madeline, by turning her head, could look into the depths below. She did not move or cry; she lay still, but for the deep gasping breaths that would not cease, though all the life had seemed to go out from her when he went down. The relief of unconsciousness did not come to her. She was aware of the soft, dry night wind growing cool, of the river's soughing, of the long grasses fluttering wildly against the moon above her head. The perfume of wild syringa blossoms, hidden in some crevice of the rock, came to her with the breeze. There were crackling, rustling noises from the depth of shadow, into which she dared not look; then silence, except the wind and the river's roar, borne strongly upwards, as it freshened. And all the words they had said to each other in their long, passionate argument kept repeating themselves, forcing themselves upon her stunned, passive consciousness, she lying there, not caring if she never stirred again, and he on the rocks below; and between them the sudden, awful silence. She might have crept to the brink and called, but she could not call to the dead.

Gradually it came to her that she must get herself back somehow to the camp with her miserable story. It would be easier, it seemed, to turn once over and drop off the cliff, and let some one else tell the story for them both. But the fascination of this impulse could not prevail over the awakening shuddering fact of her physical being. She despised herself for the caution with which she crept along the ledge and up the grass-grown crevice. If he had been cautious she would be where he was lying now. It was her own rash girl's fancy for getting on the brink of things and looking over, that had brought them first to that fatal place. But these thoughts were but pin-pricks following the shock of that benumbing horror she was carrying with her back to the camp.

As she looked down upon its lights she felt like one already long estranged from the life of which she had been the gay centre but two hours before. She knew how her sister's little girls were asleep, the night wind softly stirring the leaves outside their bedroom window; how still the house was; how empty and white in the moonlight the tents on the hill; how the camp was assembled on the beach, waiting for her return with Aldis and for the evening singing. Sing! She could have shrieked, sobbed, and cried aloud at the thought of this home-coming — she alone with the burden of her sorrow, and by and by Aldis, borne in his comrades' arms and laid on his bed in that empty tent on the hill.

But there was a hard constriction, a dumb, convulsive ache in her throat. She felt as if no sound could ever be uttered by her again.

If Aldis had been lying dead at the foot of the bluffs, as Madeline believed, this story would never have been told in print, except in a cold-blooded newpaper paragraph, which would have omitted to mention one curious fact connected with the accident; that a young girl, who was the companion of the unfortunate young man when it occurred, suffered a shock of the nerves from the sight of his fall that deprived her entirely of her voice, so that she could not speak except in whispers.

It was not Aldis who was the victim of this tragedy of the bluffs, but Aldis's successful rival, the Voice. It was hushed at the very moment of its triumph. A blow from the brain upon those nerve-chords which were its life — love shook the house in which music dwelt, jarred it to its centre, and the imperious but frail tenant had fled. At the moment when Madeline's tortured fancy was bringing him home a mangled heap, and laying him in the last of that row of tents on the hill, Aldis was getting himself home by the lower trail, as fast as his bruises would let him.

He had fallen into a scruby growth of wild syringa, which flung its wax-white blossoms out from a cranny in the cliff, less than half-way down. As he crashed into it, its tough and springy mass checked his fall enough to enable him to get a firm grasp with his hands. He hung dangling at arm's length against the cliff, groping for a temporary lodgment for his feet. In the darkness he dimly perceived something like a ledge, not too far below him, towards which the face of the bluff sloped slightly outwards.

Flattening himself against the rock he let go his hold and slid, clutching and grinding downward, till his feet struck the ledge. From this vantage, after getting his breath and taking a deliberate view of his situation, it was not a difficult feat to reach the slope of broken rock below. He sat there while the trembling in his strained muscles subsided, scarcely conscious as yet of his torn and scratched and bruised condition. He was about to raise his voice in a shout to assure Madeline of his safety, when the thought turned him sick that, unnerved as she must be with the sight of his fall, she might mistake the call for a cry for help, and venture too near that treacherous edge to look down. He kept still, while the horror grew upon him of what might happen to Madeline alone on the ledge or trying to climb the slippery crevice in the shadow of the bluff. He knew that a mass of rock had fallen when he fell; was there space enough left on the ledge by which she could safely reach the crevice? He could not resist giving one low call, speaking her name as distinctly and quietly as he could, and bidding her not move but listen. There was no answer; the roar of the rapids borne on the wind that nightly drew down the cañon, drowned his voice. Madeline did not hear him. He waited until the silence convinced him that she was no longer there; then he took his way toilsomely back to the camp.

A light showed in the window of the office, which in the evening was usually dark. He found the family assembled there in the light of a single kerosene lamp, the flame of which was streaming up the chimney unobserved, while all eyes were bent upon Madeline, seated in one of the revolving office chairs, with her back to the desk. She leaned, shivering and whispering, towards her sister, who knelt on the floor before her, holding her hands and staring with a fearful interest into the girl's colorless face.

The men who stood nearest the door turned and started as Aldis entered.

"Why, good God, Aldis!" Mr. Duncan exclaimed. "Why, man, we thought you were dead. You don't mean to say it's you — all of you?"

"I'm all here," said Aldis.

"He's all here, Madeline," Mrs. Duncan shouted hysterically to the girl, as if she were deaf as well as dumb.

The fateful voice was undoubtedly gone. Madeline could no longer plead a higher call when the common destiny of woman was offered her. But if Aldis had thought to profit immediately by her release from the claims of art, he was disappointed.

What was the new obstacle? Only some more of Madeline's high-flown nonsense, as her sister called it. She was always making a heroic situation out of everything that happened to her, and expecting her friends to bear her out in it.

On the night of the adventure on the cliff she had been put to bed, shaking with a nervous chill. Next day's packing had been suspended, and the eastward journey postponed. But in a day or two she was sufficiently recovered to be walking again with Aldis on the shore, and the old argument was resumed on a new basis. Madeline, pale and wistful, with Aldis's head very close to hers, that the river's intruding roar might not drown her whispers, protesting — sometimes with sobs, sometimes with sudden, tremulous laughter that shook her with dumb convulsions hardly more mirthful than the sobs — that she could not and she would not burden his life with the wreck she now passionately proclaimed herself to be.

But would she not give him what he wanted, had wanted, should continue to want and to try for so long as they both should live?

No, he didn't — he couldn't possibly want a ridiculous muttering shadow of a woman beside him all the days of his life. It was only his magnanimity. She wondered he could believe her capable of the meanness of taking advantage of it.

Aldis did not despair, but it was certainly difficult, with happiness almost within his reach, with the girl herself sometimes sobbing in his arms, to be obliged to treat this obstacle as seriously as Madeline insisted it should be treated. He appealed to Mrs. Duncan, who scolded and laughed at her sister alternately, and quoted with elaborate particulars a surprising number of similar cases of voices lost and found again by means of care and skillful treatment. But hers was *not* a similar case, Madeline vehemently declared. It was *not* from a cold, like Mrs. So and So's; it had not come on gradually, beginning with a hoarseness, like some one's else. It was — the girl believed in her heart that she had been made a singular and impressive example of the folly and wickedness of pride in an exceptional gift, and of triumph in its corresponding destiny. The spirit she had boasted of harboring had deserted her. She had deserved her punishment, but she would not permit another's life to be shadowed by it, especially one so generous — who, so far from resenting her refusal of the whole loaf, was content, or pretended to be, with the broken and rejected fragments. But all this Madeline was careful to keep from the cheerful irreverence of her sister's comments. She faltered something like it to Aldis in one of their long talks by the river; his low tones answering briefly and at long intervals her piercing whispers, that sometimes almost shrieked her trouble in his ear. He could feel that she was still thrilling with the double shock she had suffered. He was infinitely tender with her, and patient with her extravagant expositions of the situation between them. He longed to heap savage ridicule upon them, but he forbore. He listened and waited and let her talk until she was worn out, and then they were happiest together. For a few moments each day it seemed that she might drift back to him on the ebb of that overstrained tide of resistance, and be at rest.

Madeline was always impatient of any discussion of the chances of her recovery; but one day, just before the time of their parting, Aldis surprised and captured an admission from her that there might be such a chance. Would she then, on the strength of that possibility, consent to be engaged to him and treat him as her accepted lover, since nothing but her pride now kept them apart?

"Pride," Madeline repeated; "I don't know what I have left to be proud of."

"There is a kind of stiff-necked humility that is worse than pride," said Aldis, smiling at the easy way in which she shirked the logic of the conclusion he was forcing upon her. "You won't consent to the meanness, as you call it, of giving me what you are pleased to consider a damaged article, a thing with a flaw in it; as if a woman would be more lovable if she were proof against all wear and tear. But if the flaw can be healed, if there is a possibility that the voice may come back, why should we not be engaged on that hope?"

"And if it never does, will you promise to let me release you?"

"You can release me at any time — now, if you like."

"But will you promise to take your release when I give it to you?"

"We will see about that. Perhaps by the time your voice doesn't come back I shall have been able to make you believe that it isn't the voice I care for."

"And if it should come back," cried Madeline with sudden enthusiasm, "I shall have my triumph! I am done forever with all that nonsense about Art and Destiny. If my voice ever does come back, I shall not let it bully me. It shall not decide my fate. You will see. Oh, how I wish you *might* see! I have learned my lesson in the true, awful values of things. Thank Heaven it has cost no more! There is one less singer in the world, perhaps, but there is not one less life. Your life. If you had lost it that night, and I had kept my voice, do you think I should ever have had any joy in it again — ever lifted it up, as I boasted to you I would some day, before crowds of listeners? Could I have gone before the footlights, bowing and smiling, with my arms full of flowers, and remembered your face and your last look as you went down?"

"Then it is settled at last, voice or no voice?"

"Yes, — but I am so sorry for you! It will not come back; I know it never will, and I shall go on whispering and gibbering to the end of my days, and all your friends will pity you; it is such a painfully conspicuous thing!"

"I want to be pitied. I am just pining to be an object of general compassion. Only I want to choose what I shall be pitied for."

"Choose?" said Madeline stupidly. "What do you mean?"

"Have I not chosen? Now be as sorry for me as you like. And we'll ask for the sympathy of the camp to-night. It will be a blow to the boys — my throwing myself away like this!"

"How ridiculous you are!" sighed Madeline. It was a luxury, after all, to yield. And perhaps in the depths of her consicousness, bruised and quivering as it was, there lingered a faint image of herself, as a charming girl sees herself reflected in those flattering mirrors, the eyes of friends, kindred, and adorers. Voiceless, futureless, spoiled as was the budding prima donna, the girl remained: eighteen years old and fair to look upon, with perfect health, and all the mysterious, fitful, but unquenchable joy of youth thrilling through her pulses. Perhaps in the innocent joy of her own intentions towards him, she was not so sorry for Aldis after all. The sobs, the frantic whispers died away, and were hushed in a blissful acquiescence. She was not less fascinating to her lover — half amazed at his own sudden triumph — in her blushing, starry-eyed silences, than she had been in all the eager redundance of her lost utterance. That was a wonderful last day for the young man to dream over, in the long months before they should meet again!

The camp had moved out of the cañon and down upon the desert plains. It was an open winter. Up to the first of January the contractors had been able to keep their men at work, following closely the locating party.

Aldis rode up and down the line, putting in fresh stakes for the contractors, keeping them true to the line, and watching incidentally that they did not pad the embankments with sage brush. His summer camp-dress of broad-shouldered, breezy, flannel shirt, and slender-waisted trousers, was changed to a reefing-jacket, double-buttoned to the chin, long boots and helmet-shaped cap, pulled low down to keep the wind out of his eyes. Strong wintry reds and browns replaced, on his thin cheek, the summer's pallor.

Madeline Hendrie, dressing for dinner at the Sutherland in New York, where she and her sister were spending the winter, stood before her toilet-glass fastening her laces, her eyes fixed alternately on her own reflection in the mirror and on a dim photograph that leaned against the frame. It was not a bad specimen of amateur photography. It represented a young man on horseback in a wide and windy country, with an expression of sadness and determination in the dark eyes that looked steadfastly out of the gray, toneless picture.

They were the most beautiful eyes in the world, Madeline thought to herself; and sinking on her knees before the low table, with her arms crossed on the lace, rose-lined cover, she would brood in a fond, luxurious melancholy over the picture — over the sombre line of plain and distant mountain and the chilly little cluster of tents, huddled close together by the river's dark, swift flood flowing between icy beaches, below barren shores, where a few leafless willows shivered and the wild-twisted clumps of sage defied the cold.

A moment later she was rustling softly down the corridor at her sister's side, passing groups of ladies who looked after them with that comprehensive but impersonal scrutiny which is a woman's recognition of anything unusual in another's dress or appearance. Mrs. Duncan looked her sister over with a quick, intelligent side glance, for those silent eye comments were all turned upon Madeline. She could see nothing amiss with the girl; she was looking very lovely, a trifle absent. Madeline had a way lately of looking as if she were alone with her own thoughts, on occasions when other women's faces took on habitually a neutral and impassive expression. It made her conspicuous, as if hers were the only sensitive human countenance exposed in a roomful of masks.

"Why do you never wear your light dresses, Madeline?" said Mrs. Duncan, with the intention of rousing the girl from her untimely dream. "You are very effective in black, with your hair, but I should think you would like once in a while to vary the effect."

"Do you suppose I am studying effects for the benefit of these people? I am saving my light dresses."

"Saving them! What for?"

"Do you never save up a pretty dress that Will likes, when you are away from him?"

"No, indeed I don't. It would get out of style, and he would see there was something wrong with it, though he might not know what it was. Dresses won't keep! Besides, do you think you are never to have any new ones, now you are engaged to an engineer?"

"I shall not need many if I go West, and a year or two behind won't matter to — my engineer!"

"Oh, you poor innocent! You don't know your engineer yet; and you don't know your West, either. And one is always having to pack up and come East at short notice, and I know of nothing more insupportable than to find one's self dumped off an overland train in New York in the middle of winter, for instance, with a veteran outfit one hasn't had the strength of mind to 'give to the poor,' as Will says. You never know how your clothes look till you have packed them up on one side of the continent and unpacked them on the other. And let me tell you it pays to dress well in camp. Nothing is too good for them, poor things, so long as it's not inappropriate. Do you suppose a man ever forgets how a woman ought to look? Wear out your things, my dear, and take the good of them before they get passè, and let the future take care of itself."

Madeline was laughing and the dreamy soft abstraction had vanished. A stranger might look into her liquid, half-averted eyes, and see no more there than was meant for the passing glance.

Aldis had the promise of a month's leave of absence in March, but soon after the 1st of January the weather turned suddenly cold. The contractors took their men off the work, and the time of Aldis's leave was thus anticipated by two months. He telegraphed to Mrs. Duncan that he would be in New York by the 15th, allowing for all contingencies. Madeline's joy over the telegram was increased by one small item, of relief from the necessity of delaying a communication which she dreaded making by letter. With rest and skillful treatment her voice had come back as her sister had prophesied, in its full compass and purity. Her musical instructor had urged her to try it once upon an audience, in a not too conspicuous role, before she went abroad to study; for Madeline had not yet found courage to confess her apostasy.

The temptation to sing once as she had so often dreamed of singing, with the support of a magnificent orchestra; the longing to know just how much she was resigning in turning her back upon a musical career, were overmastering.

Moreover, her music was the sole dowry with which she could enrich her husband's life. She had a curious, persistent humility about herself, apart from the gift which she had grown to consider the essential quality of her being. She desired intensely to know just how much it was in her power to endow her lover with, over and above what his generosity, as she insisted upon calling it, demanded. For Madeline did nothing by halves. She could abandon herself to a passion of surrender as completely as she had done to the fire of resistance; and while she was about it, she wished to feel that it was no paltry thing she was giving up. But she was wise enough in her love to reflect that possibly Aldis might not be able fully to enter into the joy of her magnificent renunciation. There might be a pang, an uneasiness to him, so far away from her, in the thought that his old enemy was again in the field. So Aldis only knew this much of her recovery, that she could speak once more in her natural voice. She would reserve her triumph, if so it should prove, until his home-coming, when she could lay it at his feet with a joyous humility and such assurances of her love as no letter could convey.

On the 13th of January she was to be the soloist at a popular concert to be given that evening; one of a series where the character of the music and of the audience was exceedingly good, and the orchestral support all that a singer's heart could desire. On the 15th Aldis would come home.

It was all delightfully dramatic; and Madeline was not yet so in love with obscurity as to be quite indifferent to the scenic element in life.

In his telegram Aldis had allowed for a two day's delay on business at Denver. Arriving at that city, however, he found that, in the absence of one of the principal parties concerned, his business would have to be deferred. He was therefore due in New York on the 13th. He had not telegraphed again to his Eastern friends; it had seemed like making too much of a ceremony of his homecoming. He dropped off the train from the north at the Grand Central Depot in the white early dusk of a snowy afternoon, when the quiet up-town streets were echoing to the sound of snow-shovels, and the muffled tinkle of car-bells came at long intervals from the neighboring avenues. He hurried ahead of the long line of passengers, jumped on the rear platform of a crowded car that was just moving off, and in twenty minutes was at his hotel. He tried to master his great but tremulous joy, to dine deliberately, to do his best for his outer man, before presenting himself to Madeline; but his lonely fancy had dwelt so long and with such intensity on this meeting that now he was almost unnerved by the nearness of the reality.

The reality was after all only a neat maid, who said, as he offered his card at the door of Mrs. Duncan's apartment, that the ladies were both out. It was impossible to accept the statement simply and go away. Were the ladies out for the evening? he asked. Yes, they had gone to a concert or the opera, or something, at the Academy of Music. Mrs. Duncan always left word where she was going when she and Miss Madeline both went out, on account of the children. The maid looked at him with intelligent friendliness. She was perfectly aware of the significance of the name on the card she held. She waited while Aldis scribbled a few words on another card which he asked her to give to Mrs. Duncan when the ladies returned, in case he should miss them at the concert. In the street he debated briefly whether to endure a few more hours of waiting, or hasten on to the mixed joy of a meeting in a crowd. Yet such meetings were not always infelicitous. Delicious moments of isolation might come to two in a great assembly, hushed, driven together in a storm of music. There seemed a peculiar fascinating fitness in the situation. Music, which had threatened to part them, should, like a hireling, celebrate their reunion.

The violins were in full cry, behind the green baize doors, mingling with the clear, terse notes of a piano, as he passed into the lobby of the academy. While he waited for the concerto to end, his eyes rested mechanically upon the portraits of prima donnas, whose names were new to him, in smiles and low corsages and wonderful coiffures of the latest fashion; and he said to himself that well it was for those fair dames, but not for his ladye — his little girl, she was safe among the listeners, unknown, unpublished. *For* her, not *of* her, the loud instruments were speaking, in the vast, hushed, resounding temple of music.

He would see her first with her rapt face turned towards the stage. He would know her by the outline of her cheek, her little ear, and the soft light tangle of curls hiding her temples. She would not be exalted above him in the Olympian circle of the boxes; she would be in the balcony, not in full-dress, but with some marvel of a little bonnet framing the color and light and sweetness of her face. Her cloak would have slipped down from her smooth, silken sleeves and shoulders. In his restless, waiting dream, while the music sank and swelled in the endless cadences behind the barriers, he could see her with distracting vividness: her listening attitude, her lifted, half-averted face, her slender passive hands in her lap, her soft deep, joyous breathing stirring the lace or ribbons at her throat.

He was prepared to find her very dainty and unapproachably elegant; there had been a hint of such formidable but delightful possibilities in the cut of her simple camp dresses and in the way she wore them. He glanced disconsolately at his own modestly dressed person, with which he was so monotonously familiar, and wondered if Madeline would find him "Western."

The concerto was over at last. He passed down the aisle and along the rear wall of the balcony, keeping under the shadow of the first tier of boxes, while he took a survey of the house. It seemed bewilderingly brilliant to Aldis, seeing it in a setting of frontier life for the first itme in three years; a much more complex emotion to one born to the life around him, and estranged from it, than to him who sees it for the first time as a spectacle in which he has never had a part. It was with rather a heart-sick gaze he searched the rows and rows of laughing women's faces, banked like flowers against the crimson and white and gold of the partitions.

Suddenly the murmur pervading the house sank into an expectant silence — the musicians' chairs were filling up: but only the grayheaded first violins were leaning to their instruments and fingering their music. The leader's music-stand had been moved aside to make room for the soloist, a young debutante, so the whispers around him announced, who was now coming forward, winding her silken train past the musicians' stands, her hand in that of the leader. Now she sank before the hushed crowd, dedicating to it, as it were, herself, her beauty, her song, her whole blissful young presence there.

Aldis crushed the unfolded programme he held in his hand. He did not need to consult it for the name of the fair young candidate. The blood rushed into his face, and then left it deadly white. His heart was pounding with a raging excitement, but he did not move or take his eyes from Madeline's face. She stood, faintly smiling down upon the crowd, folding and unfolding the music in her hands, while the orchestra played the prelude. Then on the deepening silence came the first notes of her voice. Aldis had never imagined anything like the pang of delicious pain it gave him. Its personality pierced his very soul. Every word of the recitative, in the singer's pure enunciation, could be heard. The song was Heine's "Lorelei," with Liszt's music, and the orchestration was worthy of the music.

"I know not what it presages," — the recitative began, — "this heart with sadness fraught." Aldis took a deep, hard breath. He knew the story that was coming. The rocks, the river, the evening sky — he knew them all. Had she forgotten? Did the great god Music deprive a woman of her memory, her tender womanly compunction, as well as her heart? Was this beautiful creature, with eyes alight and soft throat swelling to the notes of her song, merely a voice, after all, celebrating its own triumph and another's allurement and despair? Was the heart that beat under the laces that covered that white bosom merely a subtle machine for setting free those wonderful sounds that floated down to him and seemed to bid him farewell?

Now, in a wild crescendo, with a hurry of chords in the accompaniment, the end has come; the boat and man are lost. Then an interlude, and the pure, pitiless voice again, lamenting now, not triumphing — "And this, with her magic singing, the

Lorelei hath done — the Lorelei hath done." The song died away and ceased in the mournful repetitions, and the audience gave itself up to a transport of applause. It had won — a new singer; and he had lost — only his wife. He stood there unknown and unheeded, a pitiful minority of one, and accepted his defeat.

The frantic clappings continued. They were demanding an encore. The friendly old fellows in the orchestra were looking back across the stage to welcome the singer's return. They had assisted at the triumph of so many young aspirants and queens of the hour. This one was coming back, flushed and smiling, her face beautiful in its new joy, as she sank down again with her arms full of flowers, gratefully, submissively, before the audience at whose command she was there. The great house was enchanted with her and with its own unexpected enthusiasm. A joyous thrill and murmur, the very breath of that adulation which is dearest to the goddess of the foot-lights, floated up to the intoxicated girl, wrapt in the wonder of her own success. Aldis could bear no more. He made his way out, pursued by the furious clappings, by the silence, by the first thrilling notes of the encore. He walked the streets for hours, then went to his room, and threw himself, face downward, on his bed. The lace curtains of his window let in a pallid glimmer from the electric lights in the square, — a ghastly fiction of a moon that never waxes nor wanes. The night spent itself, the tardy winter morning crept slowly over the city and wrapt it in chill sea fog.

Mrs. Duncan woke with a hoarse feverish cold, and wished that she had given Aldis's card and message to Madeline the night before. She had kept them from her, sure that they would rob the excited girl of what was left of her night's sleep. Now she felt too ill to make the disclosure and face Madeline's alarm. She waited, with cowardly procrastination, until the late breakfast was over and her little girls had been hurried off to school. She and Madeline had drawn their chairs close to the soft coal fire to talk over the concert, Madeline with a heap of morning papers in her lap, through which she was looking for the musical notices, when Mrs. Duncan gave her Aldis's note. It required no explanation or comment. It said that he hoped to find them at the Academy of Music, but if he failed to do so, this was to prepare them for an early call; he was coming as early as he could hope to see them, — nine o'clock, he suggested, with insistence that made itself felt even in the careless words of the note. It was now nearly ten o'clock; he had not come. The gray morning turned a sickly yellow and the streets looked wet and dirty. The papers were tossed into a corner of the sofa, where Mrs. Duncan had taken refuge from Madeline's restless wanderings about the room.

A mass of hot-house roses, trophies of the evening's triumph, were displayed on the closed piano, shedding their languid sweetness unheeded; except once when Madeline stopped near them, and exclaimed to her sister:

"Oh, do tell Alice to take those flowers away!" and the next moment seemed to forget they were still there.

The ladies breakfasted and lunched in their own rooms, dining only in the restaurant below. When lunch was announced, Mrs. Duncan rose from her heap of shawls and sofa-cushions and went to the window, where Madeline stood gazing out into the yellow mist that hid the square.

"Come, girlie, come out and keep me company. A watched pot never boils, you know."

"Do you want any lunch?" Madeline asked incredulously.

Mrs. Duncan did not want any, but she was willing to pretend that she did for the sake of interrupting the girl's unhappy watch. The two women sat down opposite each other in the little dark dining-room, the one window of which looked into a dingy well inclosed by the many-storied walls of the house. The gas was burning, but enough gray daylight mingled with it to give a sickly paleness to the faces it illuminated.

There was a letter lying by Madeline's plate.

"When did this come?" she demanded of Alice, the maid.

"They sent it up, miss, with the lunch tray."

"Oh!" cried Madeline. "It may have been lying there in the office for hours!"

She read a few words of the letter, got up from the table, and left the room. Mrs. Duncan gave her a few moments to herself, and then followed her. She was in the parlor, turning over the heap of papers in a distracted search for something she could not seem to find.

"Oh, Sallie," she exclaimed, looking up piteously at her sister, "won't you find when the Boston Shore line train goes out? I think it is two o'clock, and it's after one now."

"Why do you want to know about the Boston trains?"

"Read that letter — I'm going to try to see him before he starts — read the letter!" she repeated, in answer to her sister's amazed expostulatory stare. She ran out of the room while Mrs. Duncan was reading the letter, and in her own chamber tore off her wrapper and began dressing for the street. Mrs. Duncan heard bureau-drawers flying open and hurried footsteps as she read. This was Aldis's letter: —

> *Wednesday morning.*
>
> *Dear Madeline, — I saw you at the Academy last night when the verdict was given that separates us. The destiny I would not believe in has become a reality to me at last. I must stand aside, and let it fulfill itself. Last night I accused you of bitter things — you can imagine what, seeing you so, without any forewarning; but I am tolerably sane this morning. I know that nothing of all that maddened me is true, except that I love you and must give you back to your fate that claims you. You were never mine except by default.*
>
> *I am going to Boston this afternoon. I cannot trust myself to see you. I could not bear your compassion or remorse, and if you were to offer me more than that, God knows what sacrifice I might not be base enough to accept, face to face with you again.*
>
> *Good-by, my dearest, my only one. I think nothing can ever hurt me much after this. But do not grieve over what neither of us could have helped. The happiness of one man should not stand in the way of the free exercise of a divine gift like yours, and the memory of our summer in the cañon together, when my soul set itself to the music of those silences between us — that is still mine. Nothing can take that from me. Yours always.*
>
> *Hugh Aldis*

"Madeline, you are not going after him!" Mrs. Duncan protested, looking up from the letter with tears in her eyes, as her sister entered the parlor, in cloak and bonnet.

Madeline heard the protest; she did not see the tears.

"Don't *talk* to me, — help me, Sallie! Can't you see what I have done? Find me that Boston train, won't you? I know there is one in the evening, but he said afternoon. Where *is* it?" she wailed, turning over with trembling hands sheet after sheet of bewildering columns which mocked her with advertisements of musical entertainments, and even her own name staring at her in print.

"The *train* goes at two o'clock, but you shall not go racing up there after him, you crazy girl! I'd go myself, only I'm too sick. I'm awfully sorry for him, but he'll come back — they always do — and give you a chance to explain."

"Explain! I'm going to see him for one instant if I can. I've got just twenty minutes, and nothing on earth shall stop me!"

"Alice," Mrs. Duncan called down the passage, as Madeline shut the outer door, "put on your things and go after Miss Madeline, quick — Third Avenue Elevated to the Grand Central. You'll catch her if you hurry, before she gets up the steps."

Mistress and maid reached the Grand Central station together, a few minutes before the train moved out. The last of the line of passengers, ticket in hand, were filing past the door-keeper. It needed but a glance to assure Madeline that Aldis was not among them. It would be safer, she decided quickly, to get out upon the platform in broadside view from the windows of the train. If Aldis were already on the train, or, better still, on the platform, and should see her, Madeline felt sure he would instantly know why she was there.

"I only want to see a friend who is going by the Boston train," she said to the door-keeper. "I'm not going myself." He hesitated, and said something about his orders. "If I must have a ticket, my maid will get me one, but I cannot wait; you must let me through!" She handed her purse to Alice. The man at the gate said he guessed it was no matter about a ticket. He looked curiously after her as she sped along the platform — such a pretty girl, her cheeks red and her hair all out of crimp with the dampness, but with a sob in her voice and eyes strained wide with trouble!

"Last train down on the right!" he called after her. "You'll have to hurry." Ominous clouds of steam were puffing out of a smoke-stack far ahead of her; men were swinging themselves aboard from the platform where they had been walking up and down.

"Boston Shore line, miss?" a porter lounging by his empty truck called to Madeline as she came panting up to the rear car.

"Oh, yes!" she sobbed. "Is it gone?"

The train gave one heavy, clanking lurch forward. The porter laughed, caught her by the arms, and swung her lightly up to the platform of the last car. The brakeman seized her and shunted her in at the door. The train was in motion. She clung wildly to the door-handle a moment, looking back, and then sank into the nearest seat and burst into tears. Curious glances were cast at her from the neighboring seats, but Madeline was oblivious of everything but the grotesque misery of her situation. What would Alice think, and what would poor, frantic Sallie think, what even would the man at the gate think, who had taken her word instead of a ticket! The conductor came around after a while, and Madeline appealed to him. She had been put on the train by mistake. She had no money and no ticket, but there was a friend of hers aboard — would the conductor kindly find out for her if a Mr. Aldis were in any of the forward cars, and tell him that a lady, a friend of his, wished to see him?

The conductor had a broad, purple, smooth-shaven cheek, which overflowed his stiff shirt collar; he stroked a tuft of coarse beard of the end of his chin, as he assured the young lady that she need not distress herself. He would find the gentleman if he were on the train. Was he a young gentleman, for instance?

"Yes, he was young and tall, and had dark eyes" — Suddenly Madeline stopped and blushed furiously, meeting the conductor's small and merry eye fixed upon her in the abandonment of her trouble.

The door banged behind him. The car swayed and leaped on the track as the motion of the train increased. A long interval, then a loud crash of noise from the wheels as the door opened again at the forward end of the car. A gentleman was coming down the aisle, looking from side to side as if in search of someone.

Madeline squeezed herself back into the corner of her seat next the window. The blood dropped out of her hot cheeks and stifled her breathing. She turned away her face, and buried it in her muff as some one stopped at her seat, and said, leaning with one hand on the back of it, "Is this the lady who wished to see me?"

Aldis's face was as white as her own. His hand gripped the seat to hide its shaking. Madeline swept back her skirts, and he took the seat beside her. A long silence. Madeline's cheek and profile emerged from the muff and became visible in rosy silhouette against the blank white mist outside the window. Her color had come back.

"Did you get my letter?"

"Yes. That is what brought me here."

Another silence. Madeline slid the hand next to Aldis out of her muff. He took no notice of it at first, then suddenly his own closed over it, and crushed it hard.

"You must not go to Boston to-night," she whispered.

"Why not?"

"Because I am in such trouble! — I had to see you, after that letter. I ran after the train, and they caught hold of me and put me on before I knew what they were doing; and here I am without a ticket or a cent of money — and all because you would not come and let me — tell you" —   She had hidden her face again in her muff.

"Tell me — what?" His head was close to hers, his arm against her shoulder. He could feel her long, shuddering sobs.

"How *could* I come?" he said.

She did not answer. The roar and rattle of the train went sounding on. It was very interesting to the people in the car; but Madeline had forgotten them, and Aldis cared no more for the files of faces than if they had been the rocky fronts of the bluffs that had kept a summer's watch over him and the girl beside him, and the noise of the train had been the far-off river's roar. He was in a dream which could not last too long.

Madeline lifted her head, and through the lulling din he heard her voice saying: —

"Oh, the river! I seemed to hear it last night when I was singing, and the light on the rocks — do you remember? And I was so glad that the rest was not true. And then your letter came" —

"Never mind; nothing is true — only this," he roused himself to say.

The crowded train went roaring and swaying on, as it had during all the days and nights of his journey home, mingling its monotone with the dream that was coming true at last.

Somewhere in that vague and rapidly lessening region known as the frontier, there disappeared, a few years ago, a woman's voice. A soprano with a wonderful mezzo quality, those who knew it called it, and the girl, besides her beauty, had a distinct promise of dramatic power. But, they added, she seemed to have no imagination, no conception of the value of her gifts. She threw away a charming career, just at its outset, and went West with a husband — not anybody in particular. It was altogether a great pity. Perhaps she had not the artistic temperament, or was too indolent to give the time and labor required for the perfecting of her rare gift — at all events the voice was lost.

But in the camps of engineers, within the sound of unknown waters, on mountain trails, or crossing the windy cattle-ranges, or in the little churches of the valley towns, or at a lonely grave perhaps, where his comrades are burying some unwitting, unacknowledged hero, dead in the quiet doing of his duty, a voice is sometimes heard, in ballad or gay roulade, anthem or requiem, — a voice those who have heard say they will never forget.

Lost it may be to the history of famous voices, but the treasured, self-prized gifts are not those that always carry a blessing with them; and the soul of music, wherever it is purely uttered, will find its listeners; though it be a voice singing in the wilderness, in the dawn of the day of art and beauty which is coming to a new country and a new people.

~ ~ ~

Maverick
Century Magazine 1904

Traveling Buttes is a lone stage-station on the road, largely speaking, from Blackfoot to Boise. I do not know whether the stages take that road now, but ten years ago they did, and the man who kept the stage-house was a person of primitive habits and corresponding appearance named Gilroy.

The stage-house is perhaps half a mile from the foot of the largest butte, one of three that loom on the horizon, and appear to "travel" from you, as you approach them from the plains. A day's ride with the Buttes as a landmark is like a stern chase, in that you seem never to gain upon them.

From the stage-house the plain slopes up to the foot of the Big Butte, which rises suddenly in the form of an enormous tepee, as if Gitche Manito, the mighty, had here descended and pitched his tent for a council of the nations.

The country is destitute of water. To say that it is "thirsty" is to mock with vain imagery that dead and mummied land on the borders of the Black Lava. The people at the stage-house had located a precious spring, four miles up, in a cleft near the top of the Big Butte; they piped the water down to the house and they sold it to travelers on that Jericho road at so much per horse. The man was thrown in, but the man usually drank whisky.

Our guide commented unfavorably on this species of husbandry, which is common enough in the arid West, and as legitimate as selling oats or hay; but he chose to resent it in the case of Gilroy, and to look upon it as an instance of individual and exceptional meanness.

"Any man that will jump God's water in a place like this, and sell it the same as he drinks — he'd sell water to his own father in hell!"

This was our guide's opinion of Gilroy. He was equally frank, and much more explicit, in regard to Gilroy's sons. "But," he concluded, with a philosopher's acceptance of existing facts, "it ain't likely that any of that outfit will ever git into trouble, so long as Maverick is sheriff of Lemhi County."

We were about to ask why, when we drove up to the stage-house, and Maverick himself stepped out and took our horses.

"What the — infernal has happened to the man?" my companion, Ferris, exclaimed; and our guide answered indifferently, as if he were speaking of the weather, —

"Some Injuns caught him alone in an out-o'-the-way ranch, when he was a kid, and took a notion to play with him. This is what was left when they got through. I never see but one worse-looking man," he added, speaking low, as Maverick passed us with the team: "him a bear wiped over the head with its paw. 'Twas quicker over with, I expect, but he lived, and he looked worse than Maverick."

"Then I hope to the Lord I may never see him!" Ferris ejaculated; and I noticed that he left his dinner untasted, though he had boasted of a hunter's appetite.

We were two college friends on a hunting trip, but we had not got into the country of game. In two days more we expected to make Jackson's Hole, and I may mention that "hole," in this region, signifies any small, deep valley, well hidden amidst high mountains, where moisture is perennial, and grass abounds. In these pockets of plenty, herds of elk gather and feed tame as park pets; and other hunted creatures, as wild but less innocent, often find sanctuary here, and cache their stolen stock and other spoil of the road and the range.

We did not forget to put our question concerning Maverick, that unhappy man, in his character of legalized protector of the Gilroy gang. What did our free-spoken guide mean by that insinuation?

We were told that Gilroy, in his rough-handed way, had been as a father to the lad, after the savages wreaked their pleasure on him: and his people being dead or scattered, Maverick had made himself useful in various humble capacities at the stage-house, and had finally become a sort of factotum there and a member of the family. And though perfectly square himself, and much respected on account of his personal courage and singular misfortunes, he could never see the old man's crookedness, nor the more than crookedness of his sons. He was like a son of the house, himself; but most persons agreed that it was not as a brother he felt toward Rose Gilroy. And a tough lookout it was for the girl; for Maverick was one whom no man would lightly cross, and in her case he was acting as "general dog around the place," as our guide called it. The young fellows were shy of the house, notwithstanding the attraction it held. It was likely to be Maverick or nobody for Rose.

We did not see Rose Gilroy, but we heard her step in the stage-house kitchen, and her voice, as clear as a lark's, giving orders to the tall, stooping, fair young Swede, who waited on us at table, and did other work of a menial character in that singular establishment.

"How is it the watch-dog allows such a pretty sprig as that around the place?" Ferris questioned, eying our knight of the trencher, who blushed to feel himself remarked.

"He won't stay," our guide pronounced; "they don't none of 'em stay when they're good-lookin'. The old man he's failin' considerable these days — getting kind o' silly — and the boys are away the heft of the time. Maverick pretty much runs the place. I don't justly blame the critter. He's watched that little Rose grow up from a baby. How's he goin to quit being fond of her now she's a woman? I dare say he'd a heap sooner she'd stayed a little girl. And these yere boys around here they're a triflin' set, not half so able to take care of her as Maverick. He's got the sense and he's got the sand; but there's that awful head on him! I don't blame him much, lookin' the way he does, and feelin' the same as any other man."

We left Traveling Buttes and its cruel little love-story, but we had not gone a mile when a horseman overtook us with a message for Ferris from his new foreman at the ranch, a summons which called him back for a day at the least. Ferris was exceedingly annoyed: a day at the ranch meant four days on the road; but the business was imperative. We held a brief council, and decided that, with Ferris returning, our guide should push on with the animals and camp outfit into a country of grass, and look up a good camping-spot (which might not be the first place he struck) this side of Jackson's Hole. It remained for me to choose between going with the stuff, or staying for a longer look at the phenomenal Black Lava fields at Arco; Arco being another name for desolation on the very edge of that weird stone sea. This was my ostensible reason for choosing to remain at Arco; but I will not say the reflection did not cross me that Arco is only sixteen miles from Traveling Buttes — not an insurmountable distance between geology and a pretty girl, when one is five and twenty, and has not seen a pretty face for a month of Sundays.

Arco, at that time, consisted of the stage-house, a store and one or two cabins — a poor little seed of civilization dropped by the wayside between Black Lava and the hills where Lost River comes down and "sinks" on the edge of the lava. The station is somewhat back from the road, with its face — a very grimy, un-washed countenance — to the lava. Quaking asps and mountain birches follow the water, pausing a little way up the gulch behind the house, but the eager grass tracks it all the way till it vanishes; and the dry bed of the stream goes on and spreads in a mass of coarse sand and gravel, beaten flat, flailed by the feet of countless driven sheep that have gathered here. For this road is on the great overland sheep-trail from Oregon eastward — the march of the million mouths, and what the mouths do not devour the feet tramp down.

The staple topic of conversation at Arco was one very common in the far west, when a tenderfoot is of the company. The poorest place can boast of some distinction, and Arco, though hardly on the highroad of fashion and commerce, had frequently been named in print in connection with crime of a highly sensational and picturesque character. Scarcely anoth-er fifty miles of stage-road could boast of so many and such successful road-jobs; and although these affairs were of almost monthly occurrence, and might be looked for to come off always within that noted danger-limit, yet it was a fact that the law had never yet laid finger on a man of the gang, nor gained the smallest clew to their hideout. It was a difficult country around Arco, one that lent itself to secrecy. The road-agents came, and took, and vanished as if the hills were their co-partners as well as the receivers of their goods. As for the lava, which was its front dooryard, so to speak, for a hundred miles, the man did not live who could say he had crossed it. What it held or was capable of hiding, in life or in death, no man knew.

The day after Ferris left me I rode out upon that arrested tide — those silent breakers which for ages have threatened, but never reached, the shore. I tried to fancy it as it must once have been, a sluggish, vitreous flood, filling the great valley, and stiffening as it slowly pushed toward the bases of the hills. It climbed and spread, as dough rises and crawls over the edge of the pan. The Black Lava is always called a sea — that image is inevitable; yet its movement had never in the least the character of water. "This is where hell pops," an old plainsman feelingly described it, and the suggestion is perfect. The colors of the rock are those produced by fire: its texture is that of slag from a furnace. One sees how the lava hardened into a crust, which cracked and sank in places, mingling its tumbled edges with the creeping flood not cooled beneath. After all movement had ceased and the mass was still, time began upon its tortured configurations, crumbled and wore and broke, and sifted a little earth here and there, and sealed the burnt rock with fairy print of lichens, serpent-green and orange and rust-red. The spring rains left shallow pools which the summer dried. Across it, a few dim trails wander a little way and give out, like the water.

For a hundred miles to the Snake River this Plutonian gulf obliterates the land — holds it against occupation or travel. The shoes of a marching army would be cut from their feet before they had gone a dozen miles across it; horses would have no feet left; and water would have to be packed as on an ocean, or a desert, cruise.

I rode over places where the rock rang beneath my horse's hoofs like the iron cover of a manhole. I followed the hollow ridges that mounted often forty feet above my head, but always with that gruesome effect of thickening movement — that sluggish atomic crawl; and I thought how one man pursuing another into this frozen hell might lose himself, but never find the object of his quest. If he took the wrong furrow, he could not cross from one blind gut into another, nor hope to meet the fugitive at any future turning.

I don't know why the fancy of a flight and pursuit should so have haunted me, in connection with the Black Lava; probably the desperate and lawless character of our conversation at the stage-house gave rise to it.

I had fallen completely under the spell of that skeleton flood. I watched the sun sink, as it sinks at sea, beyond its utmost ragged ridges; I sat on the borders of it, and stared across it in the gray moonlight; I rode out upon it when the Buttes, in their delusive nearness, were as blue as the gates of amethyst, and the morning was as fair as one great pearl; but no peace or radiance of heaven or earth could change its aspect more than that of a mound of skulls. When I began to dream about it, I thought I must be getting morbid. This is worse than Gilroy's I said; and I promised myself I would ride up there next day and see if by chance one might get a peep at the Rose that all were praising, but none dared put forth a hand to pluck. Was it indeed so hard a case for the Rose? There are women who can love a man for the perils he has passed. Alas, Maverick! could any one get used to a face like that?

Here, surely, was the story of Beauty and her poor Beast humbly awaiting, in the mask of a brutish deformity, the recognition of Love pure enough to divine the soul beneath, and unselfish enough to deliver it. Was there such love as that at Gilroy's? However, I did not make that ride.

It was the fourth night of clear, desert moonlight since Ferris had left me: I was sleepless, and so I heard the first faint throb of a horse's feet approaching from the east, coming on at a great pace, and making the turn to the stage-house. I looked out, and on the trodden space in front I saw Maverick dismounting from a badly blown horse.

"Halloo! what's up?" I called from the open window of my bedroom on the ground-floor.

"Did two men pass here on horseback since dark?"

"Yes," I said; "about twelve o'clock: a tall man and a little short fellow."

"Did they stop to water?"

"No, they did not; and they seemed in such a tearing hurry that I watched them down the road."

"I am after those men, and I want a fresh horse," he cut in. "Call up somebody quick!"

"Shall you take one of the boys along?" I inquired, with half an eye to myself, after I had obeyed his command.

He shook his head. "Only one horse here that's good for anything: I want that myself."

"There is my horse," I suggested; "but I'd rather be the one who rides her. She belongs to a friend."

"Take her, and come on, then, but understand — this ain't a Sunday-school picnic."

"I'm with you, if you'll have me."

"I'd sooner have your horse," he remarked, shifting the quid of tobacco in his cheek.

"You can't have her without me, unless you steal her," I said.

"Git your gun, then, and shove some grub into your pockets: I can't wait for nobody."

He swung himself into the saddle.

"What road do you take?"

"There ain't but one," he shouted, and pointed straight ahead.

I overtook him easily within the hour; he was saving his horse, for this was his last chance to change until Champagne Station, fifty miles away.

He gave me rather a cynical smile of recognition as I ranged alongside, as if to say, "You'll probably get enough of this before we are through." The horses settled down to their work, and they "humped theirselves," as Maverick put it, in the cool hours before sunrise.

At daybreak his awful face struck me all afresh, as inscrutable in its strange distortion as some stone god in the desert, from whose graven hideousness a thousand years of mornings have silently drawn the veil.

"What do you want those fellows for?" I asked, as we rode. I had taken for granted that we were hunting suspects of the road-agent persuasion.

"I want 'em on general principles," he answered shortly.

"Do you think you know them?"

"I think they'll know me. All depends on how they act when we get within range. If they don't pay no attention to us, we'll send a shot across their bows. But more likely they'll speak first."

He was very gloomy, and would keep silence for an hour at a time. Once he turned on me as with a sudden misgiving.

"See here, don't you git excited; and whatever happens, don't you meddle with the little one. If the big fellow cuts up rough, he'll take his chances, but you leave the little one to me. I want him for State's evidence," he finished hoarsely.

"The little one must be the Benjamin of the family," I thought — "one of the bad young Gilroys, whose time has come at last; and sheriff Maverick finds his duty hard."

I could not say whether I really wished the men to be overtaken, but the spirit of the chase had undoubtedly entered into my blood. I felt as most men do, who are not saints or cowards, when such work as this is to be done. But I knew I had no business to be along. It was one thing for Maverick, but the part of an amateur in a man-hunt is not one to boast of.

The sun was now high, and the fresh tracks ahead of us were plain in the dust. Once they left the road and strayed off into the lava, incomprehensibly to me; but Maverick understood, and pressed forward. "We'll strike them again further on. D — fool!" he muttered, and I observed that he alluded but to one, "huntin' water holes in the lava in the tail end of August!"

They could not have found water, for at Belgian Flat they had stopped and dug for it in the gravel, where a little stream in freshet time comes down the gulch from the snow-fields higher up, and sinks, as at Arco, on the lip of the lava. They had dug, and found it, and saved us the trouble, as Maverick remarked.

Considerable water had gathered since the flight had paused here and lost precious time. We drank our fill, refreshed our horses, and shifted the saddle-girths; and I managed to stow away my lunch during the next mile or so, after offering to share it with Maverick, who refused it as if the notion of food made him sick. He had considerable whisky aboard, but he was, I judged, one of those men on whom drink has little effect; else some counter-flame of excitement was fighting it in his blood.

I looked for the development of the personal complication whenever we should come up with the chase, for the man's eye burned, and had his branded countenance been capable of any expression that was not cruelly travestied, he would have looked the impersonation of wild justice.

It was now high noon, and our horses were beginning to feel the steady work; yet we had not ridden as they brought the good news from Ghent: that is the pace of a great lyric; but it's not the pace at which justice, or even vengeance, travels in the far West.

Even the furies take it coolly when they pursue a man over these roads, and on these poor brutes of horses, in fifty-mile stages, with drought thrown in.

Maverick had had no mercy on the pony that brought him sixteen miles; but this piece of horse-flesh he now bestrode must last him through at least to Champagne Station, should we not overhaul our men before. He knew well when to press and when to spare the pace, a species of purely practical consideration which seemed habitual with him; he rode like an automaton, his baleful face borne straight before him — the Gorgon's head.

Beyond Belgian Flat — how far beyond I do not remember, for I was beginning to feel the work, too, and the country looked all alike to me as we made it, mile by mile — the road follows close along by the lava, but the hills recede, and a little trail cuts across, meeting the road again at Deadman's Flat. Here we could not trust to the track, which from the nature of the ground was indistinct. So we divided our forces, Maverick taking the trail, — which I was quite willing he should do, for it had a look of most sinister invitation, — while I continued by the longer road. Our little discussion, or some atmospheric change, — some breath of coolness from the hills, — had brought me up out of my stupor of weariness. I began to feel both alert and nervous; my heart was beating fast. The still sunshine lay around us, but where Maverick's white horse was climbing, the shadows were turning eastward, and the deep gulches, with their patches of aspen, were purple instead of brown. The aspens were left shaking where he broke through them and passed out of sight.

I kept on at a good pace, and about three o'clock I, being then as much as half a mile away, saw the spot which I knew must be Deadman's Flat; and there were our men, the tall one and his boyish mate, standing quietly by their horses in broad sunlight, as if there were no one within a hundred miles. Their horses had drunk, and were cropping the thin grass, which had set its tooth in the gravel where, as at the other places, a living stream had perished. I spurred forward, with my heart thumping, but before they saw me I saw Maverick coming down the little gulch; and from the way he came I knew that he had seen them.

The scene was awful in its treacherous peacefulness. Their shadows slept on the broad bed of sunlight, and the gulch was as cool and still as a lady's chamber. The great dead desert received the silence like a secret.

Tenderfoot as I was, I knew quite well what must happen now; yet I was not prepared — could not realize it — even when the tall one put his hand quickly behind him and stepped ahead of his horse. There was the flash of his pistol, and the loud crack echoing in the hill; a second shot, and then Maverick replied deliberately, and the tall one was down, with his face in the grass.

I heard a scream that sounded strangely like a woman's; but there were only the three, the little one, acting wildly, and Maverick bending over him who lay with his face in the grass. I saw him turn the body over, and the little fellow seemed to protest, and tried to push him away. I thought it strange he made no more of a fight, but I was not near enough to hear what those two said to each other.

Still, the tragedy did not come home to me. It was all like a scene, and I was without feeling in it except for that nervous trembling which I could not control.

Maverick stood up at length, and came slowly toward me, wiping his face. He kept his hat in his hand, and looking down at it, said huskily: —

"I gave that man his life when I found him last spring runnin' loose like a wild thing in the mountains, and now I've took it; and God above knows I had no grudge ag'in' him, if he had stayed in his place. But he would have it so."

"Maverick, I saw it all, and I can swear it was self-defense."

His face drew into the tortured grimace which was his smile. "This here will never come before a jury," he said. "It's a family affair. Did ye see how he acted? Steppin' up to me like he was a first-class shot, or else a fool. He ain't nary one; he's a poor silly tool, the whip-hand of a girl that's boltin' from her friends like they was her mortal enemies. Go and take a look at him; then maybe you'll understand."

He paused, and uttered the name of Jesus Christ, but not as such men often use it, with an inconsequence dreadful to hear: he was not idly swearing, but calling that name to witness solemnly in a case that would never come before a jury.

I began to understand.

"Is it — is the girl" —

"Yes; it's our poor little Rose — that's the little one, in the gray hat. She'll give herself away if I don't. She don't care for nothin' nor nobody. She was runnin' away with that fellow — that dish-washin' Swede what I found in the mountains eatin' roots like a ground-hog, with the ends of his feet froze off. Now you know all I know — and more than she knows, for she thinks she was fond of him. She wa'n't, never — for I watched 'em, and I know. She was crazy to git away, and she took him for the chance."

His excitement passed, and we sat apart and watched the pair at a distance. She — the little one — sat as passively by her dead as Maverick pondering his cruel deed; but with both it was a hopeless quiet.

"Come," he said at length, "I've got to bury him. You look after her, and keep her with you till I git through. I'm givin' you the hardest part," he added wistfully, as if he fully realized how he had cut himself off from all such duties, henceforth, to the girl he was consigning to a stranger's care.

I told him I thought that the funeral had more need of me than the mourner, and I shrank from intruding myself.

"I dassent leave her by herself — see? I don't know what notion she may take next, and she won't let me come within a rope's len'th of her."

I will not go over again that miserable hour in the willows, where I made her stay with me, out of sight of what Maverick was doing. Ours were the tender mercies of the wicked, I fear; but she must have felt that sympathy at least was near her, if no help. I will not say that her youth and distressful loveliness did not sharpen my perception of a sweet life wasted, gone utterly astray, which might have brought God's blessing into some man's home — perhaps Maverick's had he not been so hardly dealt with. She was not of that great disposition of heart which can love best that which has sorest need of love; but she was all woman, and helpless and distraught with her tangle of grief and despair, the nature of which I could only half comprehend.

We sat there by the sunken stream, on the hot gravel where the sun had lain, the willows sifting their inconstant shadows over us; and I thought how other things as precious as "God's water" go stray on the Jericho road, or are captured and sold for a price, while dry hearts ache with the thirst that asks a "draught divine."

The man's felt hat she wore, pulled down over her face, was pinned to her coil of braids which had slipped from the crown of her head. The hat was no longer even a protection; she cast it off, and the blond braids, that had not been smoothed for a day and night, fell like ropes down her back. The sun had burned her cheeks and neck to a clear crimson; her blue eyes were as wild with weeping as a child's. She was a rose, but a rose that had been trampled in the dust; and her prayer was to be left there, rather than that we should take her home.

I suppose I must have had some influence over her, for she allowed me to help her arrange her forlorn disguise, and put her on her horse, which was more than could have been expected from the way she had received me. And so, about four o'clock, we started back.

There was a scene when we headed the horses to the west; she protesting with wild sobs that she would not, could not, go home, that she would rather die, that we should never get her back alive, and so on. Maverick stood aside bitterly, and left her to me, and I was aware of a grotesque touch of jealousy — which after all was perhaps natural — in his dour face whenever he looked back at us. He kept some distance ahead, and waited for us when we fell too far in the rear.

This would happen when from time to time her situation seemed to overpower her, and she would stop in the road, and wring her hands, and try to throw herself out of the saddle, and pray me to let her go.

"Go where?" I would ask. "Where do you wish to go? Have you any plan, or suggestion, that I could help you to carry out?" But I said it only to show her how hopeless her resistance was. This she would own piteously, and say: "Nobody can help me. There ain't nowhere for me to go. But I can't go back. You won't let him make me, will you?"

"Why cannot you go back to your father and your brothers?"

This would usually silence her, and, setting her teeth upon her trouble, she would ride on, while I reproached myself, I knew not why.

After one of these struggles — when she had given in to the force of circumstances, but still unconsenting and rebellious — Maverick fell back, and ranged his horse by her other side.

"I know partly what's troubling you, and I'd rid you of that part quick enough," he said, with a kind of dogged patience in his hard voice; "but you can't get on there without me. You know that, don't you? You don't blame me for staying?"

"I don't blame you for anything but what you've done to-day. You've broke my heart, and ruined me, and took away my last chance, and I don't care what becomes of me, so I don't have to go back."

"You don't have to any more than you have to live. Dyin' is a good deal easier, but we can't always die when we want to. Suppose I found a little lost child on the road, and it cried to go home, and I didn't know where 'home' was, would I leave it there just because it cried and hung back? I'd take you to a better home if I knew of one; but I don't. And there's the old man. I suppose we could get some doctor to certify that he's out of his mind, and get him sent up to Blackfoot; but I guess we'd have to buy the doctor first."

"Oh, hush, do, and leave me alone," she said.

Maverick dug his spurs into his horse, and plunged ahead.

"There," she cried, "now you know part of it; but it's the least part — the least, the least! Poor father, he's awful queer. He don't more than half the time know who I am," she whispered. "But it ain't him I'm running away from. It's myself — my own life."

"What is it — can't you tell me?"

She shook her head, but she kept on telling, as if she were talking to herself.

"Father he's like I told you, and the boys — oh, that's worse! I can't get a decent woman to come there and live, and the women at Arco won't speak to me because I'm livin' there alone. They say — they think I ought to get married — to Maverick or somebody. I'll die first. I will die, if there's any way to, before I'll marry him!"

This may not sound like tragedy as I tell it, but I think it was tragedy to her. I tried to persuade her that it must be her imagination about the women at Arco; or, if some of them did talk, — as indeed I myself had heard, to my shame and disgust, — I told her I had never known that place where there was not one woman, at least, who could understand and help another in her trouble.

"I don't know of any," she said simply.

There was no more to do but ride on, feeling like her executioner; but

> "Ride hooly, ride hooly, now, gentlemen,
> Ride hooly now wi' me,"

came into my mind; and no man ever kept beside a "wearier burd," on a sadder journey.

At dusk we came to Belgian Flat, and here Maverick, dismounting, mixed a little whisky in his flask with water which he dipped from the pool. She must have recalled who dug the well, and with whom she had drunk in the morning. He held it to her lips. She rejected it with a strong shudder of disgust.

"Drink it!" he commanded. "You'll kill yourself, carryin' on like this." He pressed it on her, but she turned away her face like a sick and rebellious child.

"Maybe she'll drink it for you," said Maverick, with bitter patience, handing me the cup.

"Will you?" I asked her gently. She shook her head, but at the same time she let me take her hand, and put it down from her face, and I held the cup to her lips. She drank it, every drop. It made her deathly sick, and I took her off her horse, and made a pillow of my coat, so that she could lie down. In ten minutes she was asleep. Maverick covered her with his coat after she was no longer conscious.

We built a fire on the edge of the lava, for we were both chilled and both miserable, each for his own part in that day's work.

The flat is a little cup-shaped valley formed by high hills, like dark walls, shutting it in. The lava creeps up to it in front.

We hovered over the fire and Maverick fed it, savagely, in silence. He did not recognize my presence by a word — not so much as if I had been a strange dog. I relieved him of it after a while, and went out a little way on the lava. At first all was blackness after the strong glare of the fire; but gradually the desolation took shape, and I stumbled about in it, with my shadow mocking me in derisive beckoning, or crouching close at my heels, as the red flames towered or fell. I stayed out there till I was chilled to the bone, and then went back defiantly. Maverick sat as if he had not moved, his elbows on his knees, his face in his hands. I wondered if he were thinking of that other sleeper under the birches of Deadman's Gulch, victim of an unhappy girl's revolt. Had she loved him? Had she deceived him as well as herself? It seemed to me they were all like children who had lost their way home.

By midnight the moon had risen high enough to look at us coldly over the tops of the great hills. Their shadows crept forth upon the lava. The fire had died down. Maverick rose, and scattered the winking brands with his boot-heel.

"We must pull out," he said. "I'll saddle up, if you will" — The hoarseness in his voice choked him, and he nodded toward the sleeper.

I dreaded to waken the poor Rose. She was very meek and quiet after the brief respite sleep had given her. She sat quite still, and watched me while I shook the sand from my coat, put it on, and buttoned it to the chin, and drew my hat down more firmly. There was a kind of magnetism in her gaze; I felt it creep over me like the touch of a soft hand.

When her horse was ready, Maverick brought it, and left it standing near, and went back to his own, without looking toward us.

"Come, you poor, tired little girl," I said, holding out my hand. She could not find her way at first in the uncertain light, and she seemed half asleep still, so I kept her hand in mine, and guided her to her horse. "Now, once more up," I encouraged her; and suddenly she was clinging to me, and whispering passionately:

"Can't you take me *somewhere*? Where are those women that you know?" she cried, shaking from head to foot.

"Dear little soul, all the women I know are two thousand miles away," I answered.

"But can't you take me somewhere? There must be some place. I know you would be good to me; and you could go away afterward, and I wouldn't trouble you any more."

"My child, there is not a place under the heavens where I could take you. You must go on like a brave girl, and trust to your friends. Keep up you heart, and the way will open. God will not forget you," I said, and may he forgive me for talking cant to that poor soul in her bitter extremity.

She stood perfectly still one moment while I held her by the hands. I think she could have heard my heart beat; but there was nothing I could do. Even now I wake in the night, and wonder if there was any other way — but one; the way that for one wild moment I was half tempted to take.

"Yes; the way will open," she said very low. She cast off my hands, and in a second she was in the saddle, and off up the road, riding for her life. And we two men knew no better than to follow her.

I knew better, or I think, now, that I did. I told Maverick we had pushed her far enough. I begged him to hold up and at least not to let her see us on her track. He never answered a word, but kept straight on, as if possessed. I don't think *he* knew what he was doing. At least there was only one thing he was capable of doing — following that girl till he dropped.

Two miles beyond the Flat there is another turn, where the shoulder of a hill comes down and crowds the road, which passes out of sight. She saw us hard upon her, as she reached this bend. Maverick was ahead. Her horse was doing all he could, but it was plain he could not do much more. She looked back, and flung out her hand in the man's sleeve that half covered it. She gave a little whimpering cry, the most dreadful sound I ever heard from any hunted thing.

We made the turn after her; and there lay the road white in the moonlight, and as bare as my hand. She had escaped us.

We pulled up the horses, and listened. Not a sound came from the hills or the dark gulches, where the wind was stirring the quaking asps; the lonesome hush-sh made the silence deeper. But we heard a horse's step go clink, clinking — a loose, uncertain step wandering away in the lava.

"Look! look there! My God!" groaned Maverick.

There was her horse limping along one of the hollow ridges, but the saddle was empty.

"She has taken to the lava!"

I had no need to be told what that meant; but if I had needed, I learned what it meant before the night was through. I think that if I were a poet, I could add another "dolorous circle" to the wailing place for lost souls.

But she had found a way. Somewhere in that stony-hearted wilderness she is at rest. We shall see her again when the sea — the stupid, cruel sea that crawls upon the land — gives up its dead.

Willa Cather

~~~~~~

Although she was born in Virginia, Willa Cather (1873-1947) is most associated with the prairies of Nebraska where she was raised, and all but one of her major works are set against this Midwest background. This landscape, which she called the happiness and curse of her life, weaves through most of her fiction, imparting a sense of isolation and hardship and, yet, at the same time, a sense of accomplishment and celebration. The best of the Nebraska short stories and novels — O Pioneers!, My Antonia, and The Song of the Lark — reveal an intimate knowledge of prairie life and a strong admiration for the Scandinavian pioneers who settled the sometimes overwhelming land.

Cather's family moved to Nebraska in 1883, when she was ten, and settled in the town of Red Cloud, which became an important fictional setting for her novels, just as the people of Red Cloud provided models for many of her characters. Cather attended the University of Nebraska, where she showed her literary inclinations, and after graduation moved to Pittsburgh, Pennsylvania, where she was an editor for Home Monthly magazine and, later, for the Pittsburgh Leader. In 1901 she began to teach school so that she would have more time for her writing.

Although she published many short stories earlier, her first novel, O Pioneers!, did not appear until 1913. Other Nebraska novels followed: The Song of the Lark (1915), My Antonia (1918), One of Ours (1922), and A Lost Lady (1923).

Her best-known novel, Death Comes for the Archbishop (1927), is set entirely in the American Southwest, a land that she had visited several times. Inspired by the story of Archbishop Lamy of Santa Fe, this novel, in the words of critic *Lawrence Clark Powell, "seizes certain facts about the people, the land and the life of the Southwest, and remoulds them in a new form on a higher level."* Death marked the high point of her career and is generally considered her masterpiece, along with My Antonia, *which is usually judged the best of the Nebraska novels.*

Cather continued to publish but the later novels — Shadows on the Rock *(1931),* Obscure Destinies *(1932),* Lucy Gayheart *(1935), and* Sapphira *(1940) — were generally not as successful as the earlier works.* Sapphira *is set in Virginia, while* Lucy Gayheart *is the last of the Nebraska novels.*

Cather's work was well recognized during her lifetime. She won a Pulitzer Prize for One of Ours, *an American Academy of Arts and Letters gold medal for* Death Comes for the Archbishop, *and a Prix Femina Americaine for* Shadows on the Rock, *and she was awarded honorary degrees by several major universities, including Yale and Princeton.*

Willa Cather died in 1947. She had never married — writing apparently left little room in her life, although two women companions were important to her at various times in her life, and on one trip to the Southwest she is reported to have fallen in love with a Mexican guitarist named Julio.

The standard biography of Cather is Willa Cather: A Literary Life *by James L. Woodress (University of Nebraska Press, 1987). Sharon O'Brien's* Willa Cather: The Emerging Voice *(Oxford University Press, 1987) goes only through* O Pioneers!, *studying Cather's work from a feminist perspective. Also particularly interesting are Susan J. Rosowski's* The Voyage Perilous: Willa Cather's Romanticism *(University of Nebraska Press, 1986) and Hermione Lee's* Willa Cather: Double Lives *(Vintage Books, 1991). In addition, the University of Nebraska Press publishes a biannual journal entitled* Cather Studies.

On the Art of Fiction
The Colophon, 1931

O ne is sometimes asked about the "obstacles" that confront young writers who are trying to do good work. I
should say the greatest obstacles that writers today have to get over
are the dazzling journalistic successes of twenty years ago, stories
that surprised and delighted by their sharp photographic detail and
that were really nothing more than lively pieces of reporting. The
whole aim of that school of writing was novelty — never a very
important thing in art. They gave us, altogether, poor
standards — taught us to multiply our ideas instead of to condense
them. They tried to make a story out of every theme that occurred
to them and to get returns on every situation that suggested itself.
They got returns, of a kind. But their work, when one looks back
on it, now that the novelty upon which they counted so much is
gone, is journalistic and thin. The especial merit of a good repor-
torial story is that it shall be intensely interesting and pertinent
today and shall have lost its point by tomorrow.

Art, it seems to me, should simplify. That, indeed, is very
nearly the whole of the higher artistic process; finding what con-
ventions of form and what detail one can do without and yet
preserve the spirit of the whole — so that all that one has sup-
pressed and cut away is there to the reader's consciousness as
much as if it were in type on the page. Millet had done hundreds
of sketches of peasants growing grain, some of them very compli-
cated and interesting, but when he came to paint the spirit of them
all into one picture, "The Sower," the composition is so simple
that it seems inevitable. All the discarded sketches that went before
made the picture what it finally became, and the process was all
the time one of simplifying, of sacrificing many conceptions good
in themselves for one that was better and more universal.

Any first-rate novel or story must have in it the strength of
a dozen fairly good stories that have been sacrificed to it. A good
workman can't be a cheap workman; he can't be stingy about

wasting material, and he cannot compromise. Writing ought either to be the manufacture of stories for which there is a market demand — a business as safe and commendable as making soap or breakfast foods — or it should be an art, which is always a search for something for which there is no market demand, something new and untried, where the values are intrinsic and have nothing to do with standardized values. The courage to go on without compromise does not come to a writer all at once — nor, for that matter, does the ability. Both are phases of natural development. In the beginning, the artist, like his public, is wedded to old forms, old ideals, and his vision is blurred by the memory of old delights he would like to recapture.

Eric Hermannson's Soul
Cosmopolitan 1900

*I*t was a great night at the Lone Star schoolhouse — a night when the Spirit was present with power and when God was very near to man. So it seemed to Asa Skinner, servant of God and Free Gospeller. The schoolhouse was crowded with the saved and sanctified, robust men and women, trembling and quailing before the power of some mysterious psychic force. Here and there among this cowering, sweating multitude crouched some poor wretch who had felt the pangs of an awakened conscience, but had not yet experienced that complete divestment of reason, that frenzy born of a convulsion of the mind, which, in the parlance of the Free Gospellers, is termed "the Light." On the floor before the mourners' bench, lay the unconscious figure of a man in whom outraged nature had sought her last resort. This "trance" state is the highest evidence of grace among the Free Gospellers, and indicates a close walking with God.

Before the desk stood Asa Skinner, shouting of the mercy and vengeance of God, and in his eyes shone a terrible earnestness, an almost prophetic flame. Asa was a converted train gambler who used to run between Omaha and Denver. He was a man made for the extremes of life; from the most debauched of men he had become the most ascetic. His was a bestial face, a face that bore the stamp of Nature's eternal injustice. The forehead was low, projecting over the eyes, and the sandy hair was plastered down over it and then brushed back at an abrupt right angle. The chin was heavy, the nostrils were low and wide, and the lower lip hung loosely except in his moments of spasmodic earnestness, when it shut like a steel trap. Yet about those coarse features there were deep, rugged furrows, the scars of many a hand-to-hand struggle with the weakness of the flesh, and about that drooping lip were sharp, strenuous lines that had conquered it and taught it to pray. Over those seamed cheeks there was a certain pallor, a grayness caught from many a vigil. It was as though, after Nature had done her worst with that face, some fine chisel had gone over it, chastening and almost transfiguring it. To-night, as his muscles twitched with emotion, and the perspiration dropped from his hair and chin, there was a certain convincing power in the man. For Asa Skinner was a man possessed of a belief, of that sentiment of the sublime before which all inequalities are leveled, that transport of conviction which seems superior to all laws of condition, under which debauchees have become martyrs; which made a tinker an artist and a camel-driver the founder of an empire. This was with Asa Skinner to-night, as he stood proclaiming the vengeance of God.

It might have occurred to an impartial observer that Asa Skinner's God was indeed a vengeful God if he could reserve vengeance for those of his creatures who were packed into the Lone Star schoolhouse that night. Poor exiles of all nations; men from the south and the north, peasants from almost every country of Europe, most of them from the mountainous, night-bound coast of Norway. Honest men for the most part, but men with whom the world had dealt hardly; the failures of all countries, men sobered by toil and saddened by exile, who had been driven to fight for the dominion of an untoward soil, to sow where others should gather, the advanceguard of a mighty civilization to be.

Never had Asa Skinner spoken more earnestly than now. He felt that the Lord had this night a special work for him to do. To-night Eric Hermannson, the wildest lad on all the Divide, sat in his audience with a fiddle on his knee, just as he had dropped in on his way to play for some dance. The violin is an object of particular abhorrence to the Free Gospellers. Their antagonism to the church organ is bitter enough, but the fiddle they regard as a very incarnation of evil desires, singing forever of worldly pleasures and inseparably associated with all forbidden things.

Eric Hermannson had long been the object of the prayers of the revivalists. His mother had felt the power of the Spirit weeks ago, and special prayer-meetings had been held at her house for her son. But Eric had only gone his ways laughing, the ways of youth, which are short enough at best, and none too flowery on the Divide. He slipped away from the prayer-meetings to meet the Campbell boys in Genereau's saloon, or hug the plump little French girls at Chevalier's dances, and sometimes, of a summer night, he even went across the dewy cornfields and through the wild-plum thicket to play the fiddle for Lena Hanson, whose name was a reproach through all the Divide country, where the women are usually too plain and too busy and too tired to depart from the ways of virtue. On such occasions Lena, attired in a pink wrapper and silk stockings and tiny pink slippers, would sing to him, accompanying herself on a battered guitar. It gave him a delicious sense of freedom and experience to be with a woman who, no matter how, had lived in big cities and knew the ways of town-folk, who never worked in the fields and had kept her hands white and soft, her throat fair and tender, who had heard great singers in Denver and Salt Lake, and who knew the strange language of flattery and idleness and mirth.

Yet, careless as he seemed, the frantic prayers of his mother were not altogether without their effect upon Eric. For days he had been fleeing before them as a criminal from his pursuers, and over his pleasures had fallen the shadow of something dark and terrible that dogged his steps. The harder he danced, the louder he sang, the more was he conscious that this phantom was gaining upon him, that in time it would track him down. One Sunday afternoon, late in the fall, when he had been drinking beer with Lena Hanson and listening to a song which made his cheeks burn, a rattlesnake had crawled out of the side of the sod house and thrust its ugly head in under the screen door. He was not afraid of snakes, but he knew enough of Gospellism to feel the significance of the reptile lying coiled there upon her doorstep. His lips were cold when he kissed Lena good-by, and he went there no more.

The final barrier between Eric and his mother's faith was his violin, and to that he clung as a man sometimes will cling to his dearest sin, to the weakness more precious to him than all his strength. In the great world beauty comes to men in many guises, and art in a hundred forms, but for Eric there was only his violin. It stood, to him, for all the manifestations of art; it was his only bridge into the kingdom of the soul.

It was to Eric Hermannson that the evangelist directed his impassioned pleading that night.

"*Saul, Saul, why persecutest thou me?* Is there a Saul here tonight who has stopped his ears to that gentle pleading, who has thrust a spear into that bleeding side? Think of it, my brother; you are offered this wonderful love and you prefer the worm that dieth not and the fire which will not be quenched. What right have you to lose one of God's precious souls? *Saul, Saul, why persecutest thou me?*"

A great joy dawned in Asa Skinner's pale face, for he saw that Eric Hermannson was swaying to and fro in his seat. The minister fell upon his knees and threw his long arms up over his head.

"O my brothers! I feel it coming, the blessing we have prayed for. I tell you the Spirit is coming! Just a little more prayer, brothers, a little more zeal, and he will be here. I can feel his cooling wing upon my brow. Glory be to God forever and ever, amen!"

The whole congregation groaned under the pressure of this spiritual panic. Shouts and hallelujahs went up from every lip. Another figure fell prostrate upon the floor. From the mourners' bench rose a chant of terror and rapture:

"Eating honey and drinking wine,
Glory to the bleeding Lamb!
I am my Lord's and he is mine,
Glory to the bleeding Lamb!"

The hymn was sung in a dozen dialects and voiced all the vague yearning of these hungry lives, of these people who had starved all the passions so long, only to fall victims to the basest of them all, fear.

A groan of ultimate anguish rose from Eric Hermannson's bowed head, and the sound was like the groan of a great tree when it falls in the forest.

The minister rose suddenly to his feet and threw back his head, crying in a loud voice:

"*Lazarus, come forth!* Eric Hermannson, you are lost, going down at sea. In the name of God, and Jesus Christ his Son, I throw you the life-line. Take hold! Almighty God, my soul for his!" The minister threw his arms out and lifted his quivering face.

Eric Hermannson rose to his feet; his lips were set and the lightning was in his eyes. He took his violin by the neck and crushed it to splinters across his knee, and to Asa Skinner the sound was like the shackles of sin broken audibly asunder.

II

For more than two years Eric Hermannson kept the austere faith to which he had sworn himself, kept it until a girl from the East came to spend a week on the Nebraska Divide. She was a girl of other manners and conditions, and there were greater distances between her life and Eric's than all the miles which separated Rattlesnake Creek from New York City. Indeed, she had no business to be in the West at all; but ah! across what leagues of land and sea, by what improbable chances, do the unrelenting gods bring to us our fate!

It was in a year of financial depression that Wyllis Elliot came to Nebraska to buy cheap land and revisit the country where he had spent a year of his youth. When he had graduated from Harvard it was still customary for moneyed gentlemen to send their scapegrace sons to rough it on ranches in the wilds of Nebraska or Dakota, or to consign them to a living death in the sagebrush of the Black Hills. These young men did not always return to the ways of civilized life. But Wyllis Elliot had not married a half-breed, nor been shot in a cow-punchers' brawl, nor wrecked by bad whisky, nor appropriated by a smirched adventuress. He had been saved from these things by a girl, his sister, who had been very near to his life ever since the days when they read fairy tales together and dreamed the dreams that never come true. On this, his first visit to his father's ranch since he left it six years before, he brought her with him. She had been laid up half the winter from a sprain received while skating, and had had too much time for reflection during those months. She was restless and filled with a desire to see something of the wild country of which her brother had told her so much. She was to be married the next winter, and Wyllis understood her when she begged him to take her with him on this long, aimless jaunt across the continent, to taste the last of their freedom together. It comes to all women of her type — that desire to taste the unknown which allures and terrifies, to run one's whole length out to the wind — just once.

It had been an eventful journey. Wyllis somehow understood that strain of gypsy blood in his sister, and he knew where to take her. They had slept in sod houses on the Platte River, made the acquaintance of the personnel of a third-rate opera company on the train to Deadwood, dined in a camp of railroad constructors at the world's end beyond New Castle, gone through the Black Hills on horseback, fished for trout in Dome Lake, watched a dance at Cripple Creek, where the lost souls who bide in the hills gather for their besotted revelry. And now, last of all, before the return to thraldom, there was this little shack, anchored on the windy crest of the Divide, a little black dot against the flaming sunsets, a scented sea of cornland bathed in opalescent air and blinding sunlight.

Margaret Elliot was one of those women of whom there are so many in this day, when old order, passing, giveth place to new; beautiful, talented, critical, unsatisfied, tired of the world at twenty-four. For the moment the life and people of the Divide interested her. She was there but a week; perhaps had she stayed longer, that inexorable ennui which travels faster even than the Vestibule Limited would have overtaken her. The week she tarried there was the week that Eric Hermannson was helping Jerry Lockhart thresh; a week earlier or a week later, and there would have been no story to write.

It was on Thursday and they were to leave on Saturday. Wyllis and his sister were sitting on the wide piazza of the ranchhouse, staring out into the afternoon sunlight and protesting against gusts of hot wind that blew up from the sandy riverbottom twenty miles to the southward.

The young man pulled his cap lower over his eyes and remarked:

"This wind is the real thing; you don't strike it anywhere else. You remember we had a touch of it in Algiers and I told you it came from Kansas. It's the keynote of this country."

Wyllis touched her hand that lay on the hammock and continued gently:

"I hope it's paid you, Sis. Roughing it's dangerous business; it takes the taste out of things."

She shut her fingers firmly over the brown hand that was so like her own.

"Paid? Why, Wyllis, I haven't been so happy since we were children and were going to discover the ruins of Troy together some day. Do you know, I believe I could just stay on here forever and let the world go on its own gait. It seems as though the tension and strain we used to talk of last winter were gone for good, as though one could never give one's strength out to such petty things any more."

Wyllis brushed the ashes of his pipe away from the silk handkerchief that was knotted about his neck and stared moodily off at the sky-line.

"No, you're mistaken. This would bore you after a while. You can't shake the fever of the other life. I've tried it. There was a time when the gay fellows of Rome could trot down into the Thebaid and burrow into the sandhills and get rid of it. But it's all too complex now. You see we've made our dissipations so dainty and respectable that they've gone further in than the flesh, and taken hold of the ego proper. You couldn't rest, even here. The war-cry would follow you."

"You don't waste words, Wyllis, but you never miss fire. I talk more than you do, without saying half so much. You must have learned the art of silence from these taciturn Norwegians. I think I like silent men."

"Naturally," said Wyllis, "since you have decided to marry the most brilliant talker you know."

Both were silent for a time, listening to the sighing of the hot wind through the parched morning-glory vines. Margaret spoke first.

"Tell me, Wyllis, were many of the Norwegians you used to know as interesting as Eric Hermannson?"

"Who, Siegfried? Well, no. He used to be the flower of the Norwegian youth in my day, and he's rather an exception, even now. He has retrograded, though. The bonds of the soil have tightened on him, I fancy."

"Siegfried? Come, that's rather good, Wyllis. He looks like a dragon-slayer. What is it that makes him so different from the others? I can talk to him; he seems quite like a human being."

"Well," said Wyllis, meditatively, "I don't read Bourget as much as my cultured sister, and I'm not so well up in analysis, but I fancy it's because one keeps cherishing a perfectly unwarranted suspicion that under that big, hulking anatomy of his, he may conceal a soul somewhere. *Nicht wahr?*"

"Something like that," said Margaret, thoughtfully, "except that it's more than a suspicion, and it isn't groundless. He has one, and he makes it known, somehow, without speaking."

"I always have my doubts about loquacious souls," Wyllis remarked, with the unbelieving smile that had grown habitual with him.

Margaret went on, not heeding the interruption. "I knew it from the first when he told me about the suicide of his cousin, the Bernstein boy. That kind of blunt pathos can't be summoned at will in anybody. The earlier novelists rose to it, sometimes, unconsciously. But last night when I sang for him I was doubly sure. Oh, I haven't told you about that yet! Better light your pipe again. You see, he stumbled in on me in the dark when I was pumping away at that old parlor organ to please Mrs. Lockhart. It's her household fetish and I've forgotten how many pounds of butter she made and sold to buy it. Well, Eric stumbled in, and in some inarticulate manner made me understand that he wanted me to sing for him. I sang just the old things, of course. It's queer to sing familiar things here at the world's end. It makes one think how the hearts of men have carried them around the world, into the wastes of Iceland and the jungles of Africa and the islands of the Pacific. I think if one lived here long enough one would quite forget how to be trivial, and would read only the great books that we never get time to read in the world, and would remember only the great music, and the things that are really worth while would stand out clearly against that horizon over there. And of course I played the intermezzo from 'Cavalleria Rusticana' for him; it goes rather better on an organ than most things do. He shuffled his feet and twisted his big hands up into knots and blurted out that he didn't know there was any music like that in the world. Why, there were tears in his voice, Wyllis! Yes, like Rossetti, I *heard* his tears. Then it dawned upon me that it was probably the first good music he had ever heard in all his life. Think of it, to care for music as he does and never to hear it, never to know that it exists on earth! To long for it as we long for other perfect experiences that never come. I can't tell you what music means to that man, I never saw any one so susceptible to it. It gave him speech, he became alive. When I had finished the intermezzo, he began telling me about a little crippled brother who died and whom he loved and used to carry everywhere in his arms. He did not wait for encouragement. He took up the story and told it slowly, as if to himself, just sort of rose up and told his own woe to answer Mascagni's. It overcame me."

"Poor devil," said Wyllis, looking at her with mysterious eyes, "and so you've given him a new woe. Now he'll go on wanting Grieg and Schubert the rest of his days and never getting them. That's a girl's philanthropy for you!"

Jerry Lockhart came out of the house screwing his chin over the unusual luxury of a stiff white collar, which his wife insisted upon as a necessary article of toilet while Miss Elliot was at the house. Jerry sat down on the step and smiled his broad, red smile at Margaret.

"Well, I've got the music for your dance, Miss Elliot. Olaf Oleson will bring his accordion and Mollie will play the organ, when she isn't lookin' after the grub, and a little chap from Frenchtown will bring his fiddle — though the French don't mix with the Norwegians much."

"Delightful! Mr. Lockhart, that dance will be the feature of our trip, and it's so nice of you to get it up for us. We'll see the Norwegians in character at last," cried Margaret, cordially.

"See here, Lockhart, I'll settle with you for backing her in this scheme," said Wyllis, sitting up and knocking the ashes out of his pipe. "She's done crazy things enough on this trip, but to talk of dancing all night with a gang of half-mad Norwegians and taking the carriage at four to catch the six o'clock train out of Riverton — well, it's tommy-rot, that's what it is!"

"Wyllis, I leave it to your sovereign power of reason to decide whether it isn't easier to stay up all night than to get up at three in the morning. To get up at three, think what that means! No, sir, I prefer to keep my vigil and then get into a sleeper."

"But what do you want with the Norwegians? I thought you were tired of dancing."

"So I am, with some people. But I want to see a Norwegian dance, and I intend to. Come, Wyllis, you know how seldom it is that one really wants to do anything nowadays. I wonder when I have really wanted to go to a party before. It will be something to remember next month at Newport, when we have to and don't want to. Remember your own theory that contrast is about the only thing that makes life endurable. This is my party and Mr. Lockhart's; your whole duty tomorrow night will consist in being nice to the Norwegian girls. I'll warrant you were adept enough at it once. And you'd better be very nice indeed, for if there are many such young valkyries as Eric's sister among them, they would simply tie you up in a knot if they suspected you were guying them."

Wyllis groaned and sank back into the hammock to consider his fate, while his sister went on.

"And the guests, Mr. Lockhart, did they accept?"

Lockhart took out his knife and began sharpening it on the sole of his plowshoe.

"Well, I guess we'll have a couple dozen. You see it's pretty hard to get a crowd together here any more. Most of 'em have gone over to the Free Gospellers, and they'd rather put their feet in the fire than shake 'em to a fiddle."

Margaret made a gesture of impatience. "Those Free Gospellers have just cast an evil spell over this country, haven't they?"

"Well," said Lockhart, cautiously, "I don't just like to pass judgment on any Christian sect, but if you're to know the chosen by their works, the Gospellers can't make a very proud showin', an' that's a fact. They're responsible for a few suicides, and they've sent a good-sized delegation to the state insane asylum, an' I don't see as they've made the rest of us much better than we were before. I had a little herdboy last spring, as square a little Dane as I want to work for me, but after the Gospellers got hold of him and sanctified him, the little beggar used to get down on his knees out on the prairie and pray by the hour and let the cattle get into the corn, an' I had to fire him. That's about the way it goes. Now there's Eric; that chap used to be a hustler and the spryest dancer in all this section — called all the dances. Now he's got no ambition and he's glum as a preacher. I don't suppose we can even get him to come in to-morrow night."

"Eric? Why, he must dance, we can't let him off," said Margaret, quickly. "Why, I intend to dance with him myself."

"I'm afraid he won't dance. I asked him this morning if he'd help us out and he said, 'I don't dance now, any more,'" said Lockhart, imitating the labored English of the Norwegian.

"'The Miller of Hoffbau, the Miller of Hoffbau, O my Princess!'" chirped Wyllis, cheerfully, from his hammock.

The red on his sister's cheek deepened a little, and she laughed mischievously. "We'll see about that, sir. I'll not admit that I am beaten until I have asked him myself."

Every night Eric rode over to St. Anne, a little village in the heart of the French settlement, for the mail. As the road lay through the most attractive part of the Divide country, on several occasions Margaret Elliot and her brother had accompanied him. To-night Wyllis had business with Lockhart, and Margaret rode with Eric, mounted on a frisky little mustang that Mrs. Lockhart had broken to the side-saddle. Margaret regarded her escort very much as she did the servant who always accompanied her on long rides at home, and the ride to the village was a silent one. She was occupied with thoughts of another world, and Eric was wrestling with more thoughts than had ever been crowded into his head before. He rode with his eyes riveted on that slight figure before him, as though he wished to absorb it through the optic nerves and hold it in his brain forever. He understood the situation perfectly. His brain worked slowly, but he had a keen sense of the values of things. This girl represented an entirely new species of humanity to him, but he knew where to place her. The prophets of old, when an angel first appeared unto them, never doubted its high origin.

Eric was patient under the adverse conditions of his life, but he was not servile. The Norse blood in him had not entirely lost its self-reliance. He came of a proud fisher line, men who were not afraid of anything but the ice and the devil, and he had prospects before him when his father went down off the North Cape in the long Arctic night, and his mother, seized by a violent horror of seafaring life, had followed her brother to America. Eric was eighteen then, handsome as young Siegfried, a giant in stature, with a skin singularly pure and delicate, like a Swede's; hair as yellow as the locks of Tennyson's amorous Prince, and eyes of a fierce, burning blue, whose flash was most dangerous to women. He had in those days a certain pride of bearing, a certain confidence of approach, that usually accompanies physical perfection. It was even said of him then that he was in love with life, and inclined to levity, a vice most unusual on the Divide. But the sad history of those Norwegian exiles, transplanted in an arid soil and under a scorching sun, had repeated itself in his case. Toil and isolation had sobered him, and he grew more and more like the clods among which he labored. It was as though some red-hot instrument had touched for a moment those delicate fibers of the brain which respond to acute pain or pleasure, in which lies the power of exquisite sensation, and had seared them quite away. It is a painful thing to watch the light die out of the eyes of those Norsemen, leaving an expression of impenetrable sadness, quite passive, quite hopeless, a shadow that is never lifted. With some this change comes almost at once, in the first bitterness of homesickness, with others it comes more slowly, according to the time it takes each man's heart to die.

Oh, those poor Northmen of the Divide! They are dead many a year before they are put to rest in the little graveyard on the windy hill where exiles of all nations grow akin.

The peculiar species of hypochondria to which the exiles of his people sooner or later succumb had not developed in Eric until that night at the Lone Star schoolhouse, when he bad broken his violin across his knee. After that, the gloom of his people settled down upon him, and the gospel of maceration began its work. "*If thine eye offend thee, pluck it out,*" et cetera. The pagan smile that once hovered about his lips was gone, and he was one with sorrow. Religion heals a hundred hearts for one that it embitters, but when it destroys, its work is quick and deadly, and where the agony of the cross has been, joy will not come again. This man understood things literally: one must live without pleasure to die without fear; to save the soul it was necessary to starve the soul.

The sun hung low above the cornfields when Margaret and her cavalier left St. Anne. South of the town there is a stretch of road that runs for some three miles through the French settlement, where the prairie is as level as the surface of a lake. There the fields of flax and wheat and rye are bordered by precise rows of slender tapering Lombard poplars. It was a yellow world that Margaret Elliot saw under the wide light of the setting sun.

The girl gathered up her reins and called back to Eric, "It will be safe to run the horses here, won't it?"

"Yes, I think so, now," he answered, touching his spur to his pony's flank. They were off like the wind. It is an old saying in the West that new-comers always ride a horse or two to death before they get broken in to the country. They are tempted by the great open spaces and try to outride the horizon, to get to the end of something. Margaret galloped over the level road, and Eric, from behind, saw her long veil fluttering in the wind. It had fluttered just so in his dreams last night and the night before. With a sudden inspiration of courage he overtook her and rode beside her, looking intently at her half-averted face. Before, he had only stolen occasional glances at it, seen it in blinding flashes, always with more or less embarrassment, but now he determined to let every line of it sink into his memory. Men of the world would have said that it was an unusual face, nervous, finely cut, with clear, elegant lines that betokened ancestry. Men of letters would have called it a historic face, and would have conjectured at what old passions, long asleep, what old sorrows forgotten time out of mind, doing battle together in ages gone, had curved those delicate nostrils, left their unconscious memory in those eyes. But Eric read no meaning in these details. To him this beauty was something more than color and line; it was as a flash of white light, in which one cannot distinguish color because all colors are there. To him it was a complete revelation, an embodiment of those dreams of impossible loveliness that linger by a young man's pillow on midsummer nights; yet, because it held something more than the attraction of health and youth and shapeliness, it troubled him, and in its presence he felt as the Goths before the white marbles in the Roman Capitol, not knowing whether they were men or gods. At times he felt like uncovering his head before it, again the fury seized him to break and despoil, to find the clay in this spirit-thing and stamp upon it. Away from her, he longed to strike out with his arms, and take and hold; it maddened him that this woman whom he could break in his hands should be so much stronger than he. But near her, he never questioned this strength; he admitted its potentiality as he admitted the miracles of the Bible; it enervated and conquered him. To-night, when he rode so close to her that he could have touched her, he knew that he might as well reach out his hand to take a star.

Margaret stirred uneasily under his gaze and turned questioningly in her saddle.

"This wind puts me a little out of breath when we ride fast," she said.

Eric turned his eyes away.

"I want to ask you if I go to New York to work, if I maybe hear music like you sang last night? I have been a purty good hand to work," he asked timidly.

Margaret looked at him with surprise, and then, as she studied the outline of his face, pityingly.

"Well, you might — but you'd lose a good deal else. I shouldn't like you to go to New York — and be poor, you'd be out of atmosphere, some way," she said, slowly. Inwardly she was thinking: "There he would be altogether sordid, impossible — a machine who would carry one's trunks upstairs, perhaps. Here he is every inch a man, rather picturesque; why is it?" "No," she added aloud, "I shouldn't like that."

"Then I not go," said Eric, decidedly.

Margaret turned her face to hide a smile. She was a trifle amused and a trifle annoyed. Suddenly she spoke again.

"But I'll tell you what I do want you to do, Eric. I want you to dance with us to-morrow night and teach me some of the Norwegian dances; they say you know them all. Won't you?"

Eric straightened himself in his saddle and his eye flashed as they had done in the Lone Star schoolhouse when he broke his violin across his knee.

"Yes, I will," he said, quietly, and he believed that he delivered his soul to hell as he said it.

They had reached the rougher country now, where the road wound through a narrow cut in one of the bluffs along the creek, when a beat of hoofs ahead and the sharp neighing of horses made the ponies start and Eric rose in his stirrups. Then down the gulch in front of them and over the steep clay banks thundered a herd of wild ponies, nimble as monkeys and wild as rabbits, such as horse-traders drive east from the the plains of Montana to sell in the farming country. Margaret's pony made a shrill sound, a neigh that was almost a scream, and started up the clay bank to meet them, all the wild blood of the range breaking out in an instant. Margaret called to Eric just as he threw himself out of the saddle and caught her pony's bit. But the wiry little animal had gone mad and was kicking and biting like a devil. Her wild brothers of the range were all about her, neighing, and pawing the earth, and striking her with their fore feet and snapping at her flanks. It was the old liberty of the range that the little beast fought for.

"Drop the reins and hold tight, tight!" Eric called, throwing all his weight upon the bit, struggling under those frantic fore feet that now beat at his breast, and now kicked at the wild mustangs that surged and tossed about him. He succeeded in wrenching the pony's head toward him crowding her withers against the clay bank, so that she could not roll.

"Hold tight, tight!" he shouted again, launching a kick at a snorting animal that reared back against Margaret's saddle. If she should lose her courage and fall now, under those hoofs — He struck out again and again, kicking right and left with all his might. Already the negligent drivers had galloped into the cut, and their long quirts were whistling over the heads of the herd. As suddenly as it had come, the struggling, frantic wave of wild life swept up out of the gulch and on across the open prairie, and with a long despairing whinny of farewell the pony dropped her head and stood trembling in her sweat, shaking the foam and blood from her bit.

Eric stepped close to Margaret's side and laid his hand on her saddle. "You are not hurt?" he asked, hoarsely. As he raised his face in the soft starlight she saw that it was white and drawn and that his lips were working nervously.

"No, no, not at all. But you, you are suffering; they struck you!" she cried in sharp alarm.

He stepped back and drew his hand across his brow.

"No, it is not that," he spoke rapidly now, with his hands clenched at his side. "But if they had hurt you, I would beat their brains out with my hands, I would kill them all. I was never afraid before. You are the only beautiful thing that has ever come close to me. You came like an angel out of the sky. You are like the music you sing, you are like the stars and the snow on the mountains where I played when I was a little boy. You are like all that I wanted once and never had, you are all that they have killed in me. I die for you, to-night, to-morrow, for all eternity. I am not a coward; I was afraid because I love you more than Christ who died for me, more than I am afraid of hell, or hope for heaven. I was never afraid before. If you had fallen — oh, my God!" he threw his arms out blindly and dropped his head upon the pony's mane, leaning limply against the animal like a man struck by some sickness. His shoulders rose and fell perceptibly with his labored breathing. The horse stood cowed with exhaustion and fear. Presently Margaret laid her hand on Eric's head and said gently:

"You are better now, shall we go on? Can you get your horse?"

"No, he has gone with the herd. I will lead yours, she is not safe. I will not frighten you again." His voice was still husky, but it was steady now. He took hold of the bit and tramped home in silence.

When they reached the house, Eric stood stolidly by the pony's head until Wyllis came to lift his sister from the saddle.

"The horses were badly frightened, Wyllis. I think I was pretty thoroughly scared myself," she said as she took her brother's arm and went slowly up the hill toward the house. "No, I'm not hurt, thanks to Eric. You must thank him for taking such good care of me. He's a mighty fine fellow. I'll tell you all about it in the morning, dear. I was pretty well shaken up and I'm going right to bed now. Good-night."

When she reached the low room in which she slept, she sank upon the bed in her riding-dress face downward.

"Oh, I pity him! I pity him!" she murmured, with a long sigh of exhaustion. She must have slept a little. When she rose again, she took from her dress a letter that had been waiting for her at the village post-office. It was closely written in a long, angular hand, covering a dozen pages of foreign note-paper, and began: —

"My Dearest Margaret: If I should attempt to say *how like a winter hath thine absence been*, I should incur the risk of being tedious. Really, it takes the sparkle out of everything. Having nothing better to do, and not caring to go anywhere in particular without you, I remained in the city until Jack Courtwell noted my general despondency and brought me down here to his place on the sound to manage some open-air theatricals he is getting up. 'As You Like It' is of course the piece selected. Miss Harrison plays Rosalind. I wish you had been here to take the part. Miss Harrison reads her lines well, but she is either a maiden-all-forlorn or a tomboy; insists on reading into the part all sorts of deeper meanings and highly colored suggestions wholly out of harmony with the pastoral setting. Like most of the professionals, she exaggerates the emotional element and quite fails to do justice to Rosalind's facile wit and really brilliant mental qualities. Gerard will do Orlando, but rumor says he is épris of your sometime friend, Miss Meredith, and his memory is treacherous and his interest fitful.

"My new pictures arrived last week on the 'Gascogne.' The Puvis de Chavannes is even more beautiful than I thought it in Paris. A pale dream-maiden sits by a pale dream-cow and a stream of anemic water flows at her feet. The Constant, you will remember, I got because you admired it. It is here in all its florid splendor, the whole dominated by a glowing sensuosity. The drapery of the female figure is as wonderful as you said; the fabric all barbaric pearl and gold, painted with an easy, effortless voluptuousness, and that white, gleaming line of African coast in the background recalls memories of you very precious to me. But it is useless to deny that Constant irritates me. Though I cannot prove the charge against him, his brilliancy always makes me suspect him of cheapness."

Here Margaret stopped and glanced at the remaining pages of this strange love-letter. They seemed to be filled chiefly with discussions of pictures and books, and with a slow smile she laid them by.

She rose and began undressing. Before she lay down she went to open the window. With her hand on the sill, she hesitated, feeling suddenly as though some danger were lurking outside, some inordinate desire waiting to spring upon her in the darkness. She stood there for a long time, gazing at the infinite sweep of the sky.

"Oh, it is all so little, so little," she murmured. "When everything else is so dwarfed, why should one expect love to be great? Why should one try to read highly colored suggestions into a life like that? If only I could find one thing in it all that mattered greatly, one thing that would warm me when I am alone! Will life never give me that one great moment?"

As she raised the window, she heard a sound in the plum-bushes outside. It was only the house-dog roused from his sleep, but Margaret started violently and trembled so that she caught the foot of the bed for support. Again she felt herself pursued by some overwhelming longing, some desperate necessity for herself, like the outstretching of helpless, unseen arms in the darkness, and the air seemed heavy with sighs of yearning. She fled to her bed with the words, "I love you more than Christ, who died for me!" ringing her ears.

III

About midnight the dance at Lockhart's was at its height. Even the old men who had come to "look on" caught the spirit of revelry and stamped the floor with the vigor of old Silenus. Eric took the violin from the Frenchman, and Minna Oleson sat at the organ, and the music, made up of the folk-songs of the North, that the villagers sing through the long night in hamlets by the sea, when they are thinking of the sun, and the spring, and the fishermen so long away. To Margaret some of it sounded like Grieg's Peer Gynt music. She found something irresistibly infectious in the mirth of these people who were so seldom merry, and she felt almost one of them. Something seemed struggling for freedom in them to-night, something of the joyous childhood of the nations which exile had not killed. The girls were all boisterous with delight. Pleasure came to them rarely, and when it came, they caught at it wildly and crushed its fluttering wings in their strong brown fingers. They had a hard life enough, most of them. Torrid summers and freezing winters, labor and drudgery and ignorance, were the portion of their girlhood; a short wooing, a hasty, loveless marriage, unlimited maternity, thankless sons, premature age and ugliness, were the dower of their womanhood. But what matter? To-night there was hot liquor in the glass and hot blood in the heart; to-night they danced.

To-night Eric Hermannson had renewed his youth. He was no longer the big, silent Norwegian who had sat at Margaret's feet and looked hopelessly into her eyes. To-night he was a man, with a man's rights and a man's power. To-night he was Siegfried indeed. His hair was yellow as the heavy wheat in the ripe of summer, and his eyes flashed like the blue water between the ice-packs in the North Seas. He was not afraid of Margaret to-night, and when he danced with her he held her firmly. She was tired and dragged on his arm a little, but the strength of the man was like an all-pervading fluid, stealing through her veins, awakening under her heart some nameless, unsuspected existence that had slumbered there all these years and that went out through her throbbing finger-tips to his that answered. She wondered if the hoydenish blood of some lawless ancestor, long asleep, were calling out in her to-night, some drop of a hotter fluid that the centuries had failed to cool, and why, if this curse were in her, it had not spoken before. But was it a curse, this awakening, this wealth before undiscovered, this music set free? For the first time in her life her heart held something stronger than herself, was not this worth while? Then she ceased to wonder. She lost sight of the lights and the faces, and the music was drowned by the beating of her own arteries. She saw only the blue eyes that flashed above her, felt only the warmth of that throbbing hand which held hers and which the blood of his heart fed. Dimly, as in a dream, she saw the drooping shoulders, high white forehead and tight, cynical mouth of the man she was to marry in December. For an hour she had been crowding back the memory of that face with all her strength.

"Let us stop, this is enough," she whispered. His only answer was to tighten the arm behind her. She sighed and let that masterful strength bear her where it would. She forgot that this man was little more than a savage, that they would part at dawn. The blood has no memories, no reflections, no regrets for the past, no consideration of the future.

"Let us go out where it is cooler," she said when the music stopped; thinking, "I am growing faint here, I shall be all right in the open air." They stepped out into the cool, blue air of the night.

Since the older folk had begun dancing, the young Norwegians had been slipping out in couples to climb the windmill tower into the cooler atmosphere, as is their amusement. "How high is it?"

"Forty feet, about. I not let you fall." There was a note of irresistible pleading in his voice, and she felt that he tremendously wished her to go. Well, why not? This was a night of the unusual, when she was not herself at all, but was living an unreality. To-morrow, yes, in a few hours, there would be the Vestibule Limited and the world.

"Well, if you'll take good care of me. I used to be able to climb, when I was a little girl."

Once at the top and seated on the platform, they were silent. Margaret wondered if she would not hunger for that scene all her life, through all the routine of the days to come. Above them stretched the great Western sky, serenely blue, even in the night, with its big, burning stars, never so cold and dead and far away as in denser atmospheres. The moon would not be up for twenty minutes yet, and all about the horizon, that wide horizon, which seemed to reach around the world, lingered a pale, white light, as of a universal dawn. The weary wind brought up to them the heavy odors of the cornfields. The music of the dance sounded faintly from below. Eric leaned on his elbow beside her, his legs swinging down on the ladder. His great shoulders looked more than ever like those of the stone Doryphorus, who stands in his perfect, reposeful strength in the Louvre, and had often made her wonder if such men died forever with the youth of Greece.

"How sweet the corn smells at night," said Margaret nervously.

"Yes, like the flowers that grow in paradise, I think."

She was somewhat startled by this reply, and more startled when this taciturn man spoke again.

"You go away to-morrow?"

"Yes, we have stayed longer than we thought to now."

"You not come back any more?"

"No, I expect not. You see, it is long trip, half-way across the continent."

"You soon forget about this country, I guess." It seemed to him now a little thing to lose his soul for this woman, but that she should utterly forget this night into which he threw all his life and all his eternity, that was a bitter thought.

"No, Eric, I will not forget. You have all been too kind to me for that. And you won't be sorry you danced this one night, will you?"

"I never be sorry. I have not been so happy before. I not be so happy again, ever. You will be happy many nights yet, I only this one. I will dream sometimes, maybe."

The mighty resignation of his tone alarmed and touched her. It was as when some great animal composes itself for death, as when a great ship goes down at sea.

She sighed, but did not answer him. He drew a little closer and looked into her eyes.

"You are not always happy, too?" he asked.

"No, not always, Eric; not very often, I think."

"You have a trouble?"

"Yes, but I cannot put it into words. Perhaps if I could do that, I could cure it."

He clasped his hands together over his heart, as children do when they pray, and said falteringly, "If I own all the world, I give him you."

Margaret felt a sudden moisture in her eyes, and laid her hand on his.

"Thank you, Eric; I believe you would. But perhaps even then I should not be happy. Perhaps I have too much of it already."

She did not take her hand away from him; she did not dare. She sat still and waited for the traditions in which she had always believed to speak and save her. But they were dumb. She belonged to an ultra-refined civilization which tries to cheat nature with elegant sophistries. Cheat nature? Bah! One generation may do it, perhaps two, but the third — Can we ever rise above nature or sink below her? Did she not turn on Jerusalem as upon Sodom, upon St. Anthony in his desert as upon Nero in his seraglio? Does she not always cry in brutal triumph: "I am here still, at the bottom of things, warming the roots of life; you cannot starve me nor tame me nor thwart me; I made the world, I rule it, and I am its destiny."

This woman, on a windmill tower at the world's end with a giant barbarian, heard that cry to-night, and she was afraid! Ah! the terror and the delight of that moment when first we fear ourselves! Until then we have not lived.

"Come, Eric, let us go down; the moon is up and the music has begun again," she said.

He rose silently and stepped down upon the ladder, putting his arm about her to help her. That arm could have thrown Thor's hammer out in the cornfields yonder, yet it scarcely touched her, and his hand trembled as it had done in the dance. His face was level with hers now and the moonlight fell sharply upon it. All her life she had searched the faces of men for the look that lay in his eyes. She knew that that look had never shone for her before, would never shine for her on earth again, that such love comes to one only in dreams or in impossible places like this, unattainable always. This was Love's self, in a moment it would die. Stung by the agonized appeal that emanated from the man's whole being, she leaned forward and laid her lips on his. Once, twice and again she heard the deep respirations rattle in his throat while she held them there, and the riotous force under her heart became an engulfing weakness. He drew her up to him until he felt all the resistance go out of her body, until every nerve relaxed and yielded. When she drew her face back from his, it was white with fear.

"Let us go down, oh, my God! let us go down!" she muttered. And the drunken stars up yonder seemed reeling to some appointed doom as she clung to the rounds of the ladder. All that she was to know of love she had left upon his lips.

"The devil is loose again," whispered Olaf Oleson, as he saw Eric dancing a moment later, his eyes blazing.

But Eric was thinking with an almost savage exultation of the time when he should pay for this. Ah, there would be no quailing then! If ever a soul went fearlessly, proudly down to the gates infernal, his should go. For a moment he fancied he was there already, treading down the tempest of flame, hugging the fiery hurricane to his breast. He wondered whether in ages gone, all the countless years of sinning in which men had sold and lost and flung their souls away, any man had ever so cheated Satan, had ever bartered his soul for so great a price.

It seemed but a little while till dawn.

The carriage was brought to the door and Wyllis Elliot and his sister said goodby. She could not meet Eric's eyes as she gave him her hand, but as he stood by the horse's head, just as the carriage moved off, she gave him one swift glance that said, "I will not forget." In a moment the carriage was gone.

Eric changed his coat and plunged his head into the watertank and went to the barn to hook up his team. As he led his horses to the door, a shadow fell across his path, and he saw Skinner rising in his stirrups. His rugged face was pale and worn with looking after his wayward flock, with dragging men into the way of salvation.

"Good-morning, Eric. There was a dance here last night?" he asked, sternly.

"A dance? Oh, yes, a dance," replied Eric, cheerfully.

"Certainly you did not dance, Eric?"

"Yes, I danced. I danced all the time."

The minister's shoulders drooped, and an expression of profound discouragement settled over his haggard face. There was almost anguish in the yearning he felt for this soul.

"Eric, I didn't look for this from you. I thought God had set his mark on you if he ever had on any man. And it is for things like this that you set your soul back a thousand years from God. O foolish and perverse generation!"

Eric drew himself up to his full height and looked off to where the new day was gilding the corn-tassels and flooding the uplands with light. As his nostrils drew in the breath of the dew and the morning, something from the only poetry he had ever read flashed across his mind, and he murmured, half to himself, with dreamy exultation:

"'And a day shall be as a thousand years, and a thousand years as a day.'"

~ ~ ~

A Wagner Matinee
Everybody's Magazine 1904

I received one morning a letter, written in pale ink on glassy, blue-lined note-paper, and bearing the postmark of a little Nebraska village. This communication, worn and rubbed, looking as though it had been carried for some days in a coat pocket that was none too clean, was from my Uncle Howard and informed me that his wife had been left a small legacy by a bachelor relative who had recently died, and that it would be necessary for her to go to Boston to attend to the settling of the estate. He requested me to meet her at the station and render her whatever services might be necessary. On exactly the date indicated as that of her arrival, I found it no later than to-morrow. He had characteristically delayed writing until, had I been away from home for a day, I must have missed the good woman altogether.

The name of my Aunt Georgiana called up not alone her own figure, at once pathetic and grotesque, but opened before my feet a gulf of recollection so wide and deep, that, as the letter dropped from my hand, I felt suddenly a stranger to all the present conditions of my existence, wholly ill at ease and out of place amid the familiar surroundings of my study. I became, in short, the gangling farmer-boy my aunt had known, scourged with chilblains and bashfulness, my hands cracked and sore from the corn husking. I felt the knuckles of my thumb tentatively, as though they were raw again. I sat again before her parlour organ, fumbling the scales with my stiff, red hands, while she, beside me, made canvas mittens for the huskers.

The next morning, after preparing my landlady somewhat, I set out for the station. When the train arrived I had some difficulty in finding my aunt. She was the last of the passengers to alight, and it was not until I got her into the carriage that she seemed really to recognize me. She had come all the way in a day coach; her linen duster had become black with soot and her black bonnet grey with dust during the journey. When we arrived at my boarding-house the landlady put her to bed at once and I did not see her again until the next morning.

Whatever shock Mrs. Springer experienced at my aunt's appearance, she considerately concealed. As for myself, I saw my aunt's misshapen figure with that feeling of awe and respect with which we behold explorers who have left their ears and fingers north of Franz-Josef-Land, or their health somewhere along the Upper Congo. My Aunt Georgiana had been a music teacher at the Boston Conservatory, somewhere back in the latter sixties. One summer, while visiting in the little village among the Green Mountains where her ancestors had dwelt for generations, she had kindled the callow fancy of the most idle and shiftless of all the village lads, and had conceived for this Howard Carpenter one of those extravagant passions which a handsome country boy of twenty-one sometimes inspires in an angular, spectacled woman of thirty. When she returned to her duties in Boston, Howard followed her, and the upshot of this inexplicable infatuation was that she eloped with him, eluding the reproaches of her family and the criticisms of her friends by going with him to the Nebraska frontier. Carpenter, who, of course, had no money, had taken a homestead in Red Willow County, fifty miles from the railroad. There they had measured off their quarter section themselves by driving across the prairie in a wagon, to the wheel of which they had tied a red cotton handkerchief, and counting off its revolutions. They built a dugout in the red hillside, one of those cave dwellings whose inmates so often reverted to primitive conditions. Their water they got from the lagoons where the buffalo drank, and their slender stock of provisions was always at the mercy of bands of roving Indians. For thirty years my aunt had not been further than fifty miles from the homestead.

But Mrs. Springer knew nothing of all this, and must have been considerably shocked at what was left of my kinswoman. Beneath the soiled linen duster which, on her arrival, was the most conspicuous feature of her costume, she wore a black stuff dress, whose ornamentation showed that she had surrendered herself unquestioningly into the hands of a country dressmaker. My poor aunt's figure, however, would have presented astonishing difficulties to any dressmaker. Originally stooped, her shoulders were now almost bent together over her sunken chest. She wore no stays, and her gown, which trailed unevenly behind, rose in a sort of peak over her abdomen. She wore ill-fitting false teeth, and her skin was as yellow as a Mongolian's from constant exposure to a pitiless wind and to the alkaline water which hardens the most transparent cuticle into a sort of flexible leather.

I owed to this woman most of the good that ever came my way in my boyhood, and had a reverential affection for her. During the years when I was riding herd for my uncle, my aunt, after cooking the three meals — the first of which was ready at six o'clock in the morning — and putting the six children to bed, would often stand until midnight at her ironing-board, with me at the kitchen table beside her, hearing me recite Latin declensions and conjugations, gently shaking me when my drowsy head sank down over a page of irregular verbs. It was to her, at her ironing or mending, that I read my first Shakespere, and her old text-book on mythology was the first that ever came into my empty hands. She taught me my scales and exercises, too — on the little parlour organ, which her husband had bought her after fifteen years, during which she had not so much as seen any instrument, but an accordion that belonged to one of the Norwegian farmhands. She would sit beside me by the hour, darning and counting while I struggled with the "Joyous Farmer," but she seldom talked to me about music, and I understood why. She was a pious woman; she had the consolations of religion and, to her at least, her martyrdom was not wholly sordid. Once when I had been doggedly beating out some easy passages from an old score of *Euryanthe* I had found among her music books, she came up to me and, putting her hands over my eyes, gently drew my head back upon her shoulder, saying tremulously, "Don't love it so well, Clark, or it may be taken from you. Oh! dear boy, pray that whatever your sacrifice may be, it be not that."

When my aunt appeared on the morning after her arrival, she was still in a semi-somnambulant state. She seemed not to realize that she was in the city where she had spent her youth, the place longed for hungrily half a lifetime. She had been so wretchedly train-sick throughout the journey that she had no recollection of anything but her discomfort, and, to all intents and purposes, there were but a few hours of nightmare between the farm in Red Willow County and my study on Newbury Street. I had planned a little pleasure for her that afternoon, to repay her for some of the glorious moments she had given me when we used to milk

together in the straw-thatched cowshed and she, because I was
more than usually tired, or because her husband had spoken
sharply to me, would tell me of the splendid performance of the
Huguenots she had seen in Paris, in her youth. At two o'clock the
Symphony Orchestra was to give a Wagner programme, and I
intended to take my aunt; though, as I conversed with her, I grew
doubtful about her enjoyment of it. Indeed, for her own sake, I
could only wish her taste for such things quite dead, and the long
struggle mercifully ended at last. I suggested our visiting the
Conservatory and the Common before lunch, but she seemed
altogether too timid to wish to venture out. She questioned me
absently about various changes in the city, but she was chiefly
concerned that she had forgotten to leave instructions about feeding half-skimmed milk to a certain weakling calf, "old Maggie's
calf, you know, Clark," she explained, evidently having forgotten
how long I had been away. She was further troubled because she
had neglected to tell her daughter about the freshly-opened kit of
mackerel in the cellar, which would spoil if it were not used
directly.

I asked her whether she had ever heard any of the Wag-
nerian operas, and found that she had not, though she was perfectly familiar with their respective situations, and had once possessed the piano score of *The Flying Dutchman*. I began to think
it would have been best to get her back to Red Willow County
without waking her, and regretted having suggested the concert.

From the time we entered the concert hall, however, she was
a trifle less passive and inert, and for the first time seemed to
perceive her surroundings. I had felt some trepidation lest she
might become aware of the absurdities of her attire, or might
experience some painful embarrassment at stepping suddenly into
the world to which she had been dead for a quarter of a century.
But, again, I found how superficially I had judged her. She sat
looking about her with eyes as impersonal, almost as stony, as
those with which the granite Rameses in a museum watches the
froth and fret that ebbs and flows about his pedestal — separated
from it by the lonely stretch of centuries. I have seen this same
aloofness in old miners who drift into the Brown hotel at Denver,
their pockets full of bullion, their linen soiled, their haggard faces
unshaven; standing in the thronged corridors as solitary as though

they were still in a frozen camp on the Yukon, conscious that certain experiences have isolated them from their fellows by a gulf no haberdasher could bridge.

We sat at the extreme left of the first balcony, facing the arc of our own and the balcony above us, veritable hanging gardens, brilliant as tulip beds. The matinée audience was made up chiefly of women. One lost the contour of faces and figures, indeed any effect of line whatever, and there was only the colour of bodices past counting, the shimmer of fabrics soft and firm, silky and sheer; red, mauve, pink, blue, lilac, purple, ecru, rose, yellow, cream, and white, all the colours that an impressionist finds in a sunlit landscape, with here and there the dead shadow of a frock coat. My Aunt Georgiana regarded them as though they had been so many daubs of tube-paint on a palette.

When the musicians came out and took their places, she gave a little stir of anticipation and looked with quickening interest down over the rail at that invariable grouping, perhaps the first wholly familiar thing that had greeted her eye since she had left old Maggie and her weakling calf. I could feel how all those details sank into her soul, for I had not forgotten how they had sunk into mine when I came fresh from ploughing forever and forever between green aisles of corn, where, as in a treadmill, one might walk from daybreak to dusk without perceiving a shadow of change. The clean profiles of the musicians, the gloss of their linen, the dull black of their coats, the beloved shapes of the instruments, the patches of yellow light thrown by the green shaded lamps on the smooth, varnished bellies of the 'cellos and the bass viols in the rear, the restless, wind-tossed forest of fiddle necks and bows — I recalled how, in the first orchestra I had ever heard, those long bow strokes seemed to draw the heart out of me, as a conjurer's stick reels out yards of paper ribbon from a hat.

The first number was the *Tannhauser* overture. When the horns drew out the first strain of the Pilgrim's chorus, my Aunt Georgiana clutched my coat sleeve. Then it was I first realized that for her this broke a silence of thirty years; the inconceivable silence of the plains. With the battle between the two motives, with the frenzy of the Venusberg theme and its ripping of strings, there came to me an overwhelming sense of the waste and wear we are so powerless to combat; and I saw again the tall, naked house on the prairie, black and grim as a wooden fortress; the black pond where I had learned to swim, its margin pitted with sun-dried cattle tracks; the rain gullied clay banks about the naked house, the four dwarf ash seedlings where the dish-cloths were always hung to dry before the kitchen door. The world there was the flat world of the ancients; to the east, a cornfield that stretched to daybreak; to the west, a corral that reached to sunset; between, the conquests of peace, dearer bought than those of war.

The overture closed, my aunt released my coat sleeve, but she said nothing. She sat staring at the orchestra through a dullness of thirty years, through the films made little by little by each of the three hundred and sixty-five days in every one of them. What, I wondered, did she get from it? She had been a good pianist in her day I knew, and her musical education had been broader than that of most music teachers of a quarter of a century ago. She had often told me of Mozart's operas and Meyerbeer's, and I could remember hearing her sing, years ago, certain melodies of Verdi's. When I had fallen ill with a fever in her house she used to sit by my cot in the evening — when the cool, night wind blew in through the faded mosquito netting tacked over the window and I lay watching a certain bright star that burned red above the cornfield — and sing "Home to our mountains, O, let us return!" in a way fit to break the heart of a Vermont boy near dead of homesickness already.

I watched her closely through the prelude to *Tristan and Isolde*, trying vainly to conjecture what that seething turmoil of strings and winds might mean to her, but she sat mutely staring at the violin bows that drove obliquely downward, like the pelting streaks of rain in a summer shower. Had this music any message for her? Had she enough left to at all comprehend this power which had kindled the world since she had left it? I was in a fever of curiosity, but Aunt Georgiana sat silent upon her peak in Darien. She preserved this utter immobility throughout the number from *The Flying Dutchman*, though her fingers worked mechanically upon her black dress, as though, of themselves, they were recalling the piano score they had once played. Poor old hands! They had been stretched and twisted into mere tentacles to hold and lift and knead with; the palms unduly swollen, the fingers bent and knotted — on one of them a thin, worn band that had once been a wedding ring. As I pressed and gently quieted one of those groping hands, I remembered with quivering eyelids their services for me in other days.

Soon after the tenor began the "Prize Song," I heard a quick drawn breath and turned to my aunt. Her eyes were closed, but the tears were glistening on her checks, and I think, in a moment more, they were in my eyes as well. It never really died, then — the soul that can suffer so excruciatingly and so interminably; it withers to the outward eye only; like that strange moss which can lie on a dusty shelf half a century and yet, if placed in water, grows green again. She wept so throughout the development and elaboration of the melody.

During the intermission before the second half of the concert, I questioned my aunt and found that the "Prize Song" was not new to her. Some years before there had drifted to the farm in Red Willow County a young German, a tramp cow puncher, who had sung the chorus at Bayreuth, when he was a boy, along with the other peasant boys and girls. Of a Sunday morning he used to sit on his gingham-sheeted bed in the hands' bedroom which opened off the kitchen, cleaning the leather of his boots and saddle, singing the "Prize Song," while my aunt went about her work in the kitchen. She had hovered about him until she had prevailed upon him to join the country church, though his sole fitness for this step, in so far as I could gather, lay in his boyish face and his possession of this divine melody. Shortly afterward he had gone to town on the Fourth of July, been drunk for several days, lost his money at a faro table, ridden a saddled Texan steer on a bet, and disappeared with a fractured collar-bone. All this my aunt told me huskily, wanderingly, as though she were talking in the weak lapses of illness.

"Well, we have come to better things than the old *Trovatore* at any rate, Aunt Georgie?" I queried, with a well meant effort at jocularity.

Her lip quivered and she hastily put her handkerchief up to her mouth. From behind it she murmured, "And you have been hearing this ever since you left me, Clark?" Her question was the gentlest and saddest of reproaches.

The second half of the programme consisted of four numbers from the *Ring*, and closed with Siegfried's funeral march. My aunt wept quietly, but almost continuously, as a shallow vessel over-flows in a rainstorm. From time to time her dim eyes looked up at the lights which studded the ceiling, burning softly under their dull glass globes; doubtless they were stars in truth to her. I was still perplexed as to what measure of musical comprehension was left to her, she who had heard nothing but the singing of Gospel Hymns at Methodist services in the square frame school-house on Section Thirteen for so many years. I was wholly unable to gauge how much of it had been dissolved in soapsuds, or worked into bread, or milked into the bottom of a pail.

The deluge of sound poured on and on; I never knew what she found in the shining current of it; I never knew how far it bore her, or past what happy islands. From the trembling of her face I could well believe that before the last numbers she had been carried out where the myriad graves are, into the grey, nameless burying grounds of the sea; or into some world of death vaster yet, where, from the beginning of the world, hope has lain down with hope and dream with dream and, renouncing, slept.

The concert was over; the people filed out of the hall chattering and laughing, glad to relax and find the living level again, but my kinswoman made no effort to rise. The harpist slipped its green felt cover over his instrument; the flute-players shook the water from their mouthpieces; the men of the orchestra went out one by one, leaving the stage to the chairs and music stands, empty as a winter cornfield.

I spoke to my aunt. She burst into tears and sobbed pleadingly. "I don't want to go, Clark, I don't want to go!"

I understood. For her, just outside the door of the concert hall lay the black pond with the cattle-tracked bluffs; the tall, unpainted house, with weather-curled boards; naked as a tower, the crook-backed ash seedlings where the dish-cloths hung to dry; the gaunt, moulting turkeys picking up refuse about the kitchen door.

Mari Sandoz

〜〜〜〜〜〜〜〜〜〜〜〜〜〜〜〜〜〜〜〜〜〜

M ari Sandoz (1896-1966) had to be resilient. Born
on the uncompromising frontier of northwest Nebraska to Jules and Mary Fehr Sandoz, she was raised by a
harsh, repressive, temperamental, and violent father. Though
she loved to read, she was forced to spirit books in and out
of the household (her father discouraged reading and above
all short-story writing), yet from her formative years Mari
always wanted to be a writer. Her efforts, however, met
with repeated rejection slips

In 1914 Sandoz, then teaching at a nearby country
school, married neighboring farmer Wray Macumber, a
union that ended (apparently acrimoniously) in 1919. In
the fall of that year she moved to Lincoln and, while
attending the University of Nebraska on an intermittent
basis, worked at odd jobs when forced to but concentrated
as much as possible on her short stories. Again, she faced
rejection slip after rejection slip. But writing had become
an obsession and she refused to give up

She got a break in 1925 after winning an honorable
mention in the Harper Intercollegiate Short Story Contest
under the pen name Marie Macumber for the piece
"Fearbitten." When her father discovered her activities, he
wrote "You know I consider writers and artists the maggots
of Society." (Old Jules, p. viii) Not an auspicious start for
a budding writer.

"Poverty and lack of recognition," according to biogra-
pher Helen Stauffer, "brought on acute depression and ill
health. Thin and malnourished, she gave up writing and
retired to the sandhills in 1933. . . ." (Erisman and Etulain,
eds., Fifty Western Writers, p. 417.) Sandoz was back in Lincoln
within months, however, working for the Nebraska Historical

Society. *Two years later her first major break came with the acceptance of* Old Jules *(1935), a combination of biography, autobiography, history and fiction — a technique she employed in much of her writing. (In the pieces that follow, for example, "Marlizzie" is most likely Sandoz' mother Mary Elizabeth.) Over the next thirty years Sandoz lectured around the country, published numerous short pieces and several books including the Great Plains trilogy:* Crazy Horse: The Strange Man of the Oglalas, The Buffalo Hunters: The Story of the Hide Men, *and* Cheyenne Autumn.

In the early 1940s, Mari Sandoz moved east to be close to her publishers and to the major research institutions in the area. Although she continued to travel and lecture in the West, she died in New York City in March, 1966.

The standard biography of Sandoz is Mari Sandoz: Storycatcher of the Plains *(University of Nebraska Press, 1982) by Helen Winter Stauffer, who also edited* Letters of Mari Sandoz *(University of Nebraska Press, 1992). Stauffer is also the author of a pamphlet about Sandoz in the Boise (Idaho) Western Writers Series. "Every Husband's Right," an essay by Melody Graulich in* Western American Literature *(Spring 1983, Vol. 18 No. 1, pp. 3- 20) discusses spouse abuse in the Old West with particular reference to* Old Jules.

Pioneer Women

Editor's Note: What follows is an undated essay — probably written in 1934 or 1935 and previously unpublished in its entirety — from the University of Nebraska-Lincoln Libraries, Archives and Special Collections. In its original form the piece was unfinished, Sandoz having indicated that she intended to quote from various sources. The editors of this volume have interpreted her notations and filled in the quotes in the spirit of her intent.

This paper had its origins in an old assigned topic: "Women in Pioneer Literature," but unfortunately I found that the earlier and the more exciting portions of pioneer literature have little reference to women outside of dance hall girls, Indians, and breeds, or those mere bits of icing added for romantic interest in later rehashings of early tales. I found very few mothers, sisters, sweethearts, or wives.

It is true that the wilderness was first penetrated by lone men, or in twos and threes, their women safely and perhaps not too regretfully left behind. Dr. [John Donald] Hicks, former dean of the Arts college [at the University of Nebraska] sometimes told his classes in History of the West that if Daniel Boone and the men of his type had not become bored with their homes and their women folks, the story of the West would have been very different and surely a much more recent one.

Anyway, whatever the reason, [Rueben Gold] Thwaites [*Early] Western Travels* [1904–07], twenty-seven large volumes of frontier narratives and accounts, contains almost no references to women, white and "respectable."

In the stories of Nebraska it is the same. The early accounts of the white man's penetration up the Missouri, the Platte, the Republican, and the Niobrara sometimes mention women, usually referred to as the wife or the squaw of so-and-so, seldom the narrator's — and almost always Indians and breeds. Later came the dance hall girls of the wild west stories, the Calamity Janes, the Poker Alices, the Silver Nells. No pioneer women in the common sense of the term. These came later when actual settlement began. However, in the panhandle of the state these days are not far behind us; from the usual sources, letters, fragmentary manuscripts and particularly the old-timers, I have tried to reconstruct a March 1884 scene at Valentine, the end of the railroad at that time [in my book *Old Jules* (1935)]. If I have succeeded at all I think you will recognize it as a transitional period between the footloose frontiersman and the early pioneer, an important period in the taming of any land, be it Nebraska, the Argentine, or the Congo.

Because, in 1884, Valentine was the land office for the great expanse of free land to the west and south, Jules stopped there. The town was also the end of the railroad and the station of supply and diversion for the track crew pushing the black rails westward, for the military posts of Fort Niobrara and Fort Robinson, for the range country and for the mining camps of the Black Hills. Sioux came in every day from their great reservations to the north, warriors who as late as '77 and '81 had fought with Crazy Horse and Sitting Bull; law was remote and the broken hills or the Sioux blanket offered safe retreat for horse thief, road agent, and killer. . . . [Jules] dodged behind the horse-lined hitch-racks as a dozen galloping cowboys came into town, yelling, shooting red streaks through the darkening sky, stirring up a dust that shimmered golden in the light that spilled from the tents and shacks. In the doorway of the largest saloon and gambling house between O'Neill and the Black Hills the homeseeker hesitated.

Despite the blaze of tin lamp reflectors along the walls, the interior was murky, heavy with the stench of stale alcohol and winter-long unbathed humanity. Restless layers of smoke crept over the heads of the crowd. Hats pushed back, their hands on their hips, the frontiersmen listened to a short stocky man sitting on the wet bar. . . . Jules edged closer with the other newcomers to listen to the strange American words.

It seemed that the stocky man brought news. The vigilantes down the Niobrara were riding again. That meant . . . a cottonwood, a bridge, or a telegraph pole and a chunk of rope for somebody. The vigilantes had come as far west as Valentine before, taken men away and left them dangling for the buzzards. . . .

Jules looked curiously into the frightened faces of the land seekers about him and started away to buy a glass of beer. It was all just another joke on the greenhorns and soon the laughing would begin.

At the bar a half-drunken youth, several years younger than Jules, was talking big. "Let the viges come. We'll make 'em eat lead," he drawled. . . .

"Shut that running off the mouth, Slip," a whisper warned. . . .

"I ain't afraid of any goddamn viges," he told them all, his hand on his heavy cartridge belt.

A shot set the glasses and bottles to ringing and started a wave of relieved talk and natural laughter as Slip turned and set his glass back upon the bar. A mushroom of powder smoke rose from the crowd and crept lazily toward the dark rafters.

Jules laughed too now, not as the others, but with keen enjoyment. This was as the shooting through the darkness outside, a show, the Wild West of which he had read, with a great smell of powder and brag. It was fine. Then he stopped, a little sick. The youth was bending low over the bar and from his mouth ran a string of frothy blood. Slowly he went down, his fingers sliding from the boards.

The sun-blackened men about him melted back, their hands frankly on their guns now. A hunchback and a negro pushed between them, carrying the sagging figure out. . . . At a shoulder signal from the bartender. . . . a blond-bearded Polander climbed upon a barrel and pulled away at a red accordion. Two girls came out of the boxes at the back and slipped companionably into the double line at the bar. Gradually the crowd thickened again. Everything was as usual. (*Old Jules*, pp. 5-8)

As soon as the romantic days of the long rifle, the beaver trap, the bull boat, and the whiskey wagon began to fade and the frontiersman was compelled to settle down to make a living, his thoughts turned eastward to the women of his own kind. But after her arrival, the wife found that her husband seldom mentioned her in his letters or manuscripts save in connection with calamity. She sickened and left her work undone and so the pioneer could not plow or build or hunt. If his luck was exceeding bad, she died, and left him and his home without a housekeeper until she could be replaced. At first this seems a calloused, even a brutal attitude, but it was not so intended. The tamer of the wilderness was a doer, a man of deed, a man who had lost the ability to taste the everyday things through the satiation with the sharper spices of frontier life. Only accident or sickness or death were worth mentioning at all. The first woman I find referred to on Mirage Flats, the large plain between Alliance and Rushville, west of the sandhills, was by no means the first woman there but she furnished one man his first experience in obstetrics and so was noted in his letters. Elaborated into a scene, it might have been something like this:

But that night, while, with the point of his pocket knife, he probed frying balls of baking-powder biscuit in antelope-steak gravy, tired hoofbeats pounded over the prairie. A covered wagon broke from the darkness, the lathered flanks of the horses heaving. A man leaped down, deep shadows of night on his naked cheeks.

Jules reached for his rifle and stepped back into the darkness.

"Don't shoot! My God, man, don't shoot!" the frightened youth begged. "My wife's dying — and I can't find a woman to help her."

Suspiciously Jules came forward, scratching his beard. "In thaire?" he asked, thumbing toward the wagon.

Together they climbed the doubletrees, Jules carrying his lantern and his gun. Inside, between boxes and bundles, lay a young woman, little more than a child, her eyes unmoving caverns in the light.

Jules pushed his cap back and clambered out. He set the pan off and began eating rapidly with his knife, mouthing the hot food, his rifle still in the crook of his arm. . . .

"You can't sit there — eating — and let her die! . . . "

Slowly the man plodded to his team and gathered up the lines.

"Heah? — Oh, hell! — Put on a bucket of water to boil," Jules ordered.

At a hoarse cry from the wagon he gulped a cup of black coffee and carried the lantern into the tent, his back a black, moving shadow. From a small bottle with a red skull and crossbones he measured the equivalent of a grain of wheat of white powder into a tin cup.

"What are you giving her?" the husband whispered.

"Morphine. Kill some of the pain. Now make me room and get me some clean rags."

While the boxes and bundles came out of the wagon Jules thumbed through his doctor book, washed his hands carefully, pared his fingernails close, and pulled his blunt scissors from the boiling water with a stick. Then he carried out the instructions of the book as unfeelingly, as coldly, as though the woman were one of the animals he had so often seen his veterinary father care for, the father who still hoped that this eldest of six sons would be a doctor.

The woman was spent by long hours of labor and he needed all the ingenuity and recollection his Swiss heritage could bring to his strong narrow hands and the pitifully scant equipment he had. But she had endurance, youth, and courage, and Jules was without knowledge of pain. The horizontal rays of the early sun found the camp asleep — one more potential tiller of the soil on Mirage Flats. (*Old Jules*, pp. 22-24)

The fine thing, it seems to me, is that the early pioneer woman made the best of the situation, and usually without complaint, if one can trust the few letters available. Although her place in the literature of the time is negligible, we know that nothing happened after she arrived that did not vitally touch her. Particularly important was her place in accident or sickness, with doctors few and so far away. A good picture of the situation is given by the letters and the biography of Dr. Walter Reed, later conqueror of yellow fever, during his years [1882-1887] as post surgeon at Fort Robinson, in the northwest corner of the state. Again, because these sources are not available at this moment, I offer, with apologies, my version of the doctor's experiences:

The winter of 1884-1885 was a bad one in the panhandle, for the grangers, caught unprepared by the early winter and the severe cold, were often without food or fuel. When a half-frozen man came tearing through the snow with word that his neighbor was lying [sic] of pneumonia, or a child was choking to death with diphtheria, the doctor pulled on his great buffalo coat, threw his saddlebags across his horse and set out into the storm. Once, with the thermometer far below zero he started out at dusk against a driving snowstorm to a sick woman 12 miles away. There was no trail. He got lost, wandering until midnight. Then he saw a tiny light, the soddy he was seeking. . . .

Summer brought more grangers and smallpox, typhoid, snakebite, and the results of wind and drouth and loneliness. There was little time to ruminate except in the saddle from case to case. At the post [Reed] was busy refilling his saddlebags or making the impersonal reports: "Attended T _____ R ___, 18 miles south, mountain fever, patient resting." Sometimes he was compelled to add the hour of death. . . .

Somehow Dr. Reed wheedled food from the government stores, got transportation for those who could not stay. And often he begged his wife to let him bring home some child that needed food and kindness more than drugs. . . . (*Omaha World Herald*, June 25, 1933).

If the man of the place fell into a well or got caught in a runaway, it was usually the woman of the place who managed his rescue, cared for him, carried on his work. When drouth and hail and wind came it was the housewife who set as good a table as possible from what remained and somehow sustained the morale of her family. A fine description of what such a woman had to face is given in Keene Abbott's "The Wind Fighters," in *Outlook* [January 12], 1916. Mr. Abbott is one of the few people who have both the experiences and the art to convey these experiences to his readers. There is true drama in the following.

[It is August on the plains and in the face of a withering drouth and continuous prairie winds driving the heat, three families have decided to abandon their farms. In covered wagons they approach the modest house of James Dara and his wife. Life on the plains has not been easy for this young Irish immigrant family. They have lost two children to disease, have suffered crop losses continually. They have been through much. They do have a piano, however, and a flute, and they have spirit.]

"Only look at that now!" Dara said, contemptuously. "Deserting their homesteads!"

"Don't be scornful Jim boy. Maybe it's the winds they're going from. Maybe they can't get used to the winds grieving always, come summer, come winter, snow winds and dust winds, ice and fire forever!"

"Yes dear; the winds do be grieving in lean times. But come fat times . . . our corn all cribbed [the winds] will *sing then.* . . .

"We'll hold these people, Nora. We'll stop them; we'll play for them. If they've lost their nerve, 'tis music will be giving it back to them."

[Dara races outside and offers the families a chance to rest and water their animals.]

"There's a piano in the house. Nora will play it for you, and me with my flute knocking out tunes beside it if you would care for a bit of music — "

Con Lewis . . . laughed raucously.

"Music! There's the hot wind will make music for us."

But the frail woman on the seat with him, a baby in her arms, nudged him in the side with her elbow.

"It's the piano you got off Martin Byrne," she said to Dara. "We've heard tell your woman can finger it just grand. . . . "

The flute player had his way with these people from homesteads newly abandoned. The company assembled in the house for the concert: three men, four women, eight children, including the baby.

When the music began, the little folks grew quiet, the baby stopped fretting; and mildly interested, the men condescended to listen.

As for the women, they leaned forward, forgetting the suffocation of the heat. They drank in the simple melodies — drank of that music as if they were thirst-famished things come upon a rill of clear water. . . . (pp. 99-104)

If hardships came, with hunger and sickness, the man could escape, at least temporarily, into the fields, the woods, or perhaps to the nearest saloon where there was warmth and companion-ship. The woman faced it at home. The results are tersely told by the items in the newspapers of the day. Only sheriff sales seem to have been more numerous than the items telling of trips to the insane asylum.

But the Fourth of July brought a break in the isolation and the monotony. The first community celebration held at Rushville, then a town about ten days old, was probably much like those of other places in the same stage of pioneering. From all accounts I imagine it was something like this:

Before the Fourth of July wagons were fitted out for camping. Bows and tarps to cover excess goods or to house an old hen and her chickens, with sod along the bottom to keep the skunks out, were re-paired and mounted on wagons. Horsebackers, teams of gaunt ponies or plodding plough critters, moved like giant apparitions over the mirage lakes towards Rushville. . . .

A few weeks before, the handful of tents and shacks was moved up from Rush Creek to the railroad tracks which somehow always miss any town located along the survey. One of the first buildings to take to wheels was the saloon, pulled by fourteen horses; the single board shack swaying drunkenly over the rough road. Beside the driver rode a woman in a wine-colored silk dress. The men hailed her boisterously.

She thumbed her nose at them, quite elegantly, with a dainty lace handkerchief, so as not to offend Matilda Lahrer and her mother watching under their slat bonnets. . . .

[The saloon was in place by the Fourth.]

By ten o'clock the celebration crowd milled through the dusty street — sunburned, peeling newcomers, noisy or bewildered or overcautious, in raw contrast to the rich brown skin and easy bearing of those with some length of residence in the dry, windy Panhandle. The few women, mostly in calico and gray sunbonnets, worked about the camp wagons scattered around three sides of the town. Across the tracks was the big attraction, the broken circle camp of the Sioux under Young Man Afraid of His Horse. . . .

In the middle of the afternoon a train, an engine and a few cars puffed into sight. The crowd lined out along the new steel and ties, thrilled at the tremble of the earth, the chatter of the cars to each other, as if none had ever seen the like before. . . . Then they returned to the saloons. . . .

By evening the dust thickened until the light of the oil lamps from the doorways shivered as in a fog. On a platform couples danced polkas and square dances, others waiting their turn, the men clinging to their partners while still others elbowed six deep around any woman who demanded a moment's rest. Boots, spurs, guns, stale whiskey, loud banter, a fight or two, and over it all the noise of an accordion and a fiddle. . . . (*Old Jules*, pp. 64-65, 68)

When wind and drouth gaunted the faces of the early settlers, the sky pilots, usually afoot, appeared like magpies about a dying calf, waiting. But their revivals broke the monotony too, and gave an opportunity for a sight of one's neighbors, often living five to fifteen miles away, a long ways with plow horses and oxen. A typical revival of the periods seems to have been the one in the early Nineties up at Alkali Lake, near Hay Springs, the lake made notorious by an alleged sea monster about 1924:

When the settlers got clear down in the mouth a walking sky pilot appeared and called a revival at Alkali Lake, on the Flats, not far from Hay Springs.

"Wouldn't you jest know them critters'd have to come to pester us! Ain't we got troubles enough as 'tis?" Ma Green told Jules as she stopped her team for a rest at the river. The boys were haying and the freighting had to be done so she had climbed the heavy wagon. . . .

She was timing her loading at Hay Springs so she would make Alkali in time for the revival.

Two days later she stopped while her horses blew before they took the long climb out of the river valley. It had been a fine spectacle, with folks thick as flies around a puddle of syrup, and that sky pilot, with his red beard cut like Christ's in the Sunday-school pictures, preaching hell and damnation from the back of a grasshopper buggy, and women crying and men ripping their only shirts. Then they all moved to the lake and the preacher stuck them under like so many rag dolls until the Flats smelled of stale water and dead salamanders. "It done me more good to see that dirty parson get wet to his middle. I'll bet he ain't ever had a bath all the way up."

Mrs. Schmidt, with eight children at home and a husband laid out behind a saloon somewhere, sang all the way home from the revival. The next week they sent her to the insane asylum and scattered the children. The youngest Frahm girl took pneumonia and died, and a lone Bohemian from the breaks hung [sic] himself. Henrietta came away sad. Only Ma Green seemed to have enjoyed it. (*Old Jules*, pp. 149-150)

No pioneer account is complete without storms. Rose Wilder Lane, in her *Let the Hurricane Roar* [1933], gives a good picture of a blizzard — except that the man's walk of ten miles, as I remember it now, against a blizzard is simply incredible to us out here, where Dakota blizzards evidently out-do those of their native haunts. A good storm with a fine dramatic situation is the one in Willa Cather's *My Antonia* [1918], familiar to us all. It is beautifully and powerfully done, authentic and significant.

After considering these matters it seems a little sacrilegious to quote from my storms. However, one of mine has the advantage of being a personal experience and may, for that reason be of interest:

> . . . Now the faint green of spring was on the hills. The last day of April brought a warm rain; it turned to snow by night.
>
> "Three foot of snow by morning," Father predicted, voicing a standing exaggeration joke of the [sand] hills, but one a bit too near the truth for unadulterated humor. The next morning Mother tunneled out the door with the fire shovel and followed the yard fence to the windmill, as invisible in the flying snow as if it were in the Antarctic instead of fifteen yards from the house. The wind screeched and howled. Mother didn't return. Had she taken the wrong fence from the tank, the one that led off into the pasture? Just when I was mustering the courage to awaken the family, she came back, white, snow-covered from head to foot, her eyelashes grizzled with ice.
>
> "The cattle are gone!" she announced, exploding her bomb with characteristic abruptness. She had been to the shed and they had apparently drifted with the storm, to stumble into snow banks, to chill into pneumonia, to smother, to freeze. With them went our home on the Niobrara, our start in the cattle business. . . .
>
> That May day was a gloomy one. We foraged along the fence, tearing out alternate posts to chop up on the kitchen floor with the hatchet [for fuel]. No one was permitted out of the door without being tied to a rope. The lamp burned all day. (*North American Review*, Vol. 229 [May 1930], p. 579)

No account of pioneer women is complete without the conflict of man with man. In our region it was with the sheepmen, [the farmers], and the cattlemen. In our home, as in those around us, children grew up in the fear of expulsion or extermination by the Winchester:

> ... July 2, 1908, a young school teacher, new in the community, tore madly into our yard. His face was paper white and his day old beard was like a black smudge along his chin. Mother ran to meet him, her hands under her apron, her face anxious.
>
> "Emile's been shot!" he shouted.
>
> Mother's hands dropped heavily to her sides. "How?"
>
> "While he was branding his calves in the corral, before the whole family. R_____ N_____, the damned skunk, rode up, shot him in the back, and then rode away!"
>
> Weakly, Mother dropped to the woodblock in the front yard. So it had come. Father's brother, who never located a settler, who was, in fact, rather friendly to the small cattlemen about him. He lived only five miles away, on Pine Creek, with his wife and seven children. . . . The sheriff had not sought the murderer until the next morning. Community feeling ran high; the young teacher talked of mobbing, of searching the upper ranch. . . . Without able leadership the plan collapsed. They waited for Father, who had once been the leader of a vigilante-like group. But he was in the hills. . . .
>
> A day passed, Uncle Emile was still alive with a bullet in his lungs. Two days — three, Uncle Emile was dead. (*North American Review*, Vol. 229 [March 1930], pp. 425-426)

My resumé seems a serious indictment of writers using the early Nebraska locale. It is true that I know of only two writers, Miss Cather and Mr. Abbott, who write of the pioneer period with authenticity, sincerity, and true creative power. And both of them seem to have deserted the field.

But the story of the pioneer woman in Nebraska has not yet been written. Perhaps, when the women's magazines have turned to the south seas or the North Pole for their material and the spiritual granddaughters of the pioneers have all died off, there will rise a writer with both the insight and the detachment to give us a great American novel on the pioneer woman.

Marlizzie
Gentleman, 1935

The American Frontier is gone, we like to say, a little sadly. And with it went the frontier woman who followed her man along the dusty trail of the buffalo into the land of the hostile Indian. Never again will there be a woman like the wife of Marcus Whitman, who, exactly a hundred years ago, looked out upon a thousand miles of empty West from the bows of a wagon rolling up the Platte toward Oregon.

But there was a later, a less spectacular, and a much more persistent frontier in America, a frontier of prairie fire, drouth, and blizzard, a frontier of land fights and sickness and death far from a doctor, yet with all the characteristic gaiety, deep friendships, and that personal freedom so completely incomprehensible to the uninitiated.

Among my acquaintances are many women who walked the virgin soil of such a frontier and made good lives for themselves and those about them. And when they could they did not turn their backs upon the land they struggled to conquer. They stayed, refusing to be to be told that they occupy the last fringes of a retreating civilization, knowing that life there can be good and bountiful.

One of these frontierswomen is Marlizzie, living more than thirty miles from a railroad, over towering sandhills and through valleys that deepen and broaden to hayflats, with scarcely a house and not a tree the whole way.

No matter when you may come, you will find her away somewhere: chasing a turkey hen, looking after the cattle, repairing fence with stretchers and staples, trimming trees in the orchard, or perhaps piling cow chips for winter fuel. A blow or two on the old steel trap spring that hangs in place of a dinner bell at the gate will bring her — running, it seems to strangers, but really only at her usual gait, a gait that none of the six children towering over her can equal.

She comes smiling and curious, shading her faded blue eyes to see who you may be, and eager to welcome you in any event. And as she approaches, you see her wonderful wiry slightliness, notice that her forearms, always bare, are like steel with twisted cables under dark leather — with hands that are beautiful in the knotted vigor that has gripped the hoe and the pitchfork until the fingers can never be straightened, fingers that still mix the ingredients for the world's most divine concoction — Swiss plum pie.

And while you talk in the long kitchen-living room, she listens eagerly, demanding news of far places — the Rhineland, not so far from the place of her birth; Africa, and the political games in the Far East. Apologetically she explains that the mail is slow and uncertain here. Her daily papers come a sackful at a time, and there is no telephone. Besides, the decayed old stock station thirty miles away is little more than a post office and shipping pens. News still travels in the frontier manner, by word of mouth.

And while Marlizzie listens, perhaps she will make you a pie or two or even three — for one piece, she is certain, would be an aggravation. Gently she tests the plums between her fingers, choosing only the firmest, to halve and pit and lay in ring after ring like little saucers into crust-lined tins. Then sugar and enough of the custard, her own recipe, to cover the plums to dark submerged circles. She dots the top with thick sweet cream, dusts it with nutmeg, or you insist — but it is a serious sacrilege — with cinnamon, and slips them into her Nile-green range, gleaming as a rare piece of porcelain and heated to the exact degree with corncobs. And as she works, her hair, that she had so carefully smoothed with water before she began the pies, has come up in a halo of curls, still with a bright, glinting brown in it for all her sixty-nine years.

It is a little difficult to see in this Marlizzie, so like a timber-line tree but stanchly erect, the woman of forty years ago, delicate of skin with white hands, and what was known as "style" in the days of the leg-o'-mutton sleeve, the basque, and the shirred taffeta front. She came hopefully to Western Nebraska with eight new dresses of cashmeres and twills and figured French serges in navy, brown, gray, and green. One had a yard and a half in each sleeve, and one — a very fine light navy — had two yards of changeable gold-and-blue taffeta pleated into the front of the basque. Marlizzie got so many because she suspected that it might be difficult to find good tailoring, with good style and cloth, right at the first in this wilderness. It was, and still is; but she found no occasion for the clothes she brought, or the renewal of her wardrobe with anything except calico or denim. Gradually the fine dresses were cut up for her children.

Within three months of the day that she struggled with her absurd rosetted little hat in the wind that swept the border town and all the long road to her home in the jolting lumber wagon, Marlizzie had ceased for all time to be a city woman. She had learned to decoy the wily team of Indian ponies and had convert-ed, without a sewing machine, a fashionable gray walking skirt and cape into a pair of trousers and a cap for her new husband.

Ten years later her children found the tape loops once used to hold the trailing widths of the skirt from the dust of the street. When they asked what the loops were for, she told them and laughed a little as she buttoned her denim jacket to go out and feed the cattle. She had married an idealist, a visionary who dreamed mightily of a Utopia and worked incessantly to establish his dream and forgot that cattle must be fed to stand the white cold of thirty-below-zero weather.

By the time the calluses of her hands were as horn, her arms gnarling, and she had somehow fed every hungry wayfarer that came to her door, she had learned many things — among them that on the frontier democracy was an actuality and that, despite the hard-ships, there was a wonderful plentitude of laughter and singing, often with dancing until the cows bawled for their morning milking, or winter-long storytelling around the heater red with cow chips.

The six children of Marlizzie were brought into the world and into maturity whole and sound without a doctor in the house. Though sugar was a luxury and bread often made from grain she ground in a hand mill, they were fed. Despite the constant menace of rattlesnakes to bare feet, and range cattle and wild horses and the dare-deviltry the frontier engenders in its young, not one of the children lost so much as a little finger.

Marlizzie learned the arts of the frontier: butchering, meat care, soapmaking, and the science of the badger-oil lamp, with its underwear wick speared on a hairpin. Stores were remote, even had there been money. Not for twenty-five years, not until she was subpoenaed on a murder case, was she on a train. Finally in 1926 she was in town long enough to see her first moving picture. She stayed in the dark little opera house all the afternoon and the evening to see it over and over, and talked of it as she talked so long ago about the wonders of Faust.

During those years Marlizzie saw many spring suns rise upon the hills as she ran through the wet grass for the team, or stopped to gather a handful of wild sweet peas for her daughter, who was tied to the babies and had little time for play. Often before the fall dawnings Marlizzie stripped the milk from her cow. It was far to the field, and she and her husband must put in long days to husk the little corn before the snow came.

In those forty years Marlizzie saw large herds of range cattle driven into the country, their horns like a tangled thicket over a flowing dusty blanket of brown. She saw them give way to the white-faced Hereford, and the thick-skinned black cattle that crawled through all her fences. She saw the hard times of the East push the settler westward and the cattleman arm against the invasion. She helped mold bullets for the settlers' defense or listened silently, her knitting needles flying, to the latest account of a settler shot down between the plow handles or off his windmill before the eyes of his wife and children.

She knitted only a little more rapidly when it was her own man that was threatened, her brother-in-law that was shot. And always there was patching to be done when her husband was away for weeks on settler business and she could not sleep. In the earlier days, when there was no money for shoes, she made the slippers for the little ones from old overalls on these nights, making a double agony of it. Nothing hurt her pride more than the badly shod feet of her children.

She dug fence-post holes along lines of virgin land, hoed corn, fought prairie fires. She saw three waves of population, thousands of families, come into the free-land region, saw two-thirds of them turn back the next day and more dribble back as fast as they could get money from the folks back home, until only a handful remained.

Marlizzie still lives on the old homestead. With a hired hand — a simple, smiling boy — she runs the place that she helped build through the long years with those gnarled hands. Now that her husband has planned his last ideal community, even the larger decisions are hers to make: the time for the haying, the branding and vaccinating of the cattle, the replacing of trees in her orchards. As the frontier women before her, she looks to the sky and the earth, and their signs do not fail her.

The last time I saw Marlizzie at her home she was on a high ladder, painting the new barn built from the lumber of the old one that the wind destroyed. Winter was coming, but in her vegetable pit was enough produce for herself and her neighbors until spring, with jellies and vegetables and fruit and even roast turkey in glass jars. And in the barn, swathed in a clean old sheet, hung a yearling beef that she and the hired hand had killed and dressed.

Tomorrow she was going to town, a 120-mile trip in a son's truck, to the nearest town large enough to carry husking mittens and the things she needed for Christmas. Then there must be the special bits for the Thanksgiving dinner, such as dates, nuts, and cranberries and a few candies and other goodies.

Most of the dinner will be of her own growing. Always she roasts the largest young tom turkey from her noisy flock. The turkey is eked out with perhaps a couple of pheasants or capons and some catfish dipped from the barrel of running water where she has been fattening them all fall. And toward noon on Thanksgiving day the uninvited guests will begin to come, and come most of the afternoon, until every dish has been washed several times and the last comer fed in true frontier fashion.

And then they will all gather around the old organ, played by one of the daughters of Marlizzie. They will go through the old song books until they are all weary and sentimental and very sad and happy. Toward evening someone will surely come running. Perhaps a gate has been left open; the cattle have broken into the stackyards or a horse is sick. And Marlizzie will tuck up her skirts and fly to the emergency, much as she did the time a three-hundred-pound neighbor came down with a burst appendix and there was nothing better than the sheet-covered kitchen table for the emergency operation, with Marlizzie to stand by the doctor.

Or she will fly to the help of the new frontier woman. Economic stringency has always given the more sparsely settled regions the miraginal aspects of a refuge. During the past five years remote habitations have sprung up on deserted or isolated tracts of land that lay unclaimed.

This newer woman of the frontier lives in a log house, a soddy, a dugout, or even a haystack, much as her predecessors. Thrust from a factory, office, or from the bridge table, she comes alone or with a husband also the victim of the times. Often strong from tennis or swimming she can lay sod, hew a log, or dig a dugout, day in and out, beside most men. She learns to cook over an open fire or in a dutch oven, and, if necessary, to make an oil lamp with a wick from her husband's sock, cut round and round, and speared on an unbent hairpin across a sardine can.

I saw one of these new homemakers in the south sandhills of Nebraska not so long ago. Twenty miles from the nearest boxcar depot, an old Model T without a top, fender, or windshield drew out of the rutted trail to let us pass. In place of an engine the motive power was an old flea-bitten mare, the single-tree slack against her hoary fetlocks. The car body was rounded into a neatly tiered mound of cow chips, the native coal of the sandhills. In front, his feet reaching down to brace against the dash, sat the driver, a young man in frayed-bottom trousers. In the back was a young woman in overalls and an orange felt hat that still carried a hint of the jauntiness of a good shop. Beside her was the battered old washtub used to gather the fuel.

As we passed, they acknowledged our greeting with the salute of the hills, hand in air, palm out. A mile farther on, in a half-acre pocket, was the home of the new settlers: a low structure of Russian thistles and bunch grass tamped between layers of old chicken wire for the walls, held up by posts. There was one glassless window and a door, and through the thatch of brush on the roof rose an old stovepipe chimney with screen tied over it. Against the north side of the little house hung the pelts of a litter of half-grown coyotes, and drying from the clothesline were wreaths of green beans, covered with the skirt of a wash-faded voile dress. In a low plot spaded from the tough sod grew beans and late turnips and rutabagas and Chinese winter radishes. In a square pen shaded with an armful of weeds across a corner, a fine red shoat slept.

I felt a glow of recognition as we passed. These people were already my people. From Marlizzie and her kind they were learning all the tricks of wresting a living, even a good life, from this last frontier.

For amusement the young woman in the orange hat will go to the sandhill dances with others of her kind, perhaps in an outmoded party dress, but most likely in a mail-order print, perhaps made by hand or on the sewing machine of Marlizzie. Their men will be in overalls, turned up jauntily at the cuffs, with open shirt necks and loose ties.

The women will sit on planks over boxes along the wall as their grandmothers did. Now and then the older women, like Marlizzie, will dance to the same fiddle and accordion of forty, fifty years ago. And at midnight there will be cake and sandwiches and coffee.

And toward morning the crowd will scatter, on horseback, in wagons, and in a few old cars that cough and sputter in the sand. The women go to their homes, the straw ticks and cottonwood-leaf mattresses, and to refreshing sleep.

They are not so different from Marlizzie or even the wife of Marcus Whitman. They, too, will learn to look to the sky for the time of planting and harvest, to the earth for the wisdom and the strength she yields to those who walk her freshly turned sod.

Martha of the Yellow Braids
Prairie Schooner 1947

The day Martha came the sun was warm as May on the midwinter drifts, and I ran most of the two miles home from school in my hurry to see her. I had never been around girls much. In a frontier community they are usually scarce; besides, my father was so often embroiled in some spectacular battle for human rights or perhaps sitting out his fines in jail — a background apparently not considered the best by the local mothers of growing girls. So my few playmates were boys, often Polish boys, perhaps because they didn't seem to mind that I was spindly as a rake handle, with my hair roached close to save Mother the combing time, and that I usually had a baby astride my hip. Besides, there were always my brothers.

But the winter I was going on ten Martha came. My father was a locator, and one of his Bohemian settlers brought his family to live with us until he could plow the spring earth for the sod needed to build his house. This was common enough, except that there had never been a girl near my age before. Now there was Martha, eleven, and all the things my mother always wanted me to be: plump, white-skinned, a good bread-baker, a young lady with nice young-lady manners. Martha had grown up in town around her mother's series of boarding houses and showed no deplorable tendency to sneak off for an hour's fishing or sledding, particularly not with rude little Polaks, as she immediately labeled my playmates. Disloyally I tolerated this insult to my friends, for Martha was not only what my mother wanted me to be but all that I wanted too. She was a big girl, free of babies, and she had pale yellow braids thick as pile-driver rope to hang below her knees or to wind in a crown about her head above her garnet earrings from Vienna.

There were other things about Martha that attracted me: her father's teasing pinches at her tight, pink cheek, her mother's goodnight kiss — incredible as a storybook existence to me. But I still think it was the braids that made me desert my Polanders; the pale yellow braids and Martha's way of whispering secrets as she walked beside me with an arm chummily around my shoulders, almost as though we were two of the pretty young Hollanders from over on the Flats, or maybe even American girls.

There must have been the usual difficulties in our family that spring: snow, cold, cattle dying, bills unpaid, and surely Father's temper and his affinity for trouble. Mother must have been as impatient with him as always, and with me too, for I was certainly even less skillful at my work around the facile-handed Martha, and certainly no prettier than before. But I remember nothing much of those three months except a vague, cloudy sort of happiness in my discovery that I could have a friend like the other girls in school. There was the usual housework to be done, with Father away hunting or locating settlers, and Mother busy with the stock and the feeding, the fences to be repaired, the trees to be planted before the leaves came. Martha and I told each other stories as I did the cleaning and fed the baby — not any of those I had written myself, printed in the junior page of our daily paper. It wasn't that I didn't trust her to keep the secret of my writing from my folks; I was ashamed of the stories. Although I usually dismissed fairy tales as plain lying, I even listened to them from Martha because I couldn't bear to see the hurt that would enter into her blue eyes if I said so. And one night, after her mother allowed me to brush the long, yellow hair, I cried hours of envious tears — I who had surely put such childish things behind me long ago.

April came, with tight little clumps of Easter daisies on the greening hillsides, and finally the new sodhouse on the homestead was begun. When the swallows were back with us to skim the morning air, I stood in our yard and waved my baby sister's hand to Martha in the wagon that was taking her into the sandhills. Of course we wrote letters, long ones, every week; then shorter and not so often, for Martha's mother was down at the railroad somewhere running another boarding place, and Martha kept house for her father. Her letters were less of childish stories and more about such things as washing greasy overalls, churning, or singing for the Sunday school that a walking sky pilot had organized among the settlers. By this time there was another baby coming to our house, and while I still got away for an hour now and then, Mother needed my help more and made as much fun of the Polish boys as Martha ever did. Finally one of my brothers and I were sent to the hills to live alone on Father's new homestead, only a few miles from Martha. But I had never been allowed to go visiting and so it didn't occur to me to walk over to see her. Months later, when Mother had moved down too, Martha came for some wolf poison. A coyote was getting her turkeys. By now her skirts were to her shoetops and her talk was all of woman things to Mother. When she got into a young bachelor's top buggy in our yard I knew that I had been left years behind.

Of course we were still friendly, and in a couple of years I got my hair coaxed out into braids long enough to cross at the back. With pins in it and the hems of my faded calico dresses let down, I felt as old as anybody. By that time we had a school district organized, the teacher boarding at our house, and Father giving occasional dances in the barn. Martha came, usually with her folks, and while her mother talked about good matches for the girl, her father pulled the accordion for our dancing. Calmly, easily, Martha would put her hand on the arms of the older men, some at least twenty-five, while I stumbled around the floor with boys of my age, bickering with them about who was to lead, or perhaps talking about bronco busting or pulling a skunk from his winter hole with barbed wire. We were still known as the two good friends and sometimes Martha left the woman bench and came over to whisper giggling secrets into my ear about who was asking her to eat supper or perhaps warning me against this man or that one who had to be watched.

"He'll hold you so tight you can't breathe, if you permit him — " using grown-up words about grown-up things that I pretended to understand.

By the time I had hair enough to cover a rat I managed to have as many dances left over when daylight came as Martha, but still not with the same crowd, for hers were with bachelors who had homesteads, cookstoves, and bedsteads waiting for their wives, while mine were mostly with fuzzy-faced young ranch hands, outsiders visiting relatives in the hills, or Eastern schoolboys working in the hay camps. I was handy at picking up new steps and I had discovered that a ready foot and a glib tongue would do much to discount what I saw when I stood before the looking-glass of Mother's dresser.

"Ah, you are always wasting time with those silly boys — " Martha would try to warn me, using words from her mother's mouth against me.

The spring she was sixteen Martha came over on her flea-bitten old mare instead of sitting easy in some red-wheeled buggy. She had news, and a ring on her finger. Of course the diamond was small, she admitted before I could say it, but the setting was white gold, very stylish. Very expensive too, and much better than a big stone in cheap, old-style yellow tiffany. By then I had learned some young-lady ways too, and so I pretended that I liked the ring, although I wouldn't have been interested in a diamond the size of a boulder set in a ring of platinum the size of a wagon tire, for I was secretly planning to be a schoolteacher and have fine clothes and many beaus for years and years, maybe even write some more of my stories, but for grownups. Although certainly no romantic, I wasn't prepared for Martha's further admission — that she had never seen the man. It was all right, though, she assured me. His people and hers were friends back in the old country, and he was known as a good provider, strong, healthy, and twenty-two, right in the prime of life. Evidently Martha wasn't satisfied with what I managed to say, for she told me crossly that she hadn't expected me to appreciate a good man, not with my nose in a book all the time and without the sense to see that a girl had to do the best she could for herself while she was young.

The wedding was a year later, in June. Martha's father took them up to Rushville to be married. Although I didn't get to go along, I was supposed to pretend that I was the bridesmaid for the dinner. Mother let me cut a dress from a bolt of eleven-cent organdy on the shelf of our country store. Even with a bertha, said to be softening, the unrelieved white was so unbecoming that I dyed an old scarf for a sash. It turned out a dirty lavender, the best I could do with Father's red and blue inks. If I could have found even a stub of indelible pencil, the sash would have been a pungent but vivid purple. I tried the dress on, and while I looked no worse than I had all my sixteen years, somehow it seemed much worse. I even wondered why I had never tried holding my breath long enough to die. Of course there was the wolf poison on the top shelf of the shop, but that was a little drastic.

For the wedding present Mother cut ten yards off the family bolt of white outing flannel, and tied it up with a red ribbon from one of the candy boxes the hay waddies brought me. I came near crying over this baby bundle, which I considered most insulting and suggestive. But no one was interested in my opinion, and, besides, I had to take something. Fortunately Father's peonies were particularly fine that year, and the only clumps in all the sandhills. He let me cut a whole armful, half of them deep wine-red and the rest white. I rolled these in a newspaper twist and tied them to one side of my saddle, the outing flannel in a flour sack to the other. With my white dress rolled up around my waist over my khaki riding skirt, I rode to Martha's for the wedding dinner. She came running into the yard to meet me, holding her veil and her embroidered new dress up out of the dry manure dust with her farm-girl hands in elbow-length white silk gloves. I was overwhelmed by her strangeness, and couldn't do anything except push the peonies at her. Of course she couldn't take them, not with her gloves, and so I carried the flowers to the house and arranged them in a blue crock with Martha giving the advice. This helped us both through the embarrassment of the outing-flannel present and into the dinner, which was delayed by a discussion about the gloves. Should the bride eat with them on or might she take them off? By this time the groom got to making enough noise so that I had to notice him.

"Off!" was his firm verdict about the gloves. No use having to wash them right away. They would last a long time, years if Martha took care of them as his sisters did theirs — laid them away in blue paper to keep out the light. As the talk went around the table I looked the man over. He was that bleak age which the twenties are to the middle teens. His hair was clipped far above his ears in a highwater cut, as we called it, his knobby head showing blue around the back. The collar propping up his cleft chin was real linen, but the suit looked wooly as Grandfather's old wedding broadcloth in our trunk at home. Yet Martha seemed to like her man very much, with all his talk of "the little flat I got feathered for my little bird — " which I considered sickeningly mushy. Nor did I think he came up to any of my dancing partners, not even the one who always puffed so in the schottisches because a horse fell on him when he was small and smashed something inside.

After everybody was full of dinner and there was nothing more to do, things got particularly bad for me, with all the old-country wedding jokes and horseplay. So I managed to slip out to the clearer air of the porch. After a while Martha found me and with an arm around my back as in the old days, she looked into the yard where her flea-bitten pony stomped at the flies. And as in the old days she whispered a secret into my ear. It was about her mother. With only one daughter to be married off, she wouldn't let Martha have the dinner she wanted, with both bride's cake and *kolaches*.

"My one big day — " Martha said, blinking at the bank of tears in her blue eyes.

I tried to tell her that it didn't matter, not out here in the hills, but all I could think about was this unknown woman beside me, talking about such foolish things as bride's cake and *kolaches*, making an important secret of them. She saw my silence for something else and suddenly the kindness that was the Martha I knew broke through all the grownup woman air of the dress and the day. Laughing out loud as when she was eleven, she said that we must make a charm to bring us together again some day. She would leave me a piece of her hair that I used to love so much. Before I had to say anything she gathered up her veil over her arm and was gone to get the scissors.

But I didn't have to take the hair, for Martha's new husband followed her out and standing between us, an arm around each, reminded us that he must now be asked about everything. Maybe I'd better give him a kiss too, just to make sure he would say yes. I pulled away but no one was watching me, particularly not the old people inside the house, who were laughing, taking sides, the women encouraging Martha.

"Go ahead, cut it off. Right at the start you have to show him — " they called to her. But the men shouted them down, slapping their knees in approval at the new husband's firm stand. By golly, you could see who would rule that roost —

So the newlyweds argued a little, pouted and kissed, and then went into the house to sit on the bench along the wall while a pitcher of wine was passed around and the father played the accordion. As soon as I could I said something about going home.

"You know how the folks are about me being off the door-step a second — "

Martha knew. It was a wonder they had let me come at all, the very first time I ever managed to get away without some special errand to be done for my father. So I shook hands awkwardly all around and went to put on my riding skirt. I hated walking through the room with it hanging out below my white dress, but there was no back door. When I finally got to my horse Martha came running through the yard, her veil flying loose behind.

"Oh, I hate to go — to leave everything!" she cried, her gentle eyes swimming.

At last I got away, and as my shaggy little buckskin carried me across the wide meadow, I thought of that fine springtime on the old Niobrara when we used to lie awake nights in the attic, telling stories, Martha's always of beautiful maidens, and princes who were bewitched into frogs or cold wet stones; whispering the stories carefully so the baby wouldn't waken or Mother hear us from downstairs. But that was when I was little, a long time ago, and today the sun was shining and the first prairie roses were pink and fragrant on the upland side of the road. On the marshy side mallard ducks and their young chattered in the rushes, or dove in the open water, busy with their feeding.

And at the fence beyond the first rise a top buggy was waiting, one of the red-wheeled ones from Martha's old crowd.

"Maybe you think I got to have an automobile — ?" the serious young German settler complained when I wouldn't ride in the buggy with him, although I did let my horse idle alongside while I teased the man a little for being such a slow-poke, letting an outsider come in and take Martha away.

At the next dance I ate supper with one of my hay waddies as usual — an art student from Chicago who brought me *Lord Jim* to read and had no cookstove for a bride, no place of his own at all, not even a saddlehorse. But he was teaching me a new kind of fox trot, and anyway I knew that I could have those other things if I wanted them, for now I was really grown-up, with a bachelor in a red-wheeled buggy waiting for me along the road.

Of course I still didn't have thick yellow braids to hang as far as my knees, but that hadn't mattered for a long time.

Dorothy Johnson

~~~~~~

*T*hree stories or novellas by Dorothy Johnson (1905-
1984) have been made into movies — A Man Called
Horse, The Hanging Tree *and* The Man Who Shot
Liberty Valance. *When she died in her home state of
Montana in 1984, she left a large body of work — short
story collections, fiction, countless nonfiction pieces, even a
book called* The Bedside Book of Bastards. *She was
working, at the time of her death, on a novel about World
War II and New York City, which she called* The
Unbombed — *it has never been published.*

*Her literary reputation rests, however, on the short
story collections,* Indian Country *(1953) and* The Hanging Tree *(1957). Noted for her ability to present with
equal skill the woman's point of view and the man's, the
Indian's and the white's, Johnson fashioned her stories in
prose marked by simplicity of style, accurate historical background, positive affirmation of the strengths of ordinary
people and the bonds between them, and, frequently, extraordinary flashes of humor. Of her style, western novelist
Jack Schaefer wrote, "The stories move, flow forward with
swift, at times almost racing, vigor, and then, like a nugget
in the rewarding ore, comes the sudden singing sentence
that implies more than it says and gives depth and significance to the whole." A realist who hid a sentimental
streak, Johnson wanted things to turn out right for people — and
they often do in her stories. As a craftsman, she had an
incisive way of giving the whole idea of the story in the first
paragraph, then spinning it out in spare prose that cuts to
the bone — the opening of "Flame on the Frontier" is
typical. Her plots often utilize what she called the "switch,"
a method of turning a situation around and looking at it*

from another angle, giving her stories unusual power and impact. For instance, she wrote "The Hanging Tree" after seeing three movies in a row about men lost in the desert. Using her technique of "the switch," she wondered what would happen if a woman were lost instead of a man. The result is one of her best stories.

A more complete assessment of Johnson's life and work can be found in Judy Alter's Dorothy Johnson (Boise, Idaho: Boise State University Western Writers Series, 1980).

Jack Schaefer's People
The Short Novels of Jack Schaefer, 1967

J̲ack Schaefer burst upon the literary scene in 1949 with a quietly told story of great suspense, *Shane,* about a family of homesteaders and a mysterious man in black who rode in from nowhere and, after a while, rode on to nowhere. Shane is Lancelot, and Shane is Death.

Mr. Schaefer did not know, of course, that he was creating a classic. He thought he was writing a short story about some people who moved him, although they did not exist until he created them.

The short story turned into a novel and then a memorable motion picture. It has been published in twenty-five languages. In this collection *Shane* makes its fifty-eighth appearance in print.

There are no characters in Jack Schaefer's stories. They are all people. Still, they are the kind of people that one who lived in their time would remember with a wry smile and an admiring shake of the head, saying, "*There* was a character!"

They have this in common: They are affirmative people. They all have something or someone worth fighting for.

The nearest thing to an exception is a Cheyenne Indian in *The Canyon.* This scion of a fighting tribe doesn't want to fight. He doesn't fit his environment.

The man who doesn't fit is the stuff of comedy or of tragedy, depending on how the author-creator looks at him. There is nothing comical about the Cheyenne, Little Bear, but his story is not tragedy either, if tragedy means catastrophe. He never quits. Naturally he doesn't quit. Jack Schaefer's people don't. They endure.

A Plains Indian who did not fit into the customs of his people was an embarrassment. In the tightly knit tribal society of a nomadic tepee village, everyone's welfare depended on everyone else. There was a place for each person in the community but no room for rebels against the Establishment.

On the other hand, most of the white men who went west were rebels against something, ranging from the majesty of the law to the poverty they tried to leave behind them. A white man could be a loner, forever drifting. An Indian could not. So what Little Bear learned was this: "A man must be certain that his heart speaks the truth to him. One man cannot change a tribe. But one man can live with a tribe and not let it change him too much."

Jack Schaefer's people do things without seeming to make choices or to count the odds. They have to, because that is the kind of people they are. And we keep reading to find out what kind of people they are.

Here are some cantankerous fellows who argue at the drop of a hat, or sooner. If they're square shooters, they say just what they mean — except in expressing affection. "You ornery old scrawny hoptoad" is a term of endearment. A girl in *The Kean Land*, in a time of stress, addresses the man she loves as "you overgrown lunk-head," because love is too blinding to be stared at or mentioned without circumlocution.

These people are earthy. They smell of sweat and old leather.

Why do we read, and why do writers write, stories about the frontier West? Because the perils were different from ours.

A long-healed scar made by an Indian arrow might ache to prod a man's memory of battle. So may an ulcer hurt his great grandson — a different wound from a newer battle. We escape from the new to the old, from our conflicts to their conflicts, from our strength (which we must doubt sometimes) to strength that is dependable.

The costumes are different now, and the stage setting has changed, but Jack Schaefer's people could be someone we know, blundering, worrying, enduring, not giving up. Were people in the West, in the nineteenth century, really different from ourselves? Thomas Dimsdale, a newspaper editor in a roaring Montana gold camp in 1865, said flatly, "Middling people do not live in these regions. A man or a woman becomes better or worse by a trip towards the Pacific."

Now, of course, we have hordes of middling people. A trip toward the Pacific doesn't change anyone anymore. The journey has become too easy. We may fret because the plane is an hour late, but we don't have to fort up the wagons to fend off an Indian attack.

We are molded by different influences. Perhaps we march to a different drummer. Some of us don't march to any drummer. We saunter.

There were saunterers, drifters, in the frontier West, and a man couldn't always choose the company he kept. But a writer, re-creating the frontier, can choose, and Jack Schaefer has chosen to stress the strong, with pity in passing for the weak.

There are at least two kinds of courage. There is the sudden kind, which one summons — or fails to summon — in an emergency, the kind that requires quick action and doesn't give much time to make a decision. And there is the courage that is endurance, requiring many decisions over a long period of time that looks as if it would never have an end.

Both kinds make the story of *A Company of Cowards*, which is a story of the Civil War and not strictly a western, although it ends in the frontier West. In this one, Jack Schaefer's people are army officers who failed miserably when called upon for sudden courage but had the long, enduring kind.

In this collection there are no whiners railing against fate, defending their failure by claiming that they're searching for their own identity. Jack Schaefer's people all know who they are. *First Blood* is about a young man who found out through torment.

There is a feeling of oldness in Jack Schaefer's West. It wasn't invented just for the occasion of whatever story is at hand. It is not simply the geological oldness of mountains and prairie; it is the stability of customary things, for wherever man goes, he takes along customs and traditions and in a place he sets up new ones. He needs something to hold fast to; he is one generation in the long procession of generations.

In *First Blood*, for example, there is the oldness of an established stage line and the traditions of the firm. How refreshing, the understanding that stagecoaches constituted a business, that they didn't go bounding through the sagebrush without schedules simply so they could be held up by road agents!

Jack Schaefer's people make you want to yell, "Don't do that, man! Don't do it!" or, "Go on, hit him! What are you waiting for?" But yelling would not influence them, because they do what they must, being the kind of people they are, not puppets or paper dolls.

There can be terrible suspense just in watching a couple of old men, good friends, sitting and looking at each other. Jack Schaefer's people range from naive to sinister. *Valorous* is one thing you might call them. Another word for them is *deadly*, because strength is inherently dangerous.

Flame on the Frontier
Indian Country, 1953

On Sunday morning, wearing white man's sober clothing, a Sioux chief named Little Crow attended the church service at the Lower Agency and afterward shook hands with the preacher. On Sunday afternoon, Little Crow's painted and feathered Santee Sioux swooped down on the settlers in bloody massacre. There was no warning. . . .

Hannah Harris spoke sharply to her older daughter, Mary Amanda. "I've told you twice to get more butter from the spring. Now step! The men want to eat."

The men — Oscar Harris and his two sons, sixteen and eighteen — sat in stolid patience on a bench in front of the cabin, waiting to be called to the table.

Mary Amanda put down the book she had borrowed from a distant neighbor and went unwillingly out of the cabin. She liked to read and was proud that she knew how, but she never had another book in her hands as long as she lived. Mary Amanda

Harris was, on that day in August in 1862, just barely thirteen years old.

Her little sister Sarah tagged along down to the spring for lack of anything better to do. She was healthily hungry, and the smell of frying chicken had made her fidget until her mother had warned, "Am I going to have to switch you?"

The two girls wrangled as they trotted down the accustomed path.

"Now what'd you come tagging for?" demanded Mary Amanda. She wanted to stay, undisturbed, in the world of the book she had been reading.

Sarah said, "I guess I got a right to walk here as good as you."

She shivered, not because of any premonition but simply because the air was cool in the brush by the spring. She glanced across the narrow creek and saw a paint-striped face. Before she could finish her scream, the Indian had leaped the creek and smothered her mouth.

At the cabin they heard that single, throat-tearing scream instantly muffled. They knew what had to be done; they had planned it, because this day might come to any frontier farm.

Hannah Harris scooped up the baby boy, Willie, and hesitated only to cry out, "The girls?"

The father, already inside the cabin, handed one rifle to his eldest son as he took the other for himself. To Jim, who was sixteen, he barked, "The axe, boy."

Hannah knew what she had to do — run and hide — but that part of the plan had included the little girls, too. She was to take the four younger children, including the dull boy, Johnny. She was too sick with the meaning of that brief scream to be able to change the plan and go without the girls.

But Oscar roared, "Run for the rushes! You crazy?" and broke her paralysis. With the baby under one arm she began to run down the hill to a place by the river where the rushes grew high.

The only reason Hannah was able to get to the rushes with her two youngest boys was that the men, Oscar and Jim and Zeke, delayed the Indians for a few minutes. The white men might have barricaded themselves in the cabin and stood off the attackers for a longer period, but the approaching Indians would have seen that frantic scuttling into the rushes.

Oscar and Jim and Zeke did not defend. They attacked. With the father going first, they ran toward the spring and met the Indians in the brush. Fighting there, they bought a little time for the three to hide down by the river, and they paid for it with their lives.

Hannah, the mother, chose another way of buying time. She heard the invaders chopping at whatever they found in the cabin. She heard their howls as they found clothing and kettles and food. She stayed in the rushes as long as she dared, but when she smelled the smoke of the cabin burning, she knew the Indians would be ranging out to see what else might be found.

Then she thrust the baby into Johnny's arms and said fiercely, "You take care of him and don't you let him go until they kill you."

She did not give him any instructions about how to get to a place of safety. There might be no such place.

She kissed Johnny on the forehead and she kissed the baby twice, because he was so helpless and because he was, blessedly, not crying.

She crawled to the left, far to the left of the children, so that she would not be seen coming directly from their hiding place. Then she came dripping up out of the rushes and went shrieking up the hill straight toward the Indians.

When they started down to meet her, she hesitated and turned. She ran, still screaming, toward the river, as if she were so crazed she did not know what she was doing. But she knew. She knew very well. She did exactly what a meadowlark will do if its nest in the grass is menaced — she came into the open, crying and frantic, and lured the pursuit away from her young.

But the meadowlark acts by instinct, not by plan. Hannah Harris had to fight down her instinct, which was to try to save her own life.

As the harsh hands seized her, she threw her arm across her eyes so as not to see death . . .

Of the two girls down at the spring only Sarah screamed. Mary Amanda did not have time. A club, swung easily by a strong arm, cracked against her head.

Sarah Harris heard the brief battle and knew her father's voice, but she did not have to see the bodies, a few yards away on the path through the brush. One of the Indians held her without difficulty. She was a thin little girl, nine years old.

Mary Amanda was unconscious and would have drowned except that her guard pulled her out of the creek and laid her, face down, on the gravel bank.

The girls never saw their cabin again. Their captors tied their hands behind them and headed back the way they had come to rejoin the war party. The girls were too frightened to cry or speak. They stumbled through the brush.

Mary Amanda fell too many times. Finally she gave up and lay still, waiting to die, sobbing quietly. Her guard grunted and lifted his club.

Sarah flew at him shrieking. Her hands were tied, but her feet were free and she could still run.

The Indian, who had never had anything to do with white people except at a distance, or in furious flurries of raiding, was astonished by her courage, and impressed. All he knew of white girls was that they ran away, screaming, and then were caught. This one had the desperate, savage fury of his own women. She chattered as angrily as a bluejay. (Bluejay was the name he gave her, the name everyone called her, in the years she lived and grew up among the Sioux.)

She had knocked the wind out of him, but he was amused. He jerked the older girl, Mary Amanda, to her feet.

The mother, Hannah, was taken along by the same route, about a mile behind them, but she did not know they were still alive. One of them she saw again six years later. The other girl she never saw again.

For hours she went stumbling, praying, "Lord in thy mercy, make them kill me fast!"

When they did not, she let hope flicker, and when they camped that night, she began to ask timidly, "God, could you help me get away?"

She had no food that night, and no water. An Indian had tied her securely.

The following day her captors caught up with a larger party, carrying much loot and driving three other white women. They were younger than Hannah. That was what saved her.

When she was an old woman, she told the tale grimly: "I prayed to the Lord to let me go, and He turned the Indians' backs on me and I went into the woods, and that was how I got away."

She did not tell how she could still hear the piercing shrieks of the other women, even when she was far enough into the woods so that she dared to run.

She blundered through the woods, hiding at every sound, praying to find a trail, but terrified when she came to one, for fear there might be Indians around the next bend. After she reached the trail and began to follow it, she had a companion, a shaggy yellow dog.

For food during the two days she had berries. Then she came upon the dog eating a grouse he had killed, and she stooped, but he growled.

"Nice doggie," she crooned. "Nice old Sheppy!"

She abased herself with such praise until — probably because he had caught other game and was not hungry — he let her take the tooth-torn, dirt-smeared remnants. She picked off the feathers with fumbling fingers, washed the raw meat in the creek and ate it as she walked.

She smelled wood smoke the next morning and crawled through brush until she could see a clearing. She saw white people there in front of a cabin, and much bustling. She heard children crying and the authoritative voices of women. She stood up then and ran, screaming, toward the cabin, with the dog jumping and barking beside her.

One of the hysterical women seized a rifle and fired a shot at Hannah before a man shouted, "She's white!" and ran out to meet her.

There were sixteen persons in the cramped cabin or near it — refugees from other farms. Hannah Harris kept demanding, while she wolfed down food, "Ain't anybody seen two little girls? Ain't anybody seen a boy and a baby?"

Nobody had seen them.

The draggled-skirted women in the crowded cabin kept busy with their children, but Hannah Harris had no children any more — she who had had four sons and two daughters. She dodged among the refugees, beseeching, "Can't I help with something? Ain't there anything I can do?"

A busy old woman said with sharp sympathy, "Miz Harris, you go lay down some place. Git some sleep. All you been through!"

Hannah Harris understood that there was no room for her there. She stumbled outside and lay down in a grassy place in the shade. She slept, no longer hearing the squalling of babies and the wrangling of the women.

Hannah awoke to the crying of voices she knew and ran around to the front of the cabin. She saw two men carrying a stretcher made of two shirts buttoned around poles. A bundle sagged on the stretcher, and a woman was trying to lift it, but it cried with two voices.

Johnny lay there, clutching the baby and both of them were screaming.

Kneeling, she saw blood on Johnny's feet and thought with horror. "Did the Injuns do that?" Then she remembered, "No, he was barefoot when we ran."

He would not release the baby, even for her. He was gaunt, his ribs showed under his tattered shirt. His eyes were partly open and his lips were drawn back from his teeth. He was only half conscious, but he still had strength enough to clutch his baby brother, though the baby screamed with hunger and fear.

Hannah said in a strong voice, "Johnny, you can let go now. You can let Willie go. Johnny, this is your mother talking."

With a moan, he let his arms go slack.

For the rest of his life, and he lived another fifty years, he suffered from nightmares and often awoke screaming.

With two of her children there Hannah Harris was the equal of any woman. She pushed among the others to get to the food, to find cloth for Johnny's wounded feet. She wrangled with them, defending sleeping space for her children.

For a few months she made a home for her boys by keeping house for a widower named Lincoln Bartlett, whose two daughters had been killed at a neighbor's cabin. Then she married him.

The baby, Willie, did not live to grow up, in spite of the sacrifices that had been made for him. He died of diphtheria. While Link Bartlett dug a little grave, Hannah sat, stern but dry-eyed, on a slab bench, cradling the still body in her arms.

The dull boy, Johnny, burst out hoarsely, "It wasn't no use after all, was it?" and his mother understood.

She told him strongly, "Oh yes, it was! It was worth while, all you did. He's dead now, but he died in my arms, with a roof over him. I'll know where he's buried. It ain't as if the Indians had butchered him some place that I'd never know."

She carried the body across the room and laid it tenderly in the box that had been Willie's bed and would be his coffin. She turned to her other son and said, "Johnny, come sit on my lap."

He was a big boy, twelve years old, and he was puzzled by this invitation, as he was puzzled about so many things. Awkwardly he sat on her knees, and awkwardly he permitted her to cuddle his head against her shoulder.

"How long since your mother kissed you?" she asked, and he mumbled back, "Don't know."

She kissed his forehead. "You're my big boy. You're my Johnny."

He lay in her arms for a while, tense and puzzled. After a while, not knowing why it was necessary to cry, he began to sob, and she rocked him back and forth. She had no tears left.

Johnny said something then that he had thought over many times, often enough to be sure about it. "It was him that mattered most, I guess."

Hannah looked down at him, shocked.

"He was my child and I loved him," she said. "It was him I worried about. . . But it was you I trusted."

The boy blinked and scowled. His mother bowed her head.

"I never said so. I thought you knowed that. When I give him to you that day, Johnny boy, I put more trust in you than I did in the Lord God."

That was a thing he always remembered — the time his mother made him understand that for a while he had been more important than God.

The Harris sisters were sold twice, the second time to a Sioux warrior named Runs Buffalo, whose people ranged far to the westward.

Bluejay never had to face defeat among the Indians. The little girl who had earned her name by scolding angrily had the privileges of a baby girl. She was fed and cared for like the Indian children, and she had more freedom and less scolding than she had had in the cabin that was burned. Like the other little girls, she was freer than the boys. Her responsibility would not begin for three or four years. When the time came, she would be taught to do the slow, patient work of the women, in preparation for being a useful wife. But while she was little, she could play.

While the boys learned to shoot straight and follow tracks, while they tested and increased their endurance and strength, the little girls played and laughed in the sun. Bluejay did not even have a baby to look after, because she was the youngest child in the lodge of Runs Buffalo. She was the petted one, the darling, and the only punishment she knew was what she deserved for profaning holy objects. Once at home she had been switched by her father for putting a dish on the great family Bible. In the Indian village, she learned to avoid touching medicine bundles or sacred shields and to keep silent in the presence of men who understood religious mysteries.

Mary Amanda, stooped over a raw buffalo hide, scraping it hour after hour with tools of iron and bone, because that was women's work and she was almost a woman, heard familiar shrill arguments among the younger girls, the same arguments that had sounded in the white settlement, and in the same language: "You're it!". . ."I am not!"

That much the little Indian girls learned of English. Sarah learned Sioux so fast that she no longer needed English and would have stopped speaking it except that her older sister insisted.

Mary Amanda learned humility through blows. To her, everything about the Indians was contemptible. She learned their language simply to keep from being cuffed by the older women, who were less shocked at her ignorance of their skills than at her unwillingness to learn the work that was a woman's privilege to perform. She sickened at the business of softening hides with a mixture of clay and buffalo manure. If she had been more docile, she might have been an honored daughter in the household. Instead, she was a sullen slave. Mary Amanda remembered what Sarah often forgot: that she was white. Mary Amanda never stopped hoping that they would be rescued. The name the Indians gave her was The Foreigner.

When she tried to take Sarah aside to talk English, the old woman of the household scolded.

Mary Amanda spoke humbly in Sioux. "Bluejay forgets to talk like our own people. I want her to know how to talk."

The old woman growled, "You are Indians," and Mary Amanda answered, "It is good for Indians to be able to talk to white people."

The argument was sound. A woman interpreter would never be permitted in the councils of chiefs and captains, but who could tell when the skill might be useful? The girls were allowed to talk together, but Sarah preferred Sioux.

When The Foreigner was sixteen years old she had four suitors. She knew what a young man meant by sending a gift of meat to the lodge and later standing out in front, blanket-wrapped and silent.

When the young man came, Mary Amanda pretended not to notice, and the old woman pretended with her, but there was chuckling in the lodge as everyone waited to see whether The Foreigner would go out, perhaps to bring in water from the creek.

Her little sister teased her. "Go on out. All you have to do is let him put his blanket around you and talk. Go on. Other girls do."

"Indian girls do," Mary Amanda answered sadly. "That ain't the way boys do their courting back home."

The tall young men were patient. Sometimes as many as three at once stood out there through twilight into darkness, silent and waiting. They were eligible, respected young men, skilled in hunting, taking horses, proved in courage, schooled in the mysteries of protective charms and chanted prayer. All of them had counted coup in battle.

Mary Amanda felt herself drawn toward the lodge opening. It would be so easy to go out!

She asked Sarah humbly, "Do you think it's right, the way they buy their wives? Of course, the girl's folks give presents to pay back."

Sarah shrugged. "What other way is there? . . . If it was me, I'd go out fast enough. Just wait till I'm older!" She reminded her sister of something it was pleasanter to forget, "They don't have to wait for you to make up your mind. They could sell you to an old man for a third wife."

When Mary Amanda was seventeen, a man of forty, who had an aging wife, looked at her with favor, and she made her choice. On a sweet summer evening she arose from her place in the tepee and, without a word to anyone, stooped and passed through the lodge opening. She was trembling as she walked past Hawk and Grass Runner and eluded their reaching hands. She stopped before a young man named Snow Mountain.

He was as startled as the family back in the tepee. Courting The Foreigner had become almost a tradition with the young men, because she seemed unattainable and competition ruled their lives. He wrapped his blanket around her and felt her heart beating wildly.

He did not tell her she was pretty. He told her that he was brave and cunning. He told her he was a skilled hunter, his lodge never lacked for meat. He had many horses, most of them stolen from the Crows in quick, desperate raids.

Mary Amanda said, "You give horses to buy what you want. Will Runs Buffalo give presents to you in return?"

That was terribly important to her. The exchange of gifts was in itself the ceremony. If she went to him with no dowry, she went without honor.

"I cannot ask about that," he said. "My mother's brother will ask."

But Runs Buffalo refused.

"I will sell the white woman for horses," he announced. "She belongs to me. I paid for her."

Mary Amanda went without ceremony, on a day in autumn, to the new lodge of Snow Mountain. She went without pride, without dowry. The lodge was new and fine, she had the tools and kettles she needed, and enough robes to keep the household warm. But all the household things were from his people, not hers. When she cried, he comforted her.

For her there was no long honeymoon of lazy bliss. Her conscience made her keep working to pay Snow Mountain for the gifts no one had given him. But she was no longer a slave, she was queen in her own household. An old woman, a relative of his mother, lived with them to do heavy work. Snow Mountain's youngest brother lived with him, helping to hunt and butcher and learning the skills a man needed to know.

Mary Amanda was a contented bride — except when she remembered that she had not been born an Indian. And there was always in her mind the knowledge that many warriors had two wives, and that often the two wives were sisters.

"You work too hard," Snow Mountain told her. "Your little sister does not work hard enough."

"She is young," The Foreigner reminded him, feeling that she should apologize for Bluejay's shortcomings.

Snow Mountain said, "When she is older, maybe she will come here."

Afterward she knew he meant that in kindness. But thinking of Sarah as her rival in the tepee, as her sister-wife, froze Mary Amanda's heart. She answered only, "Bluejay is young."

Sarah Harris, known as Bluejay, already had two suitors when she was only fourteen. One of them was only two or three years older than she was, and not suitable for a husband; he had few war honors and was not very much respected by anyone except his own parents. The other was a grown man, a young warrior named Horse Ears, very suitable and, in fact, better than the flighty girl had any right to expect. When Sarah visited in her sister's lodge, she boasted of the two young men.

Mary Amanda cried out, "Oh, no! You're too young to take a man. You could wait two years yet, maybe three. Sarah, some day you will go back home."

Two years after the massacre, the first rumor that the Harris girls were alive reached the settlement, but it was nothing their mother could put much faith in. The rumor came in a roundabout way, to Link Barlett, Hannah's second husband, from a soldier at the fort, who had it from another soldier, who had it from a white trader, who heard it from a Cheyenne. And all they heard was that two white sisters were with a Sioux village far to the westward. Rumors like that drifted in constantly. Two hundred women had been missing after that raid.

Two more years passed before they could be fairly sure that there were really two white sisters out there and that they were probably the Harrises.

After still another year, the major who commanded the army post nearest the settlement was himself convinced, and negotiations began for their ransom.

Link Bartlett raised every cent he could — he sold some of his best land — to buy the gifts for that ransom.

In the sixth year of the captivity, a cavalry detachment was ordered out on a delicate diplomatic mission — to find and buy the girls back, if possible.

Link Bartlett had his own horse saddled and was ready to leave the cabin, to go with the soldiers, when Hannah cried harshly, "Link, don't you go! Don't go away and leave me and the kids!"

The children were dull Johnny and a two-year-old boy, named Lincoln, after his father, the last child Hannah ever had.

Link tried to calm her. "Now, Hannah, you know we planned I should go along to see they got back all right — if we can find 'em at all."

"I ain't letting you go," she said. "If them soldiers can't make out without you, they're a poor lot." Then she jarred him to his heels. She said, almost gently, "Link, if I was to lose you, I'd die."

That was the only time she ever hinted that she loved him. He never asked for any more assurance. He stayed at home because she wanted him there.

Mary Amanda's son was half a year old when the girls first learned there was hope of their being ransomed.

The camp crier, walking among the lodges, wailed out the day's news so that everyone would know what was planned: "Women, stay in the camp. Keep your children close to you where they will be safe. There is danger. Some white soldiers are camped on the other side of the hills. Three men will go out to talk to them. The three men are Runs Buffalo, Big Moon and Snow Mountain."

Mary Amanda did not dare ask Snow Mountain anything. She watched him ride out with the other men, and then she sat on the ground in front of his tepee, nursing her baby. Bluejay came to the lodge and the two girls sat together in silence as the hours passed.

The men from the Sioux camp did not come back until three days later. When Snow Mountain was ready to talk, he remarked, "The white soldiers came to find out about two white girls. They will bring presents to pay if the white girls want to go back."

Mary Amanda answered "O-o-oh," in a sigh like a frail breeze in prairie grass.

There was no emotion in his dark, stern face. He looked at her for a long moment, and at the baby. Then he turned away without explanation. She called after him, but he did not answer. She felt the dark eyes staring, heard the low voices. She was a stranger again, as she had not been for a long time.

Nothing definite had been decided at the parley with the white soldiers, the girls learned. The soldiers would come back sometime, bringing presents for ransom, and if the presents were fine enough, there would be talk and perhaps a bargain. Mary Amanda felt suddenly the need to prepare Sarah for life in the settlement. She told her everything she could remember that might be useful.

"You'll cook over a fire in a fireplace," she said, "and sew with thread, and you'll have to learn to knit."

Bluejay whimpered, "I wish you could come, too."

"He wouldn't let me go, of course," Mary Amanda answered complacently. "He wouldn't let me take the baby, and I wouldn't leave without him. You tell them I got a good man. Be sure to tell them that."

At night, remembering the lost heaven of the burned cabin, remembering the life that was far away and long ago, she cried a little. But she did not even consider begging Snow Mountain to let her go. She had offended him, but when he stopped brooding they would talk again. He had not said anything to her since he had tested her by telling her the ransom had been offered.

He did not even tell her that he was going away. He gave orders to the old woman in the lodge and discussed plans with his younger brother, but he ignored his wife. Five men were going out to take horses from the Crows, he said. Mary Amanda shivered.

Before he rode away with his war party, he spent some time playing with the baby, bouncing the child on his knee, laughing when the baby laughed. But he said nothing to Mary Amanda, and the whole village knew that he was angry and that she deserved his anger.

Her hands and feet were cold as she watched him go and her heart was gnawed by the fear that was part of every Indian woman's life: "Maybe he will never come back."

Not until the white soldiers had come back to parley again did she understand how cruelly she had hurt him.

She dreamed of home while they waited for news of the parley, and she tried to make Bluejay dream of it.

"You'll have to do some things different there, but Ma will remind you. I'll bet Ma will cry like everything when she sees you coming." Mary Amanda's eyes flooded with tears, seeing that meeting. "I don't remember she ever did cry," she added thoughtfully, "but I guess she must have sometimes. . . . Ma must have got out of it all right. Who else would be sending the ransom? Oh, well, sometime I'll find out all about it from Snow Mountain. . . . I wonder if she got Johnny and Willie away from the cabin safe. Tell her I talked about her lots. Be sure to tell Ma that, Sarah. Tell her how cute my baby is."

Bluejay, unnaturally silent, dreamed with her, wide-eyed, of the reunion, the half-forgotten heaven of the settlement.

"Tell her about Snow Mountain," Mary Amanda reminded her sister. "Be sure to do that. How he's a good hunter, so we have everything we want, and more. And everybody respects him. Tell her he's good to me and the baby. . . . But, Sarah, don't ever say he steals horses. They wouldn't understand back home. . . . And don't ever let on a word about scalps. If they say anything about scalps, you say our people here don't do that."

"They do, though," Sarah reminded her flatly. "It takes a brave man to stop and take a scalp off when somebody's trying to kill him."

Looking at her, Mary Amanda realized that Sarah didn't even think taking scalps was bad, so long as your own people did it and didn't have it done to them.

"You're going to have to forget some things," she warned with a sigh.

While the parley was still on Big Moon, the medicine priest, came to the lodge where The Foreigner bent over her endless work. He was carrying something wrapped in buckskin.

"Tell them the names of the people in your lodge before you came to the Sioux," he said shortly as he put down the buckskin bundle. "They are not sure you are the women they want."

In the bundle were sheets of paper and a black crayon.

Sarah came running. She sat fascinated as Mary Amanda wrote carefully on the paper: "Popa, Moma, Zeke, Jim, Johny, Wily."

Mary Amanda was breathless when she finished. She squeezed Sarah's arm. "Just think, you're going to go home!"

Sarah nodded, not speaking. Sarah was getting scared.

The following day, the ransom was paid and brought into camp. Then The Foreigner learned how much she had offended Snow Mountain.

Big Moon brought fine gifts to the lodge, and piled them inside — a gun, powder and percussion caps and bullets, bolts of cloth, mirrors and beads and tools and a copper kettle.

"The Foreigner can go now," he said.

Mary Amanda stared. "I cannot go back to the white people. I am Snow Mountain's woman. This is his baby."

"The gifts pay also for the baby," Big Moon growled. "Snow Mountain will have another wife, more sons. He does not need The Foreigner. He has sold her to the white man."

Mary Amanda turned pale. "I will not go with the white men," she said angrily. "When Snow Mountain comes back, he will see how much The Foreigner's people cared for her. They have sent these gifts as her dowry."

Big Moon scowled. "Snow Mountain may not come back. He had a dream, and the dream was bad. His heart is sick, and he does not want to come back."

As a widow in the Sioux camp, her situation would be serious. She could not go back to her parents' home, for she had no parents. But neither could she leave the camp now to go back to the settlement and never know whether Snow Mountain was alive or dead. Sarah stood staring at her in horror.

"I will wait for him," Mary Amanda said, choking. "Will Big Moon pray and make medicine for him?"

The fierce old man stared at her, scowling. He knew courage when he saw it, and he admired one who dared to gamble for high stakes.

"All these gifts will belong to Big Moon," she promised, "if Snow Mountain comes back."

The medicine priest nodded and turned away. "Bluejay must come with me," he said briefly. "I will take her to the white soldiers and tell them The Foreigner does not want to come."

She watched Sarah walk away between the lodges after the medicine priest. She waved good-bye, and then went in to the lodge. The old woman said, "Snow Mountain has a good wife.". . .

Ten days passed before the war party came back. Mary Amanda waited, hardly breathing, as they brought Snow Mountain into camp tied on a travois, a pony drag.

Big Moon said, "His shadow is gone out of his body. I do not know whether it will come back to stay."

"I think it will come back to stay," said The Foreigner, "because I have prayed and made a sacrifice."

At the sound of her voice, Snow Mountain opened his eyes. He lay quiet in his pain, staring up at her, not believing. She saw tears on his dark cheeks.

Her name was always The Foreigner, but for the rest of her life she was a woman of the Santee Sioux.

Sarah Harris, who had been called Bluejay, was hard to tame, they said in the settlement. Her mother fretted over her heathen ways. The girl could not even make bread!

"I can tan hides," Sarah claimed angrily. "I can butcher a buffalo and make pemmican. I can pitch a tepee and pack it on a horse to move."

But those skills were not valued in a white woman, and Sarah found the settlement not quite heaven. She missed the constant talk and laughter of the close-pitched tepees. She had to learn a whole new system of polite behavior. There was dickering and trading and bargaining, instead of a proud exchanging of fine gifts. A neighbor boy slouching on a bench outside the cabin, talking to her stepfather while he got up courage to ask whether Sarah was at home, was less flattering as a suitor than a young warrior, painted and feathered, showing off on a spotted horse. Sometimes Sarah felt that she had left heaven behind her.

But she never went back to it. When she was seventeen, she married the blacksmith, Herman Schwartz, and their first baby was born six months later.

Sarah's oldest child was six and her second child was three when the Indian man appeared at the door of her cabin and stood silently peering in.

"Git out of here!" she cried, seizing the broom.

He answered in the Sioux tongue, "Bluejay has forgotten."

She gave Horse Ears a shrill welcome in his own language and the three-year-old started to cry. She lifted a hand for an accustomed slap but let it fall. Indian mothers did not slap their children.

But she was not Indian any more, she recollected. She welcomed Horse Ears in as a white woman does an invited guest. In her Sunday-company voice she chattered politely. It was her privilege because she was a white woman. No need any more for the meek silence of the Indian woman.

She brought out bread and butter and ate with him. That was her privilege too.

"My sister?" she asked.

He had not seen The Foreigner for a long time. He had left that village.

"Does Bluejay's man make much meat?" Horse Ears asked. "Is he a man with many honors in war?"

She laughed shrilly. "He makes much meat. He has counted coup many times. We are rich."

"I came to find out those things," he answered. "In my lodge there is only one woman."

She understood, and her heart leaped with the flattery. He had traveled far, and in some danger, to find out that all was well with her. If it was not, there was refuge in his tepee. And not only now, she realized, but any time, forever.

A shadow fell across the threshold; a hoarse voice filled the room. "What's that bloody Injun doing here?" roared Sarah's husband. "Are you all right?"

"Sure, we're all right," she answered. "I don't know who he is. He was hungry."

His eyes narrowed with anger, "Is he one of them you used to know?"

Her body tensed with fear. "I don't know him, I told you!"

Her husband spoke to the Indian in halting Sioux, but Horse Ears was wise. He did not answer.

"Git out!" the blacksmith ordered, and the Indian obeyed without a word.

As Sarah watched him go down the path, without turning, she wished fervently that she could tell him good-bye, could thank him for coming. But she could not betray him by speaking.

Herman Schwartz strode toward her in silent, awesome, blazing fury. She did not cringe; she braced her body against the table. He gave her a blow across the face that rocked her and blinded her.

She picked up the heavy iron skillet.

"Don't you ever do that again or I'll kill you," she warned.

He glared at her with fierce pride, knowing that she meant what she said.

"I don't reckon I'll have to do it again," he said complacently. "If I ever set eyes on that savage again, I'll kill him. You know that, don't you, you damn squaw?"

She shrugged. "Talk's cheap."

As she went down to the spring for a bucket of water, she was singing.

Her girlhood was gone, and her freedom was far behind her. She had two crying children and was pregnant again. But two men loved her and both of them had just proved it.

Forty years later, her third child was elected to the state legislature, and she went, a frightened, white-haired widow, to see him there. She was proud, but never so proud as she had been on a summer day three months before he was born.

Journey to the Fort
Indian Country, 1953

S he stood where the harsh hands had pushed her. The Indians had thrown a stinking blanket over her head so that she could not see the soldiers just above her on the hill. Around her she felt the strength and menace of the Sioux; she heard rustlings and murmured growls. She listened, not breathing, trying to hear the talk of the chief with the soldiers.

She heard wagon wheels and a man's voice barking, "Whoa!" The ransom wagons! she thought. They have brought up the ransom wagons! She breathed again.

The chief's voice, old and querulous, came from a distance: "The gifts are enough. The white woman can go now to her people."

He was giving her freedom because she had healed his wound. There was angry murmuring among the Indian men around her, but someone snatched the blanket from her head and someone else pushed her so hard that she stumbled.

She walked up a hill on moccasined feet that had callused on bitter trails. But she was not walking on the ground; she was a little above it, she thought. It was safer that way, between heaven and earth, where she could not really be hurt. She had discovered many ways to keep from being hurt during the past seven months.

Now the real peril clutched her heart, because who could say that she would ever be allowed to reach the little group of waiting soldiers?

As she plodded along, she sought safety in a place no one else knew about. She had found it months before, when the Sioux had said they were going to kill her. The white soldiers had pursued them for so long that they had become irritable from the wearying retreat. Pleading was useless; Indians jeered at pleading. They had struck her when she went on her knees to beg for life.

So she had learned not to kneel or plead or even weep. Her soul simply hid behind her body for protection. Her self, her soul, was a fist-sized black cloud just in back of her heaving chest. She was hollow, she had no back. Her self, or soul, hovered behind her lungs, safe and protected.

She had stood alone before the threats, waiting for the blows, murmuring the words that the Sioux knew were magic because she had used them to calm the old chief when he was delirious from a wound. She had stared at the hating faces, whispering, "The Lord is my shepherd; I shall not want. . . . for Thou art with me, Thy rod and Thy staff they comfort me. . . . in the presence of mine enemies. . . . "

Two of the squaws had beaten her with sticks, and when her body seemed no longer a hollow hiding place, she moaned. But her self was safe. Only her body was hurt.

She had sought that hiding place often and had found peace there when the danger was most terrible. You must stay in it now, she warned herself, until we reach the fort.

The white men stood on the hill. The old chief's aides had gone down to ransack the wagons and examine the horses that had drawn them. The Indians who had been with her were running to get their share. She stumbled on.

One of the soldiers was tall. She gasped at the sight of him. Is that my husband in the blue uniform? But no, he must be dead.

The tall soldier bowed. "Lieutenant Widdicome, Mrs. Foster," he introduced himself. "We are relieved to see that you are well."

There must be some polite thing that she should say, but she could not remember. She had not slept for — how long? Staring at the tall officer, she moved her lips: "Mr. Foster? He was killed?"

"I am happy to tell you that he is safe in St. Louis. He arranged for your ransom."

She licked her lips and repeated, "Safe." Frank Foster, the tall protector, was alive instead of dead. I do not deserve him, she thought. She spoke a name: "Mary?"

The officer shook his head. "I'm sorry, ma'am. We haven't had any word of your little girl. We hope she was picked up by emigrants. Are you able to ride? We should reach the fort before dark."

She said strongly, "I can ride." She was used to walking, with heavy burdens on her back. She had not been allowed to ride since the first week of her captivity, when the war party had traveled fast.

The officer warned: "We must not seem to be in any hurry." He turned to signal a dignified farewell, with arm upraised, to the old chief. Down by the wagons, the yelling warriors were tearing apart the bundled ransom gifts, and wrangling.

A rifle shot cracked out as if the upraised arm had been a signal. The youngest soldier's horse began to shy. When he had quieted the animal, the soldier stared down at blood seeping through his trouser leg below the knee. He said gruffly, "I'm hit."

Mrs. Foster clutched at her saddle.

"Nothing's happened," the lieutenant said fiercely to the hurt soldier. "We've no time to argue."

Then they were riding, and Mrs. Foster counted the soldiers. There were six of them, exactly the number specified in the last letter she had written to the fort. The old chief had dictated the terms, as she wrote.

They are brave men, she thought, and then she preferred not to think any more except about the fort, walled in from peril.

But instead of the fort she saw, as she rode, a fair-haired child alone on the prairie that had no end or shelter, a little girl stumbling and crying, calling, "Mama! Mama!"

Mrs. Foster turned to the officer and said, "I must tell you about Mary, about my little girl." But when he answered sympathetically, she did not seem to be able to say more.

After a long time they stopped to rest. Mrs. Foster knew she should be looking after the wounded soldier — the healing that was in her hands and voice had kept her alive among the Sioux - but the officer took charge, and she did not dare push herself forward to help.

She heard the lieutenant warn: "We've got about forty miles to go yet." She heard the hurt soldier's stout answer: "I can do it, sir." But the boy could not mount his horse without help.

They rode fast until a soldier called sharply, "Dust!"

Mrs. Foster lay in a shallow ravine, and the wounded soldier was lying there too, with two other soldiers crouched down, watching something far away. When one of them glanced toward her, she said, "If the Indians come, I want you to shoot me."

He said, "Why, ma'am!" sounding shocked, and his face flushed red behind the sunburn and the dust. Mrs. Foster felt relieved, guessing that he had his orders.

She crept to the wounded boy. "Let me help you," she crooned. "I healed the chief. They called me a medicine woman."

He said stoutly, "I'm all right, ma'am."

It was a test, Mrs. Foster thought. They were deceiving her, and if she did not heal the boy, she would suffer for it. She crouched down beside him and laid her hand on his forehead. He scowled, and then she began to whisper her charm: "The Lord is my shepherd; I shall not want - "

Another soldier shouted from far away, and Mrs. Foster heard someone say she could stand up now, but she went on with her charm. If I cure him, she thought, maybe he will listen while

I tell about Mary. If I tell someone now, then perhaps later I can bear to tell Mr. Foster.

A soldier came up the hill and said, "It's five wagons of emigrants up ahead, ma'am. We're to travel with 'em to the fort."

Mrs. Foster began to tremble. "Then we won't get there tonight."

"We might," the soldier lied cheerfully. "Anyhow, we'll be a stronger party."

Mrs. Foster groped for the exact terms of the agreement with the Indians. She had written it down, translating the chief's words for the soldiers at the fort to read if the letter ever got there, if the Indians were not lying again. "Only six men were allowed," she murmured mutinously. "Only six men to take me to the fort."

And yet the contract was to be broken. The emigrants would be a terrible danger to the ransom party, for it had been promised that only six men would travel from the rendezvous to the fort. The Indians, who would be watching, would believe the promise had been broken on purpose. She preferred not to think of it. She let her thoughts lie alone in the dark caverns of her mind; she let her hands weave their spell and her voice murmur the magic charm that had saved her. Clouds were white in the clear blue sky, and wind rustled the autumn-crisp prairie grass. There was no defense.

A soldier said, "We're to catch up with the wagons, ma'am." As if coaxing a child, he added, "There's white women with the wagons. Wouldn't you like to see some white women again, after all them squaws?"

"Oh, yes!" she cried, getting to her feet. "I only saw one white woman in all that time, and she was a captive, too. She drowned herself."

I must look dreadful to be meeting white women, she thought, and her hands went to her hair. The hanging braids were crooked and mussed; the squaws had not let her borrow a comb in these last weeks, while the Indians were waiting to see whether the ransom would come. She brushed hopelessly at her dress, but brushing was no use when the dress was a greasy hand-me-down of deerskin.

As they rode on with a soldier close by the wounded man to see that he stayed in the saddle, Mrs. Foster began to feel the nearness of comfort. White women. Ladies to talk to, ladies to sympathize! They will understand when I explain, she told herself. Tears welled into her eyes, and she thought: We will cry together about my little girl.

As they came closer to the moving wagons, she could see a sunbonneted woman walking beside the last one, holding a small boy by the hand. She could not wait. She kicked her horse and rode ahead of the soldiers. She called out, choking, to the woman, "Hello! Hello!"

The woman turned a thin, dust-stained, sunburned face toward her, staring with squinted eyes. And Mrs. Foster saw not friendship but enmity, the same hatred she had seen in the dark faces of the Sioux. The woman turned away without speaking.

The lieutenant said, "I'm sorry, Mrs. Foster. The emigrants are afraid to have us with them for fear the Indians are following us — but they're afraid to go on without us for fear of Indians, too. You'll be in the second wagon, some people named Rice. A man and his daughter. You can ride in their wagon from now on. The girl's fixing a bed so you can rest."

Mrs. Foster said harshly, "I'd rather ride with the soldiers. They're not afraid to have me."

"Mrs. Foster," he asked gently, "how long is it since you've slept?"

She blinked. "I don't know. Not last night or the night before. I was afraid to sleep."

"You'll sleep well tonight, then," the lieutenant said, and she read warning into the promise. Tonight the Sioux might attack because the contract had been broken.

She spoke suddenly. "Did you say my husband is all right?"

"He is, ma'am. He recovered entirely from his wound, and he moved heaven and earth to arrange the ransom. You are to join him in St. Louis when it is safe for you to travel."

She drew a deep breath. "I don't know how I can face him. I don't see how I can tell him about Mary. It was my fault, you know."

"Nothing was your fault," the lieutenant said sharply. She heard him call her a brave woman, but it was not true. She was only desperate and enduring — and cunning when she had to be. She rode with her head down, not awake but not sleeping.

"This is Bessie Rice," she heard the lieutenant say. She opened her eyes to see a round-faced girl of perhaps sixteen staring from the back of a wagon — a fair-haired girl with blue eyes.

"Not Mary," Mrs. Foster said, shaking her head. "She was only seven."

She shut her eyes so as not to have to see the girl, who might, after all, be a cruel illusion — or could Mary have grown older in months, or had years passed on the prairie. "We're going to let our wounded man travel in the Rices' wagon," the officer said. "It would oblige me if you'd ride with him and get yourself some rest."

Rest, Mrs. Foster thought. Didn't the man understand that to rest was to die if the Sioux were following? Rest — laid to rest. That was what they did with dead people back home, laid them to rest deep in the earth, so their bones did not have to bleach in the wind-rippled grass.

But if others could speak with two tongues, she could be deceitful too. She would pretend to rest.

She answered meekly, "Yes, Lieutenant, whatever you think best." She let him help her up into the wagon where the wounded soldier lay.

The soldier was silent, but she felt him watching in the dimness, felt him wishing she were somewhere else. She lay down on quilts, and the wagon moved on. She lay in it, wide-eyed and watchful, moving with its jolting, and heard a man's voice outside the canvas say angrily, "Injun bait, that's what we picked up! Injun bait!"

Long ago she had learned that she could not afford to be angry at anyone for anything. She closed her eyes to subdue anger. Frank, I have to tell you what I did after the Indians took us. . . .

When she woke up, everything was wrong. The wagon was still, and sounds of making camp came through the canvas, hushed by fear. She wondered: Do they think that by being quiet they can hide from the Sioux? Sleep, blessed sleep, had come to her — but it was not truly blessed, because it made her mind clearer to face horror to come.

A girl's voice outside the wagon, a voice young and light, frightened her. "Miz Foster? Miz Foster?" There was pleading in it.

Could that be Mary, grown older, almost a woman from the voice, grown older and implacable, hurt and deceived beyond forgiving, calling her Miz Foster for punishment, instead of Mama for love? She answered cautiously, "Yes, dear? Yes?"

"It's Bessie, Miz Foster. Bessie Rice. Supper's ready, such as it is. We ain't got no cooking fires. You want to come out now and eat?"

"No," Mrs. Foster answered with cold determination. She could endure hunger; she had endured it before. But she would not face the accusing eyes that must be out there, the eyes of the emigrants who thought "Injun bait" even when they did not say the words. The wagon was a dark and hollow place of refuge. She would stay in it.

The young soldier spoke so suddenly that she was frightened. "Go eat, ma'am," he advised. "I already did."

She had been cuffed and ordered around for so long by the Indians that it was easier to obey than to be stubborn. She climbed down from the wagon.

The accusing eyes were not there, after all. Nobody noticed her except the waiting Bessie, who was curious and concerned but had no hatred.

"I got a little piece of soap," the girl said, "if you was wanting to wash up."

Mrs. Foster yearned toward her but remembered that no luxury of bodily cleanliness could ever wash guilt from her soul. "I've been dirty so long it doesn't matter," she said.

She wolfed the food, cold bacon and corn bread, and when she was through, she sat holding the plate on her knees, blinking back tears. "Thou preparest a table before me in the presence of mine enemies." The girl Bessie, she began to understand, was the Lord's handmaiden. One more service Bessie must provide besides this. "I want to tell you about my little girl Mary," Mrs. Foster whispered.

Bessie said, "Shh! Did you hear that? A coyote howling off there?"

Mrs. Foster had learned patience. "Yes, dear. Only a coyote. Lots of coyotes out here. You must have heard them before."

"Yes," Bessie answered. "I've heard 'em before. Heard Injuns, too. Can you tell the difference?"

Mrs. Foster did not answer. She was reliving a night seven months before, the last time she had touched little Mary. There were coyotes howling, then — or were they wolves?

The lieutenant said, "Mrs. Foster?"

"Here I am. With Bessie."

"I thought you were still in the wagon," he said.

She was on her feet instantly, remembering her duty to the wounded soldier. But her opportunity was lost already. The lieutenant was at the wagon and four men were lifting the soldier down. There was no moon, but she could see movement and form.

"Under the wagon," the officer said. "Prop him up against the wheel. Duncan, you're well enough to stand guard."

The soldier said, "Yes, sir, if I can stand it sitting down." There was a low chuckle.

Every man would stand guard, Mrs. Foster understood. And not for a part of the long night to come, but for all of it, and especially toward the end, in that gray part that is not quite morning. And with the morning would come the Sioux — who were afraid to die in the dark.

"Mrs. Foster," the lieutenant said, "I want you and Bessie to stay with the wagon. All the women and children will stay with the wagons. Don't wander around. Is that clear?"

Mrs. Foster did not answer because she was thinking that a wagon was a trap.

Bessie said, "Sure. Her and me'll stay with the wagon, like you say."

Mrs. Foster's mind went searching, into the other wagons and found the others who were trapped there — the trembling women, the children crying or asleep. Beside her she felt fear, and heard it in Bessie's breathing, She felt it under the wagon, too, where the soldier named Duncan sat propped against a wheel, staring out into the darkness, listening, listening, and everywhere around the wagons where men watched and waited.

"Your people are fools," she told Bessie, "to come with only five wagons in Sioux country. Why did you?"

The girl said, "I don't know. Some trouble among the men, and we went another way from the rest. I don't know what the trouble was."

Mrs. Foster felt pity, knowing she could not afford it — not after seven months of captivity, not when safety had been so close and the contract had been broken by the emigrants' stupidity. Pity welled into her throat; she choked it down.

Bessie must hear the story, she decided. Somebody had to hear it and try to understand. But Mrs. Foster was cunning. She would work up to the story so that Bessie would not know it was coming. "I'll bet you have some pretty clothes," she said. "In a trunk here in the wagon, I'll bet you have some."

Bessie was silent for a moment, shocked at this frivolity. "I got a red dress," she admitted.

"Show it to me. It's a long time since I saw a pretty dress." Bessie drew away. "It's pitch dark in here."

"I can touch it, anyway. Get out the dress, dear. I'll help you put it on." She thinks I'm demented, Mrs. Foster realized. Am I?

Wedged as far into the corner as she could get, Bessie whispered, "How was it when they captured you folks? Was you all waiting like this?"

"We had no warning at all," Mrs. Foster answered gently. "They were just there all of a sudden. They killed four men and captured three women and two children. I thought they killed my husband, but the lieutenant says he is safe." She would have to tell Frank Foster sometime, but she must rehearse the telling first. "I have to tell you about Mary," she said. "Will you listen?"

Bessie took a deep breath and answered, "Tell me."

Mrs. Foster was riding again with the Sioux, through a canyon. Before her on the horse's back was Mary, whimpering. "I had to let her go," she whispered. "I thought maybe I could save her that way. You see, they burned her arm."

Bessie repeated, "Let her go?"

"The Indians pushed her into the fire the first night they had us. One of them hit me with his fist when I pulled her out. Her burned arm hurt her so, she cried all night until I scared her to make her quiet." She found that she did not want to tell it after all, but Bessie prompted, "Go on."

There was good in the world, after all. There was Frank Foster, alive and safe, making possible her rescue. There were the soldiers, and a girl named Bessie, who was willing to listen.

"She was only seven. I thought an emigrant train might come along if she got back to the burned wagon. I set my little Mary down off the horse in the darkness. I set her afoot, all alone. 'Run back to where the Indians got us,' I told her. 'Try to remember where we came. I dropped bits of letters as we rode. In daylight you can find them and follow them back. Find where the wagon is. That's the emigrant road, and somebody will come along.'"

"Sure, there'd be wagons," Bessie agreed without conviction.

"Seven years old. Mary was only seven. The last thing she said, before I kissed her and let her down off the horse, was, 'Mama, I'm hungry.'"

Now it was said, the confession was ended. The horror was a burden now for young Bessie Rice, and lessened a little for Mary Foster's mother. She owed Bessie a debt. "Put on your pretty dress for me," she said. "Show me how the ruffles go."

"I'll get it." Bessie opened a chest. "It's got a ruffle around the bottom, and the dress is red."

"Pretty, it's real pretty. Put it on."

"Help me, over my head. Can you find the hooks?"

"That doesn't seem right. There, that's how it goes."

"Miz Foster, I got a knife. Right here — Them hooks ain't just straight, I guess."

"You sew very well, dear. Now, how does the neck go?"

"That's right, yes — The knife, we can both use it if —"

"Yes, dear. It's a long time since I wore a pretty dress."

"You can put it on."

"No. Wear your pretty dress."

They were silent, thinking of morning, of death in a red dress. Then they refused to think of morning.

They went through the chest, item by item, touching, questioning, describing, not seeing. When they were silent, they heard the vast silence or the howling that might be coyotes or signals from the hills.

"I want to show it to Mr. Duncan," Bessie said.

Mrs. Foster did not at first remember the name. Then she recalled that it belonged to the young soldier under the wagon, with his rifle across his knees. She wondered why Bessie should yearn toward him, almost a stranger. Then she remembered: Why, I was young once, too, when I married Mr. Foster. I am twenty-seven now.

Quietly they descended from the wagon, and Bessie's voice was velvet in the darkness: "Mr. Duncan, want to see something pretty?"

"Sure do," he answered. "Like to see ninety-'leven cavalrymen coming fast. That'd be pretty."

"I only got a red dress." Bessie said in a pouting voice.

Duncan's voice changed; there was sunlight in it. "Well, Miss Bessie, I reckon I'd rather see you in a red dress than any bunch of dirty soldiers. Don't git in front of me, though. Reckon you could both set down."

Mrs. Foster wondered: How long till dawn? And did not know she had spoken.

Duncan answered, "Can't be long now. Been here about ten years already by my figuring."

Mrs. Foster felt like crying. They were so young, the flirting girl and the boy who was a soldier. They were so much afraid, but Bessie held off fear with the ruffles of a dress unseen, and Duncan pretended there was no fear, only boredom, for a soldier.

"Miss Bessie," he said, "I'd be obliged for a drink of water."

The girl scrambled up, delighted, fluttering to serve him. When she had gone, he whispered to Mrs. Foster: "This here's a revolver, ma'am. It's loaded and primed. You know how to cock it and pull the trigger? Take it, ma'am, and don't tell her. But keep her near you if they come. Do that for me, ma'am?"

With the cold weight of the revolver in her callused hands, she pitied him, for this might be the last, as well as the first, gift he would ever have for Bessie Rice. "Yes," she answered. "I will. Mr. Duncan, do you know about my little girl?"

"Heard you lost one, ma'am. Sure sorry to know that."

"Lost, only lost, maybe not dead, Mr. Duncan." It was important to convince him, so as to convince herself. "Not as you say 'lost' about someone you've taken to the grave. I set her down in the darkness and told her to go back by following the letters I'd dropped along the way. She might be safe? She might have got back to the emigrant road?"

"Sure she might — " he agreed with conviction.

Mrs. Foster felt lighter. Anxiety was taking the place of guilt. But she could bear anxiety, now that she was learning to hope again. Twice now she had rehearsed what she must tell her husband if she still lived after this night was ended.

"There were settlers coming into the fort when we left there, ma'am," Duncan said. "Maybe some of them would have heard of your little girl."

Later, when Bessie came back, he growled, "Took you long enough. Must have gone clean back to the Missouri River." Bessie giggled as he drank. He made a bold show of cheer, sighing with satisfaction as he put down the cup. "There's men would envy me," he remarked, "sitting here talking to two purty women. Seems like daylight's coming over there."

The women stared at the paleness in the sky.

"You'd oblige me by getting back in the wagon," Duncan said. "I might need room here."

When they were back in the trap of darkness, Bessie began to cry. Mrs. Foster leaned against a barrel with the revolver under her knee. Outside, she heard the lieutenant speak briefly to Duncan. She heard the wind in the grass and a baby crying. She heard a faraway sound that cut the night like a thin, sharp knife, and her mouth went dry before she understood.

The cheering of the men in the cramped wagon circle told her the meaning, that and the glad screams of the women. The sound came clearer in the night; it was a cavalry bugle.

Bessie clung to her, crying and laughing, and Mrs. Foster warned, "Hush! I want to hear the horses!" But there was too much noise. Duncan, under the wagon, was roaring his jubilation.

Mrs. Foster threw the revolver out the back of the wagon as hard as she could. Then she began to cry with Bessie as the music of the bugle came closer and they heard faintly the drumbeat of horses' hoofs.

A captain and half a dozen troopers rode with her toward the fort. The lieutenant was following with the wagon train at a slower pace.

"We have some refugees at the fort," the captain told her. "Settlers who got a scare. They're about ready to give up and go back to the States."

"I'm thankful Mr. Foster is safe in St. Louis," Mrs. Foster said. "I will go there when it is safe to travel."

"It will be safe soon," he promised. He was squinting ahead. "Now don't be alarmed, Mrs. Foster," he urged. "That's a messenger you see coming over the hill."

A rider in cavalry blue was coming toward them at a gallop. The message was written. The captain read it and, seeing that she was tense, remarked with a little smile,

"It is not bad news, ma'am. We will ride a little faster, but it is not bad news."

Emigrant wagons were outside the fort, not too close, not so close that flames, if the Indians should set them afire, could leap to the wooden walls.

"Some new refugees have arrived," the captain commented. "Most of those wagons weren't there yesterday. There's not room for them inside."

They rode in through the cautiously opened gates. She swayed in the saddle when she heard the gates closing, the blessed gates that shut out danger. A sunbonneted woman stared, and Mrs. Foster thought: I'd like to see you look any better than I do if you'd been seven months among the savages!

The captain helped her dismount. He did not release his grip on her arms after her feet were on the ground.

"Now I can tell you what was in that message," he said. "You must not scream. You must not panic these frightened people."

"I am quite calm," she answered softly, but her voice was trembling like her body.

"There is a little girl here named Mary, came in this morning with some settlers. They picked her up on the trail months ago — don't scream, Mrs. Foster!"

She tore away from his grip at the sound of a shrill, remembered voice crying, "Mama! Mama!" In obedient silence she ran and stumbled and spread her arms as a little fair-haired girl came running from among the people.

Then she could not see because of tears, but the thin, living body was against her breast and the arms were clinging. Crooning without words, she patted the warm flesh frantically and felt the healed scar of a burn.

~ ~ ~

Lost Sister
The Hanging Tree, 1957

Our household was full of women, who overwhelmed my Uncle Charlie and sometimes confused me with their bustle and chatter. We were the only men on the place. I was nine years old when still another woman came — Aunt Bessie, who had been living with the Indians.

When my mother told me about her, I couldn't believe it. The savages had killed my father, a cavalry lieutenant, two years before. I hated Indians and looked forward to wiping them out when I got older. (But when I was grown, they were no menace any more.)

"What did she live with the hostiles for?" I demanded.

"They captured her when she was a little girl," Ma said. "She was three years younger than you are. Now she's coming home." High time she came home, I thought. I said so, promising, "If they was ever to get me, I wouldn't stay with 'em long."

Ma put her arms around me. "Don't talk like that. They won't get you. They'll never get you."

I was my mother's only real tie with her husband's family. She was not happy with those masterful women, my Aunts Margaret, Hannah and Sabina, but she would not go back East where she came from. Uncle Charlie managed the store the aunts owned, but he wasn't really a member of the family — he was just Aunt Margaret's husband. The only man who had belonged was my father, the aunts' younger brother. And I belonged, and someday the store would be mine. My mother stayed to protect my heritage.

None of the three sisters, my aunts, had ever seen Aunt Bessie. She had been taken by the Indians before they were born. Aunt Mary had known her — Aunt Mary was two years older — but she lived a thousand miles away now and was not well.

There was no picture of the little girl who had become a legend. When the family had first settled here, there was enough struggle to feed and clothe the children without having pictures made of them.

Even after Army officers had come to our house several times and there had been many letters about Aunt Bessie's delivery from the savages, it was a long time before she came. Major Harris, who made the final arrangements, warned my aunts that they would have problems, that Aunt Bessie might not be able to settle down easily into family life.

This was only a challenge to Aunt Margaret, who welcomed challenges. "She's our own flesh and blood," Aunt Margaret trumpeted. "Of course she must come to us. My poor, dear sister Bessie, torn from her home forty years ago!"

The major was earnest but not tactful. "She's been with the savages all those years," he insisted. "And she was only a little girl when she was taken. I haven't seen her myself, but it's reasonable to assume that she'll be like an Indian woman."

My stately Aunt Margaret arose to show that the audience was ended. "Major Harris," she intoned, "I cannot permit anyone to criticize my own dear sister. She will live in my home, and if I do not receive official word that she is coming within a month, I shall take steps."

Aunt Bessie came before the month was up.

The aunts in residence made valiant preparations. They bustled and swept and mopped and polished. They moved me from my own room to my mother's — as she had been begging them to do because I was troubled with nightmares. They prepared my old room for Aunt Bessie with many small comforts — fresh doilies everywhere, hairpins, a matching pitcher and bowl, the best towels and two new nightgowns in case hers might be old. (The fact was that she didn't have any.)

"Perhaps we should have some dresses made," Hannah suggested. "We don't know what she'll have with her."

"We don't know what size she'll take, either," Margaret pointed out. "There'll be time enough for her to go to the store after she settles down and rests for a day or two. Then she can shop to her heart's content."

Ladies of the town came to call almost every afternoon while the preparations were going on. Margaret promised them that, as soon as Bessie had recovered sufficiently from her ordeal, they should all meet her at tea.

Margaret warned her anxious sisters, "Now, girls, we mustn't ask her too many questions at first. She must rest for a while. She's been through a terrible experience." Margaret's voice dropped way down with those last two words, as if only she could be expected to understand.

Indeed Bessie had been through a terrible experience, but it wasn't what the sisters thought. The experience from which she was suffering, when she arrived, was that she had been wrenched from her people, the Indians, and turned over to strangers. She had not been freed. She had been made a captive.

Aunt Bessie came with Major Harris and an interpreter, a half-blood with greasy black hair hanging down to his shoulders. His costume was half Army and half primitive. Aunt Margaret swung the door open wide when she saw them coming. She ran out with her sisters following, while my mother and I watched from a window. Margaret's arms were outstretched, but when she saw the woman closer, her arms dropped and her glad cry died.

She did not cringe, my Aunt Bessie who had been an Indian for forty years, but she stopped walking and stood staring, helpless among her captors.

The sisters had described her often as a little girl. Not that they had ever seen her, but she was a legend, the captive child. Beautiful blonde curls, they said she had, and big blue eyes — she was a fairy child, a pale-haired little angel who ran on dancing feet.

The Bessie who came back was an aging woman who plodded in moccasins, whose dark dress did not belong on her bulging body. Her brown hair hung just below her ears. It was growing out; when she was first taken from the Indians, her hair had been cut short to clean out the vermin.

Aunt Margaret recovered herself and, instead of embracing this silent stolid woman, satisfied herself by patting an arm and crying, "Poor dear Bessie, I am your sister Margaret. And here are our sisters Hannah and Sabina. We do hope you're not all tired out from your journey!"

Aunt Margaret was all graciousness, because she had been assured beyond doubt that this was truly a member of the family. She must have believed — Aunt Margaret could believe anything — that all Bessie needed was to have a nice nap and wash her face. Then she would be as talkative as any of them.

The other aunts were quick-moving and sharp of tongue. But this one moved as if her sorrows were a burden on her bowed shoulders, and when she spoke briefly in answer to the interpreter, you could not understand a word of it.

Aunt Margaret ignored these peculiarities. She took the party into the front parlor — even the interpreter, when she understood there was no avoiding it. She might have gone on battling with the major about him, but she was in a hurry to talk to her lost sister.

"You won't be able to converse with her unless the interpreter is present," Major Harris said. "Not," he explained hastily, "because of any regulation, but because she has forgotten English."

Aunt Margaret gave the half-blood interpreter a look of frowning doubt and let him enter. She coaxed Bessie. "Come, dear, sit down."

The interpreter mumbled, and my Indian aunt sat cautiously on a needlepoint chair. For most of her life she had been living with people who sat comfortably on the ground.

The visit in the parlor was brief. Bessie had had her instructions before she came. But Major Harris had a few warnings for the family. "Technically, your sister is still a prisoner," he explained, ignoring Margaret's start of horror. "She will be in your custody. She may walk in your fenced yard, but she must not leave it without official permission.

"Mrs. Raleigh, this may be a heavy burden for you all. But she has been told all this and has expressed willingness to conform to these restrictions. I don't think you will have any trouble keeping her here." Major Harris hesitated, remembered that he was a soldier and a brave man, and added, "If I did, I wouldn't have brought her."

There was the making of a sharp little battle, but Aunt Margaret chose to overlook the challenge. She could not overlook the fact that Bessie was not what she had expected.

Bessie certainly knew that this was her lost white family, but she didn't seem to care. She was infinitely sad, infinitely removed. She asked one question: "Mary?" and Aunt Margaret almost wept with joy.

"Sister Mary lives a long way from here," she explained, "and she isn't well, but she will come as soon as she's able. Dear sister Mary!"

The interpreter translated this, and Bessie had no more to say. That was the only understandable word she ever did say in our house, the remembered name of her older sister.

When the aunts, all chattering, took Bessie to her room, one of them asked, "But where are her things?"

Bessie had no things, no baggage. She had nothing at all but the clothes she stood in. While the sisters scurried to bring a comb and other oddments, she stood like a stooped monument, silent and watchful. This was her prison. Very well, she would endure it.

"Maybe tomorrow we can take her to the store and see what she would like," Aunt Hannah suggested.

"There's no hurry," Aunt Margaret declared thoughtfully. She was getting the idea that this sister was going to be a problem. But I don't think Aunt Margaret ever really stopped hoping that one day Bessie would cease to be different, that she would end her stubborn silence and begin to relate the events of her life among the savages, in the parlor over a cup of tea.

My Indian aunt accustomed herself, finally, to sitting on the chair in her room. She seldom came out, which was a relief to her sisters. She preferred to stand, hour after hour, looking out the window — which was open only about a foot, in spite of all Uncle Charlie's efforts to budge it higher. And she always wore moccasins. She was never able to wear shoes from the store, but seemed to treasure the shoes brought to her.

The aunts did not, of course, take her shopping after all. They made her a couple of dresses; and when they told her, with signs and voluble explanations, to change her dress, she did.

After I found that she was usually at the window, looking across the flat land to the blue mountains, I played in the yard so I could stare at her. She never smiled, as an aunt should, but she looked at me sometimes, thoughtfully, as if measuring my worth. By performing athletic feats, such as walking on my hands, I could get her attention. For some reason, I valued it.

She didn't often change expression, but twice I saw her scowl with disapproval. Once was when one of the aunts slapped me in a casual way. I had earned the slap, but the Indians did not punish children with blows. Aunt Bessie was shocked, I think, to see that white people did. The other time was when I talked back to someone with spoiled, small-boy insolence — and that time the scowl was for me.

The sisters and my mother took turns, as was their Christian duty, in visiting her for half an hour each day. Bessie didn't eat at the table with us — not after the first meal.

The first time my mother took her turn, it was under protest. "I'm afraid I'd start crying in front of her," she argued, but Aunt Margaret insisted.

I was lurking in the hall when Ma went in. Bessie said something, then said it again, peremptorily, until my mother guessed what she wanted. She called me and put her arm around me as I stood beside her chair. Aunt Bessie nodded, and that was all there was to it.

Afterward, my mother said, "She likes you. And so do I." She kissed me.

"I don't like her," I complained. "She's queer."

"She's a sad old lady," my mother explained. "She had a little boy once, you know."

"What happened to him?"

"He grew up and became a warrior. I suppose she was proud of him. Now the Army has him in prison somewhere. He's half Indian. He was a dangerous man."

He was indeed a dangerous man, and a proud man, a chief, a bird of prey whose wings the Army had clipped after bitter years of trying.

However, my mother and my Indian aunt had that one thing in common: they both had sons. The other aunts were childless.

There was a great to-do about having Aunt Bessie's photograph taken. The aunts who were stubbornly and valiantly trying to make her one of the family wanted a picture of her for the family album. The government wanted one too, for some reason — perhaps because someone realized that a thing of historic importance had been accomplished by recovering the captive child.

Major Harris sent a young lieutenant with the greasy-haired interpreter to discuss the matter in the parlor. (Margaret, with great foresight, put a clean towel on a chair and saw to it the interpreter sat there.) Bessie spoke very little during that meeting, and of course we understood only what the half-blood said she was saying.

No, she did not want her picture made. No.

But your son had his picture made. Do you want to see it? They teased her with that offer, and she nodded.

If we let you see his picture, then will you have yours made?

She nodded doubtfully. Then she demanded more than had been offered: If you let me keep his picture, then you can make mine.

No, you can only look at it. We have to keep his picture. It belongs to us.

My Indian aunt gambled for high stakes. She shrugged and spoke, and the interpreter said, "She not want to look. She will keep or nothing."

My mother shivered, understanding as the aunts could not understand what Bessie was gambling — all or nothing.

Bessie won. Perhaps they had intended that she should. She was allowed to keep the photograph that had been made of her son. It has been in history books many times — the half-white chief, the valiant leader who was not quite great enough to keep his Indian people free.

His photograph was taken after he was captured, but you would never guess it. His head is high, his eyes stare with boldness but not with scorn, his long hair is arranged with care — dark hair braided on one side and with a tendency to curl where the other side hangs loose — and his hands hold the pipe like a royal scepter.

That photograph of the captive but unconquered warrior had its effect on me. Remembering him, I began to control my temper and my tongue, to cultivate reserve as I grew older, to stare with boldness but not scorn at people who annoyed or offended me. I never met him, but I took silent pride in him — Eagle Head, my Indian cousin.

Bessie kept his picture on her dresser when she was not holding it in her hands. And she went like a docile, silent child to the photograph studio, in a carriage with Aunt Margaret early one morning, when there would be few people on the street to stare.

Bessie's photograph is not proud but pitiful. She looks out with no expression. There is no emotion there, no challenge, only the face of an aging woman with short hair, only endurance and patience. The aunts put a copy in the family album.

But they were nearing the end of their tether. The Indian aunt was a solid ghost in the house. She did nothing because there was nothing for her to do. Her gnarled hands must have been skilled at squaws' work, at butchering meat and scraping and tanning hides, at making tepees and beading ceremonial clothes. But her skills were useless and unwanted in a civilized home. She did not even sew when my mother gave her cloth and needles and thread. She kept the sewing things beside her son's picture.

She ate (in her room) and slept (on the floor) and stood looking out the window. That was all, and it could not go on. But it had to go on, at least until my sick Aunt Mary was well enough to travel — Aunt Mary who was her older sister, the only one who had known her when they were children.

The sisters' duty visits to Aunt Bessie became less and less visits and more and more duty. They settled into a bearable routine. Margaret had taken upon herself the responsibility of trying to make Bessie talk. Make, I said, not teach. She firmly believed that her stubborn and unfortunate sister needed only encouragement from a strong-willed person. So Margaret talked, as to a child, when she bustled in:

"Now there you stand, just looking, dear. What in the world is there to see out there? The birds — are you watching the birds? Why don't you try sewing? Or you could go for a little walk in the yard. Don't you want to go out for a nice little walk?"

Bessie listened and blinked.

Margaret could have understood an Indian woman's not being able to converse in a civilized tongue, but her own sister was not an Indian. Bessie was white, therefore she should talk the language her sisters did — the language she had not heard since early childhood.

Hannah, the put-upon aunt, talked to Bessie too, but she was delighted not to get any answers and not to be interrupted. She bent over her embroidery when it was her turn to sit with Bessie and told her troubles in an unending flow. Bessie stood looking out the window the whole time.

Sabina, who had just as many troubles, most of them emanating from Margaret and Hannah, went in like a martyr, firmly clutching her Bible, and read aloud from it until her time was up.

She took a small clock along so that she would not, because of annoyance, be tempted to cheat.

After several weeks Aunt Mary came, white and trembling and exhausted from her illness and the long, hard journey. The sisters tried to get the interpreter in but were not successful. (Aunt Margaret took that failure pretty hard.) They briefed Aunt Mary, after she had rested, so the shock of seeing Bessie, would not be too terrible. I saw them meet, those two.

Margaret went to the Indian woman's door and explained volubly who had come, a useless but brave attempt. Then she stood aside, and Aunt Mary was there, her lined white face aglow, her arms outstretched. "Bessie! Sister Bessie!" she cried.

And after one brief moment's hesitation, Bessie went into her arms and Mary kissed her sun-dark, weathered cheek. Bessie spoke. "Mary," she said. "Mary." She stood with tears running down her face and her mouth working. So much to tell, so much suffering and fear — and joy and triumph, too — and the sister there at last who might legitimately hear it all and understand. But the only English word that Bessie remembered was "Mary," and she had not cared to learn any others. She turned to the dresser, took her son's picture in her work-hardened hands, reverently, and held it so her sister could see. Her eyes pleaded.

Mary looked on the calm, noble, savage face of her half-blood nephew and said the right thing: "My, isn't he handsome!" She put her head on one side and then the other. "A fine boy, sister," she approved. "You must" — she stopped, but she finished — "be awfully proud of him, dear!"

Bessie understood the tone if not the words. The tone was admiration. Her son was accepted by the sister who mattered. Bessie looked at the picture and nodded, murmuring. Then she put it back on the dresser.

Aunt Mary did not try to make Bessie talk. She sat with her every day for hours and Bessie did talk — but not in English. They sat holding hands for mutual comfort while the captive child, grown old and a grandmother, told what had happened in forty years. Aunt Mary said that was what Bessie was talking about. But she didn't understand a word of it and didn't need to.

"There is time enough for her to learn English again," Aunt Mary said. "I think she understands more than she lets on. I asked her if she'd like to come and live with me, and she nodded. We'll have the rest of our lives for her to learn English. But what she has been telling me — she can't wait to tell that. About her life, and her son."

"Are you sure, Mary dear, that you should take the responsibility of having her?" Margaret asked dutifully, no doubt shaking in her shoes for fear Mary would change her mind now that deliverance was in sight. "I do believe she'd be happier with you, though we've done all we could."

Margaret and the other sisters would certainly be happier with Bessie somewhere else. And so, it developed, would the United States government.

Major Harris came with the interpreter to discuss details, and they told Bessie she could go, if she wished, to live with Mary a thousand miles away. Bessie was patient and willing, stolidly agreeable. She talked a great deal more to the interpreter than she had ever done before. He answered at length and then explained to the others that she wanted to know how she and Mary would travel to this far country. It was hard, he said, for her to understand just how far they were going.

Later we knew that the interpreter and Bessie had talked about much more than that.

Next morning, when Sabina took breakfast to Bessie's room, we heard a cry of dismay. Sabina stood holding the tray, repeating, "She's gone out the window! She's gone out the window!"

And so she had. The window that had always stuck so that it would not raise more than a foot was open wider now. And the photograph of Bessie's son was gone from the dresser. Nothing else was missing except Bessie and the decent dark dress she had worn the day before.

My Uncle Charlie got no breakfast that morning. With Margaret shriekng orders, he leaped on a horse and rode to the telegraph station.

Before Major Harris got there with half a dozen cavalrymen, civilian scouts were out searching for the missing woman. They were expert trackers. Their lives had depended, at various times, on their ability to read the meaning of a turned stone, a broken twig, a bruised leaf. They found that Bessie had gone south. They tracked her for ten miles. And then they lost the trail, for Bessie was as skilled as they were. Her life had sometimes depended on leaving no stone or twig or leaf marked by her passage. She traveled fast at first. Then, with time to be careful, she evaded the followers she knew would come.

The aunts were stricken with grief — at least Aunt Mary was — and bowed with humiliation about what Bessie had done. The blinds were drawn, and voices were low in the house. We had been pitied because of Bessie's tragic folly in having let the Indians make a savage of her. But now we were traitors because we had let her get away.

Aunt Mary kept saying pitifully, "Oh, why did she go? I thought she would be contented with me!"

The others said that it was, perhaps, all for the best.

Aunt Margaret proclaimed, "She has gone back to her own." That was what they honestly believed, and so did Major Harris.

My mother told me why she had gone. "You know that picture she had of the Indian chief, her son? He's escaped from the jail he was in. The fort got word of it, and they think Bessie may be going to where he's hiding. That's why they're trying so hard to find her. They think," my mother explained, "that she knew of his escape before they did. They think the interpreter told her when he was here. There was no other way she could have found out."

They scoured the mountains to the south for Eagle Head and Bessie. They never found her, and they did not get him until a year later, far to the north. They could not capture him that time. He died fighting.

After I grew up, I operated the family store, disliking storekeeping a little more every day. When I was free to sell it, I did, and went to raising cattle. And one day, riding in a canyon after strayed steers, I found — I think — Aunt Bessie. A cowboy who worked for me was along, or I would never have let anybody know.

We found weathered bones near a little spring. They had a mystery on them, those nameless human bones suddenly come upon. I could feel old death brushing my back. "Some prospector," suggested my riding partner.

I thought so too until I found, protected by a log, sodden scraps of fabric that might have been a dark, respectable dress. And wrapped in them was a sodden something that might have once been a picture.

The man with me was young, but he had heard the story of the captive child. He had been telling me about it in fact. In the passing years it had acquired some details that surprised me. Aunt Bessie had become once more a fair-haired beauty, in this legend that he had heard, but utterly sad and silent. Well, sad and silent she really was.

I tried to push the sodden scrap of fabric back under the log, but he was too quick for me. "That ain't no shirt, that's a dress!" he announced. "This here was no prospector — it was a woman!" He paused and then announced with awe, "I bet you it was your Indian aunt!"

I scowled and said, "Nonsense. It could be anybody."

He got all worked up about it. "If it was my aunt," he declared, "I'd bury her in the family plot"

"No," I said, and shook my head.

We left the bones there in the canyon, where they had been for forty-odd years if they were Aunt Bessie's. And I think they were. But I would not make her a captive again. She's in the family album. She doesn't need to be in the family plot.

If my guess about why she left us is wrong, nobody can prove it. She never intended to join her son in hiding. She went in the opposite direction to lure pursuit away.

What happened to her in the canyon doesn't concern me, or anyone. My Aunt Bessie accomplished what she set out to do. It was not her life that mattered, but his. She bought him another year.

II

Other

Women's

Voices

Gertrude Atherton

In novels, short stories, sketches and tales, Gertrude Atherton (1857-1948) chronicled the history of California and the life of women in that state. Her stories reflect and study both the original Spanish and the new American culture of the area, as well as what Atherton saw as a certain isolation inherent in California life. "The Wash-Tub Mail" is from a collection of short stories and sketches about women at various ages, their relationships with themselves and each other, and with men.

The Wash-Tub Mail
The Splendid Idle Forties (1902)

Part I

"Mariquita! Thou good-for-nothing, thou art wringing that smock in pieces! Thy señora will beat thee! Holy heaven, but it is hot!"

"For that reason I hurry, old Faquita. Were I as slow as thou, I should cook in my own tallow."

"Aha, thou art very clever! But I have no wish to go back to the rancho and wash for the cooks. Ay, yi! I wonder will La Tulita ever give me her bridal clothes to wash. I have no faith that little flirt will marry the Señor Don Ramon Garcia. He did not well to leave Monterey until after the wedding. And to think — Ay! yi!"

"Thou hast a big letter for the wash-tub mail, Faquita."

"Aha, my Francesca, thou hast interest! I thought thou wast thinking only of the bandits."

Francesca, who was holding a plunging child between her knees, actively inspecting its head, grunted but did not look up, and the oracle of the wash-tubs, provokingly, with slow movements of her knotted coffee-coloured arms, flapped a dainty skirt, half-covered with drawn work, before she condescended to speak further.

Twenty women or more, young and old, dark as pine cones, stooped or sat, knelt or stood, about deep stone tubs sunken in the ground at the foot of a hill on the outskirts of Monterey. The pines cast heavy shadows on the long slope above them, but the sun was overhead. The little white town looked lifeless under its baking red tiles, at this hour of siesta. On the blue bay rode a warship flying the American colours. The atmosphere was so clear, the view so uninterrupted, that the younger women fancied they could read the name on the prow: the town was on the right; between the bay and the tubs lay only the meadow, the road, the lake, and the marsh. A few yards farther down the road rose a hill where white slabs and crosses gleamed beneath the trees. The roar of the surf came refreshingly to their hot ears. It leaped angrily, they fancied, to the old fort on the hill where men in the uniform of the United States moved about with unsleeping vigilance. It was the year 1847. The Americans had come and conquered. War was over, but the invaders guarded their new possessions.

The women about the tubs still bitterly protested against the downfall of California, still took an absorbing interest in all matters, domestic, social, and political. For those old women with grizzled locks escaping from a cotton handkerchief wound bandwise about their heads, their ample forms untrammelled by the flowing garment of calico, those girls in bright skirts and white short-sleeved smocks and young hair braided, knew all the news of the country, past and to come, many hours in advance of the dons and doñas whose linen they washed in the great stone tubs: the Indians, domestic and roving, were their faithful friends.

"Sainted Mary, but thou art more slow than a gentleman that walks!" cried Mariquita, an impatient-looking girl. "Read us the letter. La Tulita is the prettiest girl in Monterey now that the Señorita Ysabel Herrera lies beneath the rocks, and Benicia Ortega has died of her childing. But she is a flirt — that Tulita! Four of the Gringos are under her little slipper this year, and she turn over the face and roll in the dirt. But Don Ramon, so handsome, so rich — surely she will marry him."

Faquita shook her head slowly and wisely. "There — come — yesterday — from — the — South — a — young — lieutenant — of — America." She paused a moment, then proceeded leisurely, though less provokingly. "He come over the great American deserts with General Kearney last year and help our men to eat the dust in San Diego. He come only yesterday to Monterey, and La Tulita is like a little wild-cat ever since. She box my ears this morning when I tell her that the Americans are bandoleros, and say she never marry a Californian. And never Don Ramon Garcia, ay, yi!"

By this time the fine linen was floating at will upon the water, or lying in great heaps at the bottom of the clear pools. The suffering child scampered up through the pines with whoops of delight. The washing-women were pressed close about Faquita, who stood with thumbs on her broad hips, the fingers contracting and snapping as she spoke, wisps of hair bobbing back and forth about her shrewd black eyes and scolding mouth.

"Who is he? Where she meet him?" cried the audience. "Oh, thou old carreta! Why canst thou not talk faster?"

"If thou hast not more respect, Señorita Mariquita, thou wilt hear nothing. But it is this. There is a ball last night at Doña Maria Ampudia's house for La Tulita. She look handsome, that witch! Holy Mary! When she walk it was like the tule in the river. You know. Why she have that name? She wear white, of course, but that frock — it is like the cobweb, the cloud. She has not the braids like the other girls, but the hair, soft like black feathers, fall down to the feet. And the eyes like blue stars! You know the eyes of La Tulita. The lashes so long, and black like the hair. And the sparkle! No eyes ever sparkle like those. The eyes of Ysabel Herrera look like they want the world and never can get it. Benicia's, pobrecita, just dance like the child's. But La Tulita's! They sparkle like the devil sit behind and strike fire out red-hot iron — "

"Mother of God!" cried Mariquita, impatiently, "we all know thou art daft about that witch! And we know how she looks. Tell us the story."

"Hush thy voice or thou wilt hear nothing. It is this way. La Tulita have the castanets and just float up and down the sala, while all stand back and no breathe only when they shout. I am in the garden in the middle the house, and I stand on a box and look through the doors. Ay, the roses and the nasturtiums smell so sweet in that little garden! Well! She dance so beautiful, I think the roof go to jump off so she can float up and live on one the gold stars all by herself. Her little feet just twinkle! Well! The door open and Lieutenant Ord come in. He have with him another young man, not so handsome, but so straight, so sharp eye and tight mouth. He look at La Tulita like he think she belong to America and is for him. Lieutenant Ord go up to Doña Maria and say, so polite: 'I take the liberty to bring Lieutenant' — I no can remember that name, so American! 'He come to-day from San Diego and will stay with us for a while.' And Doña Maria, she smile and say, very sweet, 'Very glad when I have met all of our conquerors.' And he turn red and speak very bad Spanish and look, look, at La Tulita. Then Lieutenant Ord speak to him in English and he nod the head, and Lieutenant Ord tell Doña Maria that his friend like be introduced to La Tulita, and she say, 'Very well,' and take him over to her who is now sit down. He ask her to waltz right away, and he waltz very well, and then they dance again, and once more. And then they sit down and talk, talk. God of my soul, but the caballeros are mad! And Doña Maria! By and by she can stand it no more and she go up to La Tulita and take away from the American and say, 'Do you forget — and for a bandolero — that you are engage to my nephew?' And La Tulita toss the head and say: 'How can I remember Ramon Garcia when he is in Yerba Buena? I forget he is alive.' And Doña Maria is very angry. The eyes snap. But just then the little sister of La Tulita run into the sala, the face red like the American flag. 'Ay, Herminia!' she just gasp. 'The donas! The donas! It has come!'"

"The donas!" cried the washing-women, old and young. "Didst thou see it, Faquita? Oh, surely. Tell us, what did he send? Is he a generous bridegroom? Were there jewels? And satins? Of what was the rosary?"

"Hush the voice or you will hear nothing. The girls all jump and clap their hands and they cry: 'Come, Herminia. Come quick! Let us go and see.' Only La Tulita hold the head very high and look like the donas is nothing to her, and the Lieutenant look very surprise, and she talk to him very fast like she no want him to know what they mean. But the girls just take her hands and pull her out the house. I am after. La Tulita look very mad, but she cannot help, and in five minutes we are at the Casa Rivera, and the girls scream and clap the hands in the sala for Doña Carmen she have unpack the donas and the beautiful things are on the tables and the sofas and the chairs. Mother of God!"

"Go on! Go on!" cried a dozen exasperated voices.

"Well! Such a donas. Ay, he is a generous lover. A yellow crepe shawl embroidered with red roses. A white one with embroidery so thick it can stand up. A string of pearls from Baja California. (Ay, poor Ysabel Herrera!) Hoops of gold for the little ears of La Tulita. A big chain of California gold. A set of topaz with pearls all round. A rosary of amethyst — purple like the violets. A big pin painted with the Ascension, and diamonds all round. Silks and satins for gowns. A white lace mantilla, Dios de mi alma! A black one for the visits. And the night-gowns like cobwebs. The petticoats!" She stopped abruptly.

"And the smocks?" cried her listeners, excitedly. "The smocks? They are more beautiful than Blandina's? They were pack in rose-leaves — "

"Ay! yi! yi! yi!" The old woman dropped her head on her breast and waved her arms. She was a study for despair. Even she did not suspect how thoroughly she was enjoying herself.

"What! What! Tell us! Quick, thou old snail. They were not fine? They had not embroidery?"

"Hush the voices. I tell you when I am ready. The girls ate like crazy. They look like they go to eat the things. Only La Tulita sit on the chair in the door with her back to all and look at the windows of Doña Maria. They look like a long row of suns, those windows.

"I am the one. Suddenly I say: 'Where are the smocks?' And they all cry: 'Yes, where are the smocks? Let us see if he will be a good husband. Doña Carmen, where are the smocks?'

"'Doña Carmen turn over everything in a hurry.' I did not think of the smocks,' she say. 'But they must be here. Everything was unpack in this room.' She lift all up, piece by piece. The girls help and so do I. La Tulita sit still but begin to look more interested. We search everywhere — everywhere — for twenty minutes. There — are — no — smocks!"

"God of my life! The smocks! He did not forget!"

"He forget the smocks!"

There was an impressive pause. The women were too dumfounded to comment. Never in the history of Monterey had such a thing happened before.

Faquita continued: "The girls sit down on the floor and cry. Doña Carmen turn very white and go in the other room. Then La Tulita jump up and walk across the room. The lashes fall down over the eyes that look like she is California and have conquer America, not the other way. The nostrils just jump. She laugh, laugh, laugh. 'So!' she say, 'my rich and generous and ardent bridegroom, he forget the smocks of the donas. He proclaim as if by a poster on the streets that he will be a bad husband, a thoughtless, careless, indifferent husband. He has vow by the stars that he adore me. He has serenade beneath my window until I have beg for mercy. He persecute my mother. And now he flings the insult of insults in my teeth. And he with six married sisters!'

"The girls just sob. They can say nothing. No woman forgive that. Then she say loud, 'Ana,' and the girl run in. 'Ana,' she say, 'pack this stuff and tell Jose and Marcos take it up to the house of the Señor Don Ramon Garcia. I have no use for it.' Then she say to me: 'Faquita, walk back to Doña Maria's with me, no? I have engagement with the American.' And I go with her, of course; I think I go jump in the bay if she tell me; and she dance all night with that American. He no look at another girl — all have the eyes so red, anyhow. And Doña Maria is crazy that her nephew do such a thing, and La Tulita no go to marry him now. Ay, that witch! She have the excuse and she take it."

For a few moments the din was so great that the crows in a neighboring grove of willows sped away in fear. The women talked all at once, at the top of their voices and with no falling inflections. So rich an assortment of expletives, secular and religious, such individuality yet sympathy of comment, had not been called upon for duty since the seventh of July, a year before, when Commodore Sloat had run up the American flag on the Customhouse. Finally they paused to recover breath. Mariquita's young lungs being the first to refill, she demanded of Faquita: —

"And Don Ramon — when does he return?"

"In two weeks, no sooner."

Part II

Two weeks later they were again gathered about the tubs.

For a time after arrival they forgot La Tulita — now the absorbing topic of Monterey — in a new sensation. Mariquita had appeared with a basket of unmistakable American underwear.

"What!" cried Faquita, shrilly. "Thou wilt defile these tubs with the linen of bandoleros? Hast thou had thy silly head turned with a kiss? Not one shirt shall go in this water."

Mariquita tossed her head defiantly. "Captain Brotherton say the Indian women break his clothes in pieces. They know not how to wash anything but dish-rags. And does he not go to marry our Doña Eustaquia?"

"The Captain is not so bad," admitted Faquita. The indignation of the others also visibly diminished: the Captain had been very kind the year before when gloom lay heavy on the town. "But," continued the autocrat, with an ominous pressing of her lips, "sure he must change three times a day. Is all that Captain Brotherton's?"

"He wear many shirts," began Mariquita, when Faquita pounced upon the basket and shook its contents to the grass. "Aha! It seems that the Captain has sometimes the short legs and sometimes the long. Sometimes he put the tucks in his arms, I suppose. What meaning has this? Thou monster of hypocrisy!"

The old women scowled and snorted. The girls looked sympathetic: more than one midshipman had found favour in the lower quarter.

"Well," said Mariquita, sullenly, "if thou must know, it is the linen of the Lieutenant of La Tulita. Ana ask me to wash it, and I say I will."

At this announcement Faquita squared her elbows and looked at Mariquita with snapping eyes.

"Oho, senorita, I suppose thou wilt say next that thou knowest what means this flirtation! Has La Tulita lost her heart, perhaps? And Don Ramon — dost thou know why he leaves Monterey one hour after he comes?" Her tone was sarcastic, but in it was a note of apprehension.

Mariquita tossed her head, and all pressed close about the rivals.

"What dost thou know, this time?" inquired the girl, provok-ingly. "Hast thou any letter to read today? Thou dost forget, old Faquita, that Ana is my friend — "

"Throw the clothes in the tubs," cried Faquita, furiously. "Do we come here to idle and gossip? Mariquita, thou hussy, go over to that tub by thyself and wash the impertinent American rags. Quick. No more talk. The sun goes high."

No one dared to disobey the queen of the tubs, and in a moment the women were kneeling in irregular rows, tumbling their linen into the water, the brown faces and bright attire making a picture in the colorous landscape which some native artist would have done well to preserve. For a time no sound was heard but the distant roar of the surf, the sighing of the wind through the pines on the hill, the less romantic grunts of the women and the swish of the linen in the water. Suddenly Mariquita, the pro-scribed, exclaimed from her segregated tub: —

"Look! Look!"

Heads flew up or twisted on their necks. A party of young people, attended by a dueña, was crossing the meadow to the road. At the head of the procession were a girl and a man, to whom every gaze which should have been intent upon washing-tubs alone was directed. The girl wore a pink gown and a reboso. Her extraordinary grace made her look taller than she was; the slender figure swayed with every step. Her pink lips were parted, her blue starlike eyes looked upward into the keen cold eyes of a young man wearing the uniform of a lieutenant of the United States army.

The dominant characteristics of the young man's face, even then, were ambition and determination, and perhaps the remark-able future was foreshadowed in the restless scheming mind. But to-day his deep-set eyes were glowing with a light more peculiar to youth, and whenever bulging stones afforded excuse he grasped the girl's hand and held it as long as he dared. The procession wound past the tubs and crossing the road climbed up the hill to the little wooded cemetery of the early fathers, the cemetery where so many of those bright heads were to lie forgotten beneath the wild oats and thistles.

"They go to the grave of Benicia Ortega and her little one," said Francesca. "Holy Mary! La Tulita never look in a man's eyes like that before."

"But she have in his," said Mariquita, wisely.

"No more talk!" cried Faquita, and once more silence came to her own. But fate was stronger than Faquita. An hour later a little girl came running down, calling to the old woman that her grandchild, the consolation of her age, had been taken ill. After she had hurried away the women fairly leaped over one another in their efforts to reach Mariquita's tub.

"Tell us, tell us, chiquita," they cried, fearful lest Faquita's snubbing should have turned her sulky, "what dost thou know?"

But Mariquita, who had been biting her lips to keep back her story, opened them and spoke fluently.

"Ay, my friends! Doña Eustaquia and Benicia Ortega are not the only ones to wed Americans. Listen! La Tulita is mad for this man, who is no more handsome than the palm of my hand when it has all day been in the water. Yesterday morning came Don Ramon. I am in the back garden of the Casa Rivera with Ana, and La Tulita is in the front garden sitting under the wall. I can look through the doors of the sala and see and hear all. Such a handsome caballero, my friends! The gold six inches deep on the serape. Silver eagles on the sombrero. And the botas! Stamp with birds and leaves, ay, yi! He fling open the gates so bold, and when he see La Tulita he look like the sun is behind his face. (Such curls, my friends, tied with a blue ribbon!) But listen!

"'Mi querida!' he cry, 'mi alma!' (Ay, my heart jump in my throat like he speak to me.) Then he fall on one knee and try to kiss her hand. But she throw herself back like she hate him. Her eyes are like the bay in winter. And then she laugh. When she do that, he stand up and say with the voice that shake:

"'What is the matter, Herminia? Do you not love me any longer?'

"'I never love you,' she say. 'They give me no peace until I say I marry you, and as I love no one else — I do not care much. But now that you have insult me, I have the best excuse to break the engagement, and I do it.'

"'I insult you?' He hardly can speak, my friends, he is so surprised and unhappy.

"'Yes; did you not forget the smocks?'

"'The — smocks!' he stammer, like that. 'The smocks?'

"'No one can be blame but you,' she say. 'And you know that no bride forgive that. You know all that it means.'

"'Herminia!' he say. 'Surely you will not put me away for a little thing like that!'

'I have no more to say,' she reply, and then she get up and go in the house and shut the door so I cannot see how he feel, but I am very sorry for him if he did forget the smocks. Well! That evening I help Ana water the flowers in the front garden, and every once in the while we look through the windows at La Tulita and the Lieutenant. They talk, talk, talk. He look so earnest and she — she look so beautiful. Not like a devil, as when she talk to Don Ramon in the morning, but like an angel. Sure, a woman can be both! It depends upon the man. By and by Ana go away, but I stay there, for I like look at them. After a while they get up and come out. It is dark in the garden, the walls so high, and the trees throw the shadows, so they cannot see me. They walk up and down, and by and by the Lieutenant take out his knife and cut a shoot from the rose-bush that climb up the house.

"'These Castilian roses,' he say, very soft, but in very bad Spanish, 'they are very beautiful and a part of Monterey — a part of you. Look, I am going to plant this here, and long before it grow to be a big bush I come back and you will wear its buds in your hair when we are married in that lovely old church. Now help me,' and then they kneel down and he stick it in the ground, and all their fingers push the earth around it. Then she give a little sob and say, 'You must go?'

He lift her up and put his arms around her tight. 'I must go,' he say. 'I am not my own master, you know, and the orders have come. But my heart is here, in this old garden, and I come back for it.' And then she put her arms around him and he kiss her, and she love him so I forget to be sorry for Don Ramon. After all, it is the woman who should be happy. He hold her a long time, so long I am afraid Doña Carmen come out to look for her. I lift up on my knees (I am sit down before) and look in the window and I see she is asleep, and I am glad. Well! After a while they walk up and down again, and he tell her all about his home far away, and about some money he go to get when the law get ready, and how he cannot marry on his pay. Then he say how he go to be a great general some day and how she will be the more beautiful woman in — how you call it? — Washington, I think. And she cry and say she does not care, she only want him. And he tell her water the rose-bush every day and think of him, and he will come back before it is large, and every time a bud come out she can know he is thinking of her very hard."

"Ay, pobrecita!" said Francesca, "I wonder will he come back. These men!"

"Surely. Are not all men mad for La Tulita?"

"Yes — yes, but he go far away. To America! Dios de mi alma! And men, they forget." Francesca heaved a deep sigh. Her youth was far behind her, but she remembered many things.

"He return," said Mariquita, the young and romantic.

"When does he go?"

Mariquita pointed to the bay. A schooner rode at anchor. "He go to Yerba Buena on that to-morrow morning. From there to the land of the American. Ay, yi! Poor La Tulita! But his linen is dry. I must take it to iron for I have it promised for six in the morning." And she hastily gathered the articles from the low bushes and hurried away.

That evening as the women returned to town, talking gayly, despite the great baskets on their heads, they passed the hut of Faquita and paused at the window to inquire for the child. The little one lay gasping on the bed. Faquita sat beside her with bowed head. An aged crone brewed herbs over a stove. The dingy little house faced the hills and was dimly lighted by the fading rays of the sun struggling through the dark pine woods.

"Holy Mary, Faquita!" said Francesca, in a loud whisper. "Does Liseta die?"

Faquita sprang to her feet. Her cross old face was drawn with misery. "Go, go!" she said, waving her arms, "I want none of you."

The next evening she sat in the same position, her eyes fixed upon the shrinking features of the child. The crone had gone. She heard the door open, and turned with a scowl. But it was La Tulita that entered and came rapidly to the head of the bed. The girl's eyes were swollen, her dress and hair disordered.

"I have come to you because you are in trouble," she said. "I, too, am in trouble. Ay, my Faquita!"

The old woman put up her arms and drew the girl down to her lap. She had never touched her idol before, but sorrow levels even social barriers.

"Pobrecita!" she said, and the girl cried softly on her shoulder.

"Will he come back, Faquita?"

"Surely, niñita. No man could forget you."

"But it is so far."

"Think of what Don Vicente do for Doña Ysabel, mijita."

"But he is an American. Oh, no, it is not that I doubt him. He loves me! It is so far, like another world. And the ocean is so big and cruel."

"We ask the priest to say a mass."

"Ah, my Faquita! I will go to the church to-morrow morning. How glad I am that I came to thee." She kissed the old woman warmly, and for the moment Faquita forgot her trouble.

But the child threw out its arms and moaned. La Tulita pushed the hair out of her eyes and brought the medicine from the stove, where it simmered unsavourily. The child swallowed it painfully, and Faquita shook her head in despair. At the dawn it died. As La Tulita laid her white fingers on the gaping eyelids, Faquita rose to her feet. Her ugly old face was transfigured. Even the grief had gone out of it. For a moment she was no longer a woman, but one of the most subtle creations of the Catholic religion conjoined with racial superstitions.

"As the moon dieth and cometh to life again," she repeated with a sort of chanting cadence, "so man, though he die, will live again. Is it not better that she will wander forever through forests where crystal streams roll over golden sands, than grow into wickedness, and go out into the dark unrepenting, perhaps, to be bitten by serpents and scorched by lightning and plunged down cataracts?" She turned to La Tulita. "Will you stay here, señorita, while I go to bid them make merry?"

The girl nodded, and the woman went out. La Tulita watched the proud head and erect carriage for a moment, then bound up the fallen jaw of the little corpse, crossed its hands and placed weights on the eyelids. She pushed the few pieces of furniture against the wall, striving to forget the one trouble that had come into her triumphant young life. But there was little to do, and after a time she knelt by the window and looked up at the dark forest upon which long shafts of light were striking, routing the fog that crouched in the hollows. The town was as quiet as a necropolis.

The white houses, under the black shadows of the hills, lay like tombs. Suddenly the roar of the surf came to her ears, and she threw out her arms with a cry, dropping her head upon them and sobbed convulsively. She heard the ponderous waves of the Pacific lashing the keel of a ship.

She was aroused by shouting and sounds of merriment. She raised her head dully, but remembered in a moment what Faquita had left her to await. The dawn lay rosily on the town. The shimmering light in the pine woods was crossed and recrossed by the glare of rockets. Down the street came the sound of singing voices, the words of the song heralding the flight of a child-spirit to a better world. La Tulita slipped out of the back door and went to her home without meeting the procession. But before she shut herself in her room she awakened Ana, and giving her a purse of gold, bade her buy a little coffin draped with white and garlanded with white flowers.

Part III

"Tell us, tell, us, Mariquita, does she water the rose tree every night?"

"Every night, ay, yi!"

"And is it big yet? Ay, but that wall is high! Not a twig can I see!"

"Yes, it grows!"

"And he comes not?"

"He write. I see the letters."

"But what does he say?"

"How can I know?"

"And she goes to the balls and meriendas no more. Surely, they will forget her. It is more than a year now. Some one else will be La Favorita."

"She does not care."

"Hush the voices," cried Faquita, scrubbing diligently. "It is well that she stay at home and does not dance away her beauty before he come. She is like a lily."

"But lilies turn brown, old Faquita, when the wind blow on them too long. Dost thou think he will return?"

"Surely," said Faquita, stoutly. "Could any one forget that angel?"

"Ay, these men, these men!" said Francesca, with a sigh.

"Oh, thou old raven!" cried Mariquita. "But truly — truly — she has had no letter for three months."

"Aha, señorita, thou didst not tell us that just now."

"Nor did I intend to. The words just fell from my teeth."

"He is ill," cried Faquita, angrily. "Ay, my probrecita! Sometimes I think Ysabel is more happy under the rocks."

"How dost thou know he is ill? Will he die?" The wash-tub mail had made too few mistakes in its history to admit of doubt being cast upon the assertion of one of its officials.

"I hear Captain Brotherton read from a letter to Doña Eustaquia. Ay, they are happy!"

"When?"

"Two hours ago."

"Then we know before the town — like always."

"Surely. Do we not know all things first? Hist!"

The women dropped their heads and fumbled at the linen in the water. La Tulita was approaching.

She came across the meadow with all her old swinging grace, the blue gown waving about her like the leaves of a California lily when the wind rustled the forest. But the reboso framed a face thin and pale, and the sparkle was gone from her eyes. She passed the tubs and greeted the old women pleasantly, walked a few steps up the hill, then turned as if in obedience to an afterthought, and sat down on a stone in the shade of a willow.

"It is cool here," she said.

"Yes, señorita." They were not deceived, but they dared not stare at her, with Faquita's scowl upon them.

"What news has the wash-tub mail to-day?" asked the girl, with an attempt at lightness. "Did an enemy invade the South this morning, and have you heard it already, as when General Kearney came? Is General Castro still in Baja California, or has he fled to Mexico? Has Doña Prudencia Iturbi y Moncada given a ball this week at Santa Barbara? Have Don Diego and Doña Chonita — ?"

"The young Lieutenant is ill," blurted out one of the old women, then cowered until she almost fell into her tub. Faquita sprang forward and caught the girl in her arms.

"Thou old fool!" she cried furiously. "Thou devil! Mayst thou find a tarantula in thy bed to-night. Mayst thou dream thou art roasting in hell." She carried La Tulita rapidly across the meadow.

"Ah, I thought I should hear there," said the girl, with a laugh. "Thank heaven for the wash-tub mail."

Faquita nursed her through a long illness. She recovered both health and reason, and one day the old woman brought her word that the young Lieutenant was well again — and that his illness had been brief and slight.

THE LAST

"Ay, but the years go quick!" said Mariquita, as she flapped a piece of linen after taking it from the water. "I wonder do all towns sleep like this. Who can believe that once it is so gay? The balls! The grand caballeros! The serenades! The meriendas! No more! No more! Almost I forget the excitement when the Americanos coming. I no am young any more. Ay, yi!"

"Poor Faquita, she just died of old age," said a woman who had been young with Mariquita, spreading an article of underwear on a bush. "Her life just drop out like her teeth. No one of the old women that taught us to wash is here now, Mariquita. We are the old ones now, and we teach the young, ay, yi!"

"Well, it is a comfort that the great grow old like the low people. High birth cannot keep the skin white and the body slim. Ay, look! Who can think she is so beautiful before?"

A woman was coming down the road from the town. A woman, whom passing years had browned, although leaving the fine strong features uncoarsened. She was dressed simply in black, and wore a small American bonnet. The figure had not lost the slimness of its youth, but the walk was stiff and precise. The carriage evinced a determined will.

"Ay, who can think that once she sway like the tule!" said Mariquita, with a sigh. "Well, when she come to-day I have some news. A letter, we used to call it, dost thou remember, Brigida? Who care for the wash-tub mail now? These Americanos never hear of it, and our people — triste de mi — have no more the interest in anything."

"Tell us thy news," cried many voices. The older women had never lost their interest in La Tulita. The younger ones had heard her story many times, and rarely passed the wall before her house without looking at the tall rose-bush which had all the pride of a young tree.

"No, you can hear when she come. She will come to-day. Six months ago to-day she come. Ay, yi, to think she come once in six months all these years! And never until to-day has the wash-tub mail a letter for her."

"Very strange she did not forget a Gringo and marry with a caballero," said one of the girls, scornfully. "They say the caballeros were so beautiful, so magnificent. The Americans have all the money now, but she been rich for a little while."

"All women are not alike. Sometimes I think she is more happy with the memory." And Mariquita, who had a fat lazy husband and a swarm of brown children, sighed heavily. "She live happy in the old house and is not so poor. And always she have the rose-bush. She smile, now, sometimes, when she water it."

"Well, it is many years," said the girl, philosophically. "Here she come."

La Tulita, or Doña Herminia, as she now was called, walked briskly across the meadow and sat down on the stone which had come to be called for her. She spoke to each in turn, but did not ask for news. She had ceased long since to do that. She still came because the habit held her, and because she liked the women.

"Ah, Mariquita," she said, "the linen is not as fine as when we were young. And thou art glad to get the shirts of the Americans now. My poor Faquita!"

"Coarse things," said Mariquita, disdainfully. Then a silence fell, so sudden and so suggestive that Doña Herminia felt it and turned instinctively to Mariquita.

"What is it?" she asked rapidly. "Is there news to-day? Of what?"

"There is news, señorita," she said.

Mariquita's honest face was grave and important.

"What is it?"

The washing-women had dropped back from the tubs and were listening intently.

"Ay!" The oracle drew a long breath. "There is war over there, you know, señorita," she said, making a vague gesture toward the Atlantic states.

"Yes, I know. Is it decided? Is the North or the South victorious? I am glad that the wash-tub mail has not — "

"It is not that, señorita."

"Then what?"

"The Lieutenant — he is a great general now."

"Ay!"

"He has won a great battle — And — they speak of his wife, señorita."

Doña Herminia closed her eyes for a moment. Then she opened them and glanced slowly about her. The blue bay, the solemn pines, the golden atmosphere, the cemetery on the hill, the women washing at the stone tubs — all was unchanged. Only the flimsy wooden houses of the Americans scattered among the adobes of the town and the aging faces of the women who had been young in her brief girlhood marked the lapse of years. There was a smile on her lips. Her monotonous life must have given her insanity or infinite peace, and peace had been her portion. In a few minutes she said good-by to the women and went home. She never went to the tubs again.

Mary Austin

⦿⁓⁓⁓⁓⁓⁓⁓⁓⁓⁓⁓⁓⁓⁓⁓⁓⁓⁓⦿

*B*orn in Illinois, Mary Hunter Austin (1868-1934) moved to California's San Joaquin Valley as a young woman and began her writing career with a story for Overland Monthly. Although she eventually wrote poetry, criticism, and novels and short stories, her earliest work — and some say her most important — was sketches of western life, primarily of California. The author of twenty-five books, she is best known for The Land of Little Rain (1903), a book of California sketches. After her 1915 divorce, Austin traveled widely and lived briefly in New York City; she moved to Santa Fe, New Mexico, around 1920, where she was an active part of the colony of artists and writers there. "The Man Who Lied About a Woman" is from a collection of short fictional narratives that Austin collected from American Indian informants.

The Man Who Lied About a Woman
One Smoke Stories, 1934

*E*verybody knew that the girl who passed for the daughter of Tizessína was neither her daughter nor a Jicarilla Apache. Tizessína, being childless, had bought her, squalling, from a Navajo whose wife had died in giving birth, and she loved her inordinately. She was called Tall Flower after the hundred-belled white yucca, and carried herself always with the consciousness of superior blood. None of the Jicarilla youths, it seemed, was good enough for her. When Tizessína, who was as anxious as any real mother to see the girl well settled, asked her what she wanted,

"I shall know when I see it," said Tall Flower, and continued to give the young men who walked with her the squashes. For she was the sort that every man desired and herself desired nothing. She laughed and went her way, and whatever she did Tizessína approved.

Nevertheless, she was disappointed when the girl hunched her shoulder to Natáldin, who, besides being the richest young man of the Apaches, was much sought after and would require careful handling. "But, my mother," laughed Tall Flower, "I shall handle him not at all."

This being her way with him, Natáldin, who was used to having marriageable girls go to a great deal of trouble on his account, was hurt in his self-esteem. To keep the other young men from finding out that with the daughter of Tizessína he had to take all the trouble himself, he took the manner when he walked with her of a lover who is already successful. He stuck a flower in his hat and swung his blanket from his shoulder until Tizessína herself began to nod and wink when the other women hinted.

Then suddenly Tall Flower went off overnight with her mother and two or three other women to Taos Pueblo to gather wild plums for drying. She went without letting Natáldin know, and, when the young men of Jicarilla found this out, they laughed and presented him with a large ripe squash. Nothing like this having happened to the young man before, he stiffened his lip and swung his shoulder. "And if I did not get the young woman," he said, "I got as much as I wanted of her."

No one liked to ask him what he meant by this, for to the others the girl had been as straight and as aloof as her name flower, and to take away a maiden's honor is a serious matter among the Jicarilla Apaches. But Natáldin, for the very reason that he had had not so much from Tall Flower as the touching of her littlest finger, salved his pride with looks and shrugs and by changing the subject when her name was mentioned. The truth was that he was afraid to talk of her, not for fear he might tell more than was seemly, but for fear somebody might find out what he had lately discovered, that if he did not have the daughter of Tizessína to be his wife, his life would be as a wild gourd, smooth without, but within a mouthful of bitter ashes.

The girl and her mother went not only to Taos Pueblo where the plum branches are bent over with bright fruit, but to Taos town, where a white man persuaded Tall Flower to be painted among the plum branches. Then they gathered *osha* in the hills toward Yellow Earth, where Tizessína, who was Government school taught, stayed for a month to cook for a camp of Government surveyors. In the month of the cold touching mildly, they came to Jicarilla again.

Natáldin, who found Tall Flower more to be desired than ever, was in two minds how he should punish her, but unfortunately what was in his mind turned out to be so much less than what was in his heart that he ended by thinking only how he could persuade her to be his wife. Tizessína, he saw, was wholly on his side, but some strange fear of her daughter kept her silent. Natáldin would catch her looking at him as though she wished him to know something that she feared to tell. At other times Tizessína looked at Natáldin from behind a fold of her blanket as a wild thing watches a hunter from the rocks, while Tall Flower looked over and beyond them both. There was a dream in her eyes, and now and then it flowered around her mouth.

Presently there began to be other looks: matrons watching Tall Flower out of the tails of their eyes, young girls walking in the twilight with their arms about one another, looking the other way as she passed; young men looking slyly at Natáldin, with laughs and nudges. Natáldin, who was sick to think that another had possessed her, where he had got the squash, denied nothing. If he remembered the punishment that is due to a man who lies about a woman, he reflected that a woman who has given herself to one lover is in no position to deny that she has given herself to two. But in fact he reflected very little. He was a man jabbing at an aching tooth in the hope of driving out one pain with another.

It had been midsummer when Tizessína had taken her daughter to gather plums, and in the month of Snow Water, Tall Flower being far gone with child, the two women talked together in their house.

"I have heard," said Tizessína, "that Natáldin tells it about camp that he is the father of your child."

"Since how long?" said Tall Flower.

"Since before we had come to Taos town," said the mother, and repeated all she had heard.

"Then he has twice lied," said the girl.

"He is the richest man in Jicarilla, as well as a liar," said Tizessína, "and you will not get a husband very easily after this. I shall bring it to Council."

"What he does to another, that to him also," said the girl, which is a saying of the Apaches. "By all means take it to Council. But I shall not appear."

When Natáldin saw the *algucil* coming to call him before the Council, he was half glad, for now his tooth was about to come out. But he was sick when he saw the girl was not there; only Tizessína, who stood up and said, "O my fathers! You know that my daughter is with child, and this one says that he is the father of it. This is established by many witnesses. Therefore, if he is the father, let him take my daughter to his house. But if he has lied, then let him be punished as is the custom for a man who has lied about a woman."

Said the Council, "Have you lied?" and Natáldin saw that he was between the bow and the bowstring.

"Only Tall Flower knows if I have lied," he said, "and she does not appear against me. But I am willing to take her to my house, and the child also."

"So let it be," said the Council; and the young man's tooth was stopped, waiting to see whether it would come out or not.

But Tall Flower, when the judgment was reported to her, made conditions. "I will come to his house and cook for him and mend," she said, "but until after the child is born I will not come to his bed." And Natáldin, to whom nothing mattered except that now Tall Flower should be his wife, consented. Although he was tormented at times by the thought of that other who had had all his desire of her where Natáldin himself had got the squash, the young man salved his torment by thinking that, now the girl was his wife, nobody would be able to say that he had not been her lover. He thought that when he told the daughter of Tizessína that he had lied to save her shame, she would never shame him by telling that he had lied. What nobody knows, nobody doubts; which is also a saying of the Jicarilla Apaches. Therefore, when he walked abroad with his young wife, Natáldin carried himself as a man who has done all that can be expected of him. As for Tizessína, she walked like the mother-in-law of the richest young man in Jicarilla, and Tall Flower walked between them, dreaming.

In due time, as he worked in his field Natáldin saw Tizessína and the neighbor women hurrying to his house, after which he worked scarcely at all, but leaned upon his hoe until the sun was a bowshot from going down, and listened to the shaking of his own heart. As he came up the trail to his house at last, he saw his wife lying under the *ramada*, and beside her Tizessína with something wrapped in a blanket. "Let me see my son," he said, and wondered why the neighbor women rose and hurried away with their blankets over their faces, for with the first-born there should be compliments and present-giving. But when Tizessína turned back the blanket and showed him the child's face, he knew that after all he should not escape the punishment of a man who has lied about a woman. For the child was white!

Jeanne Williams

〰〰〰〰〰〰〰〰〰〰〰〰〰〰〰〰

Author of sixty books, all but two of them fiction, Jeanne
Williams (1930-) writes frequently of the American
West — the Mormon Handcart Emigration, the Underground
Railroad, the land boom of Oklahoma's No Man's Land,
post-Civil War dissensions in Kansas. Noted for her accurate research into daily life, she has a unique ability to
combine women's history and women's fiction in a form
that meets with commercial success. At the center of her
novels are women of strength who, finding themselves beginning anew, show daring and courage. Though her heroines
are often in love, she is by no means a romance writer, and
romance is always secondary to history in her work. In
1994, her most recent western novels include No Roof but
Heaven, Home Mountain, and The Long Road Home.

"This story grew out of an actual incident on the
Oregon trail. A man who killed another over cards was
condemned and hanged by his fellow travelers who then
took turns driving his widow's wagon to journey's end.
Forced to rely on her husband's executioners, what did she
think and feel?

"To me, women were the frontier. How they lived,
how they took care of their children, how they survived
when left without a male breadwinner — these are questions that interest me far more than do the shenanigans of
gunfighters and prostitutes. My great-grandmothers came
west in frontier days. Times were still hard for women
when my grandmothers reared their children after the turn
of the century. I spent my teenage years with my mother's
mother and heard her tell about her life in mining camps
and on the farm. In my books, I celebrate these women of

my blood and all ordinary women who did extraordinary things when conditions compelled it."

— *Jeanne Williams*

The Debt
Roundup, 1984

One of the articles agreed to by all members of the McBride Company when it was forming up in Iowa was that anyone who killed another member of the party during the trip to Oregon was to be tried and hanged. So when, a day west of Split Rock, Jed Hoffman shot Harry Drew in a card game, Jed didn't beg, though his tanned young face went pale and haggard when the other men found no way to call what he'd done anything but murder. Harry had a foul mouth, but it shouldn't have been answered with a gun.

Jed was well liked and it was a shame that his wife, Mary Ann, was big with their second child, but the article had to be followed. Make exceptions and the fifteen interdependent families would lose all order, perhaps fatally, long before they got to Oregon. So Jed was hanged with the best rope they had to the best tree they could find along the sulky Sweetwater.

After he kissed Mary Ann and four-year-old Billy, Jed looked at his friends. "I know you got to do this. But since you're taking me, you owe it to Mary Ann to get her to Oregon."

"We'll do it," promised Tam McBride, the captain, a stocky man with a grizzled spade beard and brown eyes that were merry except when he had something like this to do.

Mary Ann didn't beg, either, but though Mrs. McBride tried to lead her away, she stood and watched Jed hang. She was thin, weathered past her twenty years by farm work and the wind and sun of the trail, but her eyes were like a mountain lake, blue-green and fathomless beneath dark brows that winged up at the sides, a strange contrast to hair the pale shade of the underleaf of a cottonwood.

She kept Billy's face buried in her skirt while the women murmured with shock and pity. When Jed's legs hung slack and his poor face was something no one should see and some of the men were sick and old Mrs. Steubens fainted, Mary Ann got a knife to cut Jed down.

Talt Braden took the knife and did it for her. Rangy, broad in the shoulder, Talt had straight black hair, a lean rock-hard face, eyes like a summer storm, and a half smile that seemed to mock the world. It was whispered that he'd been a squaw man, a trapper on the Yellowstone, till his woman died. He'd joined the company at Fort Laramie and knew a lot more about the country than the little Emigrants' Guide Tam McBride had previously relied on.

Not that there was much chance of losing the way. It was a devastated swath several miles wide in places, marked with dead oxen, horses and cattle, discarded furniture and belongings that had proved too heavy for the long ordeal, and a few graves. In order to prevent looting by Indians, most burials were made in the trail and driven over so that they were obliterated.

This was how Jed and the man he'd killed were buried, wrapped first in blankets because there was no wood for coffins. Talt helped cover the grave before he came over to Mary Ann.

"I'll drive your wagon."

She stared at him as if waking from a deep sleep. Her bewildered gaze moved over the hurrying company who were eager to get away from what they had done.

"I — I can't travel with these people."

"You can't stay here!"

"I can wait till another train comes along."

He swore. "That might be a week. Indians don't bother trains much but they're always ready for easy pickings." When she said nothing, Talt demanded roughly, "What about the kid? Think of him if you don't care about yourself."

She stroked Billy's blond head as he still clung to her. "I don't want to be beholden to anyone who had a hand in — in this."

"You won't be." Talt frowned. "It's something we owe." And without allowing her further argument, he lifted her up on the seat and put Billy beside her.

Mary had always been one for keeping to herself. She had no real friends in the company and, with the reproach of Jed's death on them, people were relieved that Talt had taken on the responsibility of looking after the dead man's family. It took away the awkwardness of trying to talk to her when, no matter how friendly or matter-of-fact a body tried to be, Mary Ann just looked through you and wouldn't say anything past yes or no. She got even chillier after the children started teasing Billy.

"Your pa wet his pants when he died!" they'd taunt, when out of earshot of their elders. "His eyes booged out and his tongue was purple!"

Talt dragged a few of the boys by the scruffs of their necks over to their folks and saw they got whomped, but there's no way to stop a thing like that. Billy quit playing with the other young-sters and stuck close to his mama. Talt made him a willow flute and carved him a whole menagerie of bone animals, buffalo, horses, bear antelope, beaver and coyotes. Billy had them march to funny little whistle tunes or made up long stories about them as he moved them around on the wagon seat or the ground. Folks began to wonder if he was touched in the head but they didn't dare talk to Mary Ann about it. When Mrs. McBride ventured a question to Talt, he just rared back on his heels and stared at her till she turned redder than a turkey gobbler's wattles.

"My God, woman!" That was all he said.

So, though Mary Ann's wagon moved along with the com-pany, she and her little son were more like some kind of ghosts. That made everyone uneasy, squelched the jokes and laughter that helped ease such a grinding, monotonous journey. Still, it was an obligation to get Mary Ann to Oregon. No one questioned that. For sure, if she'd had any appetite, she could have eaten better with Talt than ever she had with Jed. Talt was far and away the best hunter in the company and when Mary Ann couldn't fancy even hump or tongue of buffalo, he brought a sage grouse or caught fish to broil till they were a mouth-watering gold. After camp was made of an evening, he often took Billy to hunt for berries and wild turnips and onions. They often had a swim before they came back and if Billy's short legs were worn out, Talt brought him back on his shoulders.

"You're good to Billy," Mary Ann said one night after the boy had gone to sleep with the bone animals arranged close to him.

Talt shrugged. "Never had any folks. I know a kid can get lonesome."

She regarded him with the first real interest she'd shown anything. "I was an orphan, too. My aunt raised me, talked on how Christian she was while she worked me like a slave. Couldn't get out of there fast enough — "

Her voice trailed off. She'd never said how she'd felt about her husband and she didn't say now. Just stared at the sunlit snow on top of the Wind Rivers to the north of where the company would cross the Continental Divide at South Pass, that broad high plain that stretched for miles between the ranges.

At Pacific Springs, where water could for the first time be seen flowing toward the Pacific, the company found what seemed to be an abandoned wagon, amid signs of a hastily broken big encampment. Tam McBride went over to look and came back in a hurry, brown eyes wide with fright.

"Cholera!" he choked. "Woman's dead and the man's close to it." This was supposed to be the night's halting place, but he gave orders to move on. Most of the drivers were already ahead of him.

Talt was climbing down as he spoke, and his storm-colored eyes had lightning in them. "Man shouldn't die alone when there are people."

"He's out of his head," McBride argued. "And you could pick up the contagion." Talt didn't answer, just started for the death wagon. "You poke around here, man, and we don't want you rejoining the company!" McBride warned, sweat popping out on his seamed forehead. "Hell, it could take away every soul of us!"

"Don't worry," said Talt. "I'll pass you up and have my land staked before you cross the Snake."

He went on toward the wagon. McBride scowled, looked unhappily at Mary Ann, and then bellowed for one of the single men to come drive her. There was a scramble. Women were scarce out west and all the bachelors had been waiting for some hint in Mary Ann's behavior that would show she had properly decided she needed a man for herself and a father for her kids. No one had pushed. Talt had the inside track there. But at this opportunity, Mary Ann could have had her pick of the unmarried fellows.

Not even looking at them as they hustled around her wagon, she said to McBride, "I'll wait for Mr. Braden."

"You can't do that!" Tam growled.

"I will."

His eyes fell under her strange blue-green ones. "But you might catch the sickness! Little Billy might! Looky here, Mrs. Hoffman, this party owes it to you — "

She made a gesture with her hand as if she were throwing something away. "I'm sick of you and your whining about a debt! Do you think you can give back a man's life? I'm sick of being tied to you on account of your duty. Go along!"

Mrs. McBride made a helpless gesture. "Now, Mrs. Hoffman, Mary Ann — " Her voice thinned to a whisper. "You can't be wicked enough to risk your little boy! Let us take him."

"So the boys can make mock of him again?" Mary Ann hugged her child against the swell of the one that was coming. "If he can't make it with us, he'd be better off dead than being kicked around like a stray cur! You better go fast. The wind might blow the cholera your direction!"

The McBrides paled and swung their wagon. One by one, under Mary Ann's sightless stare, the young single men, muttering, went back to their horses.

"Play with your animals," Mary Ann told Billy.

Heavily, she climbed down from the wagon. Talt, going for water, stopped in his tracks and shouted at her, "Go on with the others!"

She shook her head.

"You fool woman! Hurry up and rejoin the company."

"Reckon I owe you something."

"Is that the only word anyone knows? Owe?" He must have realized he couldn't budge her. "All right, wait if you're crazy enough! But you keep away from this wagon and me. If I don't come down with it in a week or two, I'd reckon we could travel along. Drive over to those willows and set up camp."

Talt dug a grave for the dead woman that afternoon. He brewed some herb drink for the man and got quite a lot of it down him but the sick man passed with next morning's dawn. Talt dug his grave, too, and burned the wagon and tainted possessions. He made his camp in sight of Mary Ann and the boy, but didn't go near them. For their meat, though, he managed to shoot a pronghorn a hundred yards from the wagon, which Mary

Ann laboriously skinned and butchered. Talt shot another for himself and feasted.

He also kept constant watch for Indians. South Pass was a favorite spot for various tribes to skirmish with each other or just come looking for excitement. Shoshoni, Sioux, Snake and Crow. He sighed, wishing he'd told Mary Ann that. Then he reflected that if cholera wouldn't send her with the company, nothing could have. She smiled sometimes at Billy. Talt wished that she would smile at him.

Five mornings after the abandoned man had died, Mary Ann climbed off the shuck mattress in the wagon and glanced toward Talt's camp. Usually, he'd wave at her, shout a greeting. This morning, he lay in his blankets.

Fear gripped and squeezed her heart. *He's just tired*, she told herself stoutly. *Man has a right to sleep late if he's not going anywhere.* And because this just had to be the answer, she got breakfast before she'd let herself look over at Talt.

He hadn't moved.

"Talt!" she shouted. There was a panicky note in her cry. Little Billy gave a whimper and ran to her. That made her get hold of herself, force herself to think.

She'd heard that about half the people who got cholera died of it, some in a day, others taking closer to a week of terrible retching agony, fever and chills. Talt Braden, if she had anything to do with it, was going to be one of those who got well.

But Billy —

What if she got the sickness, too? Terror swirled over her but she fought it down. Surely a wagon train would be along soon, it was just a fluke that none had passed while they were camped by the springs. She had often doubted there was a God. Now she had to pray that there was and that He would take care of her son.

"Billy," she said, kneeling, swallowing to steady her voice and keep it calm and reassuring. "Talt may be sick and I have to take care of him. You've got to be a big boy and take care of your animals here at the wagon. I baked bread yesterday and there's cooked meat and that I've been smoking. You can gather berries but don't get out of sight of the wagon."

His mouth trembled and his blue eyes were bewildered. "But, Mama — "

"You can see me," she assured him. "We can wave at each other and you can play some tunes on your whistle. But you mustn't come over where you could get sick." She gave him a fierce squeeze. "Whatever happens, keep away from us till I tell you it's all right."

"Talt get well?" he pleaded, tightening his grip on her dress. Gently, she unpried the chubby brown fingers, dimpled so sweetly at the knuckles.

"Yes. He's going to get well. But you have to help. Go see if you can find some berries. If you do, put them right over there by that biggest sagebrush. Then I can give them to Talt."

"I'll get a lot of berries!" Billy promised. Clutching his whistle, he went off at a trot with a little bucket.

Mary Ann gathered up things she would need and moved across the space to Talt.

Talt's sunken eyes stared at her without recognition as she coaxed him to drink the tea she'd made from the herbs left from treating the stranger. She got a few swallows down him before he convulsed in long shuddering cramps. He threw up a thin, stinking bile, kept heaving when nothing more would come. When he collapsed, she bathed him, taking off his shirt and wondering where a white scar in the shoulder had come from.

The stomach cramps tortured him again. She heated their skillets and applied them to Talt's abdomen, wrapped in one of his shirts. His legs twitched and strained. She rubbed them, trying to work out the massed rigidity of spasmed muscles. It seemed an eternity that the cramps continued. She applied heat, rubbed his arms and legs, and talked, hoping that beneath his delirium, he could know someone was there.

Billy's whistle sounded after a time. She glanced up to see that he was cautiously depositing berries on a plate by the big sagebrush.

"For Talt!" he shouted.

Rising she waved at him and went to get the fruit. Billy looked very small and vulnerable, standing uncertainly by the wagon. "Why don't you get some nice long grass for Midge and Sam?" she called.

The oxen were finding ample graze, but Billy would feel better if he had something to do. "Billy find good grass," he promised, and trotted off.

Mary Ann crushed the berries into water and got some of the thickened juice down Talt. She was encouraged when he didn't vomit at once, but within the hour, hideous cramps contorted the body which seemed to be shrinking before her eyes.

More heated skillets, more rubbing till her hands and shoulders ached. Sometimes his contortions and retching were so violent that she thought they must kill him, but his breath labored on. And thinking he surely needed fluid to replace all he was losing, she would wait for half an hour or so after a bout of retching and then get him to take tea or broth or the fruit drink.

Several times that long, hot day, Billy sounded his whistle. Mary Ann would walk as near the wagon as she dared and tell him how much the berries seemed to be helping Talt and make sure the boy was eating. Seeing her even for a few minutes seemed to reassure Billy and he would go back to playing with his animals, moving them up and down the wagon tongue.

As the setting sun made rose-gold of the high peaks of the Wind Rivers, Mary Ann looked down at Talt and thought he was resting easier. Or perhaps he was simply exhausted, slipping over that line between sleep and death?

Raising him against her breast, she gave him the rest of the fruit juice. At this altitude, the air cooled rapidly after sundown. She wrapped him warmly, went back to call good-night to Billy.

"Do you have your animals all ready to sleep?"

"All but bear. Bear's going to stand guard. He'll watch out for you and Talt, too, Mama."

"Thank him, honey. Now you cuddle up in the blankets and sleep sound."

"Talt sleep sound?"

"He's a lot better. Maybe you can find him some more berries tomorrow."

"I will." She heard him talking to his bear. Dear God, what if he should be left with only his toy animals for comfort? It didn't stand thinking about.

She wrapped up in her blankets, close enough to wake if Talt stirred much, and dropped instantly into slumber.

Twice that night, Talt's threshings roused her. She heated skillets, rubbed the knotting muscles, and got him to drink. He slept late next morning, face haggard and dark with whiskers that made his cheeks seem even more hollowed. But the dreadful vomiting and the worst cramping seemed to be over.

Billy brought more berries, and today Talt could relish their tart sweetness whole. Mary Ann enriched the broth with bits of meat and bread. Most of that day, Talt slept, but once when she was slipping berries into his mouth, his eyes looked full at her, no longer glazed.

"You're a stubborn woman," he mumbled.

"I pay my debts."

His eyebrows lifted but he was too weak to argue and lapsed back into a drowse.

He improved steadily after that. Within a week, he said he could travel though he wasn't yet up to a full day. They burned his bedding and clothes and what Mary Ann had worn while nursing him. Then, before going to Billy, they both scrubbed themselves thoroughly in water from the spring, using strong lye soap, and washing their hair as well.

"Want me to wash your back for you?" Talt called softly through the willows.

Mary Ann blushed in spite of the chuckle in his voice, but she was glad he felt good enough to be a little pesky. "I washed yours often enough," she retorted.

"But I couldn't enjoy it, ma'am. Why don't you be real sweet and do it again?"

"You — you *man!*"

He seemed to be coming through the bushes. She made for the wagon as fast as her condition permitted and stood behind it while she dried off and got into clean clothing. Then she rummaged his extra garments out of the wagon and deposited them on the willows.

"Now you can get decent," she called primly, and fled as she saw him approaching shamelessly through the wispy trees. His laughter followed her. Drat the man! Weak with cholera, he'd been safe, but now it seemed she was going to have to fight him off! It was purely ridiculous when she was big as a barn.

The baby kicked within her and she put her hands over it as if to soothe it. Anyhow, it seemed she'd escaped cholera and she didn't see any way Billy could have caught it. But her labor was before her. If only there as a woman around since there couldn't be a doctor! She'd have to deliver with no one to help but a man who was, after all, a stranger.

They got stuck in Big Sandy. In spite of Talt's warnings, Mary Ann helped push, and an hour after they were back on the road, her pains began. She hoped the birthing would hold off until they stopped for the day. Talt's sickness had made them late and every day counted now in getting through the mountains before the snows. But the muted pangs grew harsher, closer together, and within another hour, Mary Ann was chewing her lips and perspiring cold sweat.

"What's the matter?" Talt shot a sidelong glance at her involuntary moan, gasped, and stopped the oxen. "The baby?"

She nodded, panted and squeezed her eyes shut as a great hand seemed to grip the inside of her belly and wrench it around. Billy squealed and grabbed her.

"Listen, son," said Talt, lifting him down. "Your mama's going to be fine but we need some hot water. How's about you bringing in lots of sagebrush and any dried chips you can find? And then you go play over in that draw till I call you to see your new brother or sister."

"Billy want brother."

"I'll see what I can do," Talt promised. "But sometimes the good Lord decides we need a woman so there'll always be plenty of mamas. Scoot, now!"

Mary Ann wanted to lie down but Talt wouldn't let her. "You'll have that baby a lot faster if you keep walking around."

"How do you know?"

"That's how Indian women do."

"Damn you, I'm not an Indian!"

"Well, you're going to have this baby like you were, lady, because that's the only way I know how to help — and from what I've seen, it sure works better than the white way."

He made her walk while he built a fire and put water to boil. Then he drove two poles into the ground and tied a braided rawhide rope between them. "Kneel in the middle," he said, "and hang onto the rope. It'll help you push."

She was still skewered by dizzying surges of black-red pain but gradually she found that being able to push down and encourage the pains made her feel better than if she'd been lying prone amid a flock of anxious women, passively enduring her labor rather than urging it on.

Talt brought her hot tea frequently. When she was so exhausted that her sweating hands slipped from the rope, he gripped her wrists and supported her in a squat. She screamed, strangled the sound in her throat so Billy wouldn't be scared. She was splitting, being torn apart — She faded into soft darkness, conscious only of Talt's hands.

When she roused, she felt something at her breast. Wonderingly, she touched her stomach, found it flat. Bending her neck, she gazed down at a silk black head, a funny little squished-up visage.

"That's brother?" Billy was saying in disgust. "Mama, he's too little!"

"He'll grow," Talt promised.

"Bear won't like him much."

"He will later. Now why don't you and bear go find some berries?"

Billy loped off. Mary Ann sighed, blissful at being free from pain and the cumbering bigness, and drifted off to sleep.

She lay on the mattress next day as they traveled on. The baby was fretful and didn't suck much. By the fourth day, when real milk should have replaced the clear fluid, she realized that her right breast was hard and swollen, increasingly painful. By night, the other breast was caked, too, and she had to confess her condition to Talt before the baby starved.

"Fool woman!" he growled, something like panic leaping into his eyes. "Why didn't you tell me this morning?"

He made hot compresses applied with mullein leaves, made her drink herbal teas and eat, and insisted that she let the infant suck, agonizing as it was. "He won't get any milk to speak of but it'll help break up that abscess."

"He needs milk!"

"He'll get it from you when you get straightened out. Till then, don't you worry. I'll make him such a nice broth that he may not want milk, ever."

That didn't happen, but the baby stayed alive on broth till Talt's stern regime righted the misery in Mary Ann's breasts. As she cradled the child and relaxed to the sweetly painful tugging of his little jaws, it seemed natural enough for Talt to stand there watching them.

"Strong little guy. What you going to call him?"

Vaguely, she had planned to name a boy after Jed, but it seemed now that she had known the father of this child countless years ago, almost in another life. She had married Jed in the excitement of her first courtship and to escape her aunt, but had she ever loved him? He had been a habit. She was too honest to let the tragedy of his death blind her.

Looking up at Talt, she said quietly, "If — if you don't mind, I'd like to name him for you. He wouldn't be alive if you hadn't taken care of us."

"You owe it to me?"

She started to lash out at him. Then she saw a sort of hunger deep in his eyes, a look curiously like Billy's when he occasionally worried that the baby might supplant him. "I'm mighty tired of all these debts," she said levelly. "Maybe I pulled you through the cholera. You for sure saved my baby. Let's call it even."

He took a deep breath. The fire in his eyes sent a sweetness rushing through her, a sunny warmth she had never felt before. "Does that mean — well, that we're starting fresh?"

"Fresh as we can after all we've been through."

"Guess we acted like we were married — except for the best parts. Mary Ann, you reckon it's about time you got a daddy for these boys?"

She nodded. He leaned over and kissed her above the nursing baby, his kiss a promise of all they were going to share. Billy stepped out of the shadows and climbed into Talt's lap. "Bear wants someone to hold him, too!"

"Bear's come to the right place," Talt said. "And so have I."

Above the yellow head, his eyes met Mary Ann's.

Carla Kelly

~~~~~~

Carla Kelly (1947-) is a two-time winner of the Spur Award from Western Writers of America for best short story. A versatile author, she has also written one historical novel and six Regency romances. A public relations specialist, she holds a Master of Arts degree in American history.

"In 1974-75 I worked for the National Park Service at Fort Laramie National Historic Site as a seasonal ranger/historian. One of my duties was Living History. On certain days I dressed up as an officer's wife and "lived" in a tent to illustrate the misfortune of a family being bumped out of quarters by a ranking officer. This story is a result of that experience. One sidelight: As I would tell my "miseries" to the tourists, wives of present-day military men and railroad personnel often had similar contemporary experiences for me. This only confirmed something I, as a writer, had suspected all along: people don't change much; neither do situations; or, for that matter, responses."

— *Carla Kelly*

Such Brave Men
Roundup, 1984

"A little paint will make all the difference," said Hart Sanders as he and his wife surveyed the scabby walls in Quarters B.

Emma stood on tiptoe to whisper in her husband's ear. She didn't want to offend the quartermaster sergeant, who was leaning against the door and listening. "Hart, what are these walls made of?"

"Adobe," he whispered back.

"Oh."

Perhaps she could find out what adobe was later.

Hart turned to the sergeant lounging in the doorway. The man straightened up when the lieutenant spoke to him.

"Sergeant, have some men bring our household effects here. And we'll need a bed and table and chairs from supply."

"Yes, sir."

Emma took off her bonnet and watched the sergeant heading back to the quartermaster storehouse, then she turned and looked at her first army home again. Two rooms and a lean-to kitchen, the allotment of a second lieutenant.

Hart was watching her. He wanted to smile, but wasn't sure how she would take that.

"Not exactly Sandusky, is it?" he ventured.

She grinned at him and snapped his suspenders. "It's not even Omaha, Hart, and you know it!"

But she had been prepared for this, she thought to herself later as she was blacking the cookstove in the lean-to. Hart had warned her about life at Fort Laramie, Dakota Territory. He had told her about the wind and the heat and the cold and the bugs and the dirt, but sitting in the parlor of her father's house in Sandusky, she hadn't dreamed anything quite like this.

As she was tacking down an army blanket for the front room carpet, she noticed the ceiling was shedding. Every time she hammered in a tack, white flakes drifted down to the floor and settled on her hair, the folding rocking chair, and the whatnot shelf she had carried on her lap from Cheyenne Depot to Fort Laramie. She swept out the flakes after the blanket was secure, and reminded herself to step lightly in the front room.

Dinner was brought in by some of the other officers' wives, and they dined on sowbelly, hash browns and eggless custard. The sowbelly looked definitely lowbrow congealing on her Lowestoft bridal china, and she wished she had thought to bring along tin plates like Hart had suggested.

She was putting the last knickknack on the whatnot when Hart got into bed in the next room. The crackling and rustling startled her and she nearly dropped the figurine in her hand. She ran to the door "Hart? Are you all right?" she asked. He had blown out the candle, and the bedroom was dark.

"Well sure, Emma. What's the matter?"

"That awful noise!"

She heard the rustling again as he sat up in bed.

"Emma, haven't you ever slept on a straw-tick mattress?"

She shook her head. "Does it ever quiet down?"

"After you sleep on it awhile," he assured her, and the noise started up again as he lay down and rolled over.

She had finished putting the little house in order next morning when Hart came bursting into the front room. He waved a piece of paper in front of her nose.

"Guess what?" he shouted, "D Company is going on detached duty to Fetterman! We leave tomorrow!"

"Do I get to come?" she asked.

"Oh no. We'll be gone a couple months. Isn't it exciting? My first campaign!"

Well, it probably was exciting, she thought after he had left, but that meant she would have to face the house alone. The prospect gleamed less brightly than it had the night before.

Company D left the fort next morning after Guard Mount. She was just fluffing up the pillows on their bed when someone knocked at the front door.

It was the adjutant. He took off his hat and stepped into the front room, looking for all the world like a man with bad news. She wondered what could possibly be worse than seeing your husband of one month ride out toward Fetterman (wherever that was), and having to figure out how to turn that scabrous adobe box into a home.

"I hate to have to tell you this, Mrs. Sanders," he said at last.

"Tell me what?"

"You've been ranked."

Emma shook her head. Whatever was he talking about? Ranked?

"I don't understand, Lieutenant."

He took a step toward her, but he was careful to stay near the door. "Well, you know, ma'am, ranked. Bumped. Bricks falling?"

She stared at him, and wondered why he couldn't make sense. Didn't they teach them English at the Point?

"I'm afraid it's still a mystery to me, Lieutenant."

He rubbed his hand over the balding spot on the back of his head and shifted from one foot to the other.

"You'll have to move, ma'am."

"But I just did," she protested, at the same time surprised at herself for springing to the defense of such a defenseless house.

"I mean again," persisted the lieutenant. "Another lieutenant just reported in with his wife, and he outranks your husband. Yours is the only quarters available, so you'll have to leave."

It took a minute to sink in.

"But who? I can't . . ."

She was interrupted by the sound of boots on the front porch. The man who stepped inside was familiar to her, but she couldn't quite place him until he greeted her. Then she knew she would never forget that squeaky voice. He was Hart's old roommate from the Academy. She remembered that Hart had told her how the man spent all his time studying, and never was any fun at all.

"Are *you* taking my house?" she accused the lieutenant.

"I'm sorry, Mrs. Sanders," he said, and he didn't sound sorry at all.

"But . . . but . . . didn't you just graduate with my husband two months ago? How can you outrank him?" she asked, wanting to throw both officers out of her house.

He smiled again, and she resisted the urge to scrape her fingernails along his face. Instead, she stamped her foot and white flakes from the ceiling floated down.

"Yes, ma'am, we graduated together, but Hart was forty-sixth in class standing. I was fifteenth. So I still outrank him."

As she slammed the pots and pans into a box and yanked the sheets off the bed, she wished for the first time that Hart had been a little more diligent in his studies.

A corporal and two privates moved her into quarters that looked suspiciously like a chicken coop. She sniffed the air in the little one room shack and almost asked the corporal if the former tenants she ranked out had clucked and laid eggs. But he didn't speak much English, and she didn't feel like wasting her sarcasm.

Emma swept out the room with a vigor that made her cough, and by nightfall when she crawled into the rustling bed, she speculated on the cost of rail fare from Cheyenne to Sandusky.

The situation looked better by morning. The room was small, to be sure, but she was the only one using it, and if she cut up a sheet, curtains would make all the difference. She hung up the Currier and Ives lithograph of sugaring off in Vermont, and was ripping up the sheet when someone knocked at the door.

It was the adjutant again. He had to duck to get into the room, and when he straightened up, his head just brushed the ceiling.

"Mrs. Sanders," he began, and it was an effort. "I hope you'll understand what I have to tell you."

Emma sensed what was coming, but she didn't want to make it easy on him.

"What?" she asked, sitting herself in the rocking chair and folding her hands in her lap. As she waited for him to speak, she remembered a poem she had read in school called "Horatio at the Bridge."

"You've been ranked out again."

She was silent, looking at him for several moments. She noticed the drops of perspiration gathering on his forehead, and that his Adam's apple bobbed up and down when he swallowed.

"And where do I go from here?" she asked at last.

He shuffled his feet and rubbed the back of his head again, gestures she was beginning to recognize.

"All we have is a tent, ma'am."

"A tent," she repeated.

"Yes, ma'am."

At least I didn't get attached to my chicken coop, she thought as she rolled up her bedding. She felt a certain satisfaction in the knowledge that Hart's roommate had been bumped down to her coop by whoever it was that outranked him. "Serves him right," she said out loud as she carried out the whatnot and closed the door.

The same corporal and privates set up the tent at the corner of Officers Row. It wasn't even a lieutenant's tent. Because of the increased activity in the field this summer, only a sergeant's tent could be found. The bedstead wouldn't fit in, so the corporal dumped the bed sack on the grass and put the frame back in the wagon. She started to protest when he drove away, but remembering his shortage of useful English, she saved her breath. He was back soon with a cot.

She had crammed in her trunks, spread the army blanket on the grass and was setting up the rocking chair when someone rapped on the tent pole.

She knew it would be the adjutant even before she turned around. Emma pulled back the tent flap and stepped outside.

"You can't have it, Lieutenant," she stated.

He shook his head. "Oh no, ma'am, I wasn't going to bump you again." He held out a large square of green fabric. She took it.

"What's this for?" she asked.

"Ma'am, I used to serve in Arizona Territory, and most folks down there line tent ceilings with green. Easier on the eyes."

He smiled at her then, and Emma began to see that the lot of an adjutant was not to be envied. She smiled back.

"Thank you, Lieutenant. I appreciate it."

He helped her fasten up the green baize, and it did make a difference inside the tent. Before he left, he pulled her cot away from the tent wall.

"So the tent won't leak when it rains," he explained, and then laughed. "But it never rains here anyway."

Since she couldn't cook in the tent, she messed with the officers in Old Bedlam that night. There were only three. The adjutant was a bachelor, Captain Endicott was an Orphan and had left his family back in the States, and the other lieutenant was casually at post on his way from Fort Robinson to Fort D. A. Russell.

The salt pork looked more at home on a tin plate, and she discovered that plum duff was edible. The coffee burned its way down, but she knew she could get used to it.

She excused herself, ran back to her tent, and returned with the tin of peaches she had bought at the post trader's store for the extortionate sum of two dollars and twenty-five cents. The adjutant pried open the lid, and the four of them speared slices out of the can and laughed and talked until Tattoo.

Captain Endicott walked her back to her tent before Last Call. He shook his head when he saw the tent.

"Women ought to stay in the States. Good schools there, doctors, sociability. Much better," he commented.

"But don't you miss your family?" she asked.

"Lord, yes," he began, then stopped. "Beg pardon, Mrs. Sanders."

He said good-night to her, and walked off alone to his room in Old Bedlam.

Emma undressed, did up her hair, and got into bed. She lay still, listening to the bugler blow Extinguish Lights. She heard horses snuffling in the officers' stables behind Old Bedlam. When the coyotes started tuning up on the slopes rimming the fort, she pulled the blanket over her head and closed her eyes.

She knew she was not alone when she woke up before Reveille the next morning. She sat up on the cot and gasped.

A snake was curled at the foot of her blanket. She pulled her feet up until she was sitting in a ball on her pillow. She was afraid to scream because she didn't know what the snake would do, and besides, she didn't want the sergeant at arms to rush in and catch her with her hair done up rags.

As she watched and held her breath, the snake unwound itself and moved off the cot. She couldn't see any rattles on its tail, and she slowly let out her breath. The snake undulated across the grass and she stared at it, fascinated. She hadn't known a reptile could be so graceful. "How do they do that?" she asked herself, as the snake slithered into the grass at the edge of the tent. "I must remember to ask Hart."

She pulled on her wrapper and poked her head out of the tent. The sun was just coming up, and the buildings were tinted with the most delicious shade of pink. She marveled that she could ever have thought the place ugly.

Her first letter from Hart was handed to her three days later at Mail Call. She ripped open the envelope and drew out a long, narrow sheet. She read as she walked along the edge of the parade ground.

> Dearest Emma,
>
> Pardon this stationery, but I forgot to take any along and besides, this works better for letters than in the outhouse. Good news. We're going to be garrisoned here permanently, so you'll be moving quite soon, perhaps within the next few days.
>
> Bad news. Brace yourself. There aren't any quarters available, so we'll have to make do in a tent.

Emma stood still and laughed out loud. A soldier with a large P painted on the back of his shirt stopped spearing trash and looked at her, but she didn't notice. She read on.

> It won't be that bad. The CO swears there will be quarters ready by winter. Am looking forward to seeing you soon. I can't express how much I miss you.
>
> Love,
> Hart

She was almost back to her tent when the adjutant caught up with her.

"Mrs. Sanders," he began. His Adam's apple bobbed, and he started to rub his head.

"It's all right, Lieutenant," she broke in, "I've already heard. When am I leaving?"

"In the morning."

"I'll be ready."

As she was repacking her trunks that evening, she remembered something her mother had said to her when she left on the train to join Hart in Cheyenne. Mother had dabbed at her eyes and said over and over, "Such brave men, Emma, such brave men!"

Emma smiled to herself.

Judy Alter

~~~~~~~~~~~~~~~~~~~~~~~~~~~~~

*B*est known as a juvenile novelist, Judy Alter (1938-)
focuses her fiction on the experiences of women in the
American West. Her juvenile novel, Luke and the Van
Zandt County War, was named the Best Juvenile of 1984
by the Texas Institute of Letters and her adult novel,
Mattie, won a Spur Award from Western Writers of America,
Inc., as the best western novel of 1987. Her most recent
novel is Libbie, a fictional life of Elizabeth Bacon Custer,
published by Bantam in 1994. "Fool Girl" won a Western
Heritage (Wrangler) Award from the National Cowboy
Hall of Fame.

"In all my fiction I try to explore what it was like to
be a woman in the American West, mostly of a century
ago. I find it works best for me to do that in the first
person, so that I almost become the central figure as well
as the storyteller. "Fool Girl" was inspired by a brief
account in a memoir of a young boy being sent after
runaway workhorses and going too far. Naturally, I changed
the protagonist to female and the story went from there."
— Judy Alter

Fool Girl
This Place of Memory, 1992

"Josie!" Pa's voice boomed out so loud and sudden that
I almost dropped my broom.
"Yes, Pa?" I was in no hurry about sticking my head out the
door of our dogtrot cabin. Pa always wanted something — a horse's

hoof held while he repaired a shoe, someone to carry the other end of a log, someone to curry his two workhorses. Pa should have had ten sons, but he only had me, a fourteen-year-old daughter. Still, I thought I was about as good at most chores as any boy would have been.

"The workhorses are gone!" he thundered, and it's a wonder every Indian from here to the territory didn't hear him. Pa had set our cabin square in the middle of the North Texas prairie when he first came home from the War between the States. He was determined to farm, but three years running his luck had been bad and there'd been no crops to speak of, nothing but a small garden that was mostly my doing and kept us in table food of a sort. First it was a hard freeze, then the seed was moldy, and then Ma died and he couldn't work for grief. This was the year he was going to have oats and corn, he told me, and this day he had set his mind to plowing.

"The workhorses are gone," he repeated, mad as he could be at everyone — me, the horses, the world in general. "You'll have to go get 'em."

"Maybe Indians took 'em," I said. If Indians had them, they'd be beyond finding.

"Ain't no sign of Indians," he growled. "Goddamn horses broke the gate and walked away while we slept." It was almost an accusation, as if we shouldn't have slept. "I said you'll have to go get them."

"Yes, Pa." Pa was in one of his moods, and when he got that way, there wasn't much I could do to change him. Ever since Ma died, he just seemed to get stubborner and stubborner. I wanted to ask why he didn't go after them himself — after all, he couldn't plow until he found them — but experience had taught me better than that.

"Don't come home until you've found them," he said.

"What if . . . what if I can't find them?" I blurted out as a vision rose in my mind of endless days on the prairie looking for two horses too dumb to come home.

"You'll find them," he said grimly and stalked away. "Better take the six-shooter." He threw the words over his shoulder.

Figuring I might be gone long enough to get hungry, I gathered up some corn dodgers from breakfast in a clean handkerchief, one of Ma's that I treasured. Now it would have grease all over it. And I got the six-shooter off the shelf where Pa kept it. Heaven knows what he thought I'd shoot from horseback with that unwieldy weapon. By the time I got it loaded, any self-respecting Indian would have scalped me and a jackrabbit and would be clear to Oklahoma. But Pa had taught me well, and I knew better than to ride with a loaded six-shooter.

As I got my things together, I thought bitterly that if Ma hadn't died, I wouldn't be goin' out on the prairie. Ma always wanted me to be a lady, and she was the one person Pa never stood up to. When I was younger and he wanted me to ride with him, Ma would say, "Hush, Luther, she's practicing her stitches. A lady must sew neat and fine." I was almost angry at Ma for dying and leaving me.

Outside, I whistled for Maisiebelle, the mustang Pa had given me three years before. He'd been disgusted when I named her, said she needed a short name 'cause she was a short horse. Pa never did like her since she tried to bite him 'fore he even got her home to me. But Maisiebelle and I understood and trusted each other. She was about my only friend, living way out along like we did, and I told her all my hopes and dreams, for all the good it did me.

Pa had waved his arm east, and east was where I headed, pointing Maisiebelle across the vast Texas prairie. We loped along, my eyes scanning the horizon. All I saw was the great empty land covered with rolling prairie grasses and dotted with an occasional clump of mesquite or blackjack oak, treacherous outcroppings of rock, and straggly little creeks, seldom enough for fishing, and sometimes in the hot summer nothing but baked dry earth.

Expecting the horses to materialize out of the land at any moment, I rode straight on, moving at a fairly good clip. In spite of her name, Maisiebelle was all mustang and could go forever. Not, I thought, like those two heavy-footed animals that Pa linked to the plow. At first, the sun was warm and good, and I forgot my anger in the freedom of being out on the prairie, smelling all its good smells, and being away from Pa and his mood.

"Maisiebelle," I said, "we ain't always goin' to live like this. Someday, I'm gonna have me a fine house, a big house with two stories and servants to run up and down the stairs, and I'll wear beautiful gowns, and you'll eat sweet clover all day long." The little mustang nickered, and I knew she understood my dream. Content with the perfect day and my perfect dream, I almost forgot how mad I was at Pa.

But the sun climbed straight overhead, and it turned from warm and good to downright hot. I wiped my sleeve across my face and used the old battered hat I wore to fan myself. Shielding my eyes with my hand, I searched the empty land once again. I could see forever and there were no horses. No men nor houses either. Just emptiness.

What kind of a father, I thought, would send a girl out into such emptiness? He didn't care what happened to me, I told myself. Maybe he hoped I would get lost or Indians would get me — one less thing for him to worry about. But then I straightened — Pa sent me after the horses 'cause he had confidence in me. He just didn't recognize that I was a girl, with a girl's dreams.

When I judged the sun was direct overhead and it must be midday, I nooned, sitting quietly in the shade under Maisiebelle, for there were no trees nearby at that point, not even a scrub oak. It was what cowboys call a dry camp, with no water, and the corn dodgers, now hard and cold, stuck in my throat with nothing to wash them down. I threw the last one on the ground, and even Maisiebelle sniffed disdainfully at it and turned away. I wondered if Pa had warmed the dodgers on the stove and had them with cool buttermilk that had been stored in the crock. For a moment, I wished fiercely that I was back in the dogtrot, Pa's temper and all. But then I moved on.

Even that poor meal made me sleepy, hot as the sun was, and as Maisiebelle, now moving a little more slowly, headed even further east, I nodded in the saddle, overcome by weariness. Two or three times I startled myself awake and looked frantically about the prairie, as though by dozing for seconds I had missed those damn horses. But there was nothing — just me and Maisiebelle and emptiness.

I must have slept soundly, however briefly, with the saddle providing a strangely rocking kind of cradle, for this time when I came awake, I did so with great clearness of mind, the fuzzy sleepiness gone. And instantly I knew that I was alone and, though I would not have told Pa, afraid.

"Pa wouldn't have sent you if there was any danger," I lectured myself, unconsciously sitting taller in the saddle. But there was another part of me that didn't believe Pa had even thought about whether or not it was safe.

Loneliness and fright are like a fog. They settle all around you, resting on your shoulders like an invisible cloak, and no matter how you think about it logically, you cannot shake that fog. I lectured myself again and again, and I even shook my shoulders a time or two, as though to chase away that feeling. But I'd find myself checking over my shoulder more and more often as the afternoon wore on.

Ahead of me I could see the Crosstimbers, that irregular, narrow band of trees that stretched up across North Texas to the Red River and into Oklahoma. The Comanches used the timbers as a hiding place, I knew, especially in times of the full moon when they seemed more prone to raid. Fear clutched at me as I remembered that it was now a full moon, and just two days ago we'd heard of neighbors who'd lost their horses to Comanches. They were lucky, however, for they kept their scalps.

I looked around almost frantically, determined that I'd find those horses before I reached the timbers. I was convinced that once out of the open, into the wood, I'd not only lose the horses, I'd lose myself and likely, I thought, my scalp.

The sun was well on its way down when I rode within a mile of the first trees, my desperation increasing. There seemed no way I could turn and make it home before the middle of the night. I'd lose my way on the prairie a thousand times. And besides, hadn't Pa said not to come home without the horses? Yet to enter the timbers went beyond anything I was capable of in my wildest imagination. I wished desperately for Pa, unpredictable as he was.

I'd seen not so much as a pile of dung to indicate that the work horses had come this way. Perhaps Pa had been wrong, and they'd gone west and I'd been on a fool's errand all day. Half expecting the horses to be plodding along behind, I turned in the saddle, sort of standing in the stirrups as though that would give me a better view. I did not see two heavy workhorses, but I saw a lone rider coming at a good clip.

He was not Comanche, that much I could tell even from a distance by the way he sat a saddle and the broad hat on his head.

I could, of course, have headed quickly into the timbers, for I had plenty of time to beat him and lose myself among the trees. I stopped Maisiebelle and simply sat, waiting for the rider to approach.

Within minutes, I saw that it was Pa. Had he come to harangue me for my failure to find the horses? Would he holler that I was sitting still when I should be pushing on? Common sense told me I should make some last-minute effort to find those horses, dig them out of a hole in the ground if I could, but I sat, frozen, waiting for fate to come to me. Pa reined his horse to a stop in front of me, raising his hand in the traditional sign of friendship. Then he sat and stared at me, his expression unreadable.

"You've come a good twenty miles," he said, "Why did you come so far?"

Defiantly, I asked, "Why did you tell me not to come home until I found the horses?"

"Fool girl," he muttered, "don't know no better than to ride halfway to hell and gone."

Years later I figured out that was the closest he could come to showing his concern. Then, though, I took it for condemnation and burned under the phrase, "Fool girl."

We rode home together in silence, though Pa did tell me that the workhorses had come home of their own accord, shortly after midday. He never did tell me, though, and it was years before I figured out for myself that two slow workhorses could never have gone as far as my mustang and I had that day.

Josie Parker finished her story and sat silently on a bale of hay, her elbows resting on her knees as she stared at the horizon and a prairie now dotted with fences and building. She was a tall, lean woman, hardened by years of hard work. Today was a working day like any other, and she wore a pair of faded jeans, scuffed boots, a kerchief around her neck and a battered Stetson.

The young man had come from a city newspaper to interview her. His assignment was to find out how she felt about having spent her life — eighty long years — running a ranch with the help of no man, save her father who had died years before and now the few she hired.

"Why . . . ?" He stumbled over the question. "Why did you want to be a rancher, Miss Parker? Most women of your generation married . . . or taught school . . . or . . ." He was getting himself in trouble and he knew it. "Why did you choose to run your father's ranch?"

She stared at him as though he were a fool. Then she spoke very slowly, "When I was young, I lost two workhorses on the prairie."

Marcia Muller

M arcia Muller (1944-) is a native of Detroit, Michigan, who now lives in northern California. She is
the author of twenty mystery novels, including the Sharon
McCone series, and of numerous short stories, articles, and
reviews. With Bill Pronzini, she has coedited ten anthologies and a guide to mystery and detective fiction. Her tenth
McCone novel, The Shape of Dread, received the 1989
American Mystery Award, and her 1989 short story, "The
Time of Wolves," was a Spur Award finalist and the basis
for the 1991 television film, "Into the Badlands." Her
1991 short story, "Final Resting Place," received the Private
Eye Writers of America Shamus Award. In 1994 her most
recent book is Wolf in the Shadows, a Sharon McCone
mystery.

"In my western fiction, I am attempting to portray the
women of the Old West as they actually were: equal partners with their men in taming an uncharted and dangerous
territory. Often left to face life's adversities on their own,
they responded with courage, strength, and humor; and, like
the heroine of this story, they overcame physical and societal
disadvantages by finding clever solutions to their problems."
— Marcia Muller

Sweet Cactus Wine

The Arbor House Treasury of Great Western Stories, 1982

The rain stopped as suddenly as it had begun, the way it always does in the Arizona desert. The torrent had burst from a near-cloudless sky, and now it was clear once more, the land nourished. I stood in the doorway of my house, watching the sun touch the stone wall, the old buckboard and the twisted arms of the giant saguaro cacti.

The suddenness of these downpours fascinated me, even though I'd lived in the desert for close to forty years, since the day I'd come here as Joe's bride in 1866. They'd been good years, not exactly bountiful, but we'd lived here in quiet comfort. Joe had the instinct that helped bring him the crops — melons, corn, beans — from the parched soil, an instinct he shared with the Papago Indians who were our neighbors. I didn't possess the knack, so now that he was gone I didn't farm. I did share one gift with the Papagos, however — the ability to make sweet cactus wine from the fruit of the saguaro. That wine was my livelihood now — as well as, I must admit, a source of Saturday-night pleasure — and the giant cacti scattered around the ranch were my fortune.

I went inside to the big rough-hewn table where I'd been shelling peas when the downpour started. The bowl sat there half full, and I eyed the peas with distaste. Funny what age will do to you. For years I'd had an overly hearty appetite. Joe used to say, "Don't worry, Katy. I like big women." Lucky for him he did, because I'd carried around enough lard for two such admirers, and I didn't believe in divorce anyway. Joe'd be surprised if he could see me now, though. I was tall, yes, still tall. But thin. I'd guess you'd call it gaunt. Food didn't interest me anymore.

I sat down and finished shelling the peas anyway. It was market day in Arroyo, and Hank Gardner, my neighbor five miles down the road, had taken to stopping in for supper on his way home from town. Hank was widowed too. Maybe it was his way of courting. I didn't know and didn't care. One man had been enough trouble for me and, anyway, I intended to live out my days on these parched but familiar acres.

Sure enough, right about suppertime Hank rode up on his old bay. He was a lean man, browned and weathered by the sun like folks get in these parts, and he rode stiffly. I watched him dismount, then went and got the whiskey bottle and poured him a tumblerful. If I knew Hank, he'd had a few drinks in town and would be wanting another. And a glassful sure wouldn't be enough for old Hogsbreath Hank, as he was sometimes called.

He came in and sat at the table like he always did. I stirred the iron pot on the stove and sat down too. Hank was a man of few words, like my Joe had been. I'd heard tales that his drinking and temper had pushed his wife into an early grave. Sara Gardner had died of pneumonia, though, and no man's temper ever gave that to you.

Tonight Hank seemed different, jumpy. He drummed his fingers on the table and drank his whiskey.

To put him at his ease, I said, "How're things in town?"

"What?"

"Town. How was it?"

"Same as ever."

"You sure?"

"Yeah, I'm sure. Why do you ask?" But he looked kind of furtive.

"No reason," I said. "Nothing changes out here. I don't know why I asked." Then I went to dish up the stew. I set it and some corn bread on the table, poured more whiskey for Hank and a little cactus wine for me. Hank ate steadily and silently. I sort of picked at my food.

After supper I washed up the dishes and joined Hank on the front porch. He still seemed jumpy but this time I didn't try to find out why. I just sat there beside him, watching the sun spread its redness over the mountains in the distance. When Hank spoke, I'd almost forgotten he was there.

"Kathryn" — he never called me Katy; only Joe used that name — "Kathryn, I've been thinking. It's time the two of us got married."

So that was why he had the jitters. I turned to stare. "What put an idea like that in your head?"

He frowned. "It's natural."

"Natural?"

"Kathryn, we're both alone. It's foolish you living here and me living over there when our ranches sit right next to each other. Since Joe went, you haven't farmed the place. We could live at my house, let this one go, and I'd farm the land for you."

Did he want me or the ranch? I know passion is supposed to die when you're in your sixties, and as far as Hank was concerned mine had, but for form's sake he could at least pretend to some.

"Hank," I said firmly, "I've got no intention of marrying again — or of farming this place."

"I said I'd farm it for you."

"If I wanted it farmed, I could hire someone to do it. I wouldn't need to acquire another husband."

"We'd be company for one another."

"We're company now."

"What're you going to do — sit here the rest of your days scratching out a living with your cactus wine?"

"That's exactly what I plan to do."

"Kathryn . . ."

"No."

"But . . ."

"No. That's all."

Hank's jaw tightened and his eyes narrowed. I was afraid for a minute that I was going to be treated to a display of Hank's legendary temper, but soon he looked as placid as ever.

He stood, patting my shoulder.

"You think about it, " he said. "I'll be back tomorrow and I want a yes answer."

I'd think about it, all right. As a matter of fact, as he rode off on the bay I was thinking it was the strangest marriage proposal I'd ever heard of. And there was no way old Hogsbreath was getting any yesses from me.

He rode up again the next evening. I was out gathering cactus fruit. In the springtime, when the desert nights are still cool, the tips of the saguaro branches are covered with waxy white flowers. They're prettiest in the hours around dawn, and by the time the sun hits its peak, they close. When they die, the purple fruit begins to grow, and now, by mid-summer, it was splitting open to show its bright red pulp. That pulp was what I turned into wine.

I stood by my pride and joy — a fifty-foot giant that was probably two hundred years old — and watched Hank come toward me. From his easy gait, I knew he was sure I'd changed my mind about his proposal. Probably figured he was irresistible, the old goat. He had a surprise coming.

"Well, Kathryn," he said, stopping and folding his arms across his chest, "I'm here for my answer."

"It's the same as it was last night. No. I don't intend to marry again."

"You're a foolish woman, Kathryn."

"That may be. But at least I'm foolish in my own way."

"What does that mean?"

"If I'm making a mistake, it'll be one I decide on, not on one you decide for me."

The planes of his face hardened, and the wrinkles around his eyes deepened. "We'll see about that." He turned and strode toward the bay.

I was surprised he had backed down so easy, but relieved. At least he was going.

Hank didn't get on the horse, however. He fumbled at his saddle scabbard and drew his shotgun. I set down the basket of cactus fruit. Surely he didn't intend to shoot me!

He turned, shotgun in one hand.

"Don't be a fool, Hank Gardner."

He marched toward me. I got ready to run, but he kept going, past me. I whirled, watching. Hank went up to a nearby saguaro, a twenty-five footer. He looked at it, turned and walked exactly ten paces. Then he turned again, brought up the shotgun, sighted on the cactus, and began to fire. He fired at its base over and over.

I put my hand to my mouth, shutting off a scream.

Hank fired again, and the cactus toppled.

It didn't fall like a man would if he were shot. It just leaned backwards. Then it gave a sort of sigh and leaned farther and farther. As it leaned it picked up momentum, and when it hit the ground there was an awful thud.

Hank gave the cactus a satisfied nod and marched back toward his horse.

I found my voice. "Hey, you! Just what do you think you're doing?"

Hank got on the bay. "Cactuses are like people, Kathryn. They can't do anything for you once they're dead. Think about it."

"You bet I'll think about it! That cactus was valuable to me. You're going to pay!"

"What happens when there're no cactuses left?"

"What? What?"

"How're you going to scratch out a living on this miserable ranch if someone shoots all your cactuses?"

"You wouldn't dare!"

He smirked at me. "You know, there's one way cactuses *aren't* like people. Nobody ever hung a man for shooting one."

Then he rode off.

I stood there speechless. Did the bastard plan to shoot up my cacti until I agreed to marry him?

I went over to the saguaro. It lay on its back, oozing water. I nudged it gently with my foot. There were a few round holes in it — entrances to the caves where the Gila woodpeckers lived. From the silence, I guessed the birds hadn't been inside when the cactus toppled. They'd be mighty surprised when they came back and found their home on the ground.

The woodpeckers were the least of my problems, however. They'd just take up residence in one of the other giants. Trouble was, what if Hank carried out his veiled threat? Then the woodpeckers would run out of nesting places — and I'd run out of fruit to make my wine from.

I went back to the granddaddy of my cacti and picked up the basket. On the porch I set it down and myself in my rocking chair to think. What was I going to do?

I could go to the sheriff in Arroyo, but the idea didn't please me. For one thing, like Hank said, there was no law against shooting a cactus. And for another, it was embarrassing to be in this kind of predicament at my age. I could see all the locals lined up at the bar of the saloon, laughing at me. No, I didn't want to go to Sheriff Daly if I could help it.

So what else? I could shoot Hank, I supposed, but that was even less appealing. Not that he didn't deserve shooting, but they could hang you for murdering a man, unlike a cactus. And then, while I had a couple of Joe's old rifles, I'd never been comfortable with them, never really mastered the art of sighting and pulling the trigger. With my luck, I'd miss Hank and kill off yet another cactus.

I sat on the porch for a long time, puzzling and listening to the night sounds of the desert. Finally I gave up and went to bed, hoping the old fool would come to his senses in the morning.

He didn't, though. Shotgun blasts on the far side of the ranch brought me flying out of the house the next night. By the time I got over there, there was nothing around except a couple of dead cacti. The next night it happened again, and still the next night. The bastard was being cagey, too. I had no way of proving it actually was Hank doing the shooting. Finally I gave up and decided I had no choice but to see Sheriff Daly.

I put on my good dress, fixed my hair and hitched up my horse to the old buckboard. The trip to Arroyo was hot and dusty, and my stomach lurched at every bump in the road. It's no fun knowing you're about to become a laughingstock. Even if the sheriff sympathized with me, you can bet he and the boys would have a good chuckle afterwards.

I drove up Main Street and left the rig at the livery stable. The horse needing shoeing anyway. Then I went down the wooden sidewalk to the sheriff's office. Naturally, it was closed. The sign said he'd be back at two, and it was only noon now. I got out my list of errands and set off for the feed store, glancing over at the saloon on my way.

Hank was coming out of the saloon. I ducked into the shadow of the covered walkway in front of the bank and watched him, hate rising inside me. He stopped on the sidewalk and waited, and a moment later a stranger joined him. The stranger wore a frock coat and a broad-brimmed black hat. He didn't dress like anyone from these parts. Hank and the man walked toward the old adobe hotel and shook hands in front of it. Then Hank ambled over to where the bay was tied, and the stranger went inside.

I stood there, frowning. Normally I wouldn't have been curious about Hank Gardner's private business, but when a man's shooting up your cacti you develop an interest in anything he does. I waited until he had ridden off down the street, then crossed and went into the hotel.

Sonny, the clerk, was a friend from way back. His mother and I had run church bazaars together for many years, back when I still had the energy for that sort of thing. I went up to him and we exchanged pleasantries.

Then I said, "Sonny, I've got a question for you, and I'd just as soon you didn't mention me asking it to anybody."

He nodded.

"A man came in here a few minutes ago. Frock coat, black hat."

"Sure. Mr. Johnson."

"Who is he?"

"You don't know?"

"I don't get into town much these days."

"I guess not. Everybody's talking about him. Mr. Johnson's a land developer. Here from Phoenix."

Land developer. I began to smell a rat. A rat named Hank Gardner.

"What's he doing, buying up the town?"

"Not the town. The countryside. He's making offers on all the ranches." Sonny eyed me thoughtfully. "Maybe you better talk to him. You've got a fair-sized spread there. You could make good money. In fact, I'm surprised he hasn't been out to see you."

"So am I, Sonny. So am I. You see him, you tell him I'd like to talk to him."

"He's in his room now. I could . . ."

"No." I held up my hand. "I've got a lot of errands to do. I'll talk to him later."

But I didn't do any errands. Instead I went home to sit in my rocker and think.

That night I didn't light my kerosene lamp. I kept the house dark and waited at the front door. When the evening shadows had fallen, I heard a rustling sound. A tall figure slipped around the stone wall into the dooryard.

I watched as he approached one of the giant saguaros in the dooryard. He went right up to it, like he had the first one he'd shot, turned and walked exactly ten paces, then blasted away. The cactus toppled, and Hank ran from the yard.

I waited. Let him think I wasn't to home. After about fifteen minutes, I got undressed and went to bed in the dark, but I didn't rest much. My mind was too busy planning what I had to do.

The next morning I hitched up the buckboard and drove over to Hank's ranch. He was around back, mending a harness. He started when he saw me. Probably figured I'd come to shoot him. I got down from the buckboard and walked up to him, a sad, defeated look on my face.

"You're too clever for me, Hank. I should have known it."

"You ready to stop your foolishness and marry me?"

"Hank," I lied, "there's something more to my refusal than just stubbornness."

He frowned. "Oh?"

"Yes. You see, I promised Joe on his deathbed that I'd never marry again. That promise means something to me."

"I don't believe in . . ."

"Hush. I've been thinking, though, about what you said about farming my ranch. I've got an idea. Why *don't* you farm it for me? I'll move in over here, keep house and feed you. We're old enough everyone would know there weren't any shenanigans going on."

Hank looked thoughtful, pleased even. I'd guessed right; it wasn't my fair body he was after.

"That might work. But what if one of us died? Then what?"

"I don't see what you mean."

"Well, if you died, I'd be left with nothing to show for all that farming. And if I died, my son might come back from Tucson and throw you off the place. Where would you be then?"

"I see." I looked undecided, fingering a pleat in my skirt. "That *is* a problem." I paused. "Say, I think there's a way around it."

"Yeah?"

"Yes. We'll make wills. I'll leave you my ranch in mine. You do the same in yours. That way we'd both have something to show for our efforts."

He nodded, looking foxy. "That's a good idea, Kathryn. Very good." I could tell he was pleased I'd thought of it myself.

"And, Hank, I think we should do it right away. Let's go into town this afternoon and have the wills drawn up."

"Fine with me." He looked even more pleased. "Just let me finish with this harness."

The will signing, of course, was a real solemn occasion. I even sniffed a little into my handkerchief before I put my signature to the document. The lawyer, Will Jones, was a little surprised by our bequests, but not much. He knew I was alone in the world, and Hank's son John was known to be more of a ne'er-do-well than his father. Probably Will Jones was glad to see the ranch wouldn't be going to John.

I had Hank leave me off at my place on his way home. I wanted, I said, to cook him one last supper in my old house before moving to his in the morning. I went about my preparations, humming to myself. Would Hank be able to resist rushing back into town to talk to Johnson, the land developer? Or would he wait a decent interval, say a day?

Hank rode up around sundown. I met him on the porch, twisting my handkerchief in my hands.

"Kathryn, what's wrong?"

"Hank, I can't do it."

"Can't do what?"

"I can't leave the place. I can't leave Joe's memory. This whole thing's been a terrible mistake."

He scowled. "Don't be foolish. What's for supper?"

"There isn't any."

"What?"

"How could I fix supper with a terrible mistake like this on my mind?"

"Well, you just get in there and fix it. And stop talking this way."

I shook my head. "No, Hank, I mean it. I can't move to your place. I can't let you farm mine. It wouldn't be right. I want you to go now, and tomorrow I'm going into town to rip up my will."

"You what?" His eyes narrowed.

"You heard me, Hank."

He whirled and went toward his horse. "You'll never learn, will you?"

"What are you going to do?"

"What do you think? Once your damned cactuses are gone, you'll see the light. Once you can't make any more of that wine, you'll be only too glad to pack your bags and come with me."

"Hank, don't you dare!"

"I do dare. There won't be one of them standing."

"Please, Hank! At least leave my granddaddy cactus." I waved at the fifty-foot giant in the outer dooryard. "It's my favorite. It's like a child to me."

Hank grinned evilly. He took the shotgun from the saddle and walked right up to the cactus.

"Say good-bye to your child."

"Hank! Stop!"

He shouldered the shotgun.

"Say good-bye to it, you foolish woman."

"Hank, don't you pull that trigger!"

He pulled it.

Hank blasted at the giant saguaro — one, two, three times. And, like the others, it began to lean.

Unlike the others, though, it didn't lean backwards. It gave a great sigh and leaned and leaned and leaned forwards. And then it toppled. As it toppled, it picked up momentum. And when it fell on Hank Gardner, it made an awful thud.

I stood quietly on the porch. Hank didn't move. Finally I went over to him. Dead. Dead as all the cacti he'd murdered.

I contemplated his broken body a bit before I hitched up the buckboard and went to tell Sheriff Daly about the terrible accident. Sure was funny, I'd say, how that cactus toppled forwards instead of backwards. Almost as if the base had been partly cut through and braced so it would do exactly that.

Of course, the shotgun blasts would have destroyed any traces of the cutting.

~~~~ III ~~~~
Some
Men's
Voices

.

Bret Harte

~~~~~~

*B*ret Harte (1836-1902) is considered the first major American author to write short stories about the American West. Harte's best-known stories are set in the mining camps of California after the Gold Rush of 1848. Stories such as "The Luck of Roaring Camp" or "The Outcasts of Poker Flat" often feature characters now considered woefully stereotypical — the good-hearted soiled dove and the slick gambler — and may rightfully be accused of sentimentality. Although sentimental in its own way, "Miggles" shows us a woman of unusual spirit and goodness who reaches beyond the stereotype. The story is included in The Writings of Bret Harte, published in 1871; it was probably first printed in Overland Monthly, which Harte edited, during the 1860s.

Miggles
Overland Monthly, ca. 1865

We were eight including the driver. We had not spoken during the passage of the last six miles, since the jolting of the heavy vehicle over the roughening road had spoiled the Judge's last poetical quotation. The tall man beside the Judge was asleep, his arm passed through the swaying strap and his head resting upon it, — altogether a limp, helpless looking object, as if he had hanged himself and been cut down too late. The French lady on the back seat was asleep too, yet in a half-conscious propriety of attitude, shown even in the disposition of the hand-kerchief which she held to her forehead and which partially veiled her face. The lady from Virginia City, traveling with her husband, had long since lost all individuality in a wild confusion of ribbons, veils, furs, and shawls. There was no sound but the rattling of wheels and the dash of rain upon the roof. Suddenly the stage stopped and we became dimly aware of voices. The driver was evidently in the midst of an exciting colloquy with some one in the road, — a colloquy of which such fragments as "bridge gone," "twenty feet of water," "can't pass," were occasionally distinguishable above the storm. Then came a lull, and a mysterious voice from the road shouted the parting adjuration —

"Try Miggles's."

We caught a glimpse of our leaders as the vehicle slowly turned, of a horseman vanishing through the rain, and we were evidently on our way to Miggles's.

Who and where was Miggles? The Judge, our authority, did not remember the name, and he knew the country thoroughly. The Washoe traveler thought Miggles must keep a hotel. We only knew that we were stopped by high water in front and rear, and that Miggles was our rock of refuge. A ten minutes' splashing through tangled byroad, scarcely wide enough for the stage, and we drew up before a barred and boarded gate in a wide stone wall or fence about eight feet high. Evidently Miggles's, and evidently Miggles did not keep a hotel.

The driver got down and tried the gate. It was securely locked.

"Miggles! O Miggles!"

No answer.

"Migg-ells! You Miggles!" continued the driver, with rising wrath.

"Migglesy!" joined in the expressman persuasively. "O Miggy! Mig!"

But no reply came from the apparently insensate Miggles. The Judge, who had finally got the window down, put his head out and propounded a series of questions, which if answered categorically would have undoubtedly elucidated the whole mystery, but which the driver evaded by replying that "if we didn't want to sit in the coach all night we had better rise up and sing out for Miggles."

So we rose up and called on Miggles in chorus, then separately. And when we had finished, a Hibernian fellow passenger from the roof called for "Maygells!" whereat we all laughed. While we were all laughing the driver cried, "Shoo!"

We listened. To our infinite amazement the chorus of "Miggles" was repeated from the other side of the wall, even to the final and supplemental "Maygells."

"Extraordinary echo!" said the Judge.

"Extraordinary d__d skunk!" roared the driver contemptuously. "Come out of that, Miggles, and show yourself! Be a man, Miggles! Don't hide in the dark; I wouldn't if I were you, Miggles," continued Yuba Bill, now dancing about in an excess of fury.

"Miggles!" continued the voice, "O Miggles!"

"My good man! Mr. Myghail!" said the Judge, softening the asperities of the name as much as possible. "Consider the inhospitality of refusing shelter from the inclemency of the weather to helpless females. Really, my dear sir" — But a succession of "Miggles," ending in a burst of laughter, drowned his voice.

Yuba Bill hesitated no longer. Taking a heavy stone from the road, he battered down the gate, and with the expressman entered the inclosure. We followed. Nobody was to be seen. In the gathering darkness all that we could distinguish was that we were in a garden — from the rose bushes that scattered over us a minute spray from their dripping leaves — and before long, a rambling wooden building.

"Do you know this Miggles?" asked the Judge of Yuba Bill.

"No, nor don't want to," said Bill shortly, who felt the Pioneer Stage Company insulted in his person by the contumacious Miggles.

"But, my dear sir," expostulated the Judge, as he thought of the barred gate.

"Lookee here," said Yuba Bill, with fine irony, "Hadn't you better go back and sit in the coach till yer introduced? I'm going in," and he pushed open the door of the building.

A long room, lighted only by the embers of a fire that was dying on the large hearth at its farther extremity; the wall curiously papered, and the flickering firelight bringing out its grotesque pattern; somebody sitting in a large armchair by the fireplace. All this we saw as we crowded together into the room after the driver and expressman.

"Hello! be you Miggles?" said Yuba Bill to the solitary occupant.

The figure neither spoke nor stirred. Yuba Bill walked wrathfully toward it and turned the eye of his coach-lantern upon its face. It was a man's face, prematurely old and wrinkled, with very large eyes, in which there was that expression of perfectly gratuitous solemnity which I had sometimes seen in an owl's. The large eyes wandered from Bill's face to the lantern, and finally fixed their gaze on that luminous object without further recognition.

Bill restrained himself with an effort.

"Miggles! be you deaf? You ain't dumb anyhow, you know," and Yuba Bill shook the insensate figure by the shoulder.

To our great dismay, as Bill removed his hand, the venerable stranger apparently collapsed, sinking into half his size and an undistinguishable heap of clothing.

"Well, dern my skin," said Bill, looking appealingly at us, and hopelessly retiring from the contest.

The Judge now stepped forward, and we lifted the mysterious invertebrate back into his original position. Bill was dismissed with the lantern to reconnoitre outside, for it was evident that, from the helplessness of this solitary man, there must be attendants near at hand, and we all drew around the fire. The Judge, who had regained his authority, and had never lost his conversational amiability, — standing before us with his back to the hearth, — charged us, as an imaginary jury, as follows: —

"It is evident that either our distinguished friend here has reached that condition described by Shakespeare as 'the sere and yellow leaf,' or has suffered some premature abatement of his mental and physical faculties. Whether he is really the Miggles" —

Here he was interrupted by "Miggles! O Miggles! Migglesy! Mig!" and, in fact, the whole chorus of Miggles in very much the same key as it had once before been delivered unto us.

We gazed at each other for a moment in some alarm. The Judge, in particular, vacated his position quickly, as the voice seemed to come directly over his shoulder. The cause, however, was soon discovered in a large magpie who was perched upon a shelf over the fireplace, and who immediately relapsed into a sepulchral silence, which contrasted singularly with his previous volubility. It was, undoubtedly, his voice which we had heard in the road, and our friend in the chair was not responsible for the discourtesy. Yuba Bill, who reëntered the room after an unsuccessful search, was loth to accept the explanation, and still eyed the helpless sitter with suspicion. He had found a shed in which he had put up his horses, but he came back dripping and skeptical. "Thar ain't nobody but him within ten mile of the shanty, and that ar d__d old skeesicks knows it."

But the faith of the majority proved to be securely based. Bill had scarcely ceased growling before we heard a quick step upon the porch, the trailing of a wet skirt, the door was flung open, and with a flash of white teeth, a sparkle of dark eyes, and an utter absence of ceremony or diffidence, a young woman entered, shut the door, and, panting leaned back against it.

"Oh, if you please, I'm Miggles!"

And this was Miggles! this bright-eyed, full-throated young woman, whose wet gown of coarse blue stuff could not hide the beauty of the feminine curves to which it clung; from the chestnut crown of whose head, topped by a man's oil-skin sou'wester, to the little feet and ankles, hidden somewhere in the recesses of her boy's brogans, all was grace, — this was Miggles, laughing at us, too, in the most airy, frank, off-hand manner imaginable.

"You see boys," said she, quite out of breath, and holding one little hand against her side, quite unheeding the speechless discomfiture of our party or the complete demoralization of Yuba Bill, whose features had relaxed into an expression of gratuitous and imbecile cheerfulness, "— you see, boys, I was mor'n two miles away when you passed down the road. I thought you might pull up here, and so I ran the whole way, knowing nobody was home but Jim, — and — and — I'm out of breath — and — that lets me out." And here Miggles caught her dripping oil-skin hat from her head, with a mischievous swirl that scattered a shower of raindrops over us; attempted to put back her hair; dropped two hairpins in the attempt; laughed, and sat down beside Yuba Bill, with her hands crossed lightly on her lap.

The Judge recovered himself first and essayed an extravagant compliment.

"I'll trouble you for that ha'rpin," said Miggles gravely. Half a dozen hands were eagerly stretched forward; the missing hairpin was restored to its fair owner; and Miggles, crossing the room, looked keenly in the face of the invalid. The solemn eyes looked back at hers with an expression we had never seen before. Life and intelligence seemed to struggle back into the rugged face. Miggles laughed again, — it was a singularly eloquent laugh, — and turned her black eyes and white teeth once more towards us.

"This afflicted person is" — hesitated the Judge.

"Jim!" said Miggles.

"Your father?"

"No!"

"Brother?"

"No!"

"Husband?"

Miggles darted a quick, half-defiant glance at the two lady passengers, who I had noticed did not participate in the general masculine admiration of Miggles, and said gravely, "No; it's Jim!"

There was an awkward pause. The lady passengers moved closer to each other; the Washoe husband looked abstractedly at the fire, and the tall man apparently turned his eyes inward for self-support at this emergency. But Miggles's laugh, which was very infectious, broke the silence.

"Come," she said briskly, "you must be hungry. Who'll bear a hand to help me get tea?"

She had no lack of volunteers. In a few moments Yuba Bill was engaged like Caliban in bearing logs for this Miranda; the expressman was grinding coffee on the veranda; to myself the arduous duty of slicing bacon was assigned; and the Judge lent each man his good-humored and voluble counsel. And when Miggles, assisted by the Judge and our Hibernian "deck-passenger," set the table with all the available crockery, we had become quite joyous, in spite of the rain that beat against the windows, the wind that whirled down the chimney, the two ladies who whispered together in the corner, or the magpie, who uttered a satirical and croaking commentary on their conversation from his perch above. In the now bright, blazing fire we could see that the walls were papered with illustrated journals, arranged with feminine taste and discrimination. The furniture was extemporized and adapted from candle-boxes and packing cases, and covered with gay calico or the skin of some animal. The armchair of the helpless Jim was an ingenious variation of a flour-barrel. There was neatness, and even a taste for the picturesque, to be seen in the few details of the long, low room.

The meal was a culinary success. But more, it was a social triumph, — chiefly, I think, owing to the rare tact of Miggles in guiding the conversation, asking all the questions herself, yet bearing throughout a frankness that rejected the idea of any concealment on her own part, so that we talked of ourselves, of our prospects, of the journey, of the weather, of each other, — of everything but our host and hostess. It must be confessed that Miggles's conversation was never elegant, rarely grammatical, and that at times she employed expletives the use of which had generally been yielded to our sex. But they were delivered with such a lighting up of teeth and eyes, and were usually followed by a laugh — a laugh peculiar to Miggles — so frank and honest that it seemed to clear the moral atmosphere.

Once during the meal we heard a noise like the rubbing of a heavy body against the outer walls of the house. This was shortly followed by a scratching and sniffling at the door. "That's Joaquin," said Miggles, in reply to our questioning glances; "would you like to see him?" Before we could answer she had opened the door, and disclosed a half-grown grizzly, who instantly raised himself on his haunches, with his forepaws hanging down in the popular attitude of mendicancy, and looked admiringly at Miggles, with a very singular resemblance in his manner to Yuba Bill. "That's my watch-dog," said Miggles, in explanation. "Oh, he don't bite," she added as the two lady passengers fluttered into a corner. "Does he, old Toppy?" (the latter remark being addressed directly to the sagacious Joaquin). "I tell you what, boys," continued Miggles, after she had fed and closed the door on Ursa Minor, "you were in big luck that Joaquin was n't hanging round when you dropped in to-night."

"Where was he?" asked the Judge.

"With me," said Miggles. "Lord love you! he trots round with me nights like as if he was a man."

We were silent for a few moments, and listened to the wind. Perhaps we all had the same picture before us, — of Miggles walking through the rainy woods with her savage guardian at her side. The Judge, I remember, said something about Una and her lion; but Miggles received it, as she did other compliments, with quiet gravity. Whether she was altogether unconscious of the admiration she excited, — she could hardly have been oblivious of Yuba Bill's adoration, — I know not; but her very frankness suggested a perfect sexual equality that was cruelly humiliating to the younger members of our party.

The incident of the bear did not add anything in Miggles's favor to the opinions of those of her own sex who were present. In fact, the repast over, a chillness radiated from the two lady passengers that no pine boughs brought in by Yuba Bill and cast as a sacrifice upon the hearth could wholly overcome. Miggles felt it; and suddenly declaring that it was time to "turn in," offered to show the ladies to their bed in an adjoining room. "You, boys, will have to camp out here by the fire as well as you can," she added, "for thar ain't but the one room."

Our sex — by which, my dear sir, I allude of course to the stronger portion of humanity — has been generally relieved from the imputation of curiosity or a fondness for gossip. Yet I am constrained to say, that hardly had the door closed on Miggles than we crowded together, whispering, snickering, smiling and exchanging suspicions, surmises, and a thousand speculations in regard to our pretty hostess and her singular companion. I fear that we even hustled that imbecile paralytic, who sat like a voiceless Memnon in our midst, gazing with the serene indifference of the Past in his passionless eyes upon our wordy counsels. In the midst of an exciting discussion the door opened again and Miggles reëntered.

But not, apparently, the same Miggles who a few hours before had flashed upon us. Her eyes were downcast, and she hesitated for a moment on the threshold, with a blanket on her arm, she seemed to have left behind her the frank fearlessness which had charmed us a moment before. Coming into the room, she drew a low stool beside the paralytic's chair, sat down, drew the blanket over her shoulders, and saying, "If it's all the same to you, boys, as we're rather crowded, I'll stop here to-night," took the invalid's withered hand in her own, and turned her eyes upon the dying fire. An instinctive feeling that this was only premonitory to more confidential relations, and perhaps some shame at our previous curiosity, kept us silent. The rain still beat upon the roof, wandering gusts of wind stirred the embers into momentary brightness, until, in a lull of the elements, Miggles suddenly lifted up her head, and throwing her hair over her shoulder, turned her face upon the group and asked, —

"Is there any of you that knows me?"

There was no reply.

"Think again! I lived at Marysville in '53. Everybody knew me there, and everybody had the right to know me. I kept the Polka Saloon until I came to live with Jim. That's six years ago. Perhaps I've changed some."

The absence of recognition may have disconcerted her. She turned her head to the fire again, and it was some seconds before she again spoke, and then more rapidly —

"Well, you see I thought some of you must have known me. There's no great harm done anyway. What I was going to say was this: Jim here" — she took his hand in both of hers as she spoke — "used to know me, if you did n't, and spent a heap of money upon me. I reckon he spent all he had. And one day — it's six years ago this winter — Jim came into my back room, sat down on my sofy, like as you see him in that chair, and never moved again without help. He was struck all of a heap, and never seemed to know what ailed him. The doctors came and said as how it was caused all along of his way of life, — for Jim was mighty free and wild-like, — and that he would never get better, and couldn't last long anyway. They advised me to send him to Frisco to the hospital, for he was no good to any one and would be a baby all his life. Perhaps it was something in Jim's eye, perhaps it was that I never had a baby, but I said 'No.' I was rich then, for I was popular with everybody, — gentlemen like yourself, sir, came to see me, — and I sold out my business and bought this yer place, because it was sort of out of the way of travel, you see, and I brought my baby here."

With a woman's intuitive tact and poetry, she had, as she spoke, slowly shifted her position so as to bring the mute figure of the ruined man between her and her audience, hiding in the shadow behind it, as if she offered it as a tacit apology for her actions. Silent and expressionless, it yet spoke for her; helpless, crushed, and smitten with the Divine thunderbolt, it still stretched an invisible arm around her.

Hidden in the darkness, but still holding his hand, she went on: —

"It was a long time before I could get the hang of things about yer, for I was used to company and excitement. I couldn't get any woman to help me, and a man I durs n't trust; but what with the Indians hereabout, who'd do odd jobs for me, and having everything sent from the North Fork, Jim and I managed to worry through. The Doctor would run up from Sacramento once in a while. He'd ask to see 'Miggles's baby,' as he called Jim, and when he'd go away, he'd say, 'Miggles you're a trump, — God bless you,' and it didn't seem so lonely after that. But the last time he was here he said, as he opened to door to go, 'Do you know, Miggles, your baby will grow up to be a man yet and an honor to his mother; but not here, Miggles, not here!' And I thought he went away sad, — and — and" — and here Miggles's voice and head were somehow both lost completely in the shadow.

"The folks about here are very kind," said Miggles, after a pause, coming a little into the light again. "The men from the Fork used to hang around here, until they found they was n't wanted, and the women are kind, and don't call. I was pretty lonely until I picked up Joaquin in the woods yonder one day, when he was n't so high, and taught him to beg for his dinner; and then thar's Polly — that's the magpie — she knows no end of tricks, and makes it quite sociable of evenings with her talk, and so I don't feel like as I was the only living being about the ranch. And Jim here," said Miggles, with her old laugh again, and coming out quite into the firelight, — "Jim — Why, boys, you would admire to see how much he knows for a man like him. Sometimes I bring him flowers, and he looks at 'em, just as natural as if he knew 'em; and times, when we're sitting alone, I read him those things on the wall. Why, Lord!" said Miggles, with her frank laugh, "I've read him that whole side of the house this winter. There never was such a man for reading as Jim."

"Why," asked the Judge, "do you not marry this man to whom you have devoted your youthful life?"

"Well, you see," said Miggles, "it would be playing it rather low down on Jim to take advantage of his being so helpless. And then, too, if we were man and wife, now, we'd both know that I was *bound* to do what I do now of my own accord."

"But you are young yet and attractive" —

"It's getting late," said Miggles gravely, "and you'd better all turn in. Good-night, boys;" and throwing the blanket over her head, Miggles laid herself down beside Jim's chair, her head pillowed on the low stool that held his feet, and spoke no more. The fire slowly faded from the hearth; we each sought our blankets in silence; and presently there was no sound in the long room but the pattering of the rain upon the roof and the heavy breathing of the sleepers.

It was nearly morning when I awoke from a troubled dream. The storm had passed, the stars were shining, and through the shutterless window the full moon, lifting itself over the solemn pines without, looked into the room. It touched the lonely figure in the chair with an infinite compassion, and seemed to baptize with a shining flood the lowly head of the woman whose hair, as in the sweet old story, bathed the feet of him she loved. It even lent a kindly poetry to the rugged outline of Yuba Bill, half reclining on his elbow between them and his passengers, with savagely patient eyes keeping watch and ward. And then I fell asleep and only woke at broad day, with Yuba Bill standing over me, and "All aboard" ringing in my ears.

Coffee was waiting for us on the table, but Miggles was gone. We wandered about the house and lingered long after the horses were harnessed, but she did not return. It was evident that she wished to avoid a formal leave-taking, and had so left us to depart as we had come. After we had helped the ladies into the coach, we returned to the house and solemnly shook hands with the paralytic Jim, as solemnly setting him back into position after each handshake. Then we looked for the last time around the long, low room, at the stool where Miggles had sat, and slowly took our seats in the waiting coach. The whip cracked and we were off!

But as we reached the highroad, Bill's dexterous hand laid the six horses back on their haunches, and the stage stopped with a jerk. For there, on a little eminence beside the road, stood Miggles, her hair flying, her eyes sparkling, her white handkerchief waving, and her white teeth flashing a last "good-by." We waved our hats in return. And then Yuba Bill, as if fearful of further fascination, madly lashed his horses forward, and we sank back in our seats. We exchanged not a word until we reached the North Fork and the stage drew up at the Independence House. Then, the Judge leading, we walked into the bar-room and took our places gravely at the bar.

"Are your glasses charged, gentlemen?" said the Judge, solemnly taking off his white hat.

They were.

"Well, then, here's to *Miggles* — GOD BLESS HER!"

Perhaps He had. Who knows?

O. Henry

William Sydney Porter, who wrote under the name of O. Henry, is best known for short stories with a "twist" or surprise at the ending — "The Gift of the Magi" or "The Last Leaf." He is generally associated with New York City, but Porter lived in Texas for several years — first on a ranch and then as a banker in several cities — and later drew on those years for numerous short stories, most of them collected in Heart of the West (1907). Like Bret Harte, O. Henry has been accused of sentimentality, along with the use of formula plots, melodrama, and flowery language, but he was a born storyteller and a prolific author whose work continues to attract readers.

Hearts And Crosses
Heart of the West, 1907

Baldy Woods reached for the bottle, and got it. Whenever Baldy went for anything he usually — but this is not Baldy's story. He poured out a third drink that was larger by a finger than the first and second. Baldy was in consultation; and the consultee is worthy of his hire.

"I'd be king if I was you," said Baldy, so positively that his holster creaked and his spurs rattled.

Webb Yeager pushed back his flat-brimmed Stetson, and made further disorder in his straw-colored hair. The tonsorial recourse being without avail, he followed the liquid example of the more resourceful Baldy.

"If a man marries a queen, it oughtn't to make him a two-spot," declared Webb, epitomizing his grievances.

"Sure not," said Baldy, sympathetic, still thirsty, and genuine-ly solicitous concerning the relative value of the cards. "By rights you're a king. If I was you, I'd call for a new deal. The cards have been stacked on you — I'll tell you what you are, Webb Yeager."

"What?" asked Webb, with a hopeful look in his pale-blue eyes.

"You're a prince-consort."

"Go easy," said Webb. "I never black-guarded you none."

"It's a title," explained Baldy, "up among the picture-cards; but it don't take no tricks. I'll tell you, Webb. It's a brand they've got for certain animals in Europe. Say that you or me or one of them Dutch dukes marries in a royal family. Well, by and by our wife gets to be queen. Are we king? Not in a million years. At the coronation ceremonies we march between little casino and the Ninth Grand Custodian of the Royal Hall Bedchamber. The only use we are is to appear in photographs, and accept the responsi-bility for the heir-apparent. That ain't any square deal. Yes, sir, Webb, you're a prince-consort; and if I was you, I'd start a interregnum or a habeas corpus or somethin'; and I'd be king if I had to turn from the bottom of the deck."

Baldy emptied his glass to the ratification of his Warwick pose.

"Baldy," said Webb, solemnly, "me and you punched cows in the same outfit for years. We been runnin' on the same range, and ridin' the same trails since we was boys. I wouldn't talk about my family affairs to nobody but you. You was line-rider on the Nopalito Ranch when I married Santa McAllister. I was foreman then; but what am I now? I don't amount to a knot in a stake rope."

"When old McAllister was the cattle king of West Texas," continued Baldy with Satanic sweetness, "you was some tallow. You had as much to say on the ranch as he did."

"I did," admitted Webb, "up to the time he found out I was tryin' to get my rope over Santa's head. Then he kept me out on the range as far from the ranch-house as he could. When the old man died they commenced to call Santa the 'cattle queen.' I'm boss of the cattle — that's all. She 'tends to all the business; she handles all the money; I can't sell even a beef-steer to a party of campers, myself. Santa's the 'queen'; and I'm Mr. Nobody."

"I'd be a king if I was you," repeated Baldy Woods, the royalist. "When a man marries a queen he ought to grade up with her — on the hoof — dressed — dried — corned — any old way from the chaparral to the packing house. Lots of folks thinks it's funny, Webb, that you don't have the say-so on the Nopalito. I ain't reflectin' none on Miz Yeager — she's the finest little lady between the Rio Grande and next Christmas — but a man ought to be boss of his own camp."

The smooth, brown face of Yeager lengthened to a mask of wounded melancholy. With that expression, and his rumpled yellow hair and guileless blue eyes, he might have been likened to a schoolboy whose leadership had been usurped by a youngster of superior strength. But his active and sinewy seventy-two inches and his girded revolvers forbade the comparison.

"What was that you called me, Baldy?" he asked. "What kind of a concert was it?"

"A 'consort,'" corrected Baldy — "'a prince-consort.' It's a kind of short-card pseudonym. You come in sort of between Jack-high and a four-card flush."

Webb Yeager sighed, and gathered the strap of his Winchester scabbard from the floor.

"I'm ridin' back to the ranch to-day," he said, half-heartedly. "I've got to start a bunch of beeves for San Antone in the morning."

"I'm your company as far as Dry Lake," announced Baldy. "I've got a round-up camp on the San Marcos cuttin' out two-year-olds."

The two *compañeros* mounted their ponies and trotted away from the little railroad settlement, where they had foregathered in the thirsty morning.

At Dry Lake, where their routes diverged, they reined up for a party cigarette. For miles they had ridden in silence save for the soft drum of the ponies' hoofs on the matted mesquite grass, and the rattle of the chaparral against their wooden stirrups. But in Texas discourse is seldom continuous. You may fill in a mile, a meal and a murder between your paragraphs without detriment to your thesis. So, without apology, Webb offered an addendum to the conversation that had begun ten miles away.

"You remember, yourself, Baldy, that there was a time when Santa wasn't quite so independent. You remember the days when old McAllister was keepin' us apart, and how she used to send me the sign that she wanted to see me? Old man Mac promised to make me look like a colander if I ever come in gun-shot of the ranch. You remember the sign she used to send, Baldy — the heart with a cross inside of it?"

"Me?" cried Baldy, with intoxicated archness. "You old sugar-stealing coyote! Don't I remember! Why, you dad-blamed old long-horned turtle-dove, the boys in camp was all cognoscious about them hieroglyphs. The 'gizzard and crossbones' we used to call it. We used to see 'em on truck that was sent out from the ranch. They was marked in charcoal on the sacks of flour and in lead-pencil on the newspapers. I see one of 'em once chalked on the back of a new cook that old man McAllister sent out from the ranch — danged if I didn't."

"Santa's father," exclaimed Webb gently, "got her to promise that she wouldn't write to me or send me any word. That heart-and-cross sign was her scheme. Whenever she wanted to see me in particular she managed to put that mark on somethin' at the ranch that she knew I'd see. And I never laid eyes on it but what I burnt the wind for the ranch the same night. I used to see her in that coma mott back of the little horse-corral."

"We knowed it," chanted Baldy "but we never let on. We was all for you. We knowed why you always kept that fast paint in camp. And when we see that gizzard-and-crossbones figured out on the truck from the ranch we knowed old Pinto was goin' to eat up the miles that night instead of grass. You remember Scurry — that educated horse-wrangler we had — the college fellow that tangle-foot drove to the range? Whenever Scurry saw that come-meet-your-honey brand on anything from the ranch, he'd wave his hand like that, and say, 'Our friend Lee Andrews will again swim the Hell's point to-night.'"

"The last time Santa sent me the sign," said Webb, "was once when she was sick. I noticed it as soon as I hit camp, and I galloped Pinto forty mile that night. She wasn't at the coma mott. I went to the house; and old McAllister met me at the door.

'Did you come here to get killed?' says he; 'I'll disoblige you for
once. I just started a Mexican to bring you. Santa wants you. Go
in that room and see her. And then come out here and see me.'

"Santa was lyin' in bed pretty sick. But she gives out a kind
of a smile and her hand and mine lock horns, and I sets down
by the bed — mud and spurs and chaps and all. 'I've heard you
ridin' across the grass for hours, Webb,' she ways. 'I was sure
you'd come. You saw the sign?' she whispers. 'The minute I hit
camp,' says I. ''Twas marked on the bag of potatoes and onions.'
'They're always together,' says she, soft like — 'always together in
life.' 'They go well together,' I says, 'in a stew.' 'I mean hearts and
crosses,' says Santa. 'Our sign — to love and to suffer — that's
what they mean.'

"And there was old Doc Musgrove amusin' himself with
whisky and a palm-leaf fan. And by and by Santa goes to sleep;
and Doc feels her forehead; and he says to me: 'You're not such
a bad febrifuge. But you'd better slide out now, for the diagnosis
don't call for you in regular doses. The little lady'll be all right
when she wakes up."

"I seen old McAllister outside. 'She's asleep,' says I. 'And
now you can start in with your colander-work. Take your time; for
I left my gun on my saddle-horn.'

"Old Mac laughs, and he says to me: 'Pumpin' lead into the
best ranch-boss in West Texas don't seem to me good business
policy. I don't know where I could get as good a one. It's the son-
in-law idea, Webb, that makes me admire for to use you as a
target. You ain't my idea for a member of the family. But I can
use you on the Nopalito if you'll keep outside of a radius with the
ranch-house in the middle of it. You go upstairs and lay down on
a cot, and when you get some sleep we'll talk it over.'"

Baldy Woods pulled down his hat, and uncurled his leg
from his saddle-horn. Webb shortened his rein, and his pony
danced, anxious to be off. The two men shook hands with Western ceremony.

"*Adios*, Baldy," said Webb. "I'm glad I seen you and had this
talk."

With a pounding rush that sounded like the rise of a covey
of quail, the riders sped away toward different points of the compass. A hundred yards on his route Baldy reined in on the top

of a bare knoll and emitted a yell. He swayed on his horse; had he been on foot, the earth would have risen and conquered him; but in the saddle he was a master of equilibrium, and laughed at his whisky, and despised the center of gravity.

Webb turned in his saddle at the signal.

"If I was you," came Baldy's strident and perverting tones, "I'd be king!"

At eight o'clock on the following morning Bud Turner rolled from his saddle in front of the Nopalito ranch-house, and stumbled with whizzing rowels toward the gallery. Bud was in charge of the bunch of beef-cattle that was to strike the trail that morning for San Antonio. Mrs. Yeager was on the gallery watering a cluster of hyacinths growing in a red earthenware jar.

"King" McAllister had bequeathed to his daughter many of his strong characteristics — his resolution, his gay courage, his contumacious self-reliance, his pride as a reigning monarch of hoofs and horns. *Allegro* and *fortissimo* had been McAllister's tempo and tone. In Santa they survived, transposed to the feminine key. Substantially, she preserved the image of the mother who had been summoned to wander in other and less finite green pastures long before the waxing herds of kine had conferred royalty upon the house. She had her mother's slim, strong figure and grave, soft prettiness that relieved in her the severity of the imperious McAllister eye and the McAllister air of royal independence.

Webb stood on one end of the gallery giving orders to two or three sub-bosses of various camps and outfits who had ridden in for instructions.

"Morning," said Bud, briefly. "Where do you want them beeves to go in town — to Barber's, as usual?"

Now, to answer that had been the prerogative of the queen. All the reins of business — buying, selling, and banking — had been held by her capable fingers. The handling of the cattle had been entrusted fully to her husband. In the days of "King" McAllister, Santa had been his secretary and helper; and she had continued the work with wisdom and profit. But before she could reply, the prince-consort spake up with calm decision.

"You drive that bunch to Zimmerman and Nesbit's pens. I spoke to Zimmerman about it some time ago."

Bud turned on his high boot-heels.

"Wait!" called Santa quickly. She looked at her husband with surprise in her steady gray eyes.

"Why, what do you mean, Webb?" she asked, with a small wrinkle gathering between her brows. "I never deal with Zimmerman and Nesbit. Barber has handled every head of stock from this ranch in that market for five years. I'm not going to take the business out of his hands." She faced Bud Turner. "Deliver those cattle to Barber," she concluded positively.

Bud gazed impartially at the water-jar hanging on the gallery, stood on his other leg, and chewed a mesquite-leaf.

"I want this bunch of beeves to go to Zimmerman and Nesbit," said Webb, with a frosty light in his blue eyes.

"Nonsense," said Santa impatiently. "You'd better start on, Bud, so as to noon at the Little Elm waterhole. Tell Barber we'll have another lot of culls ready in about a month."

Bud allowed a hesitating eye to steal upward and meet Webb's. Webb saw apology in his look, and fancied he saw commiseration.

"You deliver them cattle," he said grimly, "to — "

"Barber," finished Santa sharply. "Let that settle it. Is there anything else you are waiting for, Bud?"

"No, m'm," said Bud. But before going he lingered while a cow's tail could have switched thrice. For a man is man's ally; and even the Philistines must have blushed when they took Samson in the way they did.

"You hear your boss!" cried Webb, sardonically. He took off his hat, and bowed until it touched the floor before his wife.

"Webb," said Santa rebukingly, "you're acting mightly foolish to-day."

"Court fool, your Majesty," said Webb, in his slow tones, which had changed their quality. "What else can you expect? Let me tell you. I was a man before I married a cattle-queen. What am I now? The laughing-stock of the camps. I'll be a man again."

Santa looked at him closely.

"Don't be unreasonable, Webb," she said calmly. "You haven't been slighted in any way. Do I ever interfere in your management of the cattle? I know the business side of the ranch much better than you do. I learned it from Dad. Be sensible."

"Kingdoms and queendoms," said Webb, "don't suit me unless I am in the pictures, too. I punch the cattle and you wear the crown. All right. I'd rather be High Lord Chancellor of a cow-camp than the eight-spot in a queen-high flush. It's your ranch; and Barber gets the beeves."

Webb's horse was tied to the rack. He walked into the house and brought out his roll of blankets that he never took with him except on long rides, and his "slicker," and his longest stake-rope of plaited raw-hide. These he began to tie deliberately upon his saddle. Santa, a little pale, followed him.

Webb swung up into the saddle. His serious, smooth face was without expression except for a stubborn light that smouldered in his eyes.

"There's a herd of cows and calves," said he, "near the Hondo Waterhole on the Frio that ought to be moved away from timber. Lobos have killed three of the calves. I forgot to leave orders. You'd better tell Simms to attend to it."

Santa laid a hand on the horse's bridle, and looked her husband in the eye.

"Are you going to leave me, Webb?" she asked quietly.

"I am going to be a man again," he answered.

"I wish you success in a praiseworthy attempt," she said, with a sudden coldness. She turned and walked directly into the house.

Webb Yeager rode to the southeast as straight as the topography of West Texas permitted. And when he reached the horizon he might have ridden on into blue space as far as knowledge of him on the Nopalito went. And the days, with Sundays at their head, formed into hebdomadal squads; and the weeks, captained by the full moon, closed ranks into menstrual companies carrying "Tempus fugit" on their banners; and the months marched on toward the vast camp-ground of the years; but Webb Yeager came no more to the dominions of his queen.

One day a being named Bartholomew, a sheep-man — and therefore of little account — from the lower Rio Grande country, rode in sight of the Nopalito ranch-house, and felt hunger assail him. *Ex consuetudine* he was soon seated at the mid-day dining-table of that hospitable kingdom. Talk like water gushed from him: he might have been smitten with Aaron's rod — that is your gentle shepherd when an audience is vouchsafed him whose ears are not overgrown with wool.

"Missis Yeager," he babbled, "I see a man the other day on the Rancho Seco down in Hidalgo County by your name — Webb Yeager was his. He'd just been engaged as manager. He was a tall, light-haired man, not saying much. Maybe he was some kin of yours, do you think?"

"A husband," said Santa cordially. "The Seco has done well. Mr. Yeager is one of the best stockmen in the West."

The dropping out of a prince-consort rarely disorganizes a monarchy. Queen Santa had appointed as *mayordomo* of the ranch, a trusty subject, named Ramsay, who had been one of her father's faithful vassals. And there was scarcely a ripple on the Nopalito ranch save when the gulf-breeze created undulations in the grass of its wide acres.

For several years the Nopalito had been making experiments with an English breed of cattle that looked down with aristocratic contempt upon the Texas long-horns. The experiments were found satisfactory; and a pasture had been set apart for the blue-bloods. The fame of them had gone forth into the chaparral and pear as far as men ride in saddles. Other ranches woke up, rubbed their eyes, and looked with new dissatisfaction upon the long-horns.

As a consequence, one day a sunburned, capable, silk-kerchiefed nonchalant youth, garnished with revolvers, and attended by three Mexican *vaqueros*, alighted at the Nopalito ranch and presented the following business-like epistle to the queen thereof.

Mrs. Yeager — the Nopalito ranch:

Dear Madam:

I am instructed by the owners of the Rancho Seco to purchase 100 head of two and three-year-old cows of the Sussex breed owned by you. If you can fill the order please deliver the cattle to the bearer; and a check will be forwarded to you at once.

Respectfully,

Webster Yeager,
Manager of the Rancho Seco.

Business is business, even — very scantily did it escape being written "especially" — in a kingdom.

That night the 100 head of cattle were driven up from the pasture and penned in a corral near the ranch-house for delivery in the morning.

When night closed down and the house was still, did Santa Yeager throw herself down, clasping that formal note to her bosom, weeping, and calling out a name that pride (either in one or the other) had kept from her lips many a day? Or did she file the letter, in her business way, retaining her royal balance and strength?

Wonder, if you will; but royalty is sacred; and there is a veil. But this much you shall learn.

At midnight Santa slipped softly out of the ranch-house, clothed in something dark and plain. She paused for a moment under the live-oak trees. The prairies were somewhat dim, and the moonlight was pale orange, diluted with particles of an impalpable, flying mist. But the mock-bird whistled on every bough of vantage; leagues of flowers scented the air; and a kindergarten of little shadowy rabbits leaped and played in an open space near by. Santa turned her face to the southeast and threw kisses thitherward; for there was none to see.

Then she sped silently to the blacksmith-shop, fifty yards away; and what she did there can only be surmised. But the forge glowed red; and there was a faint hammering such as Cupid might make when he sharpens his arrow-points.

Later she came forth with a queer-shaped, handled thing in one hand and a portable furnace, such as are seen in branding-camps, in the other. To the corral where the Sussex cattle were penned she sped with these things swiftly in the moonlight.

She opened the gate and slipped inside the corral. The Sussex cattle were mostly dark red. But among this bunch was one that was milky white — notable among the others.

And now Santa shook from her shoulder something that we had not seen before — a rope lasso. She freed the loop of it, coiling the length in her left hand, and plunged into the thick of the cattle.

The white cow was her object. She swung the lasso, which caught one horn and slipped off. The next throw encircled the forefeet and the animal fell heavily. Santa made for it like a panther; but it scrambled up and dashed against her, knocking her over like a blade of grass.

Again she made the cast, while the aroused cattle milled round the four sides of the corral in a plunging mass. This throw was fair; the white cow came to earth again; and before it could rise Santa had made the lasso fast around a post of the corral with a swift and simple knot, and had leaped upon the cow again with the rawhide hobbles.

In one minute the feet of the animal were tied (no record-breaking deed) and Santa leaned against the corral for the same space of time, panting and lax.

And then she ran swiftly to her furnace at the gate and brought the branding-iron, queerly shaped and white-hot.

The bellow of the outraged white cow, as the iron was applied, should have stirred the slumbering auricular nerves and consciences of the near-by subjects of the Nopalito, but it did not. And it was amid the deepest nocturnal silence that Santa ran like a lapwing back to the ranch-house and there fell upon a cot and sobbed — sobbed as though queens had hearts as simple ranchmen's wives have, and as though she would gladly make kings of prince-consorts, should they ride back again from over the hills and far away.

In the morning the capable, revolvered youth and his *vaqueros* set forth driving the bunch of Sussex cattle across the prairies to the Rancho Seco. Ninety miles it was; a six days' journey, grazing and watering the animals on the way.

The beasts arrived at Rancho Seco one evening at dusk; and were received and counted by the foreman of the ranch.

The next morning at eight o'clock a horseman loped out of the brush to the Nopalito ranch-house. He dismounted stiffly, and strode, with whizzing spurs, to the house. His horse gave a great sigh and swayed foam-streaked, with down drooping head and closed eyes.

But waste not your pity on Belshazzar, the flea-bitten sorrel. Today, in Nopalito horse-pasture he survives, pampered, beloved, unridden, cherished record-holder of long-distance rides.

The horseman stumbled into the house. Two arms fell around his neck and someone cried out in the voice of woman and queen alike: "Webb — oh, Webb!"

"I was a skunk," said Webb Yeager.

"Hush," said Santa, "did you see it?"

"I saw it," said Webb.

What they meant God knows; and you shall know, if you rightly read the primer of events.

"Be the cattle-queen," said Webb; "and overlook if you can. I was a mangy, sheep-stealing coyote."

"Hush!" said Santa again, laying her fingers upon his mouth. "There's no queen here. Do you know who I am? I am Santa Yeager, First Lady of the Bedchamber. Come here."

She dragged him from the gallery into the room to the right. There stood a cradle with an infant in it — a red, ribald, unintelligible, babbling, beautiful infant, sputtering at life in an unseemly manner.

"There's no queen on this ranch," said Santa again. "Look at the king. He's got your eyes, Webb. Down on your knees and look at his Highness."

But jingling rowels sounded on the gallery and Bud Turner stumbled there again with the same query that he had brought, lacking a few days a year ago.

"'Morning. Them beeves is just turned on the trail. Shall I drive 'em to Barber's or — "

He saw Webb and stopped, open-mouthed.

"Be-ba-ba-ba-ba!" shrieked the king in his cradle, beating the air with his fists.

"You hear your boss, Bud," said Webb Yeager, with a broad grin — just as he had said a year ago.

And that is all, except that when old man Quinn, owner of the Rancho Seco, went out to look over the herd of Sussex cattle that he had bought from the Nopalito ranch, he asked his new manager:

"What's the Nopalito ranch brand, Wilson?"

"X Bar Y," said Wilson.

"I thought so," said Quinn. "But look at that white heifer there; she's got another brand — a heart with a cross inside of it. What brand is that?"

Owen Wister

An aristocratic easterner who went West for his health and became a westerner at heart, Owen Wister (1860-1938) is often credited with having written, in The Virginian (1902), the archetype of the traditional western novel. It has all the ingredients — a love story between the strong and taciturn cowboy-hero and the pure schoolmarm from the East, a shootout with the villain, the lynching of a cattle thief, the gradual increase of civilization. Wister's main interest in fiction was the human experience in the West, and he frequently contrasted an eastern narrator with a western cowboy, as in this story. For Wister, the frontier — usually Wyoming — offered a pure way of life in which a man could be in touch with his better instincts; by 1902, Wister nostalgically saw that life disappearing. "Hank's Woman" is one of his earliest stories.

Hank's Woman
Harper's Weekly, ca. 1890

I

Many fish were still in the pool; and though luck seemed to have left me, still I stood at the end of the point, casting and casting my vain line, while the Virginian lay and watched. Noonday's extreme brightness had left the river and the plain in cooling shadow, but spread and glowed over the yet undimmed mountains. Westward, the Tetons lifted their peaks pale and keen as steel through the high, radiant air. Deep down between the blue gashes of their cañons the sun sank long shafts of light, and the glazed laps of their snow-fields shone separate and white upon their lofty vastness, like handkerchiefs laid out to dry. Opposite, above the valley, rose that other range, the Continental Divide, not sharp, but long and ample. It was bare in some high places, and below these it stretched everywhere, high and low, in brown and yellow parks, or in purple miles of pine a world of serene undulations, a great sweet country of silence.

A passing band of antelope stood herded suddenly together at sight of us; then a little breeze blew for a moment from us to them, and they drifted like phantoms away, and were lost in the levels of the sage-brush.

"If humans could do like that," said the Virginian, watching them go.

"Run, you mean?" said I.

"Tell a foe by the smell of him," explained the cow-puncher; "at fifty yards — or a mile."

"Yes," I said; "men would be hard to catch."

"A woman needs it most," he murmured. He lay down again in his lounging sprawl, with his grave eyes intently fixed upon my fly-casting.

The gradual day mounted up the hills farther from the floor of earth. Warm airs eddied in its wake slowly, stirring the scents of the plain together. I looked at the Southerner; and there was no guessing what his thoughts might be at work upon behind that drowsy glance. Then for a moment a trout rose, but only to look and whip down again into the pool that wedged its calm into the riffle from below.

"Second thoughts," mused the Virginian; and as the trout came no more, "Second thoughts," he repeated; "and even a fish will have them sooner than folks has them in this mighty hasty country." And he rolled over into a new position of ease.

At whom or what was he aiming these shafts of truth? Or did he moralize merely because health and the weather had steeped him in that serenity which lifts us among the spheres? Well, sometimes he went on from these beginnings and told me wonderful things.

"I reckon," said he, presently, "that knowing when to change your mind would be pretty near knowledge enough for plain people."

Since my acquaintance with him — this was the second summer of it — I had come to understand him enough to know that he was unfathomable. Still, for a moment it crossed my thoughts that perhaps now he was discoursing about himself. He had allowed a jealous foreman to fall out with him at Sunk Creek ranch in the spring, during Judge Henry's absence. The man, having a brief authority, parted with him. The Southerner had chosen that this should be the means of ultimately getting the foreman dismissed and himself recalled. It was strategic. As he put it to me: "When I am gone, it will be right easy for the judge to see which of us two he wants. And I'll not have done any talking." All of which duly befell in the autumn as he had planned: the foreman was sent off, his assistant promoted, and the Virginian again hired. But this was meanwhile. He was indulging himself in a several months' drifting, and while thus drifting he had written to me. That is how we two came to be on our way from the railroad to hunt the elk and the mountain-sheep, and were pausing to fish where Buffalo Fork joins its waters with Snake River. In those days the antelope still ran there in hundreds, the Yellowstone Park was a new thing, and mankind lived very far away. Since meeting me with the horses in Idaho the Virginian had been silent, even for him. So now I stood casting my fly, and trusting that he was not troubled with second thoughts over his strategy.

"Have yu' studied much about marriage?" he now inquired. His serious eyes met mine as he lay stretched along the ground.

"Not much," I said; "not very much."

"Let's swim," he said. "They have changed their minds."

Forthwith we shook off our boots and dropped our few clothes, and heedless of what fish we might now drive away, we went into the cool, slow, deep breadth of backwater which the bend makes just there. As he came up near me, shaking his head of black hair, the cowpuncher was smiling a little.

"Not that any number of baths," he remarked, "would conceal a man's objectionableness from an antelope — not even a she-one."

Then he went under water, and came up again a long way off.

We dried before the fire, without haste. To need no clothes is better than purple and fine linen. Then he tossed the flap-jacks, and I served the trout, and after this we lay on our backs upon a buffalo-hide to smoke and watch the Tetons grow more solemn, as the large stars opened out over the sky.

"I don't care if I never go home," said I.

The Virginian nodded. "It gives all the peace o' being asleep with all the pleasure o' feeling the widest kind of awake," said he. "Yu' might say the whole year's strength flows hearty in every waggle of your thumb." We lay still for a while. "How many things surprise yu' any more?" he next asked.

I began considering; but his silence had at length worked round to speech.

"Inventions, of course," said he, "these hyeh telephones an' truck yu' see so much about in the papers — but I ain't speaking o' such things of the brain. It is just the common things I mean. The things that a livin', noticin' man is liable to see and maybe sample for himself. How many o' them kind can surprise yu' still?"

I still considered.

"Most everything surprised me onced," the cow-puncher continued, in his gentle Southern voice. "I must have been a mighty green boy. Till I was fourteen or fifteen I expect I was astonished by ten o'clock every morning. But a man begins to ketch on to folks and things after a while. I don't consideh that when — that afteh a man is, say twenty-five, it is creditable he should get astonished too easy. And so yu've not examined yourself that-away?"

I had not.

"Well, there's two things anyway — I know them for sure — that I expect will always get me — don't care if I live to thirty-five, or forty-five, or eighty. And one's the ways lightning can strike." He paused. Then he got up and kicked the fire, and stood by it, staring at me. "And the other is the people that other people will marry."

He stopped again; and I said nothing.

"The people that other people will marry," he repeated. "That will surprise me till I die."

"If my sympathy — " I began.

But the brief sound that he gave was answer enough, and more than enough cure for my levity.

"No," said he, reflectively; "not any such thing as a family for me, yet. Never, it may be. Not till I can't help it. And *that* woman has not come along so far. But I have been sorry for a woman lately. I keep thinking what she will do. For she will have to do something. Do yu' know Austrians? Are they quick in their feelings, like Italians? Or are they apt to be sluggish, same as Norwegians and them other Dutch-speakin' races?"

I told him what little I knew about Austrians.

"This woman is the first I have ever saw of 'em," he continued. "Of course men will stampede into marriage in this hyeh Western country, where a woman is a scanty thing. It ain't what Hank has done that surprises me. And it is not on him that the sorrow will fall. For she is good. She is very good. Do yu' remember little black Hank? From Texas he claims he is. He was working on the main ditch over at Sunk Creek last summer when that Em'ly hen was around. Well, seh, yu' would not have pleasured in his company. And this year Hank is placer-mining on Galena Creek, where we'll likely go for sheep. There's Honey Wiggin and a young fello' named Lin McLean, and some others along with the outfit. But Hank's woman will not look at any of them, though the McLean boy is a likely hand. I have seen that; for I have done a right smart o' business that-a-way myself, here and there. She will mend their clothes for them, and she will cook lunches for them any time o' day, and her conduct gave them hopes at the start. But I reckon Austrians have good religion."

"No better than Americans," said I.

But the Virginian shook his head. "Better'n what I've saw any Americans have. Of course I am not judging a whole nation by one citizen, and especially her a woman. And of course in them big Austrian towns the folks has shook their virtuous sayin's loose from their daily doin's, same as we have. I expect selling yourself brings the quickest returns to man or woman all the world over. But I am speakin' not of towns, but of the back country, where folks don't just merely arrive on the cyars, but come into the world the natural way, and grow up slow. Onced a week anyway they see the bunch of old grave-stones that marks their fam'ly. Their blood and name are knowed about in the neighborhood, and it's not often one of such will sell themselves. But their religion ain't to them like this woman's. They can be rip-snortin' or'n'ary in ways.

Now she is getting naught but hindrance and temptation and meanness from her husband and every livin' thing around her — yet she keeps right along, nor does she mostly bear any signs in her face. She has cert'nly come from where they are used to believing in God and a hereafter mighty hard, and all day long. She has got one o' them crucifixes, and Hank can't make her quit prayin' to it. But what is she going to do?"

"He will probably leave her," I said.

"Yes," said the Virginian — "leave her. Alone; her money all spent; knowin' maybe twenty words of English; and thousands of miles away from everything she can understand. For our words and ways is all alike strange to her."

"Then why did he want such a person?" I exclaimed.

There was surprise in the grave glance which the cow-puncher gave me. "Why, any man would," he answered. "I wanted her myself, till I found she was good."

I looked at this son of the wilderness, standing thoughtful and splendid by the fire, and unconscious of his own religion that had unexpectedly shone forth in these last words. But I said nothing; for words too intimate, especially words of esteem, put him invariably to silence.

"I had forgot to mention her looks to yu'." he pursued, simply. "She is fit for a man." He stopped again.

"Then there was her wages that Hank saw paid to her," he resumed. "And so marriage was but a little thing to Hank — agaynst such a heap of advantages. As for her idea in takin' such as him — maybe it was that he was small and she was big; tall and big. Or maybe it was just his white teeth. Them ridiculous reasons will bring a woman to a man, haven't yu' noticed? But maybe it was just her sorrowful, helpless state, left stranded as she was, and him keeping himself near her and sober for a week.

"I had been seein' this hyeh Yellowstone Park, takin' in its geysers, and this and that, for my enjoyment; and when I found what they claimed about its strange sights to be pretty near so, I landed up at Galena Creek to watch the boys prospectin'. Honey Wiggin, yu' know, and McLean, and the rest. And so they got me to go down with Hank to Gardner for flour and sugar and truck, which we had to wait for. We lay around the Mammoth Springs and Gardner for three days, playin' cards with friends. And I got plumb inter-ested in them tourists. For I had partly forgot about Eastern people. And hyeh they came fresh every day to remind a man of the great size of his country. Most always they would talk to yu' if yu' gave 'em the chance; and I did. I have come mighty nigh regrettin' that I did not keep a tally of the questions them folks asked me. And as they seemed genu-winely anxious to believe anything at all, and the worser the thing the believinger they'd grow, why I — well, there's times when I have got to lie to keep in good health.

"So I fooled and I fooled. And one noon I was on the front poach of the big hotel they have opened at the Mammoth Springs for tourists, and the hotel kid, bein' on the watchout, he sees the dust comin' up the hill, and he yells out, 'Stage!'

"Yu've not saw that hotel yet, seh? Well, when the kid says 'Stage,' the consequences is most sudden. About as conspicuous, yu' may say, as when Old Faithful Geyser lets loose. Yu' see, one batch o' tourists pulls out right after breakfast for Norris Basin, leavin' things empty and yawnin'. By noon the whole hotel outfit has been slumberin' in its chairs steady for three hours. Maybe yu' might hear a fly buzz, but maybe not. Everything's liable to be restin', barrin' the kid. He's a-watchin' out. Then he sees the dust, and he says 'Stage!' and it touches the folks off like a hot pokeh. The Syndicate manager he lopes to a lookin' glass, and then organizes himself behind the book; and the young photograph chap bounces out o' his private door like one o' them cuckoo-clocks; and the fossil man claws his specimens and curiosities into shape, and the porters line up same as parade, and away goes the piano and fiddles up-stairs. It is mighty con-spicuous. So Hank he come runnin' out from somewheres too, and the stage drives up.

"Then out gets a tall woman, and I noticed her yello' hair. She was kind o' dumb-eyed, yet fine to see. I reckon Hank noticed her too, right away. And right away her trouble begins. For she was a lady's maid, and her lady was out of the stage and roundin' her up quick. And it's 'Where have you put the keys, Willomene?' The lady was rich and stinkin' lookin', and had come from New Yawk in her husband's private cyar.

"Well, Willomene fussed around in her pockets, and them keys was not there. So she started explaining in tanglefoot English to her lady how her lady must have took them from her before leavin' the cyar. But the lady seemed to relish hustlin' herself into a rage. She got tolerable con-spicuous, too. And after a heap o' words, 'You are discharged,' she says; and off she struts. Soon her husband came out to Willomene, still standin' like statuary, and he pays her a good sum of cash, and he goes away, and she keeps a standing yet for a spell. Then all of a sudden she says something I reckon was 'O, Jesus,' and sits down and starts a cryin'.

"I would like to have given her comfort. But we all stood around on the hotel poach, and the right thing would not come into my haid. Then the baggage-wagon came in from Cinnabar, and they had picked the keys up on the road between Cinnabar and Gardner. So the lady and her toilet was rescued, but that did no good to Willomene. They stood her trunk down along with the rest — a brass-nailed little old concern — and there was Willomene out of a job and afoot a long, long ways from her own range; and so she kept sitting, and onced in a while she'd cry some more. We got her a room in the cheap hotel where the Park drivers sleeps when they're in at the Springs, and she acted grateful like, thanking the boys in her tanglefoot English. Next mawnin' her folks druv off in a private team to Norris Basin, and she seemed dazed. For I talked with her then, and questioned her as to her wishes, but she could not say what she wished, nor if it was East or West she would go; and I reckon she was too stricken to have wishes.

"Our stuff for Galena Creek delayed on the railroad, and I got to know her, and then I quit givin' Hank cause for jealousy. I kept myself with the boys, and I played more cyards, while Hank he sca'cely played at all. One night I came on them — Hank and Willomene — walkin' among the pines where the road goes down the hill. Yu' should have saw that pair o' lovers. Her big shape was plain and kind o' steadfast in the moon, and alongside of her little black Hank! And there it was. Of course it ain't nothing to be surprised at that a mean and triflin' man tries to seem what he is not when he wants to please a good woman. But why does she get fooled, when it's so plain to other folks that are not givin' it any special thought? All the rest of the men and women at the Mammoth understood Hank. They knowed he was a worthless proposition. And I cert'nly relied on his gettin' back to his whiskey and openin' her eyes that way. But he did not. I met them next evening again by the Liberty Cap. Supposin' I'd been her brother or her mother, what use was it me warning her? Brothers and mothers don't get believed.

"The railroad brought the stuff for Galena Creek, and Hank would not look at it on account of his courtin'. I took it alone myself by Yancey's and the second bridge and Miller Creek to the camp, nor I didn't tell Willomene good-bye, for I had got disgusted at her blindness."

The Virginian shifted his position, and jerked his overalls to a more comfortable fit. Then he continued:

"They was married the Tuesday after at Livingston, and Hank must have been pow'ful pleased at himself. For he gave Willomene a wedding present, with the balance of his cash, spending his last nickel on buying her a red-tailed parrot they had for sale at the First National Bank. The son-of-a-gun hollad so freely at the bank, the president awde'd the cashier to get shed of the out-ragious bird, or he would wring its neck.

"So Hank and Willomene stayed a week up in Livingston on her money, and then he fetched her back to Gardner, and bought their grub, and bride and groom came up to the camp we had on Galena Creek.

"She had never slep' out before. She had never been on a hawss, neither. And she mighty near rolled off down into Pitch-stone Cañon, comin' up by the cut-off trail. Why, seh I would not willingly take you through that place, except yu' promised me yu' would lead your hawss when I said to. But Hank takes the woman he had married, and he takes heavy-loaded pack-hawsses. 'Tis the first time such a thing has been known of in the country. Yu' remember them big tall grass-topped mountains over in the Hoodoo country, and how they descends slam down through the cross-timber that yu' can't sca'cely work through afoot, till they pitches over into lots an' lots o' little cañons, with maybe two inches of water runnin' in the bottom? All that is East Fork water, and over the divide is Clark's Fork, or Stinkin' Water, if yu' take the country yondeli to the southeast. But any place yu' go is them undesirable steep slopes, and the cut-off trail takes along about the worst in the business.

"Well, Hank he got his outfit over it somehow, and, gentlemen, hush! but yu'd ought t've seen him and that poor girl pull into our camp. Yu'd cert'nly never have conjectured them two was a weddin' journey. He was leadin', but skewed around in his saddle to jaw back at Willomene for riding so ignorant. Suppose it was a thing she was responsible for, yu'd not have talked to her that-away even in private; and hyeh was the camp a-lookin', and a-listenin', and some of us ashamed. She was setting straddleways like a mountain, and between him and her went the three pack animals, plumb shiverin' played out, and the flour — they had two hundred pounds — tilted over hellwards, with the red-tailed parrot shoutin' landslides in his cage tied on top o' the leanin' sacks.

"It was that mean to see, that shameless and unkind, that even a thoughtless kid like the McLean boy felt offended, and favorable to some sort of remonstrance. 'The son-of-a — !' he said to me. 'The son-of-a — ! If he don't stop, let's stop him.' And I reckon we might have.

"But Hank he quit. 'Twas plain to see he'd got a genu-wine scare comin' through Pitchstone Cañon, and it turned him sour, so he'd hardly talk to us, but just mumbled 'How!' kind o' gruff, when the boys come up to congratulate him as to his marriage.

"But Willomene, she says when she saw me, 'Oh, I am so glad!' and we shook hands right friendly. And I wished I'd told her good-bye that day at the Mammoth. For she bore no spite, and maybe I had forgot her feelings in thinkin' of my own. I had talked to her down at the Mammoth at first, yu' know, and she said a word about old friends. Our friendship was three weeks old that day, but I expect her new experiences looked like years to her. And she told me how near she come to gettin' killed.

"Yu' ain't ever been over that trail, seh? Yu' cert'nly must see Pitchstone Cañon. But we'll not go there with packs. And we will get off our hawsses a good ways back. For many animals feels that there's something the matter with that place, and they act very strange about it.

"The Grand Cañon is grand, and makes yu' feel good to look at it, and a geyser is grand and all right, too. But this hyeh Pitchstone hole, if Willomene had went down into that — well, I'll tell yu', that you may judge.

"She seen the trail a-drawin' nearer and nearer the aidge, between the timber and the jumpin'-off place, and she seen how them little loose stones and the crumble stuff would slide and slide away under the hawss's feet. She could hear the stuff rattlin' continually from his steps, and when she turned her haid to look, she seen it goin' down close beside her, but into what it went she could not see. Only, there was a queer steam would come up now and agayn, and her hawss trembled. So she tried to get off and walk without saying nothin' to Hank. He kep' on ahaid, and her hawss she had pulled up started to follo' as she was half off him, and that gave her a tumble, but there was an old crooked dead tree. It growed right out o'the aidge. There she hung.

"Down below is a little green water tricklin', green as the stuff that gets on brass, and tricklin' along over soft cream-colored formation, like pie. And it ain't so far to fall but what a man might not be too much hurt for crawlin' out. But there ain't no crawlin' out o' Pitchstone Cañon, they say. Down in there is caves that yu' cannot see. 'Tis them that coughs up the stream now and agayn. With the wind yu' can smell 'em a mile away, and in the night I have been layin' quiet and heard 'em. Not that it's a big noise, even when a man is close up. It's a fluffy kind of a sigh. But it sounds as if some awful thing was a-makin' it deep down in the guts of the world. They claim there's poison air comes out o' the caves and lays low along the water. They claim if a bear or an elk strays in from below, and the caves sets up their coughin', which they don't regular every day, the animals die. I have seen it come in two seconds. And when it comes that-a-way risin' upon yu' with that fluffy kind of a sigh, yu' feel mighty lonesome, seh.

"So Hank he happened to look back and see Willomene hangin' at the aidge o' them black rocks. And his scare made him mad. And his mad stayed with him till they come into camp. She looked around, and when she seen Hank's tent that him and her was to sleep in she showed surprise. And he showed surprise when he see the bread she cooked.

"'What kind of a Dutch woman are yu',' says he, strainin' for a joke, 'if yu' can't use a Dutch-oven?'

"'You say to me you have a house to live in,' says Willomene. 'Where is that house?'

"'I did not figure on gettin' a woman when I left camp,' says Hank, grinnin', but not pleasant, 'or I'd have hurried up with the shack I'm a buildin'.'

"He was buildin' one. When I left Galena Creek and come away from that country to meet you, the house was finished enough for the couple to move in. I hefted her brass-nailed trunk up the hill from their tent myself, and I watched her take out her crucifix. But she would not let me help her with that. She'd not let me touch it. She'd fixed it up agaynst the wall her own self her own way. But she accepted some flowers I picked, and set them in a can front of the crucifix. Then Hank he come in, and seein', says to me, 'Are you one of the kind that squats before them silly dolls?' 'I would tell yu',' I answered him; 'but it would not inter-est yu'.' And I cleared out, and left him and Willomene to begin their housekeepin'.

"Already they had quit havin' much to say to each other down in their tent. The only steady talkin' done in that house was done by the parrot. I've never saw any go ahaid of that bird. I have told yu' about Hank, and how when he'd come home and see her prayin' to that crucifix he'd always get riled up. He would mention it freely to the boys. Not that she neglected him, yu' know. She done her part, workin' mighty hard, for she was a willin' woman. But he could not make her quit her religion; and Willomene she had got to bein' very silent before I come away. She used to talk to me some at first, but she dropped it. I don't know why. I expect maybe it was hard for her to have us that close in camp, witnessin' her troubles every day, and she a foreigner. I reckon if she got any comfort, it would be when we was off prospectin' or huntin', and she could shut the cabin door and be alone."

The Virginian stopped for a moment.

"It will soon be a month since I left Galena Creek," he resumed. "But I cannot get the business out o' my haid. I keep a studyin' over it."

His talk was done. He had unburdened his mind. Night lay deep and quiet around us, with no sound far or near, save Buffalo Fork plashing over its riffle.

II

We left Snake River. We went up Pacific Creek, and through Two Ocean Pass, and down among the watery willow-bottoms and beaver-dams of the Upper Yellowstone. We fished; we enjoyed existence along the lake. Then we went over Pelican Creek trail and came steeply down into the giant country of grass-topped mountains. At dawn and dusk the elk had begun to call across the stillness. And one morning in the Hoodoo country, where we were looking for sheep, we came round a jut of the strange, organ-pipe formation upon a long-legged boy of about nineteen, also hunting.

"Still hyeh?" said the Virginian, without emotion.

"I guess so," returned the boy equally matter-of-fact. "Yu' seem to be around yourself," he added.

They might have been next-door neighbors, meeting in a town street for the second time in the same day.

The Virginian made me known to Mr. Lin McLean, who gave me a brief nod.

"Any luck?" he inquired, but not of me.

"Oh," drawled the Virginian, "luck enough."

Knowing the ways of the country, I said no word. It was bootless to interrupt their own methods of getting at what was really in both their minds.

The boy fixed his wide-open hazel eyes upon me. "Fine weather," he mentioned.

"Very fine," said I.

"I seen your horses a while ago," he said. "Camp far from here?" he asked the Virginian.

"Not specially. Stay and eat with us. We've got elk meat."

"That's what I'm after for camp," said McLean. "All of us is out on a hunt to-day — except him."

"How many are yu' now?"

"The whole six."

"Makin' money?"

"Oh, some days the gold washes out good in the pan, and others it's that fine it'll float off without settlin'."

"So Hank ain't huntin' to-day?"

"Huntin'! We left him layin' out in that clump o'brush below their cabin. Been drinkin' all night."

The Virginian broke off a piece of the Hoodoo mud-rock from the weird eroded pillar that we stood beside. He threw it into a bank of last year's snow. We all watched it as if it were important. Up through the mountain silence pierced the long quivering whistle of a bull-elk. It was like an unearthly singer practising an unearthly scale.

"First time she heard that," said McLean, "she was scared."

"Nothin' maybe to resemble it in Austria," said the Virginian.

"That's so," said McLean. "That's so, you bet! Nothin' just like Hank over there, neither."

"Well, flesh is mostly flesh in all lands, I reckon," said the Virginian. "I expect yu' can be drunk and disorderly in every language. But an Austrian Hank would be liable to respect her crucifix."

"That's so!"

"He 'ain't made her quit it yet?"

"Not him. But he's got meaner."

"Drunk this mawnin', yu' say?"

"That's his most harmless condition now."

"Nobody's in camp but them two? Her and him alone?"

"Oh, he dassent touch her."

"Who did he tell that to?"

"Oh, the camp is backin' her. The camp has explained that to him several times, you bet! And what's more, she has got the upper hand of him herself. She has him beat."

"How beat?"

"She has downed him with her eye, just by endurin' him peacefully; and with her eye. I've saw it. Things changed some after yu' pulled out. We had a good crowd still, and it was pleasant, and not too lively nor yet too slow. And Willomene, she come more among us. She'd not stay shut in-doors, like she done at first. I'd have like to've showed her how to punish Hank."

"Afteh she had downed yu' with her eye?" inquired the Virginian.

Young McLean reddened, and threw a furtive look upon me, the stranger, the outsider. "Oh, well," he said, "I done nothing onusual. But that's all different now. All of us likes her and respects her, and makes allowances for her bein' Dutch. Yu' can't help but respect her. And she shows she knows."

"I reckon maybe she knows how to deal with Hank," said the Virginian.

"Shucks!" said McLean, scornfully. "And her so big and him so puny! She'd ought to lift him off the earth with one arm and lam him with a baste or two with the other, and he'd improve."

"Maybe that's why she don't," mused the Virginian, slowly; "because she is so big. Big in the spirit, I mean. She'd not stoop to his level. Don't yu' see she is kind o' way up above him and camp and everything — just her and her crucifix?"

"Her and her crucifix!" repeated young Lin McLean, staring at this interpretation, which was beyond his lively understanding. "Her and her crucifix. Turrible lonesome company! Well, them are things yu' don't know about. I kind o' laughed myself the first time I seen her at it. Hank, he says to me soft, 'Come here, Lin,' and I peeped in where she was a-prayin'. She seen us two, but she didn't quit. So I quit, and Hank came with me, sayin' tough words about it. Yes, them are things yu' sure don't know about. What's the matter with you camping with us boys to-night?"

We had been going to visit them the next day. We made it to-day, instead. And Mr. McLean helped us with our packs, and we carried our welcome in the shape of elk meat. So we turned our faces down the grass-topped mountains towards Galena Creek. Once, far through an open gap away below us, we sighted the cabin with the help of our field-glasses.

"Pity we can't make out Hank sleepin' in that brush," said McLean.

"He has probably gone into the cabin by now," said I.

"Not him! He prefers the brush all day when he's that drunk, you bet!"

"Afraid of her?"

"Well — oneasy in her presence. Not that she's liable to be in there now. She don't stay inside nowadays so much. She's been comin' round the ditch, silent-like but friendly. And she'll watch us workin' for a spell, and then she's apt to move off alone into the woods, singin' them Dutch songs of hern that ain't got no toon. I've met her walkin' that way, tall and earnest, lots of times. But she don't want your company, though she'll patch your over-alls and give yu' lunch always. Nor' she won't take pay."

Thus we proceeded down from the open summits into the close pines; and while we made our way among the cross-timber and over the little streams, McLean told us of various days and nights at the camp, and how Hank had come to venting his cowardice upon his wife's faith.

"Why, he informed her one day when he was goin' to take his dust to town, that if he come back and found that thing in the house, he'd do it up for her. 'So yu' better pack off your wooden dummy somewheres,' says he. And she just looked at him kind o' stone-like and solemn. For she don't care for his words no more.

"And while he was away she'd have us all in to supper up at the shack, and look at us eatin' while she'd walk around puttin' grub on your plate. Day time she'd come around the ditch, watchin' for a while, and move off slow, singin' her Dutch songs. And when Hank comes back from spendin' his dust, he sees the crucifix same as always, and he says, 'Didn't I tell yu' to take that down?' 'You did,' says Willomene, lookin' at him very quiet. And he quit.

"And Honey Wiggin says to him, 'Hank, leave her alone.' And Hank, bein' all trembly from spreein' in town, he says, 'You're all agin me!' like as if he were a baby."

"I should think you would run him out of camp," said I.

"Well, we've studied over that some," McLean answered. "But what's to be done with Willomene?"

I did not know. None of us seemed to know.

"The boys got together night before last," continued McLean, "and after holdin' a unanimous meetin', we visited her and spoke to her about goin' back to her home. She was slow in corrallin' our idea on account of her bein' no English scholar. But when she did, after three of us takin' their turn at puttin' the proposition to her, she would not accept any of our dust. And though she started to thank us the handsomest she knowed how, it seemed to grieve her, for she cried. So we thought, we'd better get out. She's tried to tell us the name of her home, but yu' can't pronounce such outlandishness."

As we went down the mountains, we talked of other things, but always came back to this; and we were turning it over still when the sun had departed from the narrow cleft that we were following, and shone only on the distant grassy tops which rose round us into an upper world of light.

"We'll all soon have to move out of this camp, anyway," said McLean, unstrapping his coat from his saddle and drawing it on. "It gets chill now in the afternoons. D'yu' see the quakin'-asps all turned yello', and the leaves keeps fallin' without no wind to blow 'em down? We're liable to get snowed in on short notice in this mountain country. If the water goes to freeze on us we'll have to quit workin'. There's camp."

We had rounded a corner, and once more sighted the cabin. I suppose it may have been still half a mile away, upon the further side of a ravine into which our little valley opened. But field-glasses were not needed now to make out the cabin clearly, windows and door. Smoke rose from it; for supper-time was nearing, and we stopped to survey the scene. As we were looking, another hunter joined us, coming from the deep woods to the edge of the pines where we were standing. This was Honey Wiggin. He had killed a deer, and he surmised that all the boys would be back soon. Others had met luck besides himself; he had left one dressing an elk over the next ridge. Nobody seemed to have got in yet, from appearances. Didn't the camp look lonesome?

"There's somebody, though," said McLean.

The Virginian took the glasses. "I reckon — yes, that's Hank. The cold has woke him up, and he's comin' in out o' the brush."

Each of us took the glasses in turn; and I watched the figure go up the hill to the door of the cabin. It seemed to pause and diverge to the window. At the window it stood still, head bent, looking in. Then it returned quickly to the door. It was too far to discern, even through the glasses, what the figure was doing. Whether the door was locked, whether he was knocking or fumbling with a key, or whether he spoke through the door to the person within — I cannot tell what it was that came through the glasses straight to my nerves, so that I jumped at a sudden sound; and it was only the distant shrill call of an elk. I was handing the glasses to the Virginian for him to see when the figure opened the door and disappeared in the dark interior. As I watched the square of darkness which the door's opening made, something seemed to happen there — or else it was a spark, a flash, in my own straining eyes.

But at that same instant the Virginian dashed forward upon his horse, leaving the glasses in my hand. And with the contagion of his act the rest of us followed him, leaving the pack animals to follow us as they should choose.

"Look!" cried McLean. "He's not shot her."

I saw the tall figure of a woman rush out of the door and pass quickly round the house.

"He's missed her!" cried McLean, again. "She's savin' herself."

But the man's figure did not appear in pursuit. Instead of this, the woman returned as quickly as she had gone, and entered the dark interior.

"She had something," said Wiggin. "What would that be?"

"Maybe it's all right, after all," said McLean. "She went out to get wood."

The rough steepness of our trail had brought us down to a walk, and as we continued to press forward at this pace as fast as we could, we compared a few notes. McLean did not think he saw any flash. Wiggin thought that he had heard a sound, but it was at the moment when the Virginian's horse had noisily started away.

Our trail had now taken us down where we could no longer look across and see the cabin. And the half-mile proved a long one over this ground. At length we reached and crossed the rocky ford, overtaking the Virginian there.

"These hawsses," said he, "are played out. We'll climb up to camp afoot. And just keep behind me for the present."

We obeyed our natural leader, and made ready for whatever we might be going into. We passed up the steep bank and came again in sight of the door. It was still wide open. We stood, and felt a sort of silence which the approach of two new-comers could not break. They joined us. They had been coming home from hunting, and had plainly heard a shot here. We stood for a moment more after learning this, and then one of the men called out the names of Hank and Willomene. Again we — or I at least — felt that same silence, which to my disturbed imagination seemed to be rising round us as mists rise from water.

"There's nobody in there," stated the Virginian. "Nobody that's alive," he added. And he crossed the cabin and walked into the door.

Though he made no gesture, I saw astonishment pass through his body, as he stopped still; and all of us came after him. There hung the crucifix, with a round hole through the middle of it. One of the men went to it and took it down; and behind it, sunk in the log, was the bullet. The cabin was but a single room, and every object that it contained could be seen at a glance; nor was there hiding-room for anything. On the floor lay the axe from the wood-pile; but I will not tell of its appearance. So he had shot her crucifix, her Rock of Ages, the thing which enabled her to bear her life, and that lifted her above life; and she — but there was the axe to show what she had done then. Was this cabin really empty? I looked more slowly about, half dreading to find that I had overlooked something. But it was as the Virginian had said; nobody was there.

As we were wondering, there was a noise above our heads, and I was not the only one who started and stared. It was the parrot; and we stood away in a circle, looking up at his cage. Crouching flat on the floor of the cage, his wings huddled tight to his body, he was swinging his head from side to side; and when he saw that we watched him, he began a low croaking and monotonous utterance, which never changed, but remained rapid and continuous. I heard McLean whisper to the Virginian, "You bet he knows."

The Virginian stepped to the door, and then he bent to the gravel and beckoned us to come and see. Among the recent footprints at the threshold the man's boot-heel was plain, as well as the woman's broad tread. But while the man's steps led into the cabin, they did not lead away from it. We tracked his course just as we had seen it through the glasses: up the hill from the brush to the window, and then to the door. But he had never walked out again. Yet in the cabin he was not; we tore up the half-floor that it had. There was no use to dig in the earth. And all the while that we were at this search the parrot remained crouched in the bottom of his cage, his black eye fixed upon our movements.

"She has carried him," said the Virginian. "We must follow up Willomene."

The latest heavy set of footprints led us from the door along the ditch, where they sank deep in the softer soil; then they turned off sharply into the mountains.

"This is the cut-off trail," said McLean to me. "The same he brought her in by."

The tracks were very clear, and evidently had been made by a person moving slowly. Whatever theories our various minds were now shaping, no one spoke a word to his neighbor, but we went along with a hush over us.

After some walking, Wiggin suddenly stopped and pointed.

We had come to the edge of the timber, where a narrow black cañon began, and ahead of us the trail drew near a slanting ledge, where the footing was of small loose stones. I recognized the odor, the volcanic whiff, that so often prowls and meets one in the lonely woods of that region, but at first I failed to make out what had set us all running.

"Is he looking down into the hole himself?" some one asked; and then I did see a figure, the figure I had looked at through the glasses, leaning strangely over the edge of Pitchstone Cañon, as if indeed he was peering to watch what might be in the bottom.

We came near. But those eyes were sightless, and in the skull the story of the axe was carved. By a piece of his clothing he was hooked in the twisted roots of a dead tree, and hung there at the extreme verge. I went to look over, and Lin McLean caught me as I staggered at the sight I saw. He would have lost his own foothold in saving me had not one of the others held him from above.

She was there below; Hank's woman, brought from Austria to the New World. The vision of that brown bundle lying in the water will never leave me, I think. She had carried the body to this point; but had she intended this end? Or was some part of it an accident? Had she meant to take him with her? Had she meant to stay behind herself? No word came from these dead to answer us. But as we stood speaking there, a giant puff of breath rose up to us between the black walls.

"There's that fluffy sigh I told yu' about," said the Virginian.

"He's talkin' to her! I tell yu' he's talkin' to her!" burst out McLean, suddenly, in such a voice that we stared as he pointed at the man in the tree. "See him lean over! He's sayin', 'I have yu' beat after all.'" And McLean fell to whimpering.

Wiggin took the boy's arm kindly and walked him along the trail. He did not seem twenty yet. Life had not shown this side of itself to him so plainly before.

"Let's get out of here," said the Virginian.

It seemed one more pitiful straw that the lonely bundle should be left in such a vault of doom, with no last touches of care from its fellow-beings, and no heap of kind earth to hide it. But whether the place is deadly or not, man dares not venture into it. So they took Hank from the tree that night, and early next morning they buried him near camp on the top of a little mound.

But the thought of Willomene lying in Pitchstone Cañon had kept sleep from me through that whole night, nor did I wish to attend Hank's burial. I rose very early, while the sunshine had still a long way to come down to us from the mountain-tops, and I walked back along the cut-off trail. I was moved to look once more upon that frightful place. And as I came to the edge of the timber, there was the Virginian. He did not expect any one. He had set up the crucifix as near the dead tree as it could be firmly planted.

"It belongs to her, anyway," he explained.

Some lines of verse came into my memory, and with a change or two I wrote them as deep as I could with my pencil upon a small board that he smoothed for me.

> "Call for the robin redbreast and the wren,
>   Since o'er shady groves they hover,
> And with flowers and leaves do cover
>   The friendless bodies of unburied men.
> Call to this funeral dole
>   The ant, the field-mouse, and the mole,
> To rear her hillocks that shall keep her warm."

"That kind o' quaint language reminds me of a play I seen onced in Saynt Paul," said the Virginian. "About young Prince Henry."

I told him that another poet was the author.

"They are both good writers," said the Virginian. And as he was finishing the monument that we had made, young Lin McLean joined us. He was a little ashamed of the feelings that he had shown yesterday, a little anxious to cover those feelings with brass.

"Well," he said, taking an offish, man-of-the-world tone, "all this fuss just because a woman believed in God."

"You have put it down wrong," said the Virginian; "it's just because a man didn't."

Charles Eastman

~~~~~~

Charles Eastman (1858-1939) was the best-known American Indian writer of the early twentieth century. Raised until his teen years as a member of the Sioux Nation, he was educated in the East, eventually attending Boston University Medical School. Eastman practiced at Pine Ridge Reservation briefly and lived in South Dakota, working on matters pertaining to Indian affairs, for twenty years before moving East. He began writing with an auto-biographical sketch and published two autobiographical books, Indian Boyhood *(1902) and* From the Deep Woods to Civilization *(1916). Eastman also wrote several other books, including some which repeated traditional Sioux legends for children.*

The Peace-Maker
Old Indian Days, 1907

One of the most remarkable women of her day and nation was Eyatónkawee, She-whose-Voice-is-heard-afar. It is matter of history among the Wakpáykootay band of Sioux, the Dwellers among the Leaves, that when Eyatónkawee was a very young woman she was once victorious in a hand-to-hand combat with the enemy in the woods of Minnesota, where her people were hunting the deer. At such times they often met with stray parties of Sacs and Foxes from the prairies of Iowa and Illinois.

Now, the custom was among our people that the doer of a notable warlike deed was held in highest honor, and these deeds were kept constantly in memory by being recited in public, before many witnesses. The greatest exploit was that one involving most personal courage and physical address, and he whose record was adjudged best might claim certain privileges, not the least of which was the right to interfere in any quarrel and separate the combatants. The peace-maker might resort to force, if need be, and no one dared to utter a protest who could not say that he had himself achieved an equal fame.

There was a man called Tamáhay, known to Minnesota history as the "One-eyed Sioux," who was a notable character on the frontier in the early part of the nineteenth century. He was very reckless, and could boast of many a perilous adventure. He was the only Sioux who, in the War of 1812, fought for the Americans, while all the rest of his people sided with the British, mainly through the influence of the English traders among them at that time. This same "One-eyed Sioux" became a warm friend of Lieutenant Pike, who discovered the sources of the Mississippi, and for whom Pike's Peak is named. Some say that the Indian took his friend's name, for Tamáhay in English means Pike or Pickerel.

Unfortunately, in later life this brave man became a drunkard, and after the Americans took possession of his country almost any one of them would supply him with liquor in recognition of his notable services as a scout and soldier. Thus he was at times no less dangerous in camp than in battle.

Now, Eyatónkawee, being a young widow, had married the son of a lesser chief in Tamáhay's band, and was living among strangers. Moreover, she was yet young and modest.

One day this bashful matron heard loud war whoops and the screams of women. Looking forth, she saw the people fleeing hither and thither, while Tamáhay, half intoxicated, rushed from his teepee painted for war, armed with tomahawk and scalping-knife, and approached another warrior as if to slay him. At this sight her heart became strong, and she quickly sprang between them with her woman's knife in her hand.

"It was a Sac warrior of like proportions and bravery with your own, who, having slain several of the Sioux, thus approached me with uplifted tomahawk!" she exclaimed in a clear voice, and went on to recite her victory on that famous day so that the terrified people paused to hear.

Tamáhay was greatly astonished, but he was not too drunk to realize that he must give way at once, or be subject to the humiliation of a blow from the woman-warrior who challenged him thus. The whole camp was listening; and being unable, in spite of his giant frame and well-known record, to cite a greater deed than hers, he retreated with as good a grace as possible. Thus Eyatónkawee recounted her brave deed for the first time, in order to save a man's life. From that day her name was great as a peace-maker — greater even than when she had first defended so gallant-ly her babe and home!

Many years afterward, when she had attained middle age, this woman averted a serious danger from her people.

Chief Little Crow the elder was dead, and as he had two wives of two different bands, the succession was disputed among the half-brothers and their adherents. Finally the two sons of the wife belonging to the Wabashaw band plotted against the son of the woman of the Kaposia band, His-Red-Nation by name, after-ward called Little Crow — the man who led the Minnesota mas-sacre.

They obtained a quantity of whisky and made a great feast to which many were invited, intending when all were more or less intoxicated to precipitate a fight in which he should be killed. It would be easy afterward to excuse themselves by saying that it was an accident.

Mendota, near what is now the thriving city of Saint Paul, then a queen of trading-posts in the Northwest, was the rendez-vous of the Sioux. The event brought many together, for all war-riors of note were bidden from far and near, and even the great traders of the day were present, for the succession to the chieftain-ship was one which vitally affected their interests. During the early part of the day all went well, with speeches and eulogies of the dead chief, flowing and eloquent, such as only a native orator can utter. Presently two goodly kegs of whisky were rolled into the council teepee.

Eyatónkawee was among the women, and heard their expres-sions of anxiety as the voices of the men rose louder and more threatening. Some carried their children away into the woods for safety, while others sought speech with their husbands outside the council lodge and besought them to come away in time. But more than this was needed to cope with the emergency. Suddenly a familiar form appeared in the door of the council lodge.

"Is it becoming in a warrior to spill the blood of his tribesmen? Are there no longer any Ojibways?"

It was the voice of Eyatónkawee, that strong-hearted woman! Advancing at the critical moment to the middle of the ring of warriors, she once more recited her "brave deed" with all the accompaniment of action and gesture, and to such effect that the disorderly feast broke up in confusion, and there was peace between the rival bands of Sioux.

There was seldom a dangerous quarrel among the Indians in those days that was not precipitated by the use of strong liquor, and this simple Indian woman, whose good judgment was equal to her courage, fully recognized this fact. All her life, and especially after her favorite brother had been killed in a drunken brawl in the early days of the American Fur Company, she was a determined enemy to strong drink, and it is said did more to prevent its use among her immediate band than any other person. Being a woman, her sole means of recognition was the "brave deed" which she so wonderfully described and enacted before the people.

During the lifetime of She-whose-Voice-is-heard-afar — and she died only a few years ago — it behooved the Sioux men, if they drank at all, to drink secretly and in moderation. There are many who remember her brave entrance upon the scene of carousal, and her dramatic recital of the immortal deed of her youth.

"Hanta! hanta wo! (Out of the way!)" exclaim the dismayed warriors, scrambling in every direction to avoid the upraised arm of the terrible old woman, who bursts suddenly upon them with disheveled hair, her gown torn and streaked here and there with what looks like fresh blood, her leather leggings loose and ungartered, as if newly come from the famous struggle. One of the men has a keg of whisky for which he has given a pony, and the others have been invited in for a night of pleasure. But scarcely has the first round been drunk to the toast of "great deeds," when Eyatónkawee is upon them, her great knife held high in her wrinkled left hand, her tomahawk in the right. Her black eyes gleam as she declaims in a voice strong, unterrified:

"Look! look! brothers and husbands — the Sacs
and Foxes are upon us!
Behold, our braves are surprised — they are
unprepared!
Hear the mothers, the wives and the children
screaming in affright!

"Your brave sister, Eyatónkawee, she, the newly
made mother, is serving the smoking venison
to her husband, just returned from the chase!
Ah, he plunges into the thickest of the enemy!
He falls, he falls, in full view of his young wife!

"She desperately presses her babe to her breast,
while on they come yelling and triumphant!
The foremost of them all enters her white
buffalo-skin teepee:
Tossing her babe at the warrior's feet, she stands
before him, defiant;
But he straightway levels his spear at her bosom.
Quickly she springs aside, and as quickly deals a
deadly blow with her ax:
Falls at her feet the mighty warrior!

"Closely following on comes another, unknowing
what fate has met his fellow!
He too enters her teepee, and upon his
feather-decked head her ax falls —
Only his death-groan replies!

"Another of heroic size and great prowess, as
witnessed by his war-bonnet of eagle-feathers,
Rushes on, yelling and whooping — for they
believe that victory is with them!
The third great warrior who has dared to enter
Eyatónkawee's teepee uninvited, he has already
dispatched her husband!

He it is whose terrible war-cry has scattered her
    sisters among the trees of the forest!

"On he comes with confidence and a brave heart,
    seeking one more bloody deed —
One more feather to win for his head!
Behold, he lifts above her woman's head his
    battle-ax!
No hope, no chance for her life! . . .
Ah! he strikes beyond her — only the handle of
    the ax falls heavily upon her tired shoulder!
Her ready knife finds his wicked heart, —
Down he falls at her feet!

"Now the din of war grows fainter and further.
The Sioux recover heart, and drive the enemy
    headlong from their lodges:
Your sister stands victorious over three!
"She takes her baby boy, and makes him count
    with his tiny hands the first 'coup' on each
    dead hero;
Hence he wears the 'first feathers' while yet in his
    oaken cradle.

"The bravest of the whole Sioux nation have given
    the war whoop in your sister's honor, and have
    said:
'Tis Eyatónkawee who is not satisfied with
    downing the mighty oaks with her ax —
She took the mighty Sacs and Foxes for trees,
    and she felled them with a will!"

In such fashion the old woman was wont to chant her story,
and not a warrior there could tell one to surpass it! The custom
was strong, and there was not one to prevent her when she struck
open with a single blow of her ax the keg of whisky, and the
precious liquor trickled upon the ground.

"So trickles under the ax of Eyatónkawee the blood of an
enemy to the Sioux!"

Jack London

~~~~~~

*B*est known for such masculine survival-adventure works
as the novel, Call of the Wild, and the short story,
"To Build a Fire," Jack London made women prominent in
virtually every novel and many of his short stories. By
today's standards, his Anglo women are often wooden and
uninteresting. But London had a real admiration for the
Native American women of Alaska and the Canadian
Northwest. In their lives he saw a struggle for survival as
heroic as that of the men and dogs his writing is generally
identified with, and his realistic portrayals present women
who are always courageous, never ignorant nor backward.
Of "The Wit of Porportuk" London once wrote that it
ranked among his half-dozen best stories.

The Wit of Porportuk
The Times, 1906

*E*l-Soo had been a Mission girl. Her mother had died
when she was very small, and Sister Alberta had plucked
El-Soo as a brand from the burning, one summer day, and carried
her away to Holy Cross Mission and dedicated her to God. El-Soo
was a full-blooded Indian, yet she exceeded all the half-breed and
quarter-breed girls. Never had the good sisters dealt with a girl so
adaptable and at the same time so spirited.

El-Soo was quick, and deft, and intelligent; but above all
she was fire, will, sweetness, and daring. Her father was a chief,
and his blood ran in her veins. Obedience, on the part of El-
Soo, was a matter of terms and arrangement. She had a passion

for equity, and perhaps it was because of this that she excelled in mathematics.

But she excelled in other things. She learned to read and write English as no girl had ever learned in the Mission. She led the girls in singing, and into song she carried her sense of equity. She was an artist, and the fire of her flowed toward creation. Had she from birth enjoyed a more favorable environment, she would have made literature or music.

Instead, she was El-Soo, daughter of Klakee-Nah, a chief, and she lived in the Holy Cross Mission where were no artists, but only pure-souled Sisters who were interested in cleanliness and righteousness and the welfare of the spirit in the land of immortality that lay beyond the skies.

The years passed. She was eight years old when she entered the Mission; she was sixteen, and the Sisters were corresponding with their superiors in the Order concerning the sending of El-Soo to the United States to complete her education, when a man of her own tribe arrived at Holy Cross and had talk with her. El-Soo was somewhat appalled by him. He was dirty. He was a Caliban-like creature, primitively ugly, with a mop of hair that had never been combed. He looked at her disapprovingly and refused to sit down.

"Thy brother is dead," he said, shortly.

El-Soo was not particularly shocked. She remembered little of her brother. "Thy father is an old man, and alone," the messenger went on. "His house is large and empty, and he would hear thy voice and look upon thee."

Him she remembered — Klakee-Nah, the head-man of the village, the friend of the missionaries and the traders, a large man thewed like a giant, with kindly eyes and masterful ways, and striding with a consciousness of crude royalty in his carriage.

"Tell him that I will come," was El-Soo's answer.

Much to the despair of the sisters, the brand plucked from the burning went back to the burning. All pleading with El-Soo was vain. There was much argument, expostulation, and weeping. Sister Alberta even revealed to her the project of sending her to the United States. El-Soo stared wide-eyed into the golden vista thus opened up to her, and shook her head. In her eyes persisted another vista. It was the mighty curve of the Yukon at Tana-naw

Station, with the St. George Mission on one side, and the trading post on the other, and midway between the Indian village and a certain large log house where lived an old man tended upon by slaves.

All dwellers on the Yukon bank for twice a thousand miles knew the large log house, the man and the tending slaves; and well did the Sisters know the house, its unending revelry, its feasting and its fun. So there was weeping at Holy Cross when El-Soo departed.

There was a great cleaning up in the large house when El-Soo arrived. Klakee-Nah, himself masterful, protested at the masterful conduct of his young daughter, but in the end, dreaming barbarically of magnificence, he went forth and borrowed a thousand dollars from old Porportuk, than whom there was no richer Indian on the Yukon. Also, Klakee-Nah ran up a heavy bill at the trading post. El-Soo re-created the large house. She invested it with new splendor, while Klakee-Nah maintained its ancient traditions of hospitality and revelry.

All this was unusual for a Yukon Indian, but Klakee-Nah was an unusual Indian. Not alone did he like to render inordinate hospitality, but, what of being a chief and of acquiring much money, he was able to do it. In the primitive trading days he had been a power over his people, and he had dealt profitably with the white trading companies. Later on, with Porportuk, he had made a gold-strike on the Koyokuk River. Klakee-Nah was by training and nature an aristocrat. Porportuk was bourgeois, and Porportuk bought him out of the gold-mine. Porportuk was content to plod and accumulate. Klakee-Nah went back to his large house and proceeded to spend. Porportuk was known as the richest Indian in Alaska. Klakee-Nah was known as the whitest. Porportuk was a money-lender and a usurer. Klakee-Nah was an anachronism — a medieval ruin, a fighter and a feaster, happy with wine and song.

El-Soo adapted herself to the large house and its ways as readily as she had adapted herself to Holy Cross Mission and its ways. She did not try to reform her father and direct his footsteps toward God. It is true, she reproved him when he drank overmuch and profoundly, but that was for the sake of his health and the direction of his footsteps on solid earth.

The latchstring to the large house was always out. What with the coming and the going, it was never still. The rafters of the great living room shook with the roar of wassail and of song. At table sat men from all the world and chiefs from distant tribes — Englishmen and Colonials, lean Yankee traders and rotund officials of the great companies, cowboys from the Western ranges, sailors from the sea, hunters and dog-mushers of a score of nationalities.

El-Soo drew breath in a cosmopolitan atmosphere. She could speak English as well as she could her native tongue, and she sang English songs and ballads. The passing Indian ceremonials she knew, and the perishing traditions. The tribal dress of the daughter of a chief she knew how to wear upon occasion. But for the most part she dressed as white women dress. Not for nothing was her needlework at the Mission and her innate artistry. She carried her clothes like a white woman, and she made clothes that could be so carried.

In her way she was as unusual as her father, and the position she occupied was as unique as his. She was the one Indian woman who was the social equal with the several white women at Tana-naw Station. She was the one Indian woman to whom white men honorably made proposals of marriage. And she was the one Indian woman whom no white man ever insulted.

For El-Soo was beautiful — not as white women are beautiful, not as Indian women are beautiful. It was the flame of her, that did not depend upon feature, that was her beauty. So far as mere line and feature went, she was the classic Indian type. The black hair and the fine bronze were hers, and the black eyes, brilliant and bold, keen as sword-light, proud; and hers the delicate eagle nose with the thin, quivering nostrils, the high cheekbones that were not broad apart, and the thin lips that were not too thin. But over all and through all poured the flame of her — the unanalyzable something that was fire and that was the soul of her, that lay mellow-warm or blazed in her eyes, that sprayed the cheeks of her, that distended the nostrils, that curled the lip, or, when the lip was in repose, that was still there in the lip, the lip palpitant with its presence.

And El-Soo had wit — rarely sharp to hurt, yet quick to search out forgivable weakness. The laughter of her mind played like lambent flame over all about her, and from all about her arose answering laughter. Yet she was never the centre of things. This she would not permit. The large house, and all of which it was significant, was her father's; and through it, to the last, moved his heroic figure — host, master of the revels, and giver of the law. It is true, as the strength oozed from him, that she caught up responsibilities from his failing hands. But in appearance he still ruled, dozing ofttimes at the board, a bacchanalian ruin, yet in all seeming the ruler of the feast.

And through the large house moved the figure of Porportuk, ominous, with shaking head, coldly disapproving, paying for it all. Not that he really paid, for he compounded interest in wierd ways, and year by year absorbed the properties of Klakee-Nah. Porportuk once took it upon himself to chide El-Soo upon the wasteful way of life in the large house — it was when he had about absorbed the last of Klakee-Nah's wealth — but he never ventured so to chide again. El-Soo, like her father, was an aristocrat, as disdainful of money as he, and with an equal sense of honor as finely strung.

Porportuk continued grudgingly to advance money, and ever the money flowed in golden foam away. Upon one thing El-Soo was resolved — her father should die as he had lived. There should be for him no passing from high to low, no diminution of the revels, no lessening of the lavish hospitality. When there was famine, as of old, the Indians came groaning to the large house and went away content. When there was famine and no money, money was borrowed from Porportuk, and the Indians still went away content. El-Soo might well have repeated, after the aristocrats of another time and place, that after her came the deluge. In her case the deluge was old Porportuk. With every advance of money, he looked upon her with a more possessive eye, and felt bourgeoning within him ancient fires.

But El-Soo had no eyes for him. Nor had she eyes for the white men who wanted to marry her at the Mission with ring and priest and book. For at Tana-naw Station was a young man, Akoon, of her own blood and tribe, and village. He was strong and beautiful to her eyes, a great hunter, and, in that he had wandered far and much, very poor; he had been to all the unknown wastes and places; he had journeyed to Sitka and to the United States; he had crossed the continent to Hudson Bay and back again, and as a seal-hunter on a ship he had sailed to Siberia and for Japan.

When he returned from the gold-strike in Klondike he came, as was his wont, to the large house to make report to old Klakee-Nah of all the world that he had seen; and there he first saw El-Soo, three years back from the Mission. Thereat, Akoon wandered no more. He refused a wage of twenty dollars a day as pilot on the big steamboats. He hunted some and fished some, but never far from the Tana-naw Station, and he was at the large house often and long. And El-Soo measured him against many men and found him good. He sang songs to her, and was ardent and glowed until all Tana-naw Station knew he loved her. And Porportuk but grinned and advanced more money for the upkeep of the large house.

Then came the death table of Klakee-Nah. He sat at feast, with death in his throat, that he could not drown with wine. And laughter and joke and song went around, and Akoon told a story that made the rafters echo. There were no tears or sighs at that table. It was no more than fit that Klakee-Nah should die as he had lived, and none knew this better than El-Soo, with her artist sympathy. The old roystering crowd was there, and, as of old, three frost-bitten sailors were there, fresh from the long traverse from the Arctic, survivors of a ship's company of seventy-four. At Klakee-Nah's back were four old men, all that were left him of the slaves of his youth. With rheumy eyes they saw to his needs, with palsied hands filling his glass or striking him on the back between the shoulders when death stirred and he coughed and gasped.

It was a wild night, and as the hours passed and the fun laughed and roared along, death stirred more restlessly in Klakee-Nah's throat. Then it was that he sent for Porportuk. And Porportuk came in from the outside frost to look with disapproving eyes upon the meat and wine on the table for which he had paid. But as he looked down the length of flushed faces to the far end and saw the face of El-Soo, the light in his eyes flared up, and for a moment the disapproval vanished.

Place was made for him at Klakee-Nah's side, and a glass with fervent spirits. "Drink!" he cried. "Is it not good?"

And Porportuk's eyes watered as he nodded his head and smacked his lips.

"When, in your own house, have you had such drink?" Klakee-Nah demanded.

"I will not deny that the drink is good to this old throat of mine," Porportuk made answer, and hesitated for the speech to complete the thought.

"But it costs overmuch," Klakee-Nah roared, completing it for him.

Porportuk winced at the laughter that went down the table. His eyes burned malevolently. "We were boys together, of the same age," he said. "In your throat is death. I am still alive and strong."

An ominous murmur arose from the company. Klakee-Nah coughed and strangled, and the old slaves smote him between the shoulders. He emerged gasping, and waved his hand to still the threatening rumble.

"You have grudged the very fire in your house because the wood cost overmuch!" he cried. "You have grudged life. To live cost overmuch, and you have refused to pay the price. Your life has been like a cabin where the fire is out and there are no blankets on the floor." He signalled to a slave to fill his glass, which he held aloft. "But I have lived. And I have been warm with life as you have never been warm. It is true, you shall live long. But the longest nights are the cold nights when a man shivers and lies awake. My nights have been short, but I have slept warm."

He drained the glass. The shaking hand of a slave failed to catch it as it crashed to the floor. Klakee-Nah sank back, panting, watching the upturned glasses at the lips of the drinkers, his own lips slightly smiling to the applause. At a sign, two slaves attempted to help him sit upright again. But they were weak, his frame was mighty, and the four old men tottered and shook as they helped him forward.

"But manner of life is neither here nor there," he went on. "We have other business, Porportuk, you and I, to-night. Debts are mischances, and I am in mischance with you. What of my debt, and how great is it?"

Porportuk searched in his pouch and brought forth a memorandum. He sipped at his glass and began. "There is the note of August, 1889, for three hundred dollars. The interest has never been paid. And the note of the next year for five hundred dollars.

This note was included in the note of two months later for a thousand dollars. Then there is the note — "

"Never mind the many notes!" Klakee-Nah cried out impatiently. "They make my head go around and all the things inside my head. The whole! The round whole! How much is it?"

Porportuk referred to his memorandum. "Fifteen thousand nine hundred and sixty-seven dollars and seventy-five cents," he read with careful precision.

"Make it sixteen thousand, make it sixteen thousand," Klakee-Nah said grandly. "Odd numbers were ever a worry. And now — and it is for this that I have sent for you — make me out a new note for sixteen thousand, which I shall sign. I have no thought of the interest. Make it as large as you will, and make it payable in the next world, when I shall meet you by the fire of the Great Father of all Indians. Then the note will be paid. This I promise you. It is the word of Klakee-Nah."

Porportuk looked perplexed, and loudly the laughter arose and shook the room. Klakee-Nah raised his hands. "Nay," he cried. "It is not a joke. I but speak in fairness. It was for this I sent for you, Porportuk. Make out the note."

"I have no dealings with the next world," Porportuk made answer slowly.

"Have you no thought to meet me before the Great Father!" Klakee-Nah demanded. Then he added, "I shall surely be there."

"I have no dealings with the next world," Porportuk repeated sourly.

The dying man regarded him with frank amazement.

"I know naught of the next world," Porportuk explained. "I do business in this world."

Klakee-Nah's face cleared. "This comes of sleeping cold of nights," he laughed. He pondered for a space, then said, "It is in this world that you must be paid. There remains to me this house. Take it, and burn the debt in the candle there."

"It is an old house and not worth the money," Porportuk made answer.

"There are my mines on the Twisted Salmon."

"They have never paid to work," was the reply.

"There is my share in the steamer *Koyokuk*. I am half owner."

"She is at the bottom of the Yukon."

Klakee-Nah started. "True, I forgot. It was last spring when the ice went out." He mused for a time, while the glasses remained untasted, and all the company waited upon his utterance.

"Then it would seem I owe you a sum of money which I cannot pay . . . in this world?" Porportuk nodded and glanced down the table.

"Then it would seem that you, Porportuk, are a poor business man," Klakee-Nah said slyly.

And boldly Porportuk made answer, "No; there is security yet untouched."

"What!" cried Klakee-Nah. "Have I still property? Name it, and it is yours, and the debt is no more."

"There it is." Porportuk pointed at El-Soo.

Klakee-Nah could not understand. He peered down the table, brushed his eyes, and peered again.

"Your daughter, El-Soo — her will I take and the debt be no more. I will burn the debt there in the candle."

Klakee-Nah's great chest began to heave. "Ho! ho! — a joke — Ho! ho! ho!" he laughed Homerically. "And with your cold bed and daughters old enough to be the mother of El-Soo! Ho! ho! ho!" He began to cough and strangle, and the old slaves smote him on the back. "Ho! ho!" he began again, an went off into another paroxysm.

Porportuk waited patiently, sipping from his glass and studying the double row of faces down the board. "It is no joke," he said finally. "My speech is well meant."

Klakee-Nah sobered and looked at him, then reached for his glass, but could not touch it. A slave passed it to him, and glass and liquor he flung into the face of Porportuk.

"Turn him out!" Klakee-Nah thundered to the waiting table that strained like a pack of hounds in leash. "And roll him in the snow!"

As the mad riot swept past him and out of doors, he signalled to the slaves, and the four tottering old men supported him on his feet as he met the returning revellers, upright, glass in hand, pledging them a toast to the short night when a man sleeps warm.

It did not take long to settle the estate of Klakee-Nah. Tommy, the little Englishman, clerk at the trading post, was called in by

El-Soo to help. There was nothing but debts, notes overdue, mortgaged properties, and properties mortgaged but worthless. Notes and mortgages were held by Porportuk. Tommy called him a robber many times as he pondered the compounding of the interest.

"Is it a debt, Tommy?" El-Soo asked.

"It is a robbery," Tommy answered.

"Nevertheless, it is a debt," she persisted.

The winter wore away, and the early spring, and still the claims of Porportuk remained unpaid. He saw El-Soo often and explained to her at length, as he had explained to her father, the way the debt could be cancelled. Also, he brought with him old medicine-men, who elaborated to her the ever-lasting damnation of her father if the debt were not paid. One day, after such an elaboration, El-Soo made final announcement to Porportuk.

"I shall tell you two things," she said. "First, I shall not be your wife. Will you remember that? Second, you shall be paid the last cent of the sixteen thousand dollars — "

Fifteen thousand nine hundred and sixty-seven dollars and seventy-five cents," Porportuk corrected.

"My father said sixteen thousand," was her reply. "You shall be paid."

"How?"

"I know not how, but I shall find out how. Now go, and bother me no more. If you do" — she hesitated to find fitting penalty — "if you do, I shall have you rolled in the snow again as soon as the first snow flies."

This was still in the early spring, and a little later El-Soo surprised the country. Word went up and down the Yukon from Chilcoot to the Delta, and was carried from camp to camp to the farthermost camps, that in June when the first salmon ran, El-Soo, daughter of Klakee-Nah, would sell herself at public auction to satisfy the claims of Porportuk. Vain were the attempts to dissuade her. The missionary at St. George wrestled with her, but she replied: —

"Only the debts to God are settled in the next world. The debts of men are of this world, and in this world are they settled."

Akoon wrestled with her, but she replied: "I do love thee, Akoon; but honor is greater than love, and who am I that I should blacken my father?" Sister Alberta journeyed all the way up from Holy Cross on the first steamer, and to no better end.

"My father wanders in the thick and endless forests," said El-Soo. "And there will he wander, with the lost souls crying, till the debt be paid. Then and not until then, may he go on to the house of the Great Father."

"And you believe this?" Sister Alberta asked.

"I do not know," El-Soo made answer. "It was my father's belief."

Sister Alberta shrugged her shoulders incredulously.

"Who knows but that the things we believe come true?" El-Soo went on. "Why not? The next world to you may be heaven and harps . . . because you have believed heaven and harps; to my father the next world may be a large house where he will sit always at table feasting with God."

"And you?" Sister Alberta asked. "What is your next world?"

El-Soo hesitated but for a moment. "I should like a little of both," she said. "I should like to see your face as well as the face of my father."

The day of the auction came. Tana-naw Station was populous. As was their custom, the tribes had gathered to await the salmon-run, and in the meantime spent the time in dancing and frolicking, trading, and gossiping. Then there was the ordinary sprinkling of white adventurers, traders, and prospectors, and, in addition, a large number of white men who had come because of curiosity or interest in the affair.

It had been a backward spring, and the salmon were late in running. This delay but keyed up the interest. Then, on the day of the auction, the situation was made tense by Akoon. He arose and made public and solemn announcement that whosoever bought El-Soo would forthwith and immediately die. He flourished the Winchester in his hand to indicate the manner of the taking-off. El-Soo was angered thereat; but he refused to speak with her, and went to the trading post to lay in extra ammunition.

The first salmon was caught at ten o'clock in the evening, and at midnight the auction began. It took place on top of the high bank alongside the Yukon. The sun was due north just below the horizon, and the sky was lurid red. A great crowd gathered about the table and the two chairs that stood near the edge of the bank. To the fore were many white men and several chiefs. And most prominently to the fore, rifle in hand, stood Akoon. Tommy, at El-Soo's request, served as auctioneer, but she made the opening speech and described the goods about to be sold. She was in native costume, in the dress of a chief's daughter, splendid and barbaric, and she stood on a chair, that she might be seen to advantage.

"Who will buy a wife?" she asked. "Look at me. I am twenty years old and a maid. I will be a good wife to the man who buys me. If he is a white man, I shall dress in the fashion of white women; if he is an Indian, I shall dress as" — she hesitated a moment — "a squaw. I can make my own clothes, and sew, and wash, and mend. I was taught for eight years to do these things at Holy Cross Mission. I can read and write English, and I know how to play the organ. Also I can do arithmetic and some algebra — a little. I shall be sold to the highest bidder, and to him I will make out a bill of sale of myself. I forgot to say that I can sing very well, and that I have never been sick in my life. I weigh one hundred and thirty-two pounds; my father is dead and I have no relatives. Who wants me?"

She looked over the crowd with flaming audacity and stepped down. At Tommy's request she stood upon the chair again, while he mounted the second chair and started the bidding.

Surrounding El-Soo stood the four old slaves of her father. They were age-twisted and palsied, faithful to their meat, a generation out of the past that watched unmoved the antics of younger life. In the front of the crowd were several Eldorado and Bonanza kings from the Upper Yukon, and beside them, on crutches, swollen with scurvy, were two broken prospectors. From the midst of the crowd, thrust out by its own vividness, appeared the face of a wild-eyed squaw from the remote regions of the Upper Tananaw; a strayed Sitkan from the coast stood side by side with a Stick from Lake Le Barge, and, beyond, a half-dozen French-Canadian voyageurs, grouped by themselves. From afar came the faint cries of myriads of wild-fowl on the nesting-grounds. Swallows were skimming up overhead from the placid surface of the Yukon, and robins were singing. The oblique rays of the hidden sun shot through the smoke, high-dissipated from forest fires a thousand miles away, and turned the heavens to somber red, while the earth shone red in the reflected glow. This red glow shone in the faces of all, and made everything seem unearthly and unreal.

The bidding began slowly. The Sitkan, who was a stranger in the land and who had arrived only half an hour before, offered one hundred dollars in a confident voice, and was surprised when Akoon turned threateningly upon him with the rifle. The bidding dragged. An Indian from the Tozikakat, a pilot, bid one hundred and fifty, and after some time a gambler, who had been ordered out of the Upper Country, raised the bid to two hundred. El-Soo was saddened; her pride was hurt; but the only effect was that she flamed more audaciously upon the crowd.

There was a disturbance among the onlookers as Porportuk forced his way to the front. "Five hundred dollars!" he bid in a loud voice, then looked about him proudly to note the effect.

He was minded to use his great wealth as a bludgeon with which to stun all competition at the start. But one of the voyageurs, looking on El-Soo with sparkling eyes, raised the bid a hundred.

"Seven hundred!" Porportuk returned promptly.

And with equal promptness came the "Eight hundred," of the voyageur.

Then Porportuk swung his club again. "Twelve hundred!" he shouted.

With a look of poignant disappointment the voyageur succumbed. There was no further bidding. Tommy worked hard, but could not elicit a bid.

El-Soo spoke to Porportuk. "It were good, Porportuk, for you to weigh well your bid. Have you forgotten the thing I told you — that I would never marry you!"

"It is a public auction," he retorted. "I shall buy you with a bill of sale. I have offered twelve hundred dollars. You come cheap."

"Too damned cheap!" Tommy cried. "What if I am auctioneer? That does not prevent me from bidding. I'll make it thirteen hundred."

"Fourteen hundred," from Porportuk.

"I'll buy you in to be my — my sister," Tommy whispered to El-Soo, then called aloud, "Fifteen hundred!"

At two thousand, one of the Eldorado kings took a hand, and Tommy dropped out.

A third time Porportuk swung the club of his wealth, making a clean raise of five hundred dollars. But the Eldorado king's pride was touched. No man could club him. And he swung back another five hundred.

El-Soo stood at three thousand. Porportuk made it thirty-five hundred, and gasped when the Eldorado king raised it a thousand dollars. Porportuk again raised it five hundred, and again gasped when the king raised a thousand more.

Porportuk became angry. His pride was touched; his strength was challenged, and with him strength took the form of wealth. He would not be ashamed for weakness before the world. El-Soo became incidental. The savings and scrimpings from the cold nights of all his years were ripe to be squandered. El-Soo stood at six thousand. He made it seven thousand. And then, in thousand-dollar bids, as fast as they could be uttered, her price went up. At fourteen thousand, the two men stopped for breath.

Then the unexpected happened. A still heavier club was swung. In the pause that ensued, the gambler, who had scented a speculation and formed a syndicate with several of his fellows, bid sixteen thousand dollars.

"Seventeen thousand," Porportuk said weakly.

"Eighteen thousand," said the king.

Porportuk gathered his strength. "Twenty thousand."

The syndicate dropped out. The Eldorado king raised a thousand, and Porportuk raised back; and as they bid, Akoon turned from one to the other, half menacingly, half curiously, as though to see what manner of man it was that he would have to kill. When the king prepared to make his next bid, Akoon having pressed closer, the king first loosed the revolver at his hip, then said: —

"Twenty-three thousand."

"Twenty-four thousand," said Porportuk. He grinned viciously, for the certitude of his bidding had at last shaken the king. The latter moved over close to El-Soo. He studied her carefully, for a long while.

"And five hundred," he said at last.

"Twenty-five thousand," came Porportuk's raise.

The king looked for a long space, and shook his head. He looked again, and said reluctantly, "And five hundred."

"Twenty-six thousand," Porportuk snapped.

The king shook his head and refused to meet Tommy's pleading eye. In the meantime Akoon had edged close to Porportuk. El-Soo's quick eye noted this, and, while Tommy wrestled with the Eldorado king for another bid, she bent, and spoke in a low voice in the ear of a slave. And while Tommy's "Going — going — going — " dominated the air, the slave went up to Akoon and spoke in a low voice in his ear. Akoon made no sign that he had heard, though El-Soo watched him anxiously.

"Gone!" Tommy's voice rang out. "To Porportuk, for twenty-six thousand dollars."

Porportuk glanced uneasily at Akoon. All eyes were centered upon Akoon, but he did nothing.

"Let the scales be brought," said El-Soo.

"I shall make payment at my house," said Porportuk.

"Let the scales be brought," El-Soo repeated. "Payment shall be made here where all can see."

So the gold-scales were brought from the trading post, while Porportuk went away and came back with a man at his heals, on whose shoulders was a weight of gold-dust in moose-hide sacks. Also, at Porportuk's back, walked another man with a rifle, who had eyes only for Akoon.

"Here are the notes and mortgages," said Porportuk, "for fifteen thousand nine hundred and sixty-seven dollars and seventy-five cents."

El-Soo received them into her hands and said to Tommy, "Let them be reckoned as sixteen thousand."

"There remains ten thousand dollars to be paid in gold," Tommy said.

Porportuk nodded, and untied the mouths of the sacks. El-Soo, standing at the edge of the bank, tore the papers to shreds and sent them fluttering out over the Yukon. The weighing began, but halted.

"Of course, at seventeen dollars," Porportuk had said to Tommy, as he adjusted the scales.

"At sixteen dollars," El-Soo said sharply.

"It is the custom of all the land to reckon gold at seventeen dollars for each ounce," Porportuk replied. "And this is a business transaction."

El-Soo laughed. "It is a new custom," she said. "It began this spring. Last year, and the years before, it was sixteen dollars an ounce. When my father's debt was made, it was sixteen dollars. When he spent at the store the money he got from you, for one ounce he was give sixteen dollars' worth of flour, not seventeen." Porportuk grunted and allowed the weighing to proceed.

"Weigh it in three piles, Tommy," she said. "A thousand dollars here, three thousand there, and here six thousand."

It was slow work, and, while the weighing went on, Akoon was closely watched by all.

"He but waits till the money is paid," one said; and the word went around and was accepted, and they waited for what Akoon should do when the money was paid. And Porportuk's man with the rifle waited and watched Akoon.

The weighing was finished, and the gold-dust lay on the table in three dark-yellow heaps. "There is a debt of my father to the Company for three thousand dollars," said El-Soo. "Take it, Tommy, for the Company. And here are four old men, Tommy. You know them. And here is one thousand dollars. Take it, and see that the old men are never hungry and never without tobacco."

Tommy scooped the gold into separate sacks. Six thousand dollars remained on the table. El-Soo thrust the scoop into the heap, and with a sudden turn whirled the contents out and down to the Yukon in a golden shower. Porportuk seized her wrist as she thrust the scoop a second time into the heap.

"It is mine," she said calmly. Porportuk released his grip, but he gritted his teeth and scowled darkly as she continued to scoop the gold into the river till none was left.

The crowd had eyes for naught but Akoon, and the rifle of Porportuk's man lay across the hollow of his arm, the muzzle directed at Akoon a yard away, the man's thumb on the hammer. But Akoon did nothing.

"Make out the bill of sale," Porportuk said grimly.

And Tommy made out the bill of sale, wherein all right and title in the woman El-Soo was vested in the man Porportuk. El-Soo signed the document, and Porportuk folded it and put it away in his pouch. Suddenly his eyes flashed, and in sudden speech he addressed El-Soo.

"But it was not your fathers's debt," he said. "What I paid was the price for you. Your sale is business of to-day and not of last year and the years before. The ounces paid for you will buy at the post to-day seventeen dollars of flour, and not sixteen. I have lost a dollar on each ounce. I have lost six hundred and twenty-five dollars."

El-Soo thought for a moment, and saw the error she had made. She smiled, and then she laughed.

"You are right," she laughed "I made a mistake. But it is too late. You have paid, and the gold is gone. You did not think quick. It is your loss. Your wit is slow these days, Porportuk. You are getting old."

He did not answer. He glanced uneasily at Akoon, and was reassured. His lips tightened, and a hint of cruelty came into his face. "Come," he said, "we will go to my house."

"Do you remember the two things I told you in the spring?" El-Soo asked, making no movement to accompany him.

"My head would be full with the things women say, did I heed them," he answered.

"I told you that you would be paid," El-Soo went on carefully. "And I told you that I would never be your wife."

"But that was before the bill of sale." Porportuk crackled the paper between his fingers inside the pouch. "I have bought you before all the world. You belong to me. You will not deny that you belong to me."

"I belong to you," El-Soo said steadily.

"I own you."

"You own me."

Porportuk's voice rose slightly and triumphantly. "As a dog, I own you."

"As a dog you own me," El-Soo continued calmly. "But, Porportuk, you forget the thing I told you. Had any other man bought me, I should have been that man's wife. I should have been a good wife to that man. Such was my will. But my will with you was that I should never be your wife. Wherefore, I am your dog."

Porportuk knew that he played with fire, and he resolved to play firmly. "Then I speak to you, not as El-Soo, but as a dog," he said; "and I tell you to come with me." He half reached to grip her arm, but with a gesture she held him back.

"Not so fast, Porportuk. You buy a dog. The dog runs away. It is your loss. I am your dog. What if I run away?"

"As the owner of the dog, I shall beat you — "

"When you catch me?"

"When I catch you."

"Then catch me."

He reached swiftly for her, but she eluded him. She laughed as she circled around the table. "Catch her!" Porportuk commanded the Indian with the rifle, who stood near to her. But as the Indian stretched forth his arm to her, the Eldorado king felled him with a fist blow under the ear. The rifle clattered to the ground. Then was Akoon's chance. His eyes glittered, but he did nothing.

Porportuk was an old man, but his cold nights retained for him his activity. He did not circle the table. He came across suddenly, over the top of the table. El-Soo was taken off her guard. She sprang back with a sharp cry of alarm, and Porportuk would have caught her had it not been for Tommy. Tommy's leg went out. Porportuk tripped and pitched forward on the ground. El-Soo got her start.

"Then catch me," she laughed over her shoulder, as she fled away.

She ran lightly and easily, but Porportuk ran swiftly and savagely. He outran her. In his youth he had been the swiftest of all the young men. But El-Soo dodged in a willowy, elusive way. Being in native dress, her feet were not cluttered with skirts, and her pliant body curved a flight that defied the gripping fingers of Porportuk.

With laughter and tumult, the great crowd scattered out to see the chase. It led through the Indian encampment; and ever dodging, circling, and reversing, El-Soo and Porportuk appeared and disappeared among the tents. El-Soo seemed to balance herself against the air with her arms, now one side, now on the other, and sometimes her body, too, leaned out upon the air far from the perpendicular as she achieved her sharpest curves. And Porportuk, always a leap behind, or a leap this side or that, like a lean hound strained after her.

They crossed the open ground beyond the encampment and disappeared in the forest. Tana-naw Station waited their reappearance, and long and vainly it waited.

In the meantime Akoon ate and slept, and lingered much at the steamboat landing, deaf to the rising resentment of Tana-naw Station in that he did nothing. Twenty four hours later Porportuk returned. He was tired and savage. He spoke to no one but Akoon, and with him tried to pick a quarrel. But Akoon shrugged his shoulders and walked away. Porportuk did not waste time. He outfitted half a dozen of the young men, selecting the best trackers and travellers, and at their head plunged into the forest.

Next day the steamer *Seattle*, bound up river, pulled in to the shore and wooded up. When the lines were cast off and she churned out from the bank, Akoon was on board in the pilot-house. Not many hours afterward, when it was his turn at the wheel, he saw a small birch-bark canoe put off from the shore. There was only one person in it. He studied it carefully, put the wheel over, and slowed down.

The captain entered the pilot-house. "What's the matter?" he demanded. "The water's good."

Akoon grunted. He saw a larger canoe leaving the bank, and in it were a number of persons. As the *Seattle* lost headway, he put the wheel over some more.

The captain fumed. "It's only a squaw," he protested.

Akoon did not grunt. He was all eyes for the squaw and the pursuing canoe. In the latter six paddles were flashing, while the squaw paddled slowly.

"You'll be aground," the captain protested, seizing the wheel.

But Akoon countered his strength on the wheel and looked him in the eyes. The captain slowly released the spokes.

"Queer beggar," he sniffed to himself.

Akoon held the *Seattle* on the edge of the shoal water and waited till he saw the squaw's fingers clutch the forward rail. Then he signalled for full speed ahead and ground the wheel over. The large canoe was very near, but the gap between it and the steamer was widening.

The squaw laughed and leaned over the rail. "Then catch me, Porportuk!" she cried.

Akoon left the steamer at Fort Yukon. He outfitted a small poling boat and went up the Porcupine River. And with him went El-Soo. It was a weary journey and the way led across the back-bone of the world; but Akoon had travelled it before. When they came to the head-waters of the Porcupine, they left the boat and went on foot across the Rocky Mountains.

Akoon greatly liked to walk behind El-Soo and watch the movement of her. There was a music in it that he loved. And especially he loved the well-rounded calves in their sheaths of soft-tanned leather, the slim ankles, and the small moccasined feet that were tireless through the longest days.

"You are light as air," he said, looking up at her. "It is no labor for you to walk. You almost float, so lightly do your feet rise and fall. You are like a deer, El-Soo; you are like a deer, and your eyes are like deer's eyes now as you look at me."

And El-Soo, luminous and melting, bent and kissed Akoon.

"When we reach the Mackenzie, we will not delay," Akoon said later. "We will go south before the winter catches us. We will go to the sunlands where there is no snow. But we will return. I have seen much of the world, and there is no land like Alaska, no sun like our sun, and the snow is good after the long summer."

"And you will learn to read," said El-Soo.

And Akoon said, "I will surely learn to read."

But there was delay when they reached the Mackenzie. They fell in with a band of Mackenzie Indians and, hunting, Akoon was shot by accident. The rifle was in the hands of a youth. The bullet broke Akoon's right arm and, ranging farther, broke two of his ribs. Akoon knew rough surgery, while El-Soo had learned some refinement at Holy Cross. The bones were finally set, and Akoon lay by the fire for them to knit. Also, he lay by the fire so that the smoke would keep the mosquitoes away.

Then it was that Porportuk, with his six young men, arrived. Akoon groaned in his helplessness and made appeal to the Mackenzies. But Porportuk made demand, and the Mackenzies were perplexed. Porportuk was for seizing upon El-Soo, but this they would not permit. Judgment must be given, and, as it was an affair of man and woman, the council of the old men was called — this that warm judgment might not be given by the young men, who were warm of heart.

The old men sat in a circle about the smudge-fire. Their faces were lean and wrinkled, and they gasped and panted for air. The smoke was not good for them. Occasionally they struck with withered hands at the mosquitoes that braved the smoke. After such exertion they coughed hollowly and painfully. Some spat blood, and one of them sat a bit apart with head bowed forward, and bled slowly and continuously at the mouth; the coughing sickness had gripped them. They were as dead men; their time was short. It was a judgment of the dead.

"And I paid for her a heavy price," Porportuk concluded his complaint. "Such a price you have never seen. Sell all that is yours — sell your spears and arrows and rifles, sell your skins and furs, sell your tents and boats and dogs, sell everything, and you will not have maybe a thousand dollars. Yet did I pay for the woman, El-Soo, twenty-six times the price of all your spears and arrows and rifles, your skins and furs, your tents and boats and dogs. It was a heavy price."

The old men nodded gravely, though their weazened eye-slits widened with wonder that any woman should be worth such a price. The one that bled at the mouth wiped his lips. "Is it true talk?" he asked each of Porportuk's six young men. And each answered that it was true.

"Is it true talk?" he asked El-Soo, and she answered, "It is true."

"But Porportuk has not told that he is an old man," Akoon said, "and that he has daughters older than El-Soo."

"It is true, Porportuk is an old man," said El-Soo.

"It is for Porportuk to measure the strength of his age," said he who bled at the mouth. "We be old men. Behold! Age is never so old as youth would measure it."

And the circle of old men champed their gums, and nodded approvingly, and coughed.

"I told him that I would never be his wife," said El-Soo.

"Yet you took from him twenty-six times all that we possess?" asked a one-eyed old man.

El-Soo was silent.

"It is true?" and his one eye burned and bored into her like a fiery gimlet.

"It is true," she said.

"But I will run away again," she broke out passionately, a moment later. "Always will I run away."

"That is for Porportuk to consider," said another of the old men. "It is for us to consider the judgment."

"What price did you pay for her?" was demanded of Akoon.

"No price did I pay for her," he answered. "She was above price. I did not measure her in gold-dust, nor in dogs, and tents, and furs."

The old men debated among themselves and mumbled in undertones. "These old men are ice," Akoon said in English. "I will not listen to their judgment, Porportuk. If you take El-Soo, I will surely kill you."

The old men ceased and regarded him suspiciously. "We do not know the speech you make," one said.

"He but said that he would kill me," Porportuk volunteered. "So it were well to take from him his rifle, and to have some of your young men sit by him, that he may not do me hurt. He is a young man, and what are broken bones to youth!"

Akoon, lying helpless, had rifle and knife taken from him, and to either side of his shoulders sat young men of the Mackenzies. The one-eyed old man arose and stood upright. "We marvel at the price paid for one mere woman," he began; "but the wisdom of the price is no concern of ours. We are here to give judgment, and judgment we give. We have no doubt. It is known to all that Porportuk paid a heavy price for the woman El-Soo. Wherefore does the woman El-Soo belong to Porportuk and none other." He sat down heavily, and coughed. The old men nodded and coughed.

"I will kill you," Akoon cried in English.

Porportuk smiled and stood up. "You have given true judgment," he said to the council, "and my young men will give to you much tobacco. Now let the woman be brought to me."

Akoon gritted his teeth. The young men took El-Soo by the arms. She did not resist, and was led, her face a sullen flame to Porportuk.

"Sit there at my feet till I have made my talk," he commanded. He paused a moment. "It is true," he said, "I am an old man. Yet can I understand the ways of youth. The fire has not all gone out of me. Yet am I no longer young, nor am I minded to run these old legs of mine through all the years that remain to me. El-Soo can run fast and well. She is a deer. This I know, for I have seen and run after her. It is not good that a wife should run so fast. I paid for her a heavy price, yet does she run away from me. Akoon paid no price at all, yet does she run to him.

"When I came among you people of the Mackenzie, I was of one mind. As I listened in the council and thought of the swift legs of El-Soo, I was of many minds. Now I am of one mind again, but it is a different mind from the one I brought to the council. Let me tell you my mind. When a dog runs once away from a master, it will run away again. No matter how many times it is brought back, each time it will run away again. When we have such dogs, we sell them. El-Soo is like a dog that runs away. I will sell her. Is there any man of the council that will buy?"

The old men coughed and remained silent.

"Akoon would buy," Porportuk went on, "but he has no money. Wherefore I will give El-Soo to him as he said, without price. Even now will I give her to him."

Reaching down, he took El-Soo by the hand and led her across the space to where Akoon lay on his back.

"She has a bad habit, Akoon," he said, seating her at Akoon's feet. "As she has run away from me in the past, in the days to come she may run away from you. But there is no need to fear that she will ever run away, Akoon. I shall see to that. Never will she run away from you — this the word of Porportuk. She has great wit. I know, for often has it bitten into me. Yet am I minded myself to give my wit play for once. And by my wit will I secure her to you, Akoon."

Stooping, Porportuk crossed El-Soo's feet, so that the instep of one lay over that of the other, and then, before his purpose could be divined, he discharged his rifle through the two ankles. As Akoon struggled to rise against the weight of the young men, there was heard the crunch of the broken bone rebroken.

"It is just," said the old men, one to another.

El-Soo made no sound. She sat and looked at her shattered ankles, on which she would never walk again.

"My legs are strong, El-Soo," Akoon said. "But never will they bear me away from you."

El-Soo looked at him, and for the first time in all the time he had known her, Akoon saw tears in her eyes.

"Your eyes are like deer's eyes, El-Soo," he said.

"Is it just?" Porportuk asked, and grinned from the edge of the smoke as he prepared to depart.

"It is just," the old men said. And they sat on in the silence.

Jack Schaefer

~~~~~~

A *journalist who began writing fiction for relaxation,*
Jack Schaefer (1907-1991) began his writing career
with the novel for which he is today best known, Shane,
first published in 1946 in Argosy *as a three-part serial*
titled "Rider from Nowhere." By the early 1950s Schaefer
had four books in print about the West but had never been
west of the Mississippi River. In 1953 he moved to New
Mexico, where he lived until his death. Known for his
versatility and the variety of his work, Schaefer is also the
author of many novels, including The Canyon *and* Mavericks, *the nonfiction* An American Bestiary, *and several*
collections of short stories. If any one theme may be said
to characterize his fiction, it is the strength and endurance
of individuals in the West.

Kittura Remsberg
The Collected Stories of Jack Schaefer, 1966

K ittura Remsberg was my grandmother. My mother's
mother. I knew her only the few weeks I spent at the
ranch near Kalispell one summer, and then only as little more
than a presence, dark eyes and still dark hair above the prominent
cheekbones of a permanent invalid held to her bed within the
walls of the room that compassed all that remained of her life. It
was a big room, big and quiet and cool even when the summer
burned the wide reaches of the range outside. I was in it only the
few times she asked for me. I never went in voluntarily because
I was afraid of her. She was not a storybook grandmother. She was

an impatient, sharp-tongued personality with no softness for me in her. Yet I remember that room with a clarity and a feeling that spring unfailing across the years. I remember it because she was there and she filled it with a bigness and a quietness and a strange cool strength of spirit. There was peace in that room.

I would not have spent those weeks at the ranch if my parents had not been hard-pressed and unable to hire a nurse when my sister had rheumatic fever. They felt I should be sent away for a while and there was no place else to send me. They worried for days before they did send me because my mother disapproved of Ben Remsberg, her father, my grandfather. She had married early to get away and into town and not be dependent on him. She said that he drank too much and that he had a violent temper. She said that no decent person who could get away would live long in the same house with him. From her point of view perhaps she was right. I saw him drunk more than once during those few weeks and heard him shout in frequent fury at the fat old Mexican woman who did the housework and at the one old cowhand who had stayed with him. But he was kind to me and let me tag him about asking endless questions. And he told me about the woman, his wife, my grandmother, lying quietly in the big cool room.

There was nothing peculiar about his telling me, though my mother always said he was difficult to talk to. He told me because I asked him. I asked him because I noticed he was different when he went into that room. He was loud and angry much of the time outside of it. But when he passed through that doorway he was different. He usually closed the door after him, and then for a while after he came out he would be soft-spoken and absent-minded as if he were out of focus with things immediately around him. Once he left the door partly open and I peered in. He was sitting on a chair by the bed with one of his blunt hands resting on the counterpane beside her and she was sitting in the bed with her back to a pillow and one of her thin hands was on his hand and they were just sitting there together. When he came out I asked him about her and he told me. He told me about her and about the mirror, and I saw it once in the loft of the storage barn, the heavy gilt paint of the ornate frame chipping off and only a few pieces of jagged glass left in one corner.

The whole story has come clear in my mind through the years. Some of the details and spoken words may not be true to absolute exact fact. But the whole of it means truth to me. Kittura Remsberg was my grandmother and I want to tell you about her.

Kittura Perkins was her maiden name. She was the third daughter of a prosperous landowner in Pennsylvania about thirty miles out of Philadelphia. He was a man of real substance in his part of the State. They lived in the main farmhouse on the property where he could hold sharp watch on his crops and see that the hired men earned their keep. He also owned a share in a shipping business in the city and he had filled the farmhouse with fine furniture brought from Europe at bargain intervals by his company's ships. His wife, Kittura's mother, had died when she was small, and the two older sisters had done their futile best to raise her as a proper young lady.

Kitt Perkins everyone called her during those years just after the Civil War, and she knew everyone in the neighborhood and everyone knew her as a strong-willed girl whose vital coloring and manner contrasted sharply with the pallid gentility of her sisters and whose habits of going her own way and speaking her own mind annoyed her careful father. The young men knew her and wanted to know her better. She herself was constantly disappointed in them. She knew what she wanted and one day she saw it.

What she saw was a deep-bodied young man lifting an anvil out of a wagon and setting it on the ground and kneeling to hammer horseshoes into shape on it with slow deliberate strokes. He was the son of a Belgian immigrant who had come into the neighborhood some years before and set up a blacksmith shop. She had seen him often helping his father, but now she really saw him for the first time. She liked the shape of him, solid and thick through. She liked the way he looked at her, measuring her without offense as a healthy human animal whose vitality might match his own. She did not like the way he kept silent, withdrawing as if he realized a gap between them.

She went straight to him. "Why won't you speak to me?"

He laid the hammer on the anvil and looked up at her. "That wouldn't do anybody any good. I'm not your kind."

"That's ridiculous."

"Yes? Your father wouldn't like it."

"Ben Remsberg," she said, "I am not my father."

That was the beginning. They were together each evening after that for nearly two weeks. They walked the fields long miles that seemed short, often talking eagerly and as often being silent and content to be. Then one evening she stopped and looked straight at him. "I want you to call on me tomorrow night. At home."

He came, and he was awkward in his dress-up clothes. He was uncomfortable talking to her in the fine parlor. He was more uncomfortable when her sisters stepped in to be introduced and made a point of departing quickly upstairs. He stood stiffly at attention when her father entered and greeted him coldly, and in the midst of a tight silence he turned and walked steadily out and down the flat stone path toward the road.

She sat silent, hurt anger rising, and then there was no anger and she ran after him. She called from the front stoop and he went steadily on and she caught him by the picket gate and swung him around. "Ben, don't be a fool."

He took her by the arms and shook her fiercely and her head rose defiantly and he pulled her to him. She came reaching for him, and as she felt the hard crushing strength of his body, she knew that she was right.

She stepped back, chewing on her lower lip. "Ben, be honest with me. Are you afraid of my father?"

"No, but he doesn't want me in his house so I'll never set foot in it again."

"Then I won't either."

He stared at her, startled. "Where will you go?"

"Wherever you go."

"But — but I oughtn't to marry you."

"Why not?"

"No money, that's why. I haven't got anything."

"Ben," she said, "you'll have me."

They were married that night. They sent word to her father and went home to the little house behind the blacksmith shop and his father blessed them in his flowing French and moved into the room over the shop and they were alone in the little house together. In the morning he was tall with the arrogance of possession and she was certain that she was right. She was so certain of many things.

"Ben, we'll have to set foot in father's house again, after all. To get my clothes. And of course my mirror."

They drove a wagon to the big farmhouse and her sisters watched in disapproving silence while they carried out the contents of her old mahogany wardrobe. He was surprised when he saw the mirror. It was full-length, tall enough for the tallest man, cased in a heavy frame, hand-carved and gilt-painted. He had to rest often lugging it down the stairs and to the wagon. And all the while she talked, telling him about it. "I've had it ever since I was a little girl. Father had it brought from England, some old place there, and I made such a fuss he said I could have it. I like to sit with it. Fixing myself and thinking. That's how I first knew you were the man I'd marry. Oh, not you of course, then. Someone like you."

And when he carried it into their little house, the ceiling of their bedroom was too low for it to stand upright and he had to rig a way to fasten it sideways on the wall where it looked strange and grotesque until she covered the heavy carving of the top and bottom, now the sides, with cloth like curtains, and it was a part of the room, giving depth like a seeing into and beyond the confining walls.

They lived quietly to themselves and for the first months being together was enough. But the blacksmith shop was small. Most of its meager business came from the poorer farmers who lived nearby. They would barely have scraped along except for the small income she had from her mother's estate. Then one morning he and his father were repairing the cracked axle of a loaded grain cart and suddenly the cart crumpled and overturned, sending him sprawling and pinning his father under the weight of the piled bags. Three days his father lay in the bedroom watching the mirror catch the sun through the one window and on the third day died, apologetic to his last breath over the trouble he had caused. And money was a bit easier for them after the funeral expenses because all that came into the shop was theirs.

Easier. Not easy enough. Ben Remsberg was no businessman, not in the cautious penny-watching way of the people with whom he had to deal. He used better materials and did better work than most of his customers paid for. He could not refuse a call on his time even from a man already behind in paying for past work. At the end of the month he would be short on the rent for the shop and the house and it would be her money that matched the amount. For the next days he would be irritable and too harsh demanding payment and his mouth would be tight in a straight line.

Then one evening she looked at him over the supper dishes and chewed on her lower lip. "Ben, you don't want to be a blacksmith all your life do you?'

He stared down at his empty plate, searching his own mind for her. "No. And not here. When I was a kid, I used to think some of striking out somewhere for myself."

"Why didn't you?"

"Oh, I don't know. First there was papa. Now there's you."

She looked at him, serious and perhaps a bit frightened. "Ben, be honest with me. What do you want to do with your life?"

"I guess I want to be some place where it's new. Where a man can start with nothing and show what he is. I've thought some of going West."

She chewed on her lip a long moment. She remembered many things out of the passing days, little things like his sullen naming of a price for a poor farmer when his impulse was to give freely of himself in open fellowship. She remembered the wideness of him, the stretching bigness that was not of his body alone that seemed to be shrinking at each month's end. She remembered and spoke quickly to have it said.

"You ought to do it, Ben. Go West or wherever you want."

He stared at her, startled. "You mean just do it? Just like that?"

"Yes. That's the way to do things. Or else you might never do them."

"But — but you don't mean to go and leave you?'

"I mean go find where you want to be and come back and get me."

"But — but a man can't — "

"Ben, don't ever let me be in your way."

He left her in the morning, swinging down the road to Philadelphia and a start on the first train west with an extra shirt and several pairs of socks in a neat bundle under his arm. She watched him go and turned back into the house and closed the door, and with it closed a period in her life and began another, the years of being alone.

Four years. Four years and some months. She sold the equipment in the shop and rented the building to an elderly farmer for a small grocery store. With that and her own income she was independent. She waited and sat hours in front of the mirror and steadied her mind against the waiting with thoughts of the fine big home they would build, somewhere, sometime. And she saved what she could of the money available and bought things they would need for the home. Bedclothes and linens and dishes, and on rare occasions pieces of silver. She took wooden boxes from the store and packaged the things in these, snugly packed and repacked for the journey to wherever they would be together.

With Ben gone, she began to see her family again. Once a month her sisters came to call in the family carriage. They came with a sense of duty and did not disguise the fact that they were sorry for her, and they never stayed long because she never let them see that she might be sorry for herself. Once a week her father came. He would knock on the door, and when she opened it he would take off his hat and say: "Well, Kittura, are you ready to come home now?" And when she would shake her head, he would turn and walk away in stubborn wonderment.

A few weeks after Ben left, a card came from Cincinnati. He was working his way on a river boat and moving west. Later there was another from St. Louis. He was moving on by rail tending a carload of herd bulls and thought there might be a ranch job at the end of the line. That was all. And the months stretched into years, and the note came, the hurried scrawl: "Forget about me. I'm not your kind."

She sat by the mirror and read the note again and again. She tore the paper across and dropped it on the floor and took another piece and wrote a single line on it. "Ben," she wrote, "don't be a fool." She tucked this piece in an envelope and saw the Fort Laramie postmark on his note and addressed her envelope to him care of General Delivery there and walked to the postoffice and mailed it. The months passed and she sat by the mirror and saw the straightness growing in her lips, and she cut expenses more to buy more things for the boxes beginning to fill the front room of the little house. And after four years and some months he was there, suddenly and completely and travel-worn in the doorway with paper in his hand.

"Kitt, I came damn near being a fool. This caught up with me and I pulled in sharp. Got me a stake and found a place."

"A place, Ben? Is it what you want?"

"Yes. A nice piece of range off near the mountains where nobody's spoiled it. I've got a few mavericks on it already."

"Mavericks, Ben?"

"Sure. Calves. Orphans. No one to claim them. I scoured them out of the brush and slapped my brand on them. Our brand. A straight big K."

He was sunburned and rugged with the hard fitness of tough cordwood. He stood in the doorway, a man who owned the earth in company with all men who were men. She felt the wideness spreading out from him. She dropped into a chair and her shoulders shook as the sobs fought in her throat. He leaped to kneel beside her and put out his arms and she gripped him with fingers that dug into his welcome hardness.

"Ben," she kept saying, "Ben, I was right after all, wasn't I, Ben?"

She let him sleep late in the morning while she cooked a good breakfast and she waited until he had eaten. Then she could wait no longer and hurried to show him her boxes. He followed from one to the next and on to them all, and amazement grew in him till it burst out in shout that shook the house.

"Good God, Kitt! All that stuff! It's wonderful! But do you realize where you're going? Way out to the end of nowhere. It's four hundred miles from the nearest railhead. All I've got anyway is a two-room shack. We're starting small, Kitt."

"Suppose we are. We won't always be small. We'll be building a decent place."

"Sure. That'll come. But we've got no use for stuff like this now. What we need is good breeding cows and couple of the right kind of range bulls."

"I just don't care, Ben. These things are going with us. We'll keep them till we can use them. I'll get mother's money from the bank and we'll send them by train and buy wagons for the rest of the way."

"Why, I bet you'd even try to take that mirror."

"Of course. Especially my mirror."

They waited five weeks for the shipment at the railhead out of Corinne in Utah Territory. She had time after the excitement of the long train trip to become accustomed to the change in all that had been familiar. She learned to endure the dust and the heat that swirled by day through the one street of the crowded town and the nighttime noise that penetrated the room over a saloon that was the only one they could find. She was even proud of Ben in his worn Western clothes with a gun at his side and meeting and mingling with strange kinds of men in an easy equality. But it was then that the fear began to creep into her, not a physical fear but a far-back shrinking from the newness and rawness and sprawling bigness of the land. She clung in her mind to the thought of her boxes coming and with them the wide flat crate that held the mirror, the tangible evidences of the life she had known and that she would be taking with her. She was reassured when the things came and were stowed with their supplies in two heavy wagons and they headed north, she and Ben and her boxes and the two teams pulling the wagons, and the lank silent prospector who was driving one to pay his way northward to the mining country. They moved along rapidly the first days and crossed into Idaho and pushed steadily north until the ground began to drop into the valley of the Snake River and they reached the south bank and followed upstream to cross at Fort Hall.

They had to wait two more weeks there because reports of Indian raids were drifting down country and military orders were that no wagons could travel except in companies of ten or more. When they started again, part of a long various procession of vehicles, their driver disappeared the first night out, disappeared into the darkness, and why and what happened to him they never knew, and she had to drive their second wagon after that, wincing at the grind of the hard leather until the calluses formed on her hands.

The season was far advanced by now. Grass for the horses was sparse and burned and water was often more than a full day's drive ahead. Day merged into day as the motley procession climbed the long rolling rise out of the valley and struck across the high plateau toward the mountains and the Montana line and the safety of Bannack City. Twice the company's lone point rider reported Indian signs and once they saw smoke signals rising far off in the horizon haze. The men drove for all possible distance each daylight hour and grew ever more grim in the circle of wagons at night. The nameless fear of the new land crept into her again, and she might have begged Ben to turn back if turning back would not have been worse than going forward. Their horses, straining long days into the tugs of the heavy wagons, wasted down to a weakening thinness and slowed in pace until she and Ben dropped back place by place in the procession and were among the last stragglers to reach camp at night. And then, in the forenoon of one day so relentlessly like the others, the fear took her.

They had reached a rocky dry gulch where they had expected to find at least a trickle of water still running. There were only dust and caked mud and the bare stones baking in the sun. The other wagons had crossed the dry ford and were pushing on. She had seen Ben, showing her the way for their own wagons as he always did, swing his team to hit the crossing at an angle and avoid the biggest stones. She followed and tried to do the same, and as the horses settled to the pull up the other side a rear wheel struck a rock and the wagon stopped. She urged the team sideways and forward and heard the wheel grind on the rock and drop back immovable. She saw the other wagons moving on, the distance growing, and the fear rushed through her. Frantically she slapped at the horses with the reins and they lunged forward and one of them floundered in the loose gravel of the slope and went down. She saw the horse fight upward and stand with one leg hanging useless and her scream brought men upright and pulling in their teams all along the line ahead.

She sat on the seat silent and unable to move. She saw Ben standing beside the wagon and staring at her and at the horse and then walking to meet the other men coming and stand with them in hurried talk. She saw them scatter toward their own wagons and Ben coming toward her. He looked up and managed a small tight smile for her. "This does it, Kitt. We tried anyway. Wait for me at the other wagon."

At the sound of his voice she could move and she climbed down and went forward and pulled herself up to the other driving seat. She did not dare look around until after the shot, and when she did turn he was leading the other horse unharnessed and tying it by the bridle to the tailboard behind her. She looked back at the wagon in the gulch piled with her boxes beneath the dusty canvas.

She spoke softly in simple wonder. "I don't understand, Ben. What are we going to do? Will we tow it?"

"Good God, Kitt! We're going to leave it. Damn near everything else too."

The words hit her mind, but she did not grasp them until he began to pull boxes out of the wagonbed behind her and heave them to one side. Then the fear raced through her again, and she jumped to the ground and ran headlong at him with her hands. "You can't, Ben! You can't!"

He held her from him, shaking her by the arms. "Listen, Kitt. We're miles from anywhere. No water. Horses about played out. Indians maybe near. We have to travel light and might not make it even then."

"No! You can't!" She broke from him and blocked him from the wagon. "I won't have anything left! Not anything!" Her voice rose wailing and he snapped at her in contempt. "If they can, we can." She looked and saw the other men stripping down their wagons and some of the women helping, and she was suddenly ashamed and stepped aside. She stood quietly while he stripped the wagon to the sparse necessities — food and a few tools and the two rifles and several blankets — and she drove away the fear that was not a physical fear, and the conviction came. He was throwing away her defenses against the brutal indifference of this raw land, and if she let this happen she would be alone in a strange nakedness and she would lose contact with a way of life she could never recapture.

When he finished, she spoke quietly. "All right, Ben. I won't make any more fuss. But you've forgotten my mirror." When he stared at her, she spoke again quietly, "I'll leave everything else, but I won't leave that. If we can't take it I'll stay here too." When he still stared at her, she spoke again just as quietly, "Ben, I mean it."

When they moved on, more rapidly now and the last in the long line driving for distance, he sat beside her grim and refusing to look at her as he had been getting the wide flat crate from the abandoned wagon and struggling with it end over end up the slope. She sat huddled on the seat beside him in her own taut silence, and the hours crawled by and she watched the barren burned miles passing under the horses' hooves, and for the first time when they were together they were not together and they lay apart in separate blankets that night, not sleeping and perhaps not hearing the lonely night sounds.

It was the same in the morning. She watched the dust rising under the hooves and moving backwards under the wagon, and with each passing hour the effort to speak became more difficult. Then her head began to rise and a faint suggestion of freshness touched the air, and far ahead almost beyond vision the haze began to shift and take shapes and was no longer haze, but the remote challenging solidity of the mountains. And when speaking no longer seemed possible she spoke: "I was wrong, Ben. I have you."

He swung his head to look at her and some of the grimness left his face. Speaking was easier now and her voice gained strength.

"I was wrong too about bringing all those things. I should have saved the money and we'd have some now for you to buy your cattle."

He sat up straighter on the seat and clucked to the horses. "Just as well, Kitt. Now we're starting right."

She nodded and watched the mountains emerging in sharper outline. "I guess, Ben, I just couldn't accept all this new way of doing things. This — this land. It's so big, and it doesn't seem to know that we're even here. But you don't need to worry about me any more."

"I'm not worrying," he said. "Not about you." And they were together on the seat, gaunt and tired and dusty in a creaking wagon at the tag end of a motley worn procession, but together. He stirred on the seat and licked his dry lips and grinned a little. "That mirror. I guess we've got to take it through somehow if I have to carry the damned thing."

They took it through. Flat in the wagonbed, the wide crate was a seat for two families whose own wagons had broken past repair during the last days before they rolled into Bannack City. It was there, firm ballast in the bottom, when they struck on north through the mountains to Butte and on past Deer Lodge and Gold Creek to Fort Missoula. It was there, almost the only thing left to unload, when they reached the Flathead Lake country and stopped at last by the shack that was their home for the next years.

Nothing, no trick of curtains, could make that mirror be anything but grotesque in that shack. It was out of place, out of keeping, an unbelievable burst of elegance out of another world. Yet there was a rightness in its very wrongness. It was a symbol and a signpost. A reminder and a beckoning. And certainly it was a mark of distinction. It made them quickly known through the Territory, the "looking-glass people," and the word ran and far neighbors came miles to see it. Hung sideways again, it nearly filled one end of the main room of the shack, eye-holding and impressive, and it hung there during the years they put themselves and everything possible into the ranch, reaching out, buying land and cattle, taking long chances on slim credit and always somehow pulling through, the two of them together, seen and known by everyone and always together. And then things were easy for them. He had what he wanted, miles of good range and hundreds of cattle on it, and she could have what she wanted, a house to match the mirror.

Building that house must have been an event in that growing Territory. While she was still planning it, word came that her father had died and she could draw on a third of his estate and they tossed discretion aside and built the house big, rambling and roomy with wide walls and deep-set windows and high-ceilinged with huge beams freighted down from the mountain forests. And she bought and bought things for it, sending as far as Denver and even all the way to New York for them, feeling that at last in a sense she had again and was unpacking her wooden boxes. Together they had defeated the land that had almost defeated her, and her house was her victory banner, what she had once had and known remade for her. She filled it with fine things as her father had his house, and when she was finished the mirror stood upright in their bedroom and merged into the over-all magnificence.

Her one child was born in that bedroom. One. There were no others. Perhaps that bothered her as sometimes it bothered Ben, but it did not mar the running rightness of their being together. They kept open house for all the surrounding country and lived smack up to the edge of their income and beyond and never worried because they had put that behind them years and miles before on the hard board seat of a dust-covered wagon. With heads high and eyes forward they lived straight into the bitter winter of '86.

Summer came early that year, dry and warm. As it progressed, hot winds swept through the valleys and the grass was stunted and shriveled back on its roots. Droughts far down in the Southwest sent extra numbers of cattle north and Ben jumped at the low prices and rented more range and bought till this was too crowded. As fall came he held his herds late, hoping for a rise in the market, and then it was too late. Winter dropped out of the mountains six weeks earlier than usual and gripped the land with a blizzard that blocked all movement. Deadly cold settled and stayed, and as the weeks passed blizzard after blizzard buried even the level stretches under four or five feet of dry packing snow. When the first thaw broke in mid-March, the overflowing streams were choked with the emaciated bodies of dead cattle. When the snow had gone down enough for an attempt at a spring round-up, there were only a few pitiful survivors where thousands had grazed.

Days passed and their men were paid off somehow and drifted away, and Ben Remsberg sat and looked over the ruined land and Kitt Remsberg wandered through her big house and sat by the mirror chewing on her lower lip.

She went to him and sat beside him. "How bad is it, Ben?"

"We're wiped out. Not enough left to pay taxes. And we still owe on cattle lying dead out there. We'll be lucky to hold on to your house." He tried a grin for her and it was worn thin like the feeling coming from him. "I guess I can always be a blacksmith again."

"Ben, what would it take to lick winters like that?"

"Only one way, Kitt. Wind shelters. Plenty of hay for the rough times when the grass is covered. That would take money. For lumber and equipment and barn space. We haven't got it."

"We've got a lot of things in this house that cost a lot of money."

He stared at her, startled. "You — you'd — you mean — "

"I mean we can strip down this house the way you did a wagon once. We can tear down part of it, too, and use the lumber. We'll sell everything in it and start small again."

He stared at her and he grinned again, and she felt the wideness beginning to spread again beside her. "Everything, Kitt?"

"Well, no. Of course not. Not my mirror."

Together they did it, went back to the beginning and began again. They sold everything for what they could get, everything except the mirror and the beds for themselves and the little girl, and they paid most of their debts, and he made what other furniture they needed out of old boards, rough and crude but adequate. They ripped down more than half of the house and built their first hay barn and the first of their wind shelters. They sold part of their range and bought the small first of their new herds and a used mower and a dump-rake. They worked together and progress was slow now, but they moved ahead, and the mirror stood lonely against the wall of their bedroom, but not grotesque in the emptiness of the bare room because it was still the beginning that could always be made again. And then, when they were solidly on their feet again, came the one blow that could break them.

She was riding out to find Ben across the vast stretch of level ground they kept for hay. Life sang in her and she urged the horse into full gallop and it stumbled in a small gully hidden in the tall grass and went to its knees and she pitched forward over its head and rolled with the momentum to crumple unconscious against a rock. Hours later he found the riderless horse by the home corral gate. Still later he found her, struggling toward him, clutching at the tough grasses to drag herself along in limp agony. There was little any doctor could do except ease her pain. She had fractured the base of her spine and she endured the hard cast for months, and when the pain left and the bone knit, the paralysis came, freezing the lower half of her body in a wasting immobility.

She lay in their big bedroom and drove out the despair and hopelessness. She learned to order her household through the two

Mexican women Ben hired to do for her. She held to their ranch through the hours Ben spent with her telling her about it. The months moved inevitably, and she lay in the bedroom and watched the slow changes creep into Ben and herself and their house. She saw them and she refused to see them. She shut them away in her mind and willed herself to believe that nothing of importance was changed. She lay there at night with Ben beside her and waited until he breathed with the long slow regularity of sleep and she could force herself to believe that everything was as it had been because they were there together. But the morning was always bad, the time when he left her, when she watched him disappear through the doorway. And then she discovered what the mirror could do.

Lying there, looking over the foot of the bed, she had been able to see the top of it against the far wall, the carved gilt top of the frame and a small part of the glass. Now she found that when she was raised up to sit against the pillows, she could see almost all of it and it reflected for her a view through the wide window of the side wall. It was thus itself a window, a vista for her vision into the outside world showing part of the broad porch across the front of the house and the curving lane, and beyond that a corner of the barn and the corral beside it, and farther beyond that the stretching reaches of grassland. It carried her out through the confining walls into the world Ben entered when he left the room. She could be out there with him in her thoughts. And looking out through the mirror she could watch when he moved unknowing into the frame of her vision. She could try to determine, from his appearance or actions or something carried, what he was doing, what was happening about the place. Then she could surprise him with what she knew when he came into this other world, their room, to be with her. This was her secret, her solace, her defense. The mirror was her shield until it betrayed her.

She sat in the bed and watched Ben standing on the porch and the other figure appear from somewhere on some errand, the younger of the Mexican women, and stop by him, close and conscious of the closeness. She saw but could not hear them talking and the woman turned away and tossed her head in a quick provocative sidewise glance and he took her by the shoulders and swung her around and pulled her to him. She saw the two figures molded as one in the single intensity and they separated slightly and moved away together out of the mirror, out of the rigid limits of her vision.

Kittura Remsberg lay limp against the pillows of the bed and stared across the room at the mirror. Faithfully it held open its vista into the world outside, but she did not see that. She saw there the slow changes that had been creeping into them, into Ben and herself, and that she had refused to see. She saw the lines deepening about his mouth and his temper thinning to snap ever more easily. She saw his pity for her changing, unaware, to pity for himself and the bitterness taking him. She saw herself becoming irritable, sharp-tongued, wanting and demanding to know what he did every moment he was out of the room. She saw herself slipping into resentment of him, of his untouched vitality, his ability to stand erect and move about and go through the doorway away from her. She saw these things happening and it had taken the mirror-caught sight of two figures fusing into one in a simple elemental hunger to tell her why. She lay against the pillows and her hands beat at the cover over the thin immobility of her hips and she chewed on her lower lip till it was raw with the blood showing. Yet she was still and her voice was quiet when at last he was there by the bed looking down at her.

"I want to tell you something, Ben. My mirror. You've never noticed, but from here it lets me see right out that window. Almost the same as if I could be out there."

"That's fine, Kitt. But I've been thinking maybe I could rig some kind of a special wheelchair. Then you could — "

"No, Ben. I'll never leave this room." And while he stared at her she spoke quickly to have it said. "I saw you. In that mirror. With that woman."

Deeper color climbed behind the burned brown of his face, but his voice was as steady as hers. "I'm sorry, Kitt."

"That I saw you? No. That had to be." He started to speak and she stopped him with a shake of her head. "Ben, give me your gun."

He looked down at her for a long moment.

"Ben, my life is my own. Give me your gun."

326 / Unbridled Spirits

He looked down at her, and he knew the quality of her and he was man enough for her to lift the gun from the holster by his side and lean to place it in her hands.

She lay against the pillows with the gun in her lap. "Ben, be honest with me. Would it be better for you if I were out of the way?"

Time moved past them and small drops of sweat stood out on his forehead as he pushed deep into his own mind.

"No, Kitt. I need you. I need to know that you are. Without that there'd be no meaning in my life."

A small sigh came from her and she looked at him and felt the wideness reaching out, wavering and twisted perhaps from the beating of the years, but a wideness for her to feel.

"All right, Ben," she said. "This is our room and all I can have. I don't want ever to see anything that you do outside of this room. I don't even want to know what you do, except about our ranch and what you want to tell me."

She did not falter as she raised the big gun and it bucked in her hand. The roar of the shot echoed from the walls and the mirror shattered in its ornate carved frame and when the last piece fell tinkling to the floor there was an abiding quietness in the room.

Kittura Remsberg was my grandmother. She is buried under a stone mountain of granite on the slight rise of ground behind the corral of the ranch that belongs to someone else now. There is another stone beside hers. I believe that Ben Remsberg, her husband, my grandfather, told her the truth when he looked down at her as she lay in the bed with the big gun in her lap. When I saw him at the simple funeral, he still seemed broad and strong, rugged as an oak that sheds the years like water. Yet within a year after he raised the stone on her grave, he lay down in their bed to sleep and slipped quietly away without waking in the now empty peace of that room.

Elmer Kelton

~~~~~~

*T*he author of some thirty-five novels, Elmer Kelton
(1926-) has recorded, in fiction, the history of Texas
from the years of the Republic (1836-1846) until the
present time. The son of a working cowboy and himself a
livestock journalist for over thirty years, Kelton finds cowboy life less myth than reality, and his close association
with that life is evident in his fiction. Yet his is not
traditional, pulp western fiction. His classic The Time It
Never Rained, based on Texas' seven-year drouth of the
1950s, has been called one of the dozen or so best novels
by an American of the twentieth century. Kelton uses the
western setting as a vehicle for studying mankind, rather
than an end in itself. His novels are characterized themat-
ically by the moral complexities wrought in men's lives by
change and stylistically by a narrative voice that speaks
clearly of his home territory of West Texas. As of this
writing, his most recent novel is Slaughter (1992).

"Much more has been written about the men of the
frontier than about the women. The truth is, of course, that
the women faced the same physical hardships and dangers,
carrying a heavy workload plus the extra burden of bearing
and raising their children, often in isolation and loneliness.
The demands upon their courage were as great as that upon
the men's, and sometimes greater. This story was suggested
by the late cowboy cartoonist Ace Reid, attributed to a son
of Captain Charles Schreiner, Ranger, ranchman and pioneer banker. He said the captain and his wife were on
their way to their hill country ranch in a buckboard when
an Indian stepped out of the brush and into the road. The
captain fired a shot at him and missed. The Indian quickly

*disappeared back into the brush, and none was ever seen
in that area again. Mrs. Schreiner bore a son shortly
afterward. Thus, the son was always able to say that he
was present at the last great Indian fight in Kerr County."*
— Elmer Kelton

The Last Indian Fight in Kerr County
Roundup, 1984

*I*n later times, Burkett Wayland liked to say he was in the
last great Indian battle of Kerr County, Texas. It happened
before he was born.

It started one day while his father, Matthew Wayland, then
not much past twenty, was breaking a new field for fall wheat
planting, just east of a small log cabin on one of the creeks
tributary to the Guadalupe River. The quiet of autumn morning
was broken by a fluttering of wings as a covey of quail flushed
beyond a heavy stand of oak timber past the field. Startled, Matthew jerked on the reins and quickly laid his plow over on its side
in the newly broken sod. His bay horse raised its head and
pointed its ears toward the sound.

Matthew caught a deep breath and held it. He thought he
heard a crackling of brush. He reached back for the rifle slung over
his shoulder and quickly unhitched the horse. Standing behind it
for protection, he watched and listened another moment or two,
then jumped up bareback and beat his heels against the horse's ribs,
moving in a long trot for the cabin in the clearing below.

He wanted to believe ragged old Burk Kennemer was coming
for a visit from his little place three miles down the creek, but the
trapper usually rode in the open where Matthew could see him
coming, not through the brush.

Matthew had not been marking the calendar in his almanac,
but he had not needed to. The cooling nights, the curing of the
grass to a rich brown, had told him all too well that this was
September, the month of the Comanche moon. This was the time
of year — their ponies strong from the summer grass — that the

warrior Comanches could be expected to ride down from the high plains. Before winter they liked to make a final grand raid through the rough limestone hills of old hunting grounds west of San Antonio, then retire with stolen horses and mules — and sometimes captives and scalps — back to sanctuary far to the north. They had done it every year since the first settlers had pushed into the broken hill country. Though the military was beginning to press in upon their hideaways, all the old settlers had been warning Matthew to expect them again as the September moon went full, aiding the Comanches in their nighttime prowling.

Rachal opened the roughhewn cabin door and looked at her young husband in surprise, for normally he would plow until she called him in for dinner at noon. He was trying to finish breaking the ground and dry-sow the wheat before fall rains began.

She looked as if she should still be in school somewhere instead of trying to make a home in the wilderness; she was barely eighteen. "What is it, Matthew?"

"I don't know," he said tightly. "Get back inside."

He slid from the horse and turned it sideways to shield him. He held the rifle ready. It was always loaded.

A horseman broke out of the timber and moved toward the cabin. Matthew let go a long-held breath as he recognized Burk Kennemer. Relief turned to anger for the scare. He walked out to meet the trapper, trying to keep the edginess from his voice, but he could not control the flush of color that warmed his face.

He noted that the old man brought no meat with him. It was Kennemer's habit, when he came visiting, to fetch along a freshly killed deer, or sometimes a wild turkey, or occasionally a ham out of his smokehouse, and stay and eat some of it cooked by Rachal's skillful hands. He ran a lot of hogs in the timber, fattening them on the oak mast. He was much more of a hogman and trapper than a farmer. Plow handles did not fit his hands, Kennemer claimed. He was of the restless breed that moved westward ahead of the farmers, and left when they crowded him.

Kennemer had a tentative half smile. "Glad I wasn't a Comanche. You'd've shot me dead."

"I'd've tried," Matthew said, his heart still thumping. He lifted a shaky hand to show what Kennemer had done to him. "What did you come sneaking in like an Indian for?"

Kennemer's smile was gone. "For good reason. That little girl inside the cabin?"

Matthew nodded. Kennemer said, "You'd better keep her there."

As if she had heard the conversation, Rachal Wayland opened the door and stepped outside, shading her eyes with one hand. Kennemer's gray-bearded face lighted at the sight of her. Matthew did not know if Burk had ever had a wife of his own; he had never mentioned one. Rachal shouted, "Come on up, Mr. Kennemer. I'll be fixing us some dinner."

He took off his excuse of a hat and shouted back, for he was still at some distance from the cabin. "Can't right now, girl. Got to be traveling. Next time maybe." He cut his gaze to Matthew's little log shed and corrals. "Where's your other horse?"

"Grazing out yonder someplace. Him and the milk cow both."

"Better fetch him in," Kennemer said grimly. "Better put him and this one in the pen closest to the cabin if you don't want to lose them. And stay close to the cabin yourself, or you may lose more than the horses."

Matthew felt the dread chill him again. "Comanches?"

"Don't know. Could be. Fritz Dieterle come by my place while ago and told me he found tracks where a bunch of horses crossed the Guadalupe during the night. Could've been cowboys, or a bunch of hunters looking to lay in some winter meat. But it could've been Comanches. The horses wasn't shod."

Matthew could read the trapper's thoughts. Kennemer was reasonably sure it had not been cowboys or hunters. Kennemer said, "I come to warn you, and now I'm going west to warn that bunch of German farmers out on the forks. They may want to fort-up at the best house."

Matthew's thoughts were racing ahead. He had been over to the German settlement twice since he and Rachal had arrived here late last winter, in time to break out their first field for spring planting. Burk Kennemer had told him the Germans — come west from the older settlements around New Braunfels and Fredericksburg — had been here long enough to give him sound advice about farming this shallow-soil land. And perhaps they might, if he could have understood them. They had seemed friendly enough, but they spoke no English, and he knew nothing of German. Efforts at communication had led him nowhere but back here, his shoulders slumped in frustration. He had counted Burk Kennemer as his only neighbor — the only one he could talk with.

"Maybe I ought to send Rachal with you," Matthew said. "It would be safer for her there, all those folks around her."

Kennemer considered that for only a moment. "Too risky traveling by daylight, one man and one girl. Even if you was to come along, two men and a girl wouldn't be no match if they jumped us."

"You're even less of a match, traveling by yourself."

Kennemer patted the shoulder of his long-legged brown horse. "No offense, boy, but old Deer-catcher here can run circles around them two of yours, and anything them Indians is liable to have. He'll take care of me, long as I'm by myself. You've got a good strong cabin there. You and that girl'll be better off inside it than out in the open with me." He frowned. "If it'll make you feel safer, I'll be back before dark. I'll stay here with you, and we can fort-up together."

That helped, but it was not enough. Matthew looked at the cabin, which he and Kennemer and the broken-English-speaking German named Dieterle had put up after he finished planting his spring crops. Until then, he and Rachal had lived in their wagon, or around and beneath it. "I wish she wasn't here, Burk. All of a sudden, I wish I'd never brought her here."

The trapper frowned. "Neither one of you belongs here. You're both just shirttail young'uns, not old enough to take care of yourselves."

Matthew remembered that the old man had told him as much, several times. A pretty girl like Rachal should not be out here in a place like this, working like a mule, exposed to the dangers of the thinly settled frontier. But Matthew had never heard a word of complaint from her, not since they had started west from the piney-woods country in the biting cold of a wet winter, barely a month married. She always spoke of this as *our* place, *our* home.

He said, "It seemed all right, till now. All of a sudden I realize what I've brought her to. I want to get her out of here, Burk."

The trapper slowly filled an evil black pipe while he pondered and twisted his furrowed face. "Then we'll go tonight. It'll be safer traveling in the dark because I've been here long enough to know this country better than them Indians do. We'll make Fredericksburg by daylight. But one thing you've got to make up your mind to, Matthew. You've got to leave her there, or go back to the old home with her yourself. You've got no business bringing her here again to this kind of danger."

"She's got no home back yonder to go to. This is the only home she's got, or me either."

Kennemer's face went almost angry. "I buried a woman once in a place just about like this. I wouldn't want to help bury that girl of yours. *Adiós,* Matthew. See you before dark." He circled Deer-catcher around the cabin and disappeared in a motte of live-oak timber.

Rachal stood in the doorway, puzzled. She had not intruded on the conversation. Now she came out on to the foot-packed open ground. "What was the matter with Mr. Kennemer? Why couldn't he stay?"

He wished he could keep it from her. "Horse tracks on the Guadalupe. He thinks it was Indians."

Matthew watched her closely, seeing the sudden clutch of fear in her eyes before she firmly put it away. "What does he think we ought to do?" she asked, seeming calmer than he thought she should.

"Slip away from here tonight, go to Fredericksburg."

"For how long, Matthew?"

He did not answer her. She said, "We can't go far. There's the milk cow, for one thing. She's got to be milked."

The cow had not entered his mind. "Forget her. The main thing is to have you safe."

"We're going to need that milk cow."

Impatiently he exploded, "Will you grow up, and forget that damned cow? I'm taking you out of here."

She shrank back in surprise at his sharpness, a little of hurt in her eyes. They had not once quarreled, not until now. "I'm sorry, Rachal. I didn't go to blow up at you that way."

She hid her eyes from him. "You're thinking we might just give up this place and never come back. . . ." She wasn't asking him; she was telling him what was in his mind.

"That's what Burk thinks we ought to do."

"He's an old man, and we're young. And this isn't his home. He hasn't even got a home, just that old rough cabin, and those dogs and hogs. . . . He's probably moved twenty times in his life. But we're not like that, Matthew. We're the kind of people who put down roots and grow where we are."

Matthew looked away. "I'll go fetch the dun horse. You bolt the door."

Riding away, he kept looking back at the cabin in regret. He knew he loved this place where they had started their lives together. Rachal loved it too, though he found it difficult to understand why. Life had its shortcomings back in east Texas, but her upbringing there had been easy compared to the privations she endured here. When she needed water she carried it in a heavy oaken bucket from the creek, fully seventy-five yards. He would have built the cabin nearer the water, but Burk had advised that once in a while heavy rains made that creek rise up on its hind legs and roar like an angry bear.

She worked her garden with a heavy-handled hoe, and when Matthew was busy in the field from dawn to dark she chopped her own wood from the pile of dead oak behind the cabin. She cooked over an ill-designed open fireplace that did not draw as well as it should. And, as much as anything, she put up with a deadening loneliness. Offhand, he could not remember that she had seen another woman since late in the spring, except for a German girl who stopped by once on her way to the forks. They had been unable to talk to each other. Even so, Rachal had glowed for a couple of days, refreshed by seeing someone besides her husband and the unwashed Burk Kennemer.

The cabin was as yet small, just a single room which was kitchen, sleeping quarters and sitting room combined. It had been in Matthew's mind, when he had nothing else to do this coming winter, to start work on a second section that would become a bedroom. He would build a roof and an open dog run between that part and the original, in keeping with Texas pioneer tradition, with a sleeping area over the dog run for the children who were sure to come with God's own time and blessings. He and Rachal had talked much of their plans, of the additional land he would break out to augment the potential income from their dozen or so beef critters scattered along the creek. He had forcefully put the dangers out of his mind, knowing they were there but choosing not to dwell upon them.

He remembered now the warnings from Rachal's uncle and aunt, who had brought her up after her own father was killed by a falling tree and her mother was taken by one of the periodic fever epidemics. They had warned of the many perils a couple would face on the edge of the settled lands, perils which youth and love and enthusiasm had made to appear small, far away in distance and time, until today. Now, his eyes nervously searching the edge of the oak timber for anything amiss, fear rose up in him. It was a primeval, choking fear of a kind he had never known, and a sense of shame for having so thoughtlessly brought Rachal to this sort of jeopardy.

He found the dun horse grazing by the creek, near a few of the speckled beef cows which a farmer at the old home had given him in lieu of wages for two years of backbreaking work. He had bartered for the old wagon and the plow and a few other necessary tools. Whatever else he had, he and Rachal had built with their hands. For Texans, cash money was still in short supply.

He thought about rounding up the cows and corralling them by the cabin, but they were scattered. He saw too much risk in the time it might take him to find them all, as well as the exposure to any Comanches hidden in the timber. From what he had heard, the Indians were much less interested in cattle than in horses. Cows were slow. Once the raiders were ready to start north, they would want speed to carry them to sanctuary. Matthew pitched a rawhide *reata* loop around the dun's neck and led the animal back in a long trot. He had been beyond sight of the cabin for a while, and he prickled with anxiety. He breathed a sigh of relief when he broke into the open. The smoke from the chimney was a welcome sight.

He turned the horses into the pole corral and closed the gate, then poured shelled corn into a crude wooden trough. They eagerly set to crunching the grain with their strong teeth, a sound he had always enjoyed when he could restrain himself from thinking how much that corn would be worth in the settlements. The horses were blissfully unaware of the problems that beset their owners. Matthew wondered how content they would be if they fell into Indian hands and were driven or ridden the many long, hard days north into that mysterious hidden country. It would serve them right!

Still, he realized how helpless he and Rachal would be without them. He could not afford to lose the horses.

Rachal slid the heavy oak bar from the door and let him into the cabin. He immediately replaced the bolt while she went back to stirring a pot of stew hanging on an iron rod inside the fireplace. He avoided her eyes, for the tension stretched tightly between them.

"See anything?" she asked, knowing he would have come running.

He shook his head. "Not apt to, until night. If they're here, that's when they'll come for the horses."

"And find us gone?" Her voice almost accused him.

He nodded. "Burk said he'll be back before dark. He'll help us find our way to Fredericksburg."

Firelight touched her face. He saw a reflection of tears. She said, "They'll destroy this place."

"Better this place than *you*. I've known it from the start, I guess, and just wouldn't admit it. I shouldn't have brought you here."

"I came willingly. I've been happy here. So have you."

"We just kept dancing and forgot that the piper had to be paid."

A silence fell between them, heavy and unbridgeable. When the stew was done they sat at the roughhewn table and ate without talking. Matthew got up restlessly from time to time to look out the front and back windows. These had no glass. They were like small doors in the walls. They could be closed and bolted shut. Each had a loophole which he could see out of, or fire through. Those, he remembered, had been cut at Burk Kennemer's insistence. From the first, Matthew realized now, Burk had been trying to sober him, even to scare him away. Matthew had always put him off with a shrug or a laugh. Now he remembered what Burk had said today about having buried a woman in a place like this. He thought he understood the trapper, and the man's fears, in a way he had not before.

The heavy silence went unrelieved. After eating what he could of the stew, his stomach knotted, he went outside and took a long look around, cradling the rifle. He fetched a shovel and began to throw dirt onto the roof to make it more difficult for the Indians to set afire. It occurred to him how futile this labor was if they were going to abandon the place anyway, but he kept swinging the shovel, trying to work off the tension.

The afternoon dragged. He spent most of it outside, pacing, watching. In particular he kept looking to the west, anticipating Burk Kennemer's return. Now that he had made up his mind to it, he could hardly wait for darkness, to give them a chance to escape this place. The only thing which came from that direction — or any other — was the brindle milk cow, drifting toward the shed at her own slow pace and in her own good time for the evening milking and the grain she knew awaited her. Matthew owned no watch, but he doubted that a watch kept better time than that cow, her udder swinging in rhythm with her slow and measured steps. Like the horses, she had no awareness of anything except her daily routine, of feeding and milking and grazing. Observing her patient pace, Matthew could almost assure himself that this day was like all others, that he had no reason to fear.

He milked the cow, though he intended to leave the milk unused in the cabin, for it was habit with him as well as with the cow. The sun was dropping rapidly when he carried the bucket of milk to Rachal. Her eyes asked him, though she did not speak.

He shook his head. "No sign of anything out there. Not of Burk, either."

Before sundown he saddled the dun horse for Rachal, making ready. He would ride the plow horse bareback. He climbed up onto his pole fence, trying to shade his eyes from the sinking sun while he studied the hills and the open valley to the west. All of his earlier fears were with him, and a new one as well.

Where is he? He wouldn't just have left us here. Not old Burk.

Once he thought he heard a sound in the edge of the timber. He turned quickly and saw a flash of movement, nothing more. It was a feeling as much as something actually seen. It *could* have been anything, a deer, perhaps, or even one of his cows. It could have been.

He remained outside until the sun was gone, and until the last golden remnant faded into twilight over the timbered hills that stretched into the distance like a succession of blue monuments.

The autumn chill set him to shivering, but he held out against going for his coat. When the night was full dark, he knew it was time.

He called softly at the cabin door. Rachal lifted the bar. He said, "The moon'll rise directly. We'd better get started."

"Without Burk? Are you really sure, Matthew?"

"If they're around, they'll be here. Out yonder, in the dark, we've got a chance."

She came out, wrapped for the night chill, carrying his second rifle, handing him his coat. Quietly they walked to the corral, where he opened the gate, untied the horses and gave her a lift up into the saddle. The stirrups were too long for her, and her skirts were in the way, but he knew she could ride. He threw himself up onto the plow horse, and they moved away from the cabin in a walk, keeping to the grass as much as possible to muffle the sound of the hoofs. As quickly as he could, he pulled into the timber, where the darkness was even more complete. For the first miles, as least, he felt that he knew the way better than any Indian who might not come here once in several years.

It was his thought to swing first by Burk's cabin. There was always a chance the old man had changed his mind about things. . . .

He had held onto this thought since late afternoon. Maybe Burk had found the tracks were not made by Indians after all, and he had chosen to let the young folks have the benefit of a good, healthy scare.

Deep inside, Matthew knew that was a vain hope. It was not Burk's way. He might have let Matthew sweat blood, but he would not do this to Rachal.

They both saw the fire at the same time, and heard the distant barking of the dogs. Rachal made a tiny gasp and clutched his arm.

Burk's cabin was burning.

They reined up and huddled together for a minute, coming dangerously close to giving in to their fears and riding away in a blind run. Matthew gripped the rawhide reins so tightly that they seemed to cut into his hands. "Easy, Rachal," he whispered.

Then he could hear horses moving through the timber, and the crisp night air carried voices to him.

"They're coming at us, Matthew," Rachal said tightly. "They'll catch us out here."

He had no way of knowing if they had been seen, or heard. A night bird called to the left of him. Another answered, somewhere to the right. At least, they sounded like night birds.

"We've got to run for it, Rachal!"

"We can't run all the way to Fredericksburg. Even if we could find it. They'll catch us."

He saw only one answer. "Back to the cabin! If we can get inside, they'll have to come in there to get us."

He had no spurs; a farmer did not need them. He beat his heels against the horse's sides and led the way through the timber in a run. He did not have to look behind him to know Rachal was keeping up with him. Somehow the horses had caught the fever of their fear.

"Keep low, Rachal," he said. "Don't let the low limbs knock you down." He found a trail that he knew and shortly burst out into the open. He saw no reason for remaining in the timber now, for the Indians surely knew where they were. The timber would only slow their running. He leaned out over the horse's neck and kept thumping his heels against its ribs. He glanced back to be sure he was not outpacing Rachal.

Off to the right he thought he saw figures moving, vague shapes against the blackness. The moon was just beginning rise, and he could not be sure. Ahead, sensed more than seen, was the clearing. Evidently the Indians had not been there yet, or the place would be in flames as Burk's cabin had been.

He could see the shape of the cabin now. "Right up to the door, Rachal!"

He jumped to the ground, letting his eyes sweep the yard and what he could see of the corrals. "Don't get down," he shouted. "Let me look inside first."

The door was closed, as they had left it. He pushed it open and stepped quickly inside, the rifle ready. The dying embers in the fireplace showed him he was alone. "It's all right, Rachal. Get down quick, and into the cabin!"

She slid down and fell, and he helped her to her feet. She pointed and gave a cry. Several figures were moving rapidly toward the shed. Matthew fired the rifle in their general direction and gave Rachal a push toward the door. She resisted stubbornly. "The horses," she said. "Let's get the horses into the cabin."

She led her dun through the door, though it did not much want to go into that dark and unaccustomed place.

Matthew would have to admit later — though now he had no time for such thoughts — that she was keeping her head better than he was. He would have let the horses go, and the Indians would surely have taken them. The plow horse was gentler and entered the cabin with less resistance, though it made a nervous sound in its nose at sight of the glowing coals.

Matthew heard something *plunk* into the logs as he pushed the door shut behind him and dropped the bar solidly into place. He heard a horse race up to the cabin, and felt the jarring weight of a man's body hurled against the door, trying to break through. Matthew pushed his own strength upon the bar, bracing it. A chill ran through him, and he shuddered at the realization that only the meager thickness of that door lay between him and an intruder who intended to kill him. He heard the grunting of a man in strain, and he imagined he could feel the hot breath. His hair bristled.

Rachal opened the front-window loophole and fired her rifle.

Thunder seemed to rock the cabin. It threw the horses into a panic that made them more dangerous, for the moment, than those Indians outside. One of them slammed against Matthew and pressed him to the wall so hard that he thought all his ribs were crushed. But that was the last time an Indian tried the door. Matthew could hear the man running, getting clear of Rachal's rifle.

A gunshot sounded from out in the night. A bullet struck the wall but did not break through between the logs. Periodically Matthew would hear a shot, first from one direction, then from another. After the first three or four, he was sure.

"They've just got one gun. We've got two."

The horses calmed, after a time. So did Matthew. He threw ashes over the coals to dim their glow, which had made it difficult for him to see out into the night. The moon was up, throwing a silvery light across the yard.

"I'll watch out front," he said. "You watch the back."

All his life he had heard that Indians did not like to fight at night because of a fear that their souls would wander lost if they died in the darkness. He had no idea if the stories held any truth. He knew that Indians were skillful horsethieves, in darkness or light, and that he and Rachal had frustrated these by bringing their mounts into the cabin.

Burk had said the Indians on these September raids were more intent on acquiring horses than on taking scalps, though they had no prejudice against the latter. He had said Indians did not like to take heavy risks in going against a well-fortified position, that they were likely to probe the defenses and, if they found them strong, withdraw in search of an easier target.

But they had a strong incentive for breaking into this cabin.

He suggested, "They might leave if we turn the horses out."

"And what do we do afoot?" she demanded. Her voice was not a schoolgirl's. It was strong, defiant. "If they want these horses, let them come through that door and pay for them. These horses are ours!"

Her determination surprised him, and shamed him a little. He held silent a while, listening, watching for movement. "I suppose those Indians feel like they've got a right here. They figure this land belongs to them."

"Not if they just come once a year. We've come here to stay."

"I wish we hadn't. I wish I hadn't brought you."

"Don't say that. I've always been glad that you did. I've loved this place from the time we first got here and lived in the wagon, because it was ours. It *is* ours. When this trouble is over it will *stay* ours. We've earned the right to it."

He fired seldom, and only when he thought he had a good target, for shots inside the cabin set the horses to plunging and threshing.

He heard a cow bawl, in fear and agony. Later, far beyond the shed, he could see a fire building. Eventually he caught the aroma of meat, roasting.

"They've killed the milk cow," he declared.

Rachal said, "We'll need another one, then. For the baby."

That was the first she had spoken of it, though he had had reason lately to suspect. "I shouldn't have put you through that ride tonight."

"That didn't hurt me. I'm not so far along yet. That's one reason we've got to keep the horses. We may need to trade the dun for a milk cow."

They watched through the long hours, he at the front window, she at the rear. The Indians had satisfied their hunger, and they were quiet, sleeping perhaps, waiting for dawn to storm the cabin without danger to their mortal souls. Matthew was tired, and his legs were cramped form the long vigil, but he felt no sleepiness. He thought once that Rachal had fallen asleep, and he made no move to awaken her. If trouble came from that side he thought he would probably hear it.

She was not asleep. She said, "I hear a rooster way off somewhere. Burk's, I suppose. Be daylight soon."

"They'll hit us then. They'll want to overrun us in a hurry."

"It's up to us to fool them. You and me together, Matthew, we've always been able to do whatever we set our minds to."

They came as he expected, charging horseback out of the rising sun, relying on the blazing light to blind the eyes of the defenders. But with Rachal's determined shouts ringing in his ears, he triggered the rifle at darting figures dimly seen through the golden haze. Rachal fired rapidly at those horsemen who ran past the cabin and came into her field of view on the back side. The two horses just trembled and leaned against one another.

One bold, quick charge and the attack was over. The Comanches swept on around, having tested the defense and found it unyielding. They pulled away, regrouping to the east as if considering another try.

"We done it, Rachal!" Matthew shouted. "We held them off."

He could see her now in the growing light, her hair stringing down, her face smudged with black, her eyes watering from the sting of the gunpowder. He had never seen her look so good.

She said triumphantly, "I tried to tell you we could do it, Matthew. You and me, we can do anything."

He thought the Indians might try again, but they began pulling away. He could see now that they had a considerable number of horses and mules, taken from other settlers. They drove these before them, splashing across the creek and moving north in a run.

"They're leaving," he said, not quite believing.

"Some more on this side," Rachal warned. "You'd better come over here and look."

Through the loophole in her window, out of the west, he saw a dozen or more horesmen loping toward the cabin. For a minute he thought he and Rachal would have to fight again. Strangely, the thought brought him no particular fear.

We can handle it. Together, we can do anything.

Rachal said, "Those are white men."

They threw their arms around each other and cried. They were outside the cabin, the two of them, when the horsemen circled warily around it, rifles ready for a fight. The men were strangers, except the leader. Matthew remembered him from up at the forks. Excitedly the man spoke in a language Matthew knew was German. Then half the men were talking at once. They looked Rachal and Matthew over carefully, making sure neither was hurt.

The words were strange, but the expressions were universal. They were of relief and joy at finding the young couple alive and on their feet.

The door was open. The bay plow horse stuck its head out experimentally, nervously surveying the crowd, then breaking into a run to get clear of the oppressive cabin. The dun horse followed, pitching in relief to be outdoors. The German rescuers stared in puzzlement for a moment, then laughed as they realized how the Waylands had saved their horses.

One of them made a sweeping motion, as if holding a broom, and Rachal laughed with him. It was going to take a lot of work to clean up that cabin.

The spokesman said something to Matthew, and Matthew caught the name of Burk Kennemer. The man made a motion of drawing a bow, and of an arrow striking him in the shoulder.

"Dead?" Matthew asked worriedly.

The man shook his head. "*Nein, nicht tod.* Not dead." By the motions, Matthew perceived that the wounded Burk had made it to the German settlement to give warning, and that the men had ridden through the night to get here.

Rachal came up and put her arm around Matthew, leaning against him. She said, "Matthew, do you think we killed any of those Indians?"

"I don't know that we did."

"I hope we didn't. I'd hate to know all of my life that there is blood on this ground."

Some of the men seemed to be thinking about leaving. Matthew said, "You-all pen your horses, and we'll have breakfast directly." He realized they did not understand his words, so he pantomimed and put the idea across. He made a circle, shaking hands with each man individually, telling him thanks, knowing each followed his meaning whether the words were understood or not.

"Rachal," he said, "these people are our neighbors. Somehow we've got to learn to understand each other."

She nodded. "At least enough so you can trade one of them out of another milk cow. For the baby."

When the baby came, late the following spring, they named it Burkett Kennemer Wayland, after the man who had brought them warning, and had sent them help.

That was the last time the Comanches ever penetrated so deeply into the hill country, for the military pressure was growing stronger.

And all of his life Burkett Kennemer Wayland was able to say, without taking sinful advantage of the truth, that he had been present at the last great Indian fight in Kerr County.

Robert Flynn

~~~~~~

One of Texas' major novelists, Robert Flynn (1932-) is the author of four novels, including Wanderer Springs, which won a Spur Award from Western Writers of America as the Best Novel of the West of 1987, and North to Yesterday which won a Western Heritage (Wrangler) Award from the National Cowboy Hall of Fame as the best novel of 1967 and was named the best novel of the year by the Texas Institute of Letters. Flynn is also the author of one short story collection, Seasonal Rain from which this short story is taken, and several nonfiction works. First published as a short story, "The Great Plain" was later incorporated into Wanderer Springs.

"The most striking thing about the Great Plains is that they are plain. Not ugly but unadorned, without frills or pretense, beauty on the thrift plain. Not ordinary. There is nothing ordinary about the plains or the women who conquered the dust, distance, insects, predators, wind, heat, cold, rain, sleet, hail, drought, and their romantic dreams. To read their diaries and letters is to see the depth of their misery and the height of their courage. Those who could not conquer the plains, or their dreams of a fresh and seamless life, went home, or crazy, or fanatical. The best of them, the most of them, endured."

— Robert Flynn

The Great Plain
Seasonal Rain, 1986

Grover and Edna married, when Grover Turrill was six-teen, at the request of both families. Crowded out by younger children they set out for a life on their own. Grover's father gave them a milk cow and Edna's father gave them a steer. It was the best their families could do. Grover yoked the cow and steer together and they started to California in a wagon. It was his promise to Edna.

They crossed Red River and stopped near Preston where Edna had a baby boy with no one to help her but Grover. They named him Grover, too. They started moving again as soon as Edna was able to travel, Edna and the baby in the wagon, and Grover walking beside the wagon, prodding the ox and milk cow, and picking up firewood. After Preston there was little wood and Grover picked up whatever sticks he saw for the evening fire.

One day, tired of sitting, Edna placed the sleeping baby in the back of the wagon and got out to walk beside the cow. Grover found a tree stump and, not knowing the baby was in the back of the wagon, he threw in the stump, killing his child. Some cowboys found them, two teenagers traveling across the prairie with a dead baby wrapped in a quilt and carried in Edna's lap.

The cowboys dug a grave and buried the child, still wrapped in the quilt Edna's mother had given them. After the cowboys had gone, Grover and Edna made a cross of two pieces of firewood. For a long time they sat by the grave, trying to decide whether to abandon the grave of their firstborn. Despite their youth their faces were lined and drawn. Already they were beginning to share that common look that was supposed to come only with years of togetherness.

"California is purty," Grover said, renewing his plight. Grover had been stunted and hardened by a life of misfortune, but Edna's steel had been warmed by motherhood. "It'll be easier to forget."

"We still got four hours of daylight," Edna said, getting to her feet. Her eyes acknowledged that life was hard, but her jaw was set for the long haul as she turned her face forever from the grave of her son.

Grover and Edna were still on their way to California when the milk cow died near Wanderer Springs. They lived in the wagon while Grover broke the land, with the steer and Edna pulling the plow, and planted a crop. The corn was to buy oxen to take them to California. Grover had a good harvest and Edna had a baby girl named Polly. The wagon was no place for a mother and baby. Grover built a lean-to for the winter.

In the spring Grover and the steer pulled, and Edna plowed, leaving the baby at the end of the row. By fall there was enough corn for an ox, but Edna had another son, this one called Billo. Grover traded the corn for a milk cow. He enclosed the lean-to and put in a door.

The land Grover had chosen was not good enough to make him forget his dreams, not rich enough to provide the means to accomplish it. There was always enough but the more than enough was soon required by boils, fevers, broken bones. Drought alternated with flood. Hail alternated with grasshoppers. There was high wind, early frost, unseasonal rain. Grover and Edna still talked of California but they built a regular house for the children. Grover traded the harvest for mules to pull the plow.

Others came to settle the land, break the soil, to share the joys and trials. While the children played, the adults talked about the friends and family they had left never to see again, and the freedom they hoped to find in the hard land. They sat or squatted near the earth, looking out across the prairie that was as silent and empty as a dream. They waited for the sun to fade and the wind to rise. "Best time of the day," they said.

Edna told of the gentle life Grover had promised her in California. "It's purty," Grover said. But the son they had left behind was buried in their own hearts.

Billo was small and tough like his father, and like his father, he was always in a hurry. When he was eight, Billo went coon hunting one night with some older boys. They ran a coon up a dead tree on the creek, and Billo climbed the tree to shake the coon down. A pile of brush had been washed up under the tree and the older boys set it afire so that Billo could see. The dead tree caught fire and Billo was burned so that he couldn't lie down and Edna and Grover took turns holding him the four days it took him to die.

The neighbors came to tend the fields and livestock, to look after Polly, and to feed Edna and Grover, who sat like double images, their faces set to bear all, do all, to spare Billo pain. They scarcely moved except to shift Billo from one lap to another.

When Billo died, the neighbors dug his grave, and Grover took him from Edna and laid him in it. The neighbors buried him, and sat for a while with Edna, and Grover, and Polly. They stared at the unforgiving earth and talked of the land where Billo had gone, a land without memory, without tears.

When the neighbors had gone, Edna and Grover held Polly close and told her of California and the sweetness of life there. "It's purty," Grover said.

"When?" Polly asked.

"As soon as I sell the land we'll have enough to go," Grover said.

When Polly was thirteen, she complained of a stomachache. Polly was not fat but, like Edna, she was slope-shouldered, solid, and a good eater. Polly was no whiner, but she tossed all night on her bed and was unable to eat breakfast. Grover hitched the team to the wagon, made a pallet in the back, and with Edna to comfort Polly they started for the doctor at Wanderer Springs, several miles away. The wagon had no springs, the road was just a set of ruts across the prairie. Polly whimpered the whole way although Grover drove as slowly as he dared.

When they got to Wanderer Springs they found that Dr. Vestal had been called out of town. Over near Medicine Hill folks thought, expected to be gone all day. Polly was too sick to wait for his return, so they started for Medicine Hill, sending word ahead by fourteen-year-old Buster Bryant who volunteered to ride with the message.

It was August and the sun was hot and Polly cried out at every bump, so Edna stood and held a quilt to shade her, and Grover drove the mules as fast as he dared for Medicine Hill. They met Buster coming back. He had missed Dr. Vestal who was on his way to Bull Valley. Grover turned the mules towards Bull

Valley with Buster racing ahead. Somewhere along that road, Grover stopped to kill a rattlesnake that was so big when it coiled it reached the hub of the wagon wheel. Polly was dying, but Grover was a father and there were other children to think of.

Dr. Vestal had left Bull Valley for Red Top. Buster rode to head off the wagon, telling Grover to go home. He would find Dr. Vestal and meet them there. The mules had played out and Grover was walking beside them to lighten the load. Edna was standing with her feet spread, holding the stout little girl in her arms, trying to absorb the bumps and shocks of the wagon with her own body.

It was almost dark when the wagon got back home and Buster and the doctor were waiting. Edna was sitting beside Grover holding the child so that she lay across both their laps. The mules stopped of their own accord and neither Grover nor Edna made a move to get down. Dr. Vestal started to the wagon but Grover said, "I don't want you to touch her. We've been praying for you all day and listening to her die. I know it ain't your fault, but I don't want to see you now.

Grover got down, lifted Polly, and followed by Edna he started towards the house. "Are you sure, Grover?" Dr. Vestal asked.

"She's not screaming any more is she?" Grover said. "I'd rather have her dead than have to listen to that."

Dr. Vestal left but Buster stayed with the Turrills, although he didn't dare go in the house. He unhitched the mules and fed them and sat on the graceless porch. After a while Grover came out to water the single tree in the yard, a stunted, ugly pear tree that Edna had planted and watered until it had finally dropped a few sun-baked pears as warty as horseapples.

Grover sat on the porch and stared out at the empty treeless miles over which he had ridden that day, listening to the shriek of the wagon wheels and the dying cries of his last child.

After a while Edna came out also and leaned against the porch post, hugging the porch post as though it were a child, her head hanging down a little as though permanently bent from ironing clothes and chopping cotton. She waited while the last light of day faded and one by one the stars came out, watching the prairie that under moonlight had a sheen like a silent sea.

"If that cow hadn't died we'd be in California," Grover said.

"Old Boss," Edna said, remembering the name over all the years, recalling the dreams they had as they traveled across the prairie in the wagon.

"Damn country. Washes away every time it rains. Blows away every time there's a wind. Hail or grasshoppers every year. I've sweated over it. I've broken my back. It has taken every thing I have and given me nothing."

"Yeah," Edna said, looking out over the miles and years they had traveled together. "But ain't it purty."

Grover, whose eyes had darkened but not dimmed, nodded his agreement.

Elmore Leonard

~~~~~~~~~~~~~~~~~~~~~~~~~~~~~~~~~~~~~~

*E*lmore Leonard (1925-) began writing western short
stories during the 1950s and was published in The
Saturday Evening Post, Argosy, and a number of pulp
magazines, including Dime Western. Films adapted from
Leonard's work include Hombre, Valdez Is Coming, and
3:10 to Yuma. He still writes an occasional western short
story while concentrating on crime novels. A native of New
Orleans, he makes his home in Michigan. In 1994, his
most recent title is Pronto, a crime novel set partly in Italy
where they answer the phone by saying "Pronto!"

>   "The first time I planned to use a woman as a
> central character was in 1969 when I was writing Valdez
> Is Coming. There were women playing important roles in
> western novels I wrote before that — three women in Hombre
> with quite different attitudes — but none was pivotal in
> the development of the plot. Later, in the 1980s, women
> became more and more important in my writing. In two of
> my last four crime novels, in fact, a woman drives the plot
> and is responsible for the outcome."
>
> — Elmore Leonard

The Tonto Woman
Roundup, 1984

A time would come, within a few years, when Ruben Vega
would go to the church in Benson, kneel in the con-
fessional and say to the priest, "Bless me, Father, for I have
sinned. It has been thirty-seven years since my last confession. . . .

Since then I have fornicated with many women, maybe eight hundred. No, not that many, considering my work. Maybe six hundred only." And the priest would say, "Do you mean bad women or good women?" And Ruben Vega would say, "They are all good, Father." He would tell the priest he had stolen, in that time, about twenty thousand head of cattle but only maybe fifteen horses. The priest would ask him if he had committed murder. Ruben Vega would say no. "All that stealing you've done," the priest would say, "you've never killed anyone?" And Ruben Vega would say, "Yes, of course, but it was not to commit murder. You understand the distinction? Not to kill someone to take a life, but only to save my own."

Even in this time to come, concerned with dying in a state of sin, he would be confident. Ruben Vega knew himself, when he was right, when he was wrong.

Now, in a time before, with no thought of dying, but with the same confidence and caution that kept him alive, he watched a woman bathe. Watched from a mesquite thicket on the high bank of a wash.

She bathed at the pump that stood in the yard of the adobe, the woman pumping and then stooping to scoop the water from the basin of the irrigation ditch that led off to a vegetable patch of corn and beans. Her dark hair was pinned up in a swirl, piled on top of her head. She was bare to her gray skirt, her upper body pale white, glistening wet in the late afternoon sunlight. Her arms were very thin, her breasts small, but there they were with rosy blossoms on the tips and Ruben Vega watched them as she bathed, as she raised one arm and her hand rubbed soap under the arm and down over her ribs. Ruben Vega could almost feel those ribs, she was so thin. He felt sorry for her, for all the women like her, stick women drying up in the desert, waiting for a husband to ride in smelling of horse and sweat and leather, lice living in his hair.

There was a stock tank and rickety windmill off in the pasture, but it was empty graze, all dust and scrub. So the man of the house had moved his cows to grass somewhere and would be coming home soon, maybe with his sons. The woman appeared old enough to have young sons. Maybe there was a little girl in the house. The chimney appeared cold. Animals stood in a mesquite-pole corral off to one side of the house, a cow and a calf and a dun-colored horse, that was all. There were a few chickens. No buckboard or wagon. No clothes drying on the line. A lone woman here at day's end.

From fifty yards he watched her. She stood looking this way now, into the red sun, her face raised. There was something strange about her face. Like shadow marks on it, though there was nothing near enough to her to cast shadows.

He waited until she finished bathing and returned to the house before he mounted his bay and came down the wash to the pasture. Now as he crossed the yard, walking his horse, she would watch him from the darkness of the house and make a judgment about him. When she appeared again it might be with a rifle, depending on how she saw him.

Ruben Vega said to himself, Look, I'm a kind person. I'm not going to hurt nobody.

She would see a bearded man in a cracked straw hat with the brim bent to his eyes. Black beard, with a revolver on his hip and another beneath the leather vest. But look at my eyes, Ruben Vega thought. Let me get close enough so you can see my eyes.

Stepping down from the bay he ignored the house, let the horse drink from the basin of the irrigation ditch as he pumped water and knelt to the wooden platform and put his mouth to the rusted pump spout. Yes, she was watching him. Looking up now at the doorway he could see part of her: a coarse shirt with sleeves too long and the gray skirt. He could see strands of dark hair against the whiteness of the shirt, but could not see her face.

As he rose, straightening, wiping his mouth, he said, "May we use some of your water, please?"

The woman didn't answer him.

He moved away from the pump to the hardpack, hearing the ching of his spurs, removed his hat and gave her a little bow. "Ruben Vega, at your service. Do you know Diego Luz, the horsebreaker?" He pointed off toward a haze of foothills. "He lives up there with his family and delivers horses to the big ranch, the Circle-Eye. Ask Diego Luz, he'll tell you I'm a person of trust." He waited a moment. "May I ask how you're called?" Again he waited.

"You watched me," the woman said.

Ruben Vega stood with his hat in his hand facing the woman who was half in shadow in the doorway. He said, "I waited. I didn't want to frighten you."

"You watched me," she said again.

"No, I respect your privacy."

She said, "The others look. They come and watch."

He wasn't sure who she meant. Maybe anyone passing by. He said, "You see them watching?"

She said, "What difference does it make?" She said then, "You come from Mexico, don't you?"

"Yes, I was there. I'm here and there, working as a drover." Ruben Vega shrugged. "What else is there to do, uh?" Showing her he was resigned to his station in life.

"You'd better leave," she said.

When he didn't move, the woman came out of the doorway into light and he saw her face clearly for the first time. He felt a shock within him and tried to think of something to say, but could only stare at the blue lines tattooed on her face: three straight lines on each cheek that extended from her cheekbones to her jaw, markings that seemed familiar, though he could not in this moment identify them.

He was conscious of himself standing in the open with nothing to say, the woman staring at him with curiosity, as though wondering if he would hold her gaze and look at her. Like there was nothing unusual about her countenance. Like it was common to see a woman with her face tattooed and you might be expected to comment, if you said anything at all, "Oh, that's a nice design you have there. Where did you have it done?" That would be one way — if you couldn't say something interesting about the weather or about the price of cows in Benson.

Ruben Vega, his mind empty of pleasantries, certain he would never see the woman again, said, "Who did that to you?"

She cocked her head in an easy manner, studying him as he studied her, and said, "Do you know, you're the first person who's come right out and asked."

"Mojave," Ruben Vega said, "but there's something different. Mojaves tattoo their chins only, I believe."

"And look like they were eating berries," the woman said. "I told them if you're going to do it, do it all the way. Not like a blue dribble."

It was in her eyes and in the tone of her voice, a glimpse of the rage she must have felt. No trace of fear in the memory, only cold anger. He could hear her telling the Indians — this skinny woman, probably a girl then — until they did it her way and marked her good for all time. Imprisoned her behind the blue marks on her face.

"How old were you?"

"You've seen me and had your water," the woman said, "now leave."

It was the same type of adobe house as the woman's but with a great difference. There was life here, the warmth of family: children sleeping now, Diego Luz's wife and her mother cleaning up after the meal as the two men sat outside in horsehide chairs and smoked and looked at the night. At one time they had both worked for a man named Sundeen and packed running irons to vent the brands on the cattle they stole. Ruben Vega was still an outlaw, in his fashion, while Diego Luz broke green horses and sold them to cattle companies.

They sat at the edge of the ramada, an awning made of mesquite, and stared at pinpoints of light in the universe. Ruben Vega asked about the extent of graze this season, where the large herds were that belonged to the Maricopa and the Circle-Eye. He had been thinking of cutting out maybe a hundred — he wasn't greedy — and drive them south to sell to the mine companies. He had been scouting the Circle-Eye range, he said, when he came to the strange woman. . . .

The Tonto woman, Diego Luz said. Everyone called her that now.

Yes, she had been living there, married a few years, when she went to visit her family who lived on the Gila above Painted Rock. Well, some Yavapai came looking for food. They clubbed her parents and two small brothers to death and took the girl north with them. The Yavapai traded her to the Mojave as a slave. . . .

"And they marked her," Ruben Vega said.

"Yes, so when she died the spirits would know she was Mojave and not drag her soul down into a rathole," Diego Luz said.

"Better to go to heaven with your face tattooed," Ruben Vega said, "than not at all. Maybe so."

During a drought the Mojave traded her to a band of Tonto Apaches for two mules and a bag of salt and one day she appeared at Bowie with the Tontos that were brought in to be sent to Oklahoma. Among the desert Indians twelve years and returned home last spring.

"It put age on her," Ruben Vega said. "But what about her husband?"

"Her husband? He banished her," Diego Luz said, "like a leper. Unclean from living among the red niggers. No one speaks of her to him, it isn't allowed."

Ruben Vega frowned. There was something he didn't understand. He said, "Wait a minute — "

And Diego Luz said, "Don't you know who her husband is? Mr. Isham himself, man, of the Circle-Eye. She comes home to find her husband a rich man. He don't live in that hut no more. No, he owns a hundred miles of graze and a house it took them two years to build, the glass and bricks brought by the Southern Pacific. Sure, the railroad comes and he's a rich cattleman in only a few years."

"He makes her live there alone?"

"She's his wife, he provides for her. But that's all. Once a month his segundo named Bonnet rides out there with supplies and has someone shoe her horse and look at the animals."

"But to live in the desert," Ruben Vega said, still frowning, thoughtful, "with a rusty pump. . . ."

"Look at her," Diego Luz said. "What choice does she have?"

It was hot down in this scrub pasture, a place to wither and die. Ruben Vega loosened the new willow-root straw that did not yet conform to his head, though he had shaped the brim to curve down on one side and rise slightly on the other so that the brim slanted across the vision of his left eye. He held on his lap a nearly flat cardboard box that bore the name *L.S. Weiss Mercantile Store*.

The woman gazed up at him, shading her eyes with one hand. Finally she said, "You look different."

"The beard began to itch," Ruben Vega said, making no mention of the patches of gray he had studied in the hotel-room mirror. "So I shaved it off." He rubbed a hand over his jaw and smoothed down the tips of his mustache that was still full and seemed to cover his mouth. When he stepped down from the bay and approached the woman standing by the stick-fence corral she looked off into the distance and back again.

She said, "You shouldn't be here."

Ruben Vega said, "Your husband doesn't want nobody to look at you. Is that it?" He held the store box, waiting for her to answer. "He has a big house with trees and the San Pedro River in his yard. Why doesn't he hide you there?"

She looked off again and said, "If they find you here, they'll shoot you."

"They," Ruben Vega said. "The ones who watch you bathe? Work for your husband and keep more than a close eye on you and you'd like to hit them with something, wipe the grins from their faces."

"You better leave," the woman said.

The blue lines on her face were like claw marks, though not as wide as fingers: indelible lines of dye etched into her flesh with a cactus needle, the color worn and faded but still vivid against her skin, the blue matching her eyes.

He stepped close to her, raised his hand to her face and touched the markings gently with the tips of his fingers, feeling nothing. He raised his eyes to hers. She was staring at him. He said, "You're in there, aren't you? Behind these little bars. They don't seem like much. Not enough to hold you."

She said nothing, but seemed to be waiting.

He said to her, "You should brush your hair. Brush it every day. . . ."

"Why?" the woman said.

"To feel good. You need to wear a dress. A little parasol to match."

"I'm asking you to leave," the woman said. But didn't move from his hand, with its yellowed, stained nails, that was like a fist made of old leather.

"I'll tell you something if I can," Ruben Vega said. "I know women all my life, all kinds of women in the way they look and dress, the way they adorn themselves according to custom. Women are always a wonder to me. When I'm not with a woman, I think of them as all the same because I'm thinking of one thing. You understand?"

"Put a sack over their head," the woman said.

"Well, I'm not thinking of what she looks like then, when I'm out in the mountains or somewhere," Ruben Vega said. "That part of her doesn't matter. But when I'm *with* the woman, ah, then I realize how they are all different. You say, of course. This isn't a revelation to you. But maybe it is when you think about it some more."

The woman's eyes changed, turned cold. "You want to go to bed with me? Is that what you're saying, why you bring a gift?"

He looked at her with disappointment, an expression of weariness. But then he dropped the store box and took her to him gently, placing his hands on her shoulders, feeling her small bones in his grasp as he brought her in against him and his arms went around her.

He said, "You're gonna die here. Dry up and blow away."

She said, "Please. . . ." Her voice hushed against him.

"They wanted only to mark your chin," Ruben Vega said, "in the custom of those people. But you wanted your own marks, didn't you? Your marks, not like anyone else. . . . Well, you got them." After a moment he said to her, very quietly, "Tell me what you want."

The hushed voice close to him said, "I don't know."

He said, "Think about it and remember something. There is no one else in the world like you."

He reined the bay to move out and saw the dust trail rising out of the old pasture, three riders coming, and heard the woman say, "I told you. Now it's too late."

A man on a claybank and two young riders eating his dust, finally separating to come in abreast, reined to walk as they reached the pump and the irrigation ditch. The woman, walking from the corral to the house, said to them, "What do you want? I don't need anything, Mr. Bonnet."

So this would be the Circle-Eye foreman on the claybank. The man ignored her, his gaze holding on Ruben Vega with a solemn expression, showing he was going to be dead serious. A chew formed a lump in his jaw. He wore army suspenders and sleeve garters, his shirt buttoned up at the neck. As old as you are, Ruben Vega thought, a man who likes a tight feel of security and is serious about his business.

Bonnet said to him finally, "You made a mistake."

"I don't know the rules," Ruben Vega said.

"She told you to leave her be. That's the only rule there is. But you bought yourself a dandy new hat and come back here."

"That's some hat," one of the young riders said. This one held a single-shot Springfield across his pommel. The foreman, Bonnet, turned in his saddle and said something to the other rider who unhitched his rope and began shaking out a loop, hanging it nearly to the ground.

It's a show, Ruben Vega thought. He said to Bonnet, "I was leaving."

Bonnet said, "Yes, indeed, you are. On the off end of a rope. We're gonna drag you so you'll know the ground and never cross this land again."

The rider with the Springfield said, "Gimme your hat, mister, so's you don't get it dirty."

At this point Ruben Vega nudged his bay and began moving in on the foreman who straightened, looking over at the roper and said, "Well, tie onto him."

But Ruben Vega was close to the foreman now, the bay taller than the claybank and would move the claybank if the man on his back told him to. Ruben Vega watched the foreman's eyes moving and knew the roper was coming around behind him. Now the foreman turned his head to spit and let go a stream that spattered the hard-pack close to the bay's forelegs.

"Stand still," Bonnet said, "and we'll get her done easy. Or you can run and get snubbed out of your chair. Either way."

Ruben Vega was thinking that he could drink with this ramrod and they'd tell each other stories until they were drunk. The man had thought it would be easy: chase off a Mexican gunnysacker who'd come sniffing the boss's wife. A kid who was good with a rope and another one who could shoot cans off the fence with an old Springfield should be enough.

Ruben Vega said to Bonnet, "Do you know who I am?"

"Tell us," Bonnet said, "so we'll know what the cat drug in and we drug out."

And Ruben Vega said, because he had no choice, "I hear the rope in the air, the one with the rifle is dead. Then you. Then the roper."

His words drew silence because there was nothing more to be said. In the moments that Ruben Vega and the one named Bonnet stared at each other, the woman came out to them holding a revolver, an old Navy colt, which she raised and laid the barrel against the muzzle of the foreman's claybank.

She said, "Leave now, Mr. Bonnet, or you'll walk nine miles to shade."

There was no argument, little discussion, a few grumbling words. The Tonto woman was still Mrs. Isham. Bonnet rode away with his young hands and a new silence came over the yard.

Ruben Vega said, "He believes you'd shoot his horse."

The woman said, "He believes I'd cut steaks, and eat it, too. It's how I'm seen after twelve years of that other life."

Ruben Vega began to smile. The woman looked at him and in a few moments she began to smile with him. She shook her head then, but continued to smile. He said to her, "You could have a good time if you want to."

She said, "How, scaring people?"

He said, "If you feel like it." He said, "Get the present I brought you and open it."

He came back for her the next day in a Concord buggy, wearing his new willow-root straw and a cutaway coat over his revolvers, the coat he'd rented at a funeral parlor. Mrs. Isham wore the pale blue and white lace-trimmed dress he'd bought at Weiss's store, sat primly on the bustle and held the parasol against the afternoon sun all the way to Benson, ten miles, and up the main street to the Charles Crooker Hotel where the drummers and cattlemen and railroad men sitting in their front-porch rockers stared and stared.

They walked past the manager and into the dining room before Ruben Vega removed his hat and pointed to the table he liked, one against the wall between two windows. The waitress in her starched uniform was wide-eyed taking them over and getting them seated. It was early and the dining room was not half filled.

"The place for a quiet dinner," Ruben Vega said. "You see how quiet it is?"

"Everybody's looking at me," Sarah Isham said to the menu in front of her.

Ruben Vega said, "I thought they were looking at me. All right, soon they'll be used to it."

She glanced up and said, "People are leaving."

He said, "That's what you do when you finish eating, you leave."

She looked at him, staring, and said, "Who are you?"

"I told you."

"Only your name."

"You want me to tell you the truth, why I came here?"

"Please."

"To steal some of your husband's cattle."

She began to smile and he smiled. She began to laugh and he laughed, looking openly at the people looking at them, but not bothered by them. Of course they'd look. How could they help it? A Mexican rider and a woman with blue stripes on her face sitting at a table in the hotel dining room, laughing. He said, "Do you like fish? I know your Indian brothers didn't serve you none. It's against their religion. Some things are for religion, as you know, and some things are against it. We spend all our lives learning customs. Then they change them. I'll tell you something else if you promise not to be angry or point your pistol at me. Something else I could do the rest of my life. I could look at you and touch you and love you."

Her hand moved across the linen tablecloth to his and with the cracked, yellowed nails and took hold of it, clutched it.

She said, "You're going to leave."

He said, "When it's time."

She said, "I know you. I don't know anyone else."

He said, "You're the loveliest woman I've ever met. And the strongest. Are you ready? I think the man coming now is your husband."

It seemed strange to Ruben Vega that the man stood looking at him and not at his wife. The man seemed not too old for her, as he had expected, but too self-important. A man with a very serious demeanor, as though his business had failed or someone in his family had passed away. The man's wife was still clutching the hand with the gnarled fingers. Maybe that was it. Ruben Vega was going to lift her hand from his, but then thought, Why? He said as pleasantly as he was able, "Yes, can I help you?"

Mr. Isham said, "You have one minute to mount up and ride out of town."

"Why don't you sit down," Ruben Vega said, "Have a glass of wine with us?" he paused and said, "I'll introduce you to your wife."

Sarah Isham laughed; not loud but with a warmth to it and Ruben Vega had to look at her and smile. It seemed all right to release her hand now. As he did he said, "Do you know this gentleman?"

"I'm not sure I've had the pleasure," Sarah Isham said. "Why does he stand there?"

"I don't know," Ruben Vega said. "He seems worried about something."

"I've warned you," Mr. Isham said. "You can walk out or be dragged out."

Ruben Vega said, "He has something about wanting to drag people. Why is that?" And again heard Sarah's laugh, a giggle now that she covered with her hand. Then she looked up at her husband, her face with its blue tribal lines raised to the soft light of the dining room.

She said, "John, look at me. . . . Won't you please sit with us?"

Now it was as if the man had to make a moral decision, first consult his conscience, then consider the manner in which he would pull the chair out — the center of attention. When finally he was seated, upright on the chair and somewhat away from the table, Ruben Vega thought, All that to sit down. He felt sorry for the man now, because the man was not the kind who could say what he felt.

Sarah said, "John, can you look at me?"

He said, "Of course I can."

"Then do it. I'm right here."

"We'll talk later," her husband said.

She said, "When? Is there a visitor's day?"

"You'll be coming to the house, soon."

"You mean to see it?"

"To live there."

She looked at Ruben Vega with just the trace of a smile, a sad one. Then said to her husband, "I don't know if I want to. I don't know you. So I don't know if I want to be married to you. Can you understand that?"

Ruben Vega was nodding as she spoke. He could understand it. He heard the man say, "But we *are* married. I have an obligation to you and I respect it. Don't I provide for you?"

Sarah said, "Oh, my God — " and looked at Ruben Vega. "Did you hear that? He provides for me." She smiled again, not able to hide it, while her husband began to frown, confused.

"He's a generous man," Ruben Vega said, pushing up from the table. He saw her smile fade, though something warm remained in her eyes. "I'm sorry I have to leave. I'm going on a trip tonight, south, and first I have to pick up a few things." He moved around the table to take one of her hands in his, not caring what the husband thought. He said, "You'll do all right, whatever you decide. Just keep in mind that there's no one else in the world like you."

She said, "I can always charge admission. Do you think ten cents a look is too high?"

"At least that," Ruben Vega said. "But you'll think of something better."

He left her there in the dining room of the Charles Crooker Hotel in Benson, Arizona — maybe to see her again sometime, maybe not — and went out with a good conscience to take some of her husband's cattle.

Further Reading

Armitage, Susan, and Elizabeth Jameson, eds. *The Women's West*. Norman: University of Oklahoma Press, 1987.

Erisman, Fred, and Richard W. Etulain, eds. *Fifty Western Writers*. Westport, Connecticut: Greenwood Press, 1982.

Lee, L.L., and Merrill Lewis, eds. *Women, Women Writers, and the West*. Troy, New York: Whitston Publishing Co., 1979.

Moynihan, Ruth B., Susan Armitage, and Christiane Fischer Dichamp, eds. *So Much to be Done: Women Settlers on the Mining and Ranching Frontier*. Lincoln: University of Nebraska Press, 1990.

Myres, Sandra. *Westering Women and the Frontier Experience, 1800–1915*. Albuquerque: University of New Mexico Press, 1982.

Riley, Glenda. *The Female Frontier: A Comparative View of Women on the Prairie and the Plains*. Lawrence: University Press of Kansas, 1988.

Stauffer, Helen Winter, and Susan J. Rosowski, eds. *Women and Western American Literature*. Troy, New York: Whitston Publishing Co., 1982.

The Anthologists

Judy Alter is director of Texas Christian University Press and the author of several novels about women in the American West. Her most recent novel is *Libbie,* based on the life of Mrs. George Armstrong Custer.

A. T. Row is the editor of Texas Christian University Press. He served formerly as director of publications for the Arizona Historical Society in Tucson and editor of *The Journal of Arizona History.*

Fred Erisman is Lorraine Sherley Professor of Literature at Texas Christian University, a co-editor of *Fifty Western Writers,* contributor to the *Literary History of the American West* and author of a monograph on Frederic Remington.